The Ship
Faithful Steward

A Story of
Scots-Irish, English, and Irish Migration to
Pennsylvania

"Delaware's Worst Maritime Tragedy – 1785"

The Ship
Faithful Steward

A Story of
Scots-Irish, English, and Irish Migration to
Pennsylvania

"Delaware's Worst Maritime Tragedy – 1785"

Harry Allen Wenzel

Yellowtail Snapper Publishing

Copyright 2021 Harry Allen Wenzel
ISBN: 979-8-9851047-0-7

Yellowtail Snapper Publishing

Ulster – 1785

Londonderry Quay - 1793
John Nixon

Book cover design by
Lee Carol Wenzel

Front cover – picture of the three-mast ship
provided courtesy of
Cape Gazette
Lewes, Delaware

Back cover and interior
painting of
Londonderry Quay – 1793
by John Nixon, merchant and
Revolutionary War Veteran

CONTENTS

Author's Preface
Londonderry Journal - Extracts
Characters
From the Deck of Faithful Steward
Prologue

Chapters

APPENDICES

AUTHOR'S PREFACE

Historical news accounts claim 249 people boarded the ship, *Faithful Steward*, manned by a captain and twelve seamen at Londonderry on July 9, 1785. James McIntire recounts in his historical narrative there were more than 300. There are familial historical references to others, the Thomas Lee family for example, who attempted to board the ship and were unable to obtain passage as the ship was filled.

Approximately seventy percent of the passengers were Ulster-Scots, or as described in America, Scots-Irish; people with names depicting Scots who previously crossed the North Channel settling in the north of Ireland, or those that were born in Ulster. During the 1600s Scots from the lowland region surrounding Ayrshire and English from multiple locations in England participated in the Plantation of Ulster.

Circa mid-1700s, Scots-Irish and others of English ancestry, now identifying as Irish, and native Irish became part of a new mass migration. They left behind the fields, streams, brooks, farms, market towns, and places of burial of their ancestors, selling land leases and personal possessions – seeking an opportunity in British America with Pennsylvania receiving the greater influx.

American descendants of these people report the existence of familial naming patterns as they trace the historic roots of the people who sailed on the *Faithful Steward*. The forename of the firstborn male could be identical to the forename of the paternal grandfather, and the forename of the second-born male could be identical to the forename of the maternal grandfather. The third son would be named after his father, and the fourth son would be named after the eldest paternal uncle. There are other instances where the first son was named after the father and the third son likewise. Junior or III might be added after the son's name, or not at all. And if not so named, the liberty was taken to distinguish between my characters. Such was the case with the family of James Lee and his spouse Isabella Boscawen Lee, emigrating with their son James Lee II and their grandson James Lee III. In naming daughters, the first-born daughter may have been named after her maternal grandmother, and the second-born daughter was named after the paternal grandmother. The third daughter was named after her mother, and the fourth daughter was named after the eldest aunt on her mother's side.

The following story was constructed using researched names of real people – those who boarded the ship, and the storyline was built upon other names of relatives, and other passengers who knew or became acquainted with those on the ship. History records the names of Scots-Irish and Irish, people who made their home in or nearby Philadelphia decades before 1785, and willingly volunteered and sacrificed much of what they had, including their lives in the War of Independence. James McIntire II of Ardstraw Bridge sailed on the ship with his entire family except for one brother. He believed and so stated he was sailing to a land where heroes lived.

Names can be important – and when chosen with thought and purpose – they convey meaning, perhaps a description or a message. I poured over many historical accounts of ships, merchant ships, including the names of sail ships that transported cargo or passengers to British America during the 1700s.

Many ship's names bore the forenames of a male or a female. Others were named after a person such as a count, countess, or duke; and the remainder of names included a place such as a market town, or a location in Ulster, or perhaps a city in British America. Some of the ships were employed in the Royal Navy and the ship's name was prefaced by HMS (His or Her Majesty's Ship), declaring the source of ownership. Other names depicted a state of action such as *Defiance, Perseverance,* or Gustavus Conyngham's *Revenge.*

I remember the day I plucked the name of a ship from a map of shipwrecks along the Mid-Atlantic Coast. There wasn't an inkling of what words would form the thoughts for the pages to follow. Archibald Stewart, originally from Ballintoy, later a Rhode Island merchant, had a sail ship of 300 tons built in British America. He sailed together with his young son, Charles, on his new ship, *Stewart*, for Londonderry in 1784.

Archibald later transferred ownership in *Stewart* to a partnership including himself and two others, a ship captain from Limavady and his merchant brother. The origin of the new name of the ship departing Londonderry, July 9, 1785, remains in obscurity, however; a case can be made for the derivation to be biblically based, describing one who cares for the condition of another. A ship steward looks after the passengers or a person who assumes responsibility to care for another's property. Ironically, and sadly, the ship that made only four voyages in its entire history failed to live up to its name – *Faithful Steward.*

Londonderry Journal, Tuesday, March 16, 1784
Londonderry Ship News

Entered from Rhode Island, ship Stewart, owner Archibald Stewart – Master Joseph Haynes – flaxseed

Auction of Flaxseed

A cargo lately imported in the ship Stewart from Rhode Island, and to be sold by Mr. Archibald Stewart, on Wednesdays and Saturdays and to continue until the whole is sold. The sales to begin exactly at 1 o'clock each of said days on the Ship Quay. Cash, or good bills of exchange at 31 days sight, will only be taken as payment.

Any person inclinable to purchase by private sale may find Mr. Stewart at Mrs. H. Miller's near the Ferry Quay, where he will be ready to treat with any person for freight or passage to Newcastle or Rhode Island in the above ship, which will sail about the middle of May next. Said vessel was built last year, is upwards of 300 tons burthen, a prime sailer, and completely calculated for the passenger trade.

Mr. Stewart takes the liberty of acquainting the public that the place of his nativity was near Ballintoy, in the County of Antrim, but hath been a resident in America these twenty-two years last past; and as he intends to return in the ship to his family in America, he will take particular care that an ample store of provisions of the best quality shall be laid in for the voyage and that he will see every passenger treated with the greatest justice and humanity.

Coopers and house carpenters may meet with great encouragement from Mr. Stewart.

Londonderry Journal, Tuesday, March 22, 1784

For NEWCASTLE AND RHODE ISLAND
The Ship
FAITHFUL STEWARD
Burthen 300 Tons
Jos. Haynes, Master

Will be clear to sail for the above ports the 15th of May next. This vessel was built last year (1783), sails remarkably fast, and is in every respect well calculated for the passenger trade. For freight or passage apply to Mr. Archibald Stewart at Mrs. H. Miller's next to the Ferry Quay, or the captain on board said vessel.

Tuesday, April 20, 1784

As Abraham McCausland, merchant, and Captain Connolly McCausland have purchased two-thirds of the ship Faithful Steward (Stewart), they pledge themselves to every person that would wish to take passage in the said ship, to have the greatest plenty of provisions laid in, so that they may have a pleasant and agreeable voyage. Captain Connolly McCausland goes out the master of said ship with Captain Jos. Haynes, who is well known to have made many fortunate voyages to America. Any passenger that would choose to go in the said ship will have two free houses at each side of Culmore Point until said ship sails, and any passengers coming from County Antrim will have also free stores at Coleraine or Portrush, by applying to Robert McCausland, Esq: Custom House, Coleraine, who will give every encouragement necessary.

Londonderry Journal Tuesday, June 15, 1784
Londonderry Ship News
Cleared for Philadelphia – Faithful Steward, McCausland

Londonderry Journal Tuesday, June 22, 1784
Since our last, the ships St. Patrick and Faithful Steward sailed for America having about 1,000 passengers on board.

Londonderry Journal Tuesday, October 12, 1784

Since our last arrived in the river from Philadelphia, the brig Peggy, Captain G. Stewart, after a passage of 30 days. By this vessel, we have an account of the safe arrival of the ships St. Patrick and Faithful Steward, and the brigs Buckskin and Jenny from this port. By the above vessel we have received several American newspapers, but they contain no material intelligence.

CHARACTERS

Archibald Stewart, Merchant & Shipowner
Charles Stewart (son)
Connolly McCausland, Captain & Shipowner
Abraham McCausland, Merchant & Shipowner

The Crew
Mr. Stanfield, First Mate
Mr. Gwyn, Second Mate
Edward McCaffrey, Boatswain
Pelig Hudson, Steward
John Quigley, Helmsman
Samuel Irwin, Carpenter
John Brown, Sailmaker
William Dalrymple
Robert Kelley
William Linn
Patrick Mourn
Owen Phillips

Passengers (in order of appearance)
James McIntire I
Rebecca McIntire
James McIntire II
Rebecca McIntire (daughter)
Gustavus Colhoun, Merchant
Thomas Colhoun, Mariner/Supercargo
James Lee I
Isabella Boscawen Lee
James Lee II
Mary Lee
James Lee III
Simon Elliott I
James Elliott
Simon Elliott II
Hugh Espey Sr.
John Espey
James Espey
Samuel Hepburn
John Hepburn
Matthew Caldwell

PROLOGUE

March - 1937

There were three of them, all friends, inspecting the shoreline during an incoming tide; one of them waded into the Atlantic Ocean. The sun was bright, illuminating spectacles from the sea washing on the shore when suddenly he was knocked off balance by an unsuspecting wave. With his composure regained, his pupils dilated as he gazed into the saltwater spotting an old chest approximately three feet square held together by copper ribbing and encrusted with barnacles.

He yelled to attract the attention of his companions further down the beach. The chest was old, the Atlantic cold, and the seawater soaked his pants as he grabbed underneath a corner of the chest. Heavy and immovable, his senses could only react to what his eyes could now see. Together the three determined to move the chest to safer ground, but the object's weight was too great. Lindsley managed to pry open one compartment to the chest, but there was nothing inside to their disappointment.

Lindsley L. Beach was born in the year 1888, and by 1900, he resided in Floyd County, the northwestern corner of Georgia. Time advanced, and with his childhood spent, he found himself volunteering to serve his country in the United States Army. The Great War, World War I, was winding down when he was assigned to Camp Lewis located by the American Lake in the state of Washington. The Thirteenth Division was undergoing training during 1918 when on November 11th news of an armistice was announced to the world. Major Beach, Quartermaster, found himself relieved of his command and discharged from the United States Army. While the Thirteenth Division had not seen overseas combat, their commander had addressed all, highlighting their willingness and readiness had they been called to fight.

Years later, he relocated to Sussex, Delaware, and at the age of forty-nine, spent time making frequent trips to Indian River Inlet. Spring of 1937 was cold, and there was no hint that Mother Nature was willing to let winter die along the sun-drenched coast. Before the ocean uncovered the old chest, Major Beach and his friends collected more than one hundred copper coins stamped with an imprint of King William III of England – dated 1749 - 1775.

With their wet fingers numbed by the cold and pants soaked nearly

1

to the waist, the three feverishly attempted to remove the old chest to safer ground. There was no time to pry open other passages to the old chest's interior as the saltwater continued its assault, bringing an incoming tide. The chest was covered quickly and the three could only watch a very old artifact, someone's possession, disappear beneath the waves.

FROM THE DECK OF *FAITHFUL STEWARD*

"We sailed from Londonderry with the design of landing in Philadelphia. The day was extremely fine; the wind favorable, and all on board appeared to be happy. Each one, no doubt, anticipated a quick and delightful voyage. As for myself, I suffered a commixture of uncommon feelings. I stood on the deck to view the fading shore. I was leaving my homeland, forever. My parents, my brother, and my sisters were in my company. I, therefore, could not have mourned the absence of any kindred. I was a youth of twenty-two; just emerging into complete manhood and active adult life. I was therefore a suitable person to seek the wilds of America. The picture was indeed fair.

I saw in my imagination beyond the bright expanse of water which lay before us, a country where heroes lived, where genius expanded to full perfection, where every good was possessed. I saw or thought I saw, another paradise, a new and flowery land, such as mortals can never see, such as mortals can never enjoy."

James McIntire II
July 9, 1785

1

Catastrophe

John Quigley nervously stood behind the ship's wheel. It was dark, clouds hid the moon, and there was no sight of land when there should have been. A veteran helmsman and a Massachusetts sailor, he was apprehensive, and the crew knew it. It became evident after the party ended, his anxiety was absorbed by many of the passengers, particularly the women. Their ship was fifty-three days into a voyage departing Londonderry Quay (port) on July 9th – it was the length of the sail and the absence of the captain that was the cause of consternation. Quigley was familiar with the Atlantic; he crossed it multiple times. It was the captain's indifferent attitude that caused his nervousness. The weather had been fair. The sail to Philadelphia averaged seven weeks – and that included tacking into the westerlies off the coast of North America. Nightfall set in once again, and there was no discovery of land and the mouth of the Delaware Bay.

Mr. and Mrs. Gregg, together with their guests, retired for the evening, sufficiently filled with food and spirits. James McIntire II thought it a carousal filled with all kinds of mirth. People were celebrating the Gregg's first wedding anniversary hours before.

Mary Lee, the Irish beauty, led those inclined in the old English hornpipe dance. Pelig Hudson, the ship's steward, joined in. The crew loved the hornpipe; and when they danced, they held a belaying pin in each arm to strengthen muscles. Mary needed none of that. She was well proportioned, shapely, adorned with shiny black hair with captivating deep blue eyes. Pelig laid two of the pins on the deck as she smiled and stepped and pranced around them in a circle. The captain, married a few years prior, couldn't take his eyes off the beauty from Donegal. Mary Maginnis played the fiddle, and the dancing continued into the late evening. There was sufficient food, laughter, and for some, plenty of Madeira stocked weeks before. The Greggs' honored guests, the captain, his officers, and selected passengers, both men and women, returned to their cabins and berths. Captain McCausland and Mr. Stanfield, First Mate, lay below deck in the officer quarters, each having fallen into an alcohol-induced slumber.

Pelig, a handsome sailor of muscular build, tipped the hourglass at four bells of the first dog watch. Thickening clouds rolled in since the afternoon watch, bringing signs of a change in weather and hiding many of the stars. A half-moon, now barely visible, shed minimal light over Neptune's domain. Wind speed, ever-increasing, enveloped the stunsails, forcing them outward over the bowsprit. It was ten o'clock in the evening – the air temperature balmy – and two more hours until midnight and September 1st.

Mr. Gwyn, Second Mate, fell when the ship pitched leeward from a strong gust of wind. Embarrassed and springing to his feet, he grumbled at his helmsman. "Why haven't we spotted land?"

He was not alone in pondering their location. Captain McCausland was preoccupied hours earlier – or was he hiding his concern, something a commander must do before his passengers, and sometimes his crew.

The prospect of entering the Delaware Bay without a fixed position and decreased visibility brought on by dark skies was a mariner's nightmare filled with risk – risk not to be engaged. The obvious course for safety was to identify land and the ship's position during the light of day, and sail into the bay, and navigate the Delaware River with the assistance of a pilot boat captain from Lewestown, if necessary.

Captain McCausland, weeks before, spoke to his crew of the fate of the captain and mates of the sail ship *Philadelphia Packet*. They left the port of Belfast, and the ship *America*, left the eastern port of Newry, bound for Philadelphia, two years prior. Both shipwrecked near Sinepuxent and Cape Henlopen. Captains knew that navigating the waters to the bay separating Delaware from New Jersey was fraught with danger.

"Mr. Gwyn," Second Mate called loudly to one of the crew. An experienced second mate, he signed the Crewman's Agreement for one trans-Atlantic sail at the port of Londonderry.

"Aye," Mr. Phillips responded.

"Haul out the lead and take a sounding," directed Mr. Gwyn.

Minutes passed – Mr. Quigley moved the wheel one point to port, attempting to right the ship from another strong gust of wind. The crewman pulled the bucket from storage, untangled a knot in the lead, and proceeded to the port side, lowering the bucket with the line streaming into the sea.

An instant passed, and he could feel the bucket drag on the bottom. He pulled in the line far enough to eliminate any drag, paused, and lowered it again. The bucket dug into a sandy bottom, dragged, and was retrieved. The marking on the line invoked surprise, then panic.

"Mr. Gwyn – six fathoms," Mr. Phillips yelled, his face in shock. "Six fathoms (twenty-four feet) – I took the drag twice," he repeated.

"Give me the lead," screamed Mr. Gwyn, grabbing the line then lowering the bucket to verify another sounding. It hit bottom and dragged.

"Hard to port – damn, hard to port!" Mr. Gwyn screamed in alarm while hauling in the lead and dropping the bucket on the deck. "Hard to port," he tripped as he scrambled to get to the wheel.

John Quigley was in shock. William Linn, the Boatswain, bounded up the ladder to the la poupe deck, realizing something had gone wrong. His first contact was with Mr. Phillips, his eyes dilated, in a state of panic.

"Six fathoms Mr. Linn – six fathoms," Mr. Gwyn repeated. "Summon Captain McCausland and Mr. Stanfield – fast – move!"

Mr. Gwyn realized his ship had left the safety of deep water and was gliding through dangerous shallow water, with the southeast wind blowing their vessel toward the shore and eventual stranding. Mr. Quigley, hands gripping the wheel tightly, steered portside as fast and as hard as he could, awaiting further instruction.

Mr. Linn, perched on the first step leading down to the fo'cs'le, reared and yelled, "ALL HANDS ON DECK – SHALLOW WATER, ALL HANDS ON DECK – BANG ON THE CAPTAIN'S DOOR – WAKE HIM – WAKE MR. STANFIELD TOO." There was no mistaking the urgency in the boatswain's shrill voice.

Crewmen Patrick Mourn and Edward McCaffrey jumped from their berth, tumbled to the floor, and ran to the ladder, shoulders colliding as they scrambled to ascend the ladder to the deck. William Dalrymple and Robert Kelley scurried up the ladder with little time to spare. Samuel Irwin and John Brown responded to Mr. Linn's command. The remainder of the crew on the main deck dashed to move the foremast braces and reposition the sails. Mr. Linn was shaking – his senses on high alert.

Mr. Quigley, frozen behind the wheel, watched in surprise while the bosun and his crew of ten ascended the rigging to the foremast. The wind brought humidity, but there was no presence of rain.

"Tighten the halyards – reign in the topgallant – move fast," Mr. Gwyn yelled through the wind.

William Dalrymple lost his footing while climbing the ratline – but managed to grab the netting with his left hand while pulling himself up to regain his footing. Eight crewmen spread across the spars, struggling to haul in the topgallant to tie it to the brace. Samuel Irwin, ship's carpenter, secured the buntlines to the topgallant. Mr. Gwyn turned his back to the wind to shout to the crew – he was knocked off his feet and thrown to the deck following a loud rubbing sound and a sudden unsuspected jar. Panic seized his inner being – his instinct prepared him for the eventuality to follow. The passing seconds seemed like an eternity to the crew atop the deck. *Faithful Steward*, but two years dispensed from her berth along Rhode Island's shore, was in peril. Those of the crew standing on deck were thrown off their feet as the wooden hull cut through the ocean floor, scraping upon the hard surface of an unknown object, lying on the sandy bottom. No one knew the distance she traveled as the wooden hull scraped over the object and plowed into the sand, grinding a path over the floor of the ocean, rubbing and screeching until at last the ship came to rest.

Below deck, Captain McCausland, wrapped inside a swaying hammock, lay limp and relaxed, the result of an intoxicated induced rest. The force of the impact of the hull scraping bottom slammed the hammock against the wall. Awoken and thrown to the floor, he heard Mr. Irwin's alarmed voice, sounding a sense of urgency and impending doom.

"Captain McCausland – Captain," Mr. Irwin yelled. The cabin was dark – a moan was distinguishable.

"CAPTAIN – WE STRUCK BOTTOM – WE HIT BOTTOM CAPTAIN!" he exploded with fright.

His captain sat upright, gathered himself, and staggered to the door.

"CAPTAIN McCAUSLAND – RISE – GET UP – THE UNTHINKABLE HAS HAPPENED!" Mr. Irwin's voice rang with alarm.

Captain McCausland stumbled, straightened up, and opened the door, his senses returning as his mind grasped the severity of his ship's current state of affairs.

"CAPTAIN," Mr. Irwin continued. "CAPTAIN – MR. GWYN IS ATOP DECK BY THE HELM," he yelled.

Captain McCausland – now standing – his senses returning, brushed past Mr. Irwin, heading for the ladder to the deck.

The wind strengthened, causing *Faithful Steward* to dislodge from the ocean seabed, continuing her glide over the water for a short distance. The force of the impact and the hull scraping the bottom of the sea caused the mainmast to shift from the braces holding it in place. A violent jarring caused the rails of some of the berths to move, collapsing one of them upon two young children. The force of the impact was sudden, the sound a loud thud, and two victims lay buried below, wrapped in their clothes provided by their mother hours before. It was dark in steerage, and the sounds of men and women could be heard on the main deck – shrills, gasps, screams, and moaning – sounds of alarm. Everyone was frightened. Two children were hidden by the darkness. No cries for help were heard.

Captain McCausland stumbled to the la poupe deck, scrambling to the bridge. Mr. Gwyn, standing by the ship's wheel, looked shocked – dumbfounded. The wind increased and was blowing, howling, and ripping through the canvas sails. The ship pitched slowly to starboard, rocked, and now lay motionless on the seabed. The look on the captain's face was indescribable – a mixture of shock, bewilderment, yet a sense of the urgent prevailed. Darkness ruled the scene – the cloud cover thickened – the absence of any light from stars or moon was far from one's thought – panic and confusion set in making their presence known to all. Mr. Quigley, ship's wheel in his hands, yelled aloud – "my God what have we done!"

2

Emigration – Decades Before

Dr. Hugh Boulter, Archbishop of Armagh, spoke with pain in his voice. "After laboring with all my body, soul, and mind to reduce the horrible plague of famine in Ireland, there are now seven ships docked at Belfast, ready to depart with nearly 1,000 passengers destined for Pennsylvania and the middle colonies."

∞

Alexander Hewat was born in Roxburgh, Scotland, in 1739, and at age twenty-four, migrated to Charlestown, South Carolina. His ancestors came from a long line of farmers and churchmen. He added the title of reverend to his name after he became a minister. Alexander observed the desire for people seeking emigration to British America was so strong in the northern counties of Ireland, circa the 1760s and 1770s, there was a threat of a vast depopulation.

During the 1770s, the value of brown linens increased to extravagant prices, and comparable increases in leasehold rents followed suit. Economic conditions placed the weavers and spinners in an increased credit crisis. People had no option but to leave their homes.

Many residents of *Ulster* undertook to sell their belongings to pay for passage to British American ports. Some were motivated because friends took the step to escape the same difficulties, and often they landed in close-by locations. Colonel Alexander McNutt led immigrants to settle in Nova Scotia, promoting land in 300-acre increments available to each. But land promotions failed to generate enough emigrants compared to the effort and cost required to transport them.

In the 1770s, the brig *Peggy* sailed with 207 residents from Ulster, the brig *Agnes* left Belfast carrying 220, and the ship *Minerva* left Newry with about 400 on board. These sailings were in addition to the sail ship *Betsy*, departing the port of Newry with 361. *Needham* also left Newry with 500, and the vessel *Robert* carrying 420 advertised they would sail to Philadelphia and New Castle, Delaware.

Many merchants, mariners, and shipowners were involved in trans-Atlantic trade, including transportation of passengers. Some were motivated by humanitarian reasons and others for profit, and; some blended both into their logic. Land promoters toured the counties to locate potential servants. Some promoted an ad securing servants for passage and purposely delayed the ad until two weeks before sailing. Those merchants importing servants realized about £10 per servant. If a passenger ship carried fifty servants from a total of 400 passengers, they could earn £500 in addition to revenue realized from paying passengers.

Competition in transporting passengers increased, and merchants placed advertisements in the Londonderry Journal and the Belfast Newsletter. Families with accumulated wealth signed up for passage in the cabin section, a handful of private berths. Passengers with lesser means secured accommodations in steerage. They were joined by those with little to average means to cover payment for passage. Others wanted to leave but had little to no means for the cost of trans-Atlantic passage. Desperate passengers signed a contract for redemption or servitude to be fulfilled once they arrived portside.

Passengers paid their fare upfront in full to the captain or merchant. Redemptioners were required to cover part of their fare before setting sail. Upon arriving at the port of destination, the redemptioner left the ship, however, they were responsible once shore-side, to seek relatives, possibly friends, or any other means to secure the balance of funds required to cover the cost for their passage.

Transporting redemptioners was fraught with risk. Some never returned to ship with payment, and the captain of the vessel had to hunt for them, bringing them before local law officials to secure payment, if possible.

Some Scots-Irish chose New Castle, Delaware, but most sailed up the Delaware River to Philadelphia, their port of destination. Word spread rapidly that land in Pennsylvania was fertile and excellent for tilling, suitable for farming. They knew that north of the middle colonies, free labor existed, and in the south, some people were enslaved to work on plantations. Pennsylvania was a natural choice for those who sought indentured labor, thereby attracting many from Ireland who would pay for their passage to get there.

Over time Philadelphia emerged as the popular marketplace for migrating servants from Ireland. Anyone traveling on a ship as a servant would contact a merchant specializing in the servant trade. Servants were required to agree to terms of an indenture before the mayor of the port of embarkation. The contract was a written agreement, often between the servant and a local merchant or possibly the ship's captain.

The indenture, a binding contract, specified the number of years, usually four, whereby the servant was required to work to pay for the cost of their fare. Once signed and registered before the mayor, the indenture was sold to a buyer at a price near £12 to £14. One out of every ten passengers indentured themselves as a servant. Most servants were comprised of people leaving ports located along the southeast coast of Ireland – specifically Cork, Dublin, and Waterford.

Parliamentary authority wasn't in favor of emigration before the revolution spawned in British America. They viewed the situation by comparing the number of people leaving to the loss of power and the resulting reduction in the wealth of a nation. A loss of people could be quantified by a decrease in Protestants, a loyal group, impacting rents by lowering them and reducing the competition to lease land.

James Caldwell, a merchant raised in Londonderry, emigrated to Philadelphia in 1768 to set up a business branch for his brother, William, and cousin, Andrew Caldwell, who remained home. Andrew engaged in securing passage for his brethren, those impoverished from lack of economic opportunity, and victims of persecution.

Andrew recorded a total of 17,000 leaving Ulster in 1771. Not surprisingly, 12,000 people departed their homeland in 1772. The Londonderry Journal, June 3, 1772 edition, reported statistics for those emigrating. The departure port, number of vessels transporting passengers, and the total tonnage of each ship were recorded.

Leaving in 1771	Ships	Tons
Londonderry	13	3,650
Belfast	7	1,750
Newry	9	2,800
Portrush	1	250
Larne	2	450
Total	32	8,900 *

Leaving in 1772	Ships	Tons
Londonderry	9	2,650
Belfast	10	2,650
Newry	5	1,600

Portrush	1	250
Larne	5	1,300
Total	30	8,450 *

*For safety or other reasons, the number of passengers estimated to be near the ship's tonnage, approximately 17,000 for the two years.

The Belfast Newsletter, circa 1770s published Philadelphia and New Castle, Delaware as the preferred ports of entry for Irish emigrants. Advertisements for sails to Philadelphia in 1771 totaled nineteen, in 1772, seventeen; and in 1773 the number increased to twenty-one. Many of the servant passengers leaving Londonderry made arrangements with the merchant firm of Caldwell, Vance, & Caldwell. There was mention in their advertisements of the servants leaving Dublin and Cork.

Carsan, Barclay, & Mitchell, a competing merchant firm, exported a significant number of passengers in addition to flaxseed and other general merchant trade. Samuel Carsan left Ulster to open a branch in Baltimore to facilitate their business connections and endeavors. Meanwhile, Thomas Barclay labored to build up the mercantile firm of Carsan and Davey, to the point where his accumulated wealth enabled him to invest in joint ownership in twenty vessels.

John Maxwell Nesbitt and Redmond Conyngham formed a partnership and were known for bringing Irish servants to Philadelphia. They also owned multiple ships employed in the flaxseed trade. One vessel, *Culloden,* was owned by a partnership between Conyngham, Nesbitt, Robert Alexander, and John Knox of Londonderry. Redmond Conyngham owned the ship *Hayfield,* and he amassed a fortune owning estates in Donegal. Redmond's son, David Hayfield Conyngham, emigrated to Philadelphia seeking an apprenticeship with the merchant firm and becoming a partner. John Maxwell Nesbitt decided to stay and live in Philadelphia to conduct the merchant business from the colonies.

∞

Unresolved frustration led to desperation, and a movement sprung forth from the Protestant community in County Antrim. Irate farmers cheated from the profits of their toil were angered, and they took their grievances against the unfair increases in rents to the street. Rent increases placed some of them in the company of brethren, all facing eviction from their homesteads.

Intermediaries acting as opportunists sprung forth as speculators securing rights to lands from the absentee landlord. They made an increased profit after inflating rental rates, and afterward, the tenant was left poor, or about to find themselves in this economic state.

Angered Protestant farmers (Church of Ireland and the Presbyterian Church) formed an organized group with numbers increasing in the thousands. The Hearts of Steel movement was born in County Antrim, as a result of increased frustration and economic hardship. Dissatisfaction led to acts of protest and eventual violence. Word spread of the movement, and in a short time, the Hearts of Steel infiltrated Counties Armagh, Down, and Londonderry, eventually merging with another group, the Hearts of Oak. Unlawful oaths, administered by leaders, and acts of anger, and outrage were encouraged, leading to dictating terms to land proprietors. After several years, in 1772, legislative attempts designed to restore stability failed. The Irish Parliament ordered the army to put down the Hearts of Steel rebellion. People were killed and those captured hung.

In June 1772, the London-based banking house, Fordyce & Company Bankers, failed. Orders from British America peaked, producing a glut in the market, and the linen trade came to a standstill. The price of land and rents rose to an excessive level. Relatively few owned their estates in fee simple, which meant that everyone else, from landlords to humble laborers known as cottagers, were tenants.

Landed gentry was fortunate to own estates of several thousand acres, and they could derive income from leasing land to farmers. On occasion, some of the lessors obligated themselves to a lease of a hundred or more acres, and in turn, they would divide portions of the land and sub-lease to others. By 1772 the average farm size was less than thirty acres. Those considered wealthy with established revenue streams afforded finer living conditions, however, everyone remaining suffered.

Failed attempts to alleviate poor living conditions produced a steady uninterrupted flow of people leaving Ireland. In June 1773, the sail ship *Prince of Wales* departed with passengers for Baltimore, Maryland. A newspaper ad published the following to attract immigrants.

"The town of Baltimore is situated for ready communication with all the back parts of Pennsylvania, Maryland, and Virginia, to which most of the new settlers resort. It is one hundred miles nearer than Philadelphia to Fort Pitt on the Ohio River – a new province of vast extent, of the most fertile fine lands in North America, and in the most agreeable moderate climate, is now settling very fast along the banks of that famous river, where tracts of the richest land in the world and greater extent than most kingdoms in Europe, are yet unsettled, and will for many ages to come to afford the happiest asylum for all that choose to exchange a land of poverty, for freedom, wealth, and happiness."

∞

Ninety years previous (1683), the southeast corner of Pennsylvania was undergoing settlement. The geographic settlement of the colony occurred in waves and appeared as bands of fertile land displayed on a map, covering a northeast by southwest direction. By 1684 people from England and western Europe settled directly north of Philadelphia, and in 1718 a large tract, Chester County, was undergoing settlement. From 1732 to 1736, a narrow band of acreage stretching from the northern corner of Pennsylvania bordering the Delaware River, southwest to Maryland, was settled. In 1749, a strip of land in the northeast corner extending to the southwest was settled. The two bands covering 1732 to 1749 were occupied by a significant influx of farmers leaving Germany. By 1754, a large section located in the central portion of the colony stretching south to the Maryland border was next. Fourteen years later, in 1768, the largest tract of land covering a vast amount of acreage from the northeast tip spreading southwest to the border colony of Maryland was available for occupation. Lastly, the 1770s saw many immigrants from Ulster settling the northwest quadrant of the territory, an area about one-third the size of the commonwealth and a locale once occupied by the tribes of the Six Nations.

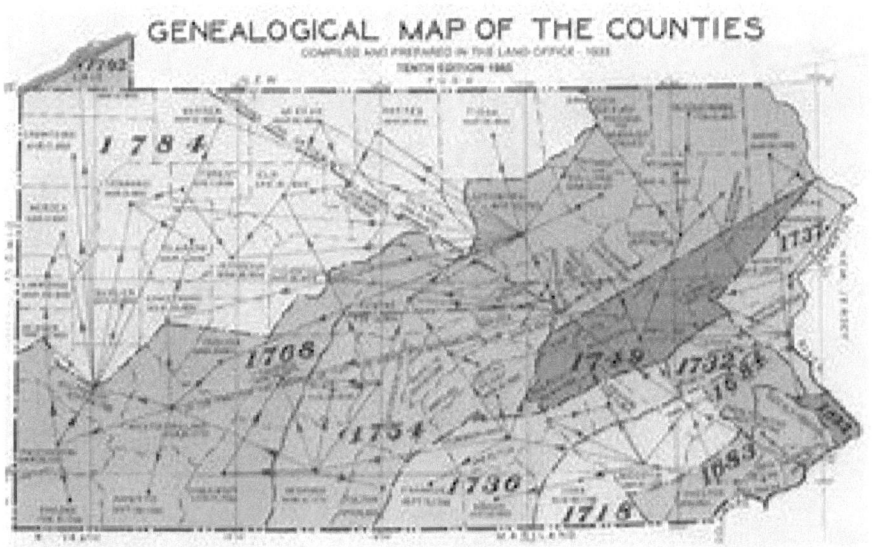

GENEALOGICAL MAP OF THE COUNTIES

The Settlement (East to West) of William Penn's Commonwealth of
Pennsylvania

Waves of people continued to leave through the port of
Londonderry in 1773. Residents were informed of events occurring where
they lived by reading the Londonderry Journal or the Belfast Newsletter. The
Newsletter ran the following account listing sail ships scheduled to embark
Londonderry for British American ports in 1773.

Date	Vessel Name	Passengers	Port
March 2	*Jenny*	250	Philadelphia
March 9	*Hannah*	400	"
March 12	*Jupiter*	300	"
March 16	*Walworth*	300	"
April 15	*Alexander*	400	"
April 27	*Hellen*	200	Charlestown
May 1	*Louisa*	200	"
June 1	*Rose*	300	Philadelphia
June 8	*Prince of Wales*	350	Baltimore
June 18	*Ann*	300	Charlestown
July 6	*Philadelphia*	250	Philadelphia
August 3	*Boscawen*	250	"
August 10	*George*	250	"
August 13	*Elizabeth*	300	Charlestown

The same newspaper published an account of the total ships, gross cargo weight, and ports of embarkation, all carrying a combination of passengers and trade goods in 1773.

Port	Ships	Tons
Londonderry	14	4,050
Belfast	13	3,400
Newry	8	2,550
Larne	4	1,300
Total	39	11,300

3

Baile an Tuaigh - Ballintoy

Many years before, people exchanging goods emigrated from the western shores of Scotland, navigating a short passage of nearly twenty miles sailing across the *Strath na Maoile* – Straits of Moyle, passing the sharp descending cliffs of Sheep Island. The strait is a beautiful hue of blue and provides a stark contrast with the green grass hills of County Antrim, descending to the shoreline to the brown sandy beaches. Further down the coastal cliffs of limestone drop toward the ocean floor.

A variety of seabirds including cormorant, fulmar, kittiwake, and black-billed gulls, make their home on Sheep Island. After a short flight across the channel, they frequent the cliffs along the coastline of Ballintoy, the English version of the Irish word *Baile an Tuaigh*. The interpretation of the word is a northern townland and the quaint coastal village, Ballintoy, lies in County Antrim.

Ballintoy Castle, a structure surrounded by a thick stone wall, stands nearly sixty-five feet high. The Stewart clan built the structure after migrating from Scotland to County Antrim many years before. The Stewarts were landowners near Ballintoy for many generations. Those of Scottish descent dominated the Parish of Ballintoy, a people who spoke with a broad dialect and accent.

Archibald Stewart was born near the village and the castle. By 1763 he chose to leave the homeland of his family and ancestors and set sail from nearby Londonderry for British America. Stories circulated for two decades of a new frontier ripe with opportunity, and he would take advantage of it.

The port of Philadelphia produced a record number of indentures recorded some years before his departure. Near 570 servants were recorded in the registry: 240 arrived from Dublin, 108 from Londonderry, and 73 from Cork, all natives of Ireland. Of the twenty-nine ships that brought them to Pennsylvania, twelve departed from Londonderry, six from Dublin, and two from Cork. People signed indentures of servitude for two to four years to pay for the cost of their passage. The buyers of the contracts paid upward of £12 to £14 per person.

Archibald Stewart, a wealthy merchant emigrated to Rhode Island, bringing with him an ample supply of linen product, strong and well colored, a yard wide to 7/8ths, to start a business. Upon arrival in Providence and locating suitable accommodations, he set about the task of expanding his family connections and developing new contacts to build his trade. Residents grew an abundance of the blue-flowered flax due to the cooler northern climate. Merchants or their agents met at a weekly town market to sell their wares.

During the following twenty years, Stewart sailed to Londonderry, shipping flaxseed for sale at the weekly marketplace and purchasing linen and other assorted products to be sold in Rhode Island. Profits grew, and Archibald increased his wealth. As was customary at the time, he directed profits into investing in shares of ownership of a sail ship, one newly constructed by the shipbuilder, or through the sale of an existing ownership share.

Archibald determined it was advantageous to partner with Alexander Black, also an Ulster emigrant. They imported *Bohea* tea, a black tea with a light smoky aroma, indigo, cotton, wool, Irish linen, silk handkerchiefs, and sold them at their store located at the west end of Great Bridge in Providence. Between the two, they could combine capital and contacts and build their business of buying and shipping their primary product – flaxseed, along with other agricultural products on return shipments to Londonderry.

By 1767, after Alexander Black succumbed to disease, Archibald dissolved the partnership and formed a new one with Robert Taylor, also of Ulster origin. In 1770 Archibald married Anstis, the widow of Captain James Hutton of Newport, Rhode Island.

In 1782 the British Parliament decided to end the hostilities with the thirteen colonies. General Washington, commanding an army outnumbering the army of Lord Cornwallis, forced his surrender at the Yorktown siege. Shipbuilders in New England realized it was time to transition from constructing brigantines armed with upward of one hundred cannons to redesigned decks for cargo carrying and passenger accommodation. And on September 3, 1783 the Treaty of Paris was consummated and England officially recognized the sovereignty of the colonies, now formed under the United States of America. But hostilities between England and France escalated and their navies were engaged in battle on the high seas.

Designers and builders of brigantines from Providence to Boston determined to make changes to the shape of the hull, the sail design, and rigging, to increase the speed of their vessel. They were well acquainted with naval captains who would transition to commanding the merchant navies of America. While the hostilities officially ceased between nations, one could not predict what another captain of an English ship, or a French ship or *privateer*, might undertake by firing upon one of the American vessels.

American shipbuilders focused on securing materials to construct the best sail ship possible. Their vessels were designed to carry great *lading* proportionate to its size, and they sailed efficiently away from the coast to avoid danger. If the vessel leaned toward the leeward side, it was dangerous to maneuver away from shore. The new design must allow the crew to work well with the ship size in proportion to the weight of the cargo. And their new ship must be stable given a small amount of ballast. New England shipbuilders reasoned the new design and increased sail capacity meant any ship could distance itself from an engagement. And accordingly, new shipowners and merchants did not hesitate to describe their ships by placing ads in the newspapers depicting, fast sailer.

Philadelphia – 1783

The ship *Stewart*

Archibald Stewart strode through the doorway at 23 Water Street leading to the offices of the Eyre brothers, shipbuilders, located at Kensington nearby Philadelphia. His dark blue frock coat flowed to the knees, partially covering a black vest buttoned down to the waistline of his brown breeches. White silk stockings met with shiny buckles attached to the shoes. Indeed, he presented a picture of a prosperous merchant.

Determined to secure ownership in a sail ship, Mr. Stewart came to discuss the details of building a new wooden vessel. Manuel, Jehu, and Benjamin Eyre were accomplished shipwrights, now focusing on constructing ships for the merchant trade. The Revolutionary War, of which they were veterans, was over. Opportunities existed to increase trade with the east coast ports of Philadelphia south to Charlestown and with the islands in the Caribbean.

Manuel Eyre stood six feet, was squarely built, and muscular. His hair was black, and a prominent nose was set between dark eyes. Those who dealt with him spoke of an independent-minded man but not an arrogant person of sorts. And when he spoke, his English was accented differently from the Scotsman who migrated to the north of Ireland and then to Rhode Island.

Mr. Stewart, curious by nature, wanted to know all sorts of details.

"Mr. Eyre – I want a vessel built, and I need your help."

Manuel Eyre surveyed Mr. Stewart's appearance. "For what purpose?"

"My trans-Atlantic merchant trade – I ship flax to Ireland and import linen goods on the return."

Manuel nodded. "You will need a brig or a ship."

"Describe the difference to me."

Manuel turned to a set of wooden drawers and secured two sets of plans, placing them on the table in front of Mr. Stewart.

"You have some important considerations before you make your decision. It will be necessary to evaluate the type of construction, a brig, for instance, or a ship, which is my preference for trans-Atlantic trade."

"Tell me about the brig first."

"There will be two masts, the length and breadth of the brig are smaller than a ship, and all sails will be square-rigged."

"And a ship?"

Manuel reached for the ship plans to place them in the center of the table. "There will be three masts, the foremast, mainmast, and mizzenmast. We design each mast to be built with a lower mast, top-mast, and the top-gallant mast, all square-rigged."

Mr. Stewart studied the plans. "What are these?"

"Tops and cross-trees – we place the tops as wooden platforms over the heads of the lower masts, and the cross-trees are placed at each top-mast head. Their purpose is to spread the rigging supporting the sails."

"Tell me about the construction process from start to finish."

"We can cover the process – but before we discuss that, think about wood. We have adequate supplies of a variety of wood, Mr. Stewart – I'm awaiting a fresh supply of live oak from South Carolina."

"Live oak?" queried Mr. Stewart.

"Yes, it is the strongest of the oaks – we prefer to use it for the hull – and this wood will resist rotting better than any other wood."

Foreign countries were envious of the forests located in Massachusetts extending south along the eastern seaboard to South Carolina. The varying species of oak and other hardwoods grew in abundance to a towering height. The newly formed states of Massachusetts, Rhode Island, Connecticut, and Pennsylvania are strategically situated for shipbuilding.

Skilled construction workers migrated from England and Europe to secure positions in shipbuilding. Suppliers could move logs through inland waterways and tributaries from inland forests. And fisheries made their appearance along the coast and bays. The Eyre brothers were fortunate – North American shipbuilders remained at a competitive advantage compared to their counterparts located in England, Holland, or France.

"Mr. Stewart – your decision concerning the wood chosen for the hull of your sail ship will impact my final price."

"Please explain."

"There is a shipment of live oak harvested in South Carolina coming by schooner," Manuel advised. "The wood is the strongest of oaks. The hull will last for thirty years or more after we salt her in the timbers."

The carpenter, upon applying salt between the planks, preserves the wood from rotting for an extended time. American vessels were constructed with oak and live oak hulls, assuming the shipowner desired to purchase a more durable vessel for a higher price. European shipbuilders had no local access to live oak, and importing oak from North America added to their production costs. A sail ship constructed in Pennsylvania was of higher value than the European ship, which had a hull laid of fir or larch wood and the interior fitted with pine.

"When we lay the keel, it will be a long one – the longer the keel, the less the ship will pitch in bad weather." Manuel pointed to the plans lying on the table.

"What will be the height of each of the three masts?" asked Mr. Stewart.

"The foremast – near sixty-one feet – the mainmast – sixty-six feet – and the mizzenmast – fifty-eight feet. The diameter of the mainmast will be nineteen inches, and the width of the main top-mast and yard will be near thirty-eight feet wide."

"Will there be a bowsprit?" Mr. Stewart followed.

Manuel pointed to the plans. "Forty-one feet long – suitable for flying two stunsails."

"Can we estimate the price?" Mr. Stewart was direct. He knew his business and always planned to reduce or control costs.

Manuel knew how to build ships – and he was one of the best. "My ship laid with an oak hull fully fitted for the sea will fetch twenty-four Spanish silver milled dollars per ton." Archibald didn't blink. "I can build the same ship laid with live oak and cedar. The price will increase to thirty-six per ton."

A similar-sized vessel constructed at ports along the Baltic would command a price near thirty-five Spanish coins per ton. A ship built of oak in England, Holland, or France, fully fitted for the sea, would cost between fifty-five to sixty coins per ton. Manuel knew his ships were valuable based upon news brought by trans-Atlantic merchants.

Mr. Stewart thought about his outlay of funds for the ship. Upon first meeting Manuel, he was struck by his knowledge, and when he spoke, he exhibited integrity and respect. He estimated a ship built of oak – 300 tons @ 24 Spanish coins per ton would cost nearly 7,200. If the shipbuilder uses live oak and cedar, the cost increases to 300 tons @ 36 coins per ton or 10,800. What will be gained if he spends 3,600 additional coins and sells his ship?

Manuel inquired. "What will be your purpose in securing a ship?"

"With the ship complete, I plan to purchase a load of flax and other desired wares to deliver the cargo to Londonderry. Trans-Atlantic trade is booming."

"Mr. Stewart – we can fill an order to complete the construction of the ship. What will you carry on your return trip?"

"Passengers – the below decks need to accommodate passengers comfortably."

"How many? We can adjust the height between decks to increase headroom and the size of the berths if desired."

Archibald wanted to be known as a merchant who planned for the welfare of passengers, and he had competition. "I like that idea – it will increase the value of the ship in the event I sell it."

"I'm going to design the hull to measure one hundred fifty feet. This length will accommodate your cabin, steerage, and cargo-carrying capacity," Manuel estimated.

Archibald thought about the measurement. "What will this do to the cost?"

"The additional charge will be minimal – I will require a three-step payment process, in Spanish coin."

"We agree – specify your process."

"One-third of the contract price to be paid within the first two weeks of the start of construction – one third upon completion of the hull, and the final third upon receipt and installing the rigging," Manuel explained.

"Agreed – draw up a contract and we can fix our signatures to it. I have another matter. I may seek an investor who would purchase a limited share, and I will require a captain. Do you have any suggestions?"

Manuel contemplated but a few seconds. "Contact Captain Joseph Haynes – he may have an interest. You'll find him at the ship's chandlery."

Providence

Upon the arrival of 1784, the Eyre brothers completed the vessel for Archibald Stewart, readying his prize for the maiden voyage to Providence and then Londonderry. The ship measured one hundred fifty feet in length and was three hundred tons burthen; a measurement applied to the maximum weight of the cargo transported in the ship's hold. Mr. Stewart opted for the construction price to be the lesser of the two choices presented. Time was essential, and waiting for live oak shipped from South Carolina would extend the construction process.

A ship carpenter attached the flag of the United States to the flagstaff at the stern. It had seven horizontal red stripes, six white stripes, and thirteen white stars set against a rich blue background. Archibald Stewart christened his newly built vessel – *Stewart.*

His new ship was a grand spectacle – all sail ships look that way when docked at a port, only moments before setting sail for the first time. The ship was three-mast, adorned with five square sails set to the foremast, five square sails to the mainmast, four sails to the mizzenmast, and four stunsails set to the bowsprit.

Dockworkers loaded a cargo of flaxseed, grown and harvested in the counties surrounding Philadelphia, combined with an ample supply of barrel staves and timber. Mr. Stewart negotiated an investment from Captain Joseph Haynes who agreed to sail their new ship to Providence. From there they would cross the Atlantic to Londonderry in a winter crossing.

Joseph Haynes, age forty-two, was from Caroline County, Virginia. An experienced shipmaster, he made many Atlantic crossings over the years. With the additional cargo loaded at Providence, the captain selected the crew of ten, and Crew Agreements was signed. A deckhand cast the lines and *Stewart* was ready to embark upon her maiden voyage to Londonderry.

Captain Haynes and the crew navigated the eight-mile-long Providence River that emptied into the Narragansett Bay. Roger Williams, a Reformed Baptist theologian founded the town of Providence in 1636.

Stewart left the Narragansett Bay entering the Providence River passing Gooseberry Island. A short distance later, they spotted Shell Island to the west, then Castle Island, followed by Hog Island to the east off the starboard bow. Their next sighting was Patience Island then Prudence Island, all of the names designated by Roger Williams.

Charles Stewart, age twelve, never having sailed before, thought it time he should accompany his father on the ship's first trans-Atlantic voyage to Londonderry. Archibald's wife, Anstis, a forename originating from the west coast, Cornwall, England, would remain at home in Providence. Archibald's brother, Richard Stewart, remained at his home in Ireland, as did his sister Rose; both were from Clare, Drummaul Parish, County Antrim.

Stewart sailed from the Narragansett Bay into the North Atlantic, and Master Haynes directed the helmsman to set the wheel to the north, navigating outside the Nantucket Shoals, sailing east of the island. Experienced New England seamen navigated the boundaries of the Gulf Stream where the current was swift, as fast as five to six miles per hour. The increased flow of the current coupled with the circling trade winds would hasten their speed. Captain Haynes sailed within the parameters of the stream as it too turned toward Great Britain. His sail plan took them off the coast of Nova Scotia, followed by Newfoundland, before turning northeast to navigate crossing the Atlantic to Ireland.

4

Limavady

Leim an Mhadaiclh – "Leap of the dog" is the Gaelic word for a small village in the northern portion of County Londonderry. The area was a planned market town, developed from the plantation settlement and founded by Sir Thomas Phillips, circa 1612. Sir Thomas was a servitor, an English soldier, and served the king by driving out the Gaelic Lords. He was a loyal subject and efficient, propelling him to become a leading figure representing the king in the settling of Ulster.

Sir Thomas advised his king regarding plans for developing County Londonderry. Before his appointment, Clan O'Cahan ruled the area for many years. Following their defeat and departure, Sir Thomas, granted 13,100 acres including the O'Cahan castle, set about repairing and improving the castle by constructing a ditch dug around the perimeter.

Limavady, located on the River Roe, is seventeen miles east of Londonderry and fourteen miles southwest of Coleraine. During the 1600s the area was settled primarily by Presbyterian Scots. Sir Thomas engaged in constructing Newtown of Limavady, nearly a mile from the O'Cahan castle, and he encouraged the Scots to build Georgian architected homes therein. Roads were laid in the pattern of a cruciform, exhibiting the shape of a cross.

Scottish fortune seekers settled in the area and built a town, and with it, a concentration of employment in the linen industry and distilling Irish whiskey ensued. English settlers followed over time, however, Scots remained dominant and outnumbered the English twenty to one. The settlement was all part of the planned population by loyal subjects of the king.

During the latter 1600s, William Connolly, a wealthy individual, and speaker in the Irish Parliament, purchased a vast land at Limavady. His estate comprising 12,886 acres was named Fruit Hill. With the passing of years, William's daughter, Hannah, married Colonel Robert McCausland, and in 1729 he inherited Fruit Hill upon the demise of William Connolly. Robert McCausland was the grandson of Baron Alexander McCausland of Dunbartonshire, a county in the west-central Lowlands of Scotland, settling in Strabane many years prior.

Robert and Hannah McCausland raised three sons: Connolly, who in time would settle at Fruit Hill, Marcus, settling at Daisy Hill, and Frederick, at Streeve Hill, all nearby Limavady. Owning and leasing land to farmers was a profitable endeavor for generating an income stream, and the colonel was no stranger to employing this method to improve his wealth. His sons and grandsons apprenticed as merchants, shippers of flaxseed, eventually transporting residents from their homeland to foreign ports.

By the mid-1700s, Frederick McCausland had two sons, Connolly, born in 1750, and his older brother Abraham, born in 1745. Frederick's wife descended from the family of Hillhouse, with mercantile connections to Belfast. Son Connolly, circa 1765–1776, apprenticed on a ship engaged in merchant trans-Atlantic trade, and Abraham, settling nearly two miles away in Culmore, followed a similar vocation.

Times were changing – increasing land rents, crop failure, religious persecution, and the advent of penal laws restricting one's civil rights passed by parliament discouraged many Scots and Irish, forcing them to press on and persevere. There was an attempt to legislate, prohibiting tenants from selling their equipment and leases and leaving Limavady, but to no avail. At the age of fifty-six, Colonel Robert McCausland watched many people from Limavady to Londonderry, descendants of those who participated in the plantation, leave their homeland forever.

A small island produces a limited quantity of timber available for constructing sail ships. As early as the 1730s, Ulster merchants engaging in trans-Atlantic trade placed orders for new vessels built in Boston, Providence, and Philadelphia. Shipwrights imported hardwoods growing in abundance along the coast of British America, because of the scarcity of wood in Ulster. The preferred method for merchants to increase the supply of ships while limiting risk was to form joint ventures.

The McCausland family invited a family member, John Stirling of Walworth, married to Connolly and Abraham's sister, to participate in a joint venture. The new partnership devised a plan and engaged a shipbuilder to build the *Walworth* and *Jane*, and funds for the vessels were secured by Thomas Barclay, a merchant born in Strabane who emigrated to Philadelphia years prior.

Free Passengers & Redemptioners

By 1768, Connolly McCausland, now a ship captain, took command of *Walworth*, sailing from Londonderry to Charlestown, South Carolina, arriving on May 21, 1769, then departing for North Carolina before arriving at Liverpool. During the years 1770 and 1771-1773, Connolly commanded voyages between Londonderry and Philadelphia. Abraham, together with business partner James Mitchell, served in the capacity of transporting Ulster passengers. A portion of the emigrants were McCausland leaseholders from nearby Limavady.

In 1771 *Walworth* arrived at the port of Philadelphia. Captain McCausland placed an ad in the Pennsylvania Chronicle advertising the ship was carrying *redemptioners* (indentured servants). Contracts bound redemptioners in exchange for the payment of their voyage costs, and the contracts were sold to interested parties after the ship docked. They were an assortment of men and women with occupations defined by their skills, including tailoring, weaving, blacksmithing, and laborers. At port arrival, redemptioners left the vessel to secure contact, often with a relative, who would share in the cost of paying the contract balance to the captain or the responsible merchant to secure their freedom. Some ran away from their obligation and the captain was forced to chase after them or post an ad in the newspaper, offering a reward for their capture and return. Anyone interested in purchasing a contract was instructed to contact Connolly McCausland, Master of *Walworth*, or contact the agents, Carsan, Barclay, and Mitchell.

Londonderry Journal – April 21, 1772
"Ship *Walworth* – 250 tons, a stout ship, almost new and a fast sailer to sail with nearly 300 passengers and provisions to Philadelphia."

Walworth arrived June 22, all healthy and all well, the duration of the voyage being eight weeks as reported in the Journal on November 13.

Throughout 1773 Connolly McCausland remained as master of the *Walworth*. He, or his brother Abraham, placed advertisements in the Journal as residents in Ulster continued to leave their homeland, destined to embrace new opportunities in British America. An ad published March 12 notified readers the *Walworth* would sail for Philadelphia and docking at New Castle before arriving at the final destination, April 6 to May 10. The timing depended on the number of passengers signing with the agents securing their passage, and favorable winds were always a determining factor for the sail.

Walworth was cleared for sail on May 25 but set her sails on June 7. On this voyage, the Journal notified everyone there was a change in destination. *Walworth* would sail to Charlestown, South Carolina, then Cape Fear in North Carolina. Agents responsible for securing the passengers and providing provisions and assigning accommodations were James Mitchell, Andrew McCausland, a relative of the captain, and James Stirling, all listed as merchants.

∞

Lough Swilley means lake of shadows, and the body of water is a glacial fjord situated between the western side of the Innishowen Peninsula and the Fanal Peninsula in County Donegal. Ships, often named after people and places, and in this instance, *Lough Swilley* was the subject of an advertisement in the Journal on January 19, 1774. The sail ship arrived from Philadelphia carrying water casks ready to fill. She was an excellent stout ship, relatively new. Residents of Ulster received news of events occurring in British America and other places, all the result of ship captains bringing local newspapers on their return voyage.

On March 12 *Lough Swilley* set sail, however, the destination was changed due to the request of some passengers, very respectable families. She departed Londonderry on April 6th and arrived safely at the Port of Charlestown, according to a report published in the South Carolina Gazette, on August 31st, carried back to Londonderry.

Over the years, *Walworth* made multiple voyages from Londonderry, Liverpool, and Cork, sailing to Philadelphia, Charlestown, and New York. Upon sailing from Londonderry, *Walworth* transported passengers, linens, and assorted goods such as butter and provisions from Cork.

The McCausland family embraced the increasing flow of people desiring to leave Ulster by providing them additional opportunities for passage. Being of Protestant descent, they sympathized with their plight and poor living conditions. Was the issue causing people to migrate determined solely by one's religion? Indeed not – the combination of economics and parliamentary law drove residents to consider alternatives. In addition to cargo trade, providing people trans-Atlantic passage was a profitable enterprise, and there was lots of money to be made. Abraham McCausland placed the following ad in the Londonderry Journal, 1784.

FOR NEWCASTLE AND PHILADELPHIA
The Remarkable stout New Brig
CULMORE PACKET 300 Tons

Micah Campbell, Master, will be clear to sail from this Port, the 1st day of August next. Passengers, Redemptioners, and Servants that wish to go in the completest Brig ever left Derry are desired to apply to Abm. McCausland, Merchant, Connolly McCausland, Master, Streeve Hill, or Mr. Rob. McCausland, Coleraine. – *Mefs* beef (beef liver), and the best of Provisions will be put on Board, and Water in Abundance. Free houses will be at Culmore, and no Passenger shall be at a Penny Expense in going in and out. Captain Campbell has had as much Experience in the Passenger Line as any other out of this Port. L:Derry 22nd June 1784. Whoever wishes to be at Sea, I beg they will make no Delay, But give their Earnest the right of way. A. McCausland

5

The Colquhouns of Luss

Ulster materialized into a land of names; people's names, names of baronies, a historical subdivision of a county. Undertakers, wealthy men from England and Scotland were granted land and brought tenants. Still, others were servitors, military, and administrators serving the king. And there were names of townlands and parishes, areas administered by a church, and names of estates, a division of land owned by a family. Each name defined the location or description of the land or identified those who settled within the land. One could guess the source or point of their migration. And most importantly, Ulster was filled with names of people who identified with power and the basis for their power.

Across the North Channel in the Kingdom of Scotland dwelt a clan in the County of Dunbartonshire, occupying the lowlands in the parish of Luss, situated on the west bank of Loch Lamond. A Gaelic word, luss stood for plant or herb. The region became a designated lieutenancy, an area where Lord-Lieutenants ruled the lives of people. They were appointed by the reigning monarch upon consultation with legal advisers to the king or queen, whoever happened to occupy the throne at the time.

Records exist for Clan Colquhoun as far back as the 1200s. Dunbartonshire and Dunbarton Castle became the center for the well-connected, even upper-class Colquhouns. The reigning monarch bestowed titles upon people creating a society of nobles (a social class ranked immediately below royalty), landed gentry (a social class of landowners), and those who derived fortunes as merchants. Titles and honors such as mister, esquire, gentleman, or sir were attached to their names.

After the passing of hundreds of years and the advent of the Plantation at Ulster, in 1625, Sir Walter Stewart of Minto, an undertaker from County Roxburghshire, sold to Sir John Colquhoun of Luss, one of twelve land parcels containing one thousand acres in the Laggan Valley. Within the acreage were portions of rich fertile soil lying to the west of the River Foyle in County Donegal. In the same year, King James I bestowed upon Sir John Colquhoun the title of Baronet (the lowest titled hereditary British order) of Nova Scotia.

Near the same time, Sir Walter Stewart negotiated another sale of 1,000 acres to Alexander Colquhoun, Laird of Luss, of Scotland. Upon Alexander's passing, the Colquhoun estate at Corkagh, inherited by his descendants, built a house and barn.

One hundred years pass by. Throughout the century, more Colquhouns migrated from Scotland, purchasing land and investing in land leases in many townlands within County Donegal and parts of County Tyrone. Given their class of landed gentry, they remained in the good graces of the crown and parliament by aligning with the Protestant Church of Ireland. Their Gaelic language was different from that of the Irish, and while similarities in spelling existed, the pronunciation of Scottish Gaelic words was different from Irish Gaelic. Over time Clan Colquhoun shortened their surname to Colhoun.

By 1727 William C. Colhoun of Crosh House, County Tyrone, entered into a deed of lease with James Mayes for lands at Knockgarren. By 1740 Audley Colhoun of Newtownstewart, County Tyrone became a common source of multiple real estate transactions for many years. He alleged fraud perpetrated by William Hamilton of Belltrim, in specified land agreements. In 1740, 3rd Viscount Lord Mountjoy of Ramelton, County Donegal, entered into a lease with David Colhoun for the benefit of his sons, David, William, and John Colhoun.

In 1756 the will of William Colhoun, husband of Patience McCausland was registered. She was a relative of the landowning and merchant McCausland family of Limavady. William left a vast land including townland locations to his inheritors.

Clergy also participated in land ownership and leasing as in 1766, Reverend Alexander Colhoun of Tullyrash, County Tyrone, sold land parcels in Inniskillin for £500 to his son, Alexander. In 1773 William and Thomas Colhoun from Glenmaqueen, and Pat Colhoun of Robertspencetown, both in Donegal, sold to William Boyd one-half of the townland of Glenmaqueen.

The Registry of Deeds in County Donegal over time became filled with many land transactions listing multiple names of Colhouns, and the location of the transactions was in the Laggan Valley, County Donegal, and parts of County Tyrone.

∞

A family of Hamiltons from the settlement at Paisley, situated in the west-central lowlands near Glasgow, Scotland, migrated near Dunalong, midway between Londonderry and the market town Strabane, County Tyrone. Lord Claud Hamilton, the son of the First Earl of Abercorn, James Hamilton, married Jane Colquhoun, the daughter of Alexander Colquhoun from Luss. Before the plantation, he received the title of Baron Paisley by King James VI, and his son James became the Second Baron Paisley. During the Plantation of Ulster, Lord Hamilton received 3,000 acres near Strabane and Dunalong, County Tyrone.

The Colquhouns of Luss, together with the Hamiltons of Paisley, now resided in Ulster and brought with them a degree of wealth and prestige. Sir Frederick Hamilton, brother to the First Earl, volunteered to take up arms and fought in the army of Gustavus Adolphus, the King of Sweden. Sir Frederick married Sidney, daughter to Sir John Vaughn, then Governor of Londonderry, serving in this capacity from a British military appointment.

Gustavus Hamilton (1642-1723), First Viscount Boyne, was a distinguished military officer in service to William of Orange, King William III of England. Gustavus raised six regiments for fighting in the Battle of the Boyne during the siege of Londonderry, 1690. Alexander Colhoun married Judith Hamilton (1664-1705), the niece of the First Viscount.

Through these years marriages occur between branches of the Colhouns with members of the Hamilton and McCausland families. Their wealth and societal position increased in importance in Ulster, and within a generation, the mid-1700s, three Colhoun brothers, Thomas, the eldest, followed by Gustavus, and Hugh, all single men, are destined to migrate as their forefathers did many years before. Thomas, born in 1760, Gustavus, born in 1765, and Hugh, 1767, are undergoing apprenticeships designed to educate and secure skills to formulate a trade, becoming merchants, cargo carriers, and mariners. Their migration will take them to the port of Philadelphia in British America, and just as their ancestors left Scotland for Ulster, the three brothers over multiple years will leave Ulster for Philadelphia.

6

Londonderry 1784

Tuesday, March 16th arrived after a quick passage of more than three thousand miles and less than one month. Captain Haynes guided *Stewart* through the northwestern coast of Ulster, entering *Lough Foyle*. His ship sailed through a narrow passage between Magilligan Point, a vast peninsula lying to the east, and filled with a lush green-grassed pasture, past sandy banks, and the rolling hills near Greencastle, *Innishowen*, with County Donegal to the west.

"Mr. Quigly," called Captain Haynes to his helmsman, "One point to starboard."

John Quigly sailed with Captain Haynes often. He was twenty-five years of age and came from Worcester, Massachusetts. Years before, in 1778, he enlisted as a private serving in Captain March Chase's Company, a contingent in Colonel Nathan Sparhawk's Regiment. He intended to fight for the citizens of Massachusetts in the War of Independence, however, his tour of duty was cut short after three months and an injury.

Lough Foyle is a body of water protected from the westerly winds of the Atlantic. There would be ships of varying sizes navigating the waters of the channel on this day.

"One point starboard," responded Mr. Quigley. *Stewart* responded as westerly breezes filled the topgallants. His ship was sailing the channel through the widening Lough Foyle, leading to the waterway to Culmore Point and eventually Londonderry.

Charles Stewart pointed to a lonely tall stone structure in the distance. "Father – what is that?"

"Charles – that's a spire – the top of a church."

"But what church?" Charles asked.

There appeared a magnificent view of the spire and other nearby buildings as they approached the wharves at *Ship Quay*, Londonderry.

"St. Columb's Cathedral, son."

Charles's eyes fixated on the shore. "Old – it must be ancient."

"Yes, Charles – it has been there a very long time – over one hundred years. Workers laid the foundation in 1633."

"Father, there is no building as magnificent as this in Providence."

"Yes, son – King Henry VIII decreed the Church of Ireland as the state church in 1536, and in 1633, the church existed to serve the people who became part of a new settlement."

Charles, enamored, ran to the bowsprit. His father followed his son. "The color of the stone is unusual."

"It was built of green-gray *schist* (shelf-like grains in the stone)."

Eight years before, Frederick Hervey, 4th Earl of Bristol and the Bishop of Londonderry, added to the tower's height by erecting the stone spire. The church building, located inside the stone wall, measured one and one-half miles in circumference. It was a fortification surrounding Londonderry, built in varying heights of twelve to thirty-five feet, and about twenty-nine feet thick.

A two-mast schooner with five sails and a staysail attached to the bowsprit navigated the river. Several small *currachs* (rowboats) were floating near the riverbank, and a small ferry carried five men and two small horses toward the townland. A two-mast brig near two hundred tons sat motionless at the quay. The brig flew the British flag and was loaded with one hundred and fifty passengers.

"Father, why are those people standing on the deck of that brig?" Charles inquired, pointing to the ship docked at the quay.

"They are leaving son – leaving their homes, farms, and their livelihood."

"But why are they leaving?" Charles persisted.

"They need work, son – some have lost their employment – some are seeking new employment in a new land. The reasons for their departure are greater than you can imagine son."

Many people – fathers, mothers, children, young ones, and others nearing the threshold of adulthood, leaned on the *gunwale* of the brig, waving to Archibald and Charles. Others pressed against the gunwale on the port side waving to family and friends standing at the quay.

"Many of those passengers are farmers, son," Archibald continued. "They have lost their farms – landlords raised their rents – they can no longer meet payments, and they are saying goodbye."

"Where are they sailing to – where will they go?"

"To one of the thirteen states son – no longer British colonies. There is fertile land in central Pennsylvania. Settlers are moving west of the Susquehanna River – a new frontier is ripe for settling son."

Captain Haynes stood on watch at the quarterdeck. With one-half of the sails lowered, he guided his ship toward the quay.

"What other places, father – is Pennsylvania the only state with available land suitable for farming?"

"No, son – the ship may be headed to Nova Scotia, but I think it probable the captain is sailing to Philadelphia or Baltimore. There is farmland available in Maryland and Virginia too."

"Virginia – the homeland of General Washington and Thomas Jefferson," Charles added.

"Yes son, and don't forget Captain Haynes is from Virginia."

"And Philadelphia is the capitol?" Charles followed.

"Yes – you learn your lessons well. Who is our President under the Articles of Federation?"

Charles hesitated. "I don't know father, who is?"

"Thomas Mifflin, a Pennsylvanian – served under General Washington in the war," replied his father teaching for the moment.

∞

More than one hundred fifty years before, this land was granted to twelve London Guild Companies, providing they would invest funds and develop the ports of Londonderry and Coleraine. Throughout the following years, these ports received an influx of merchants and artisans. While the English controlled the ownership of land, many people from Scotland settled alongside them.

Years before 1784, colonists were purchasing more linen from Londonderry than their British counterparts. Merchants filled ships returning to North American ports with linen goods and passengers. About thirty percent of Scots-Irish, near 75,000, left the port of Londonderry, destined for the colonies and Canada. Londonderry merchants accounted for the ownership of near seventy ships. In these years, close to one-tenth of passengers were indentured servants securing passage to American ports. The majority of indentured servants left through the ports of Cork, located near the southern coast, and Dublin, on the east coast, and Waterford, situated at the southeastern side of the island.

Archibald and Charles stayed on the *Stewart*, docked at Ship Quay. It was convenient to organize and auction their cargo of flaxseed, potash – a fine white powder, pearl ash, and barrel staves. Charles placed a sign advertising the date and details of the sale next to the gangplank. They wanted gunsmiths, a house carpenter, blacksmiths, a cooper, and a bricklayer. If Archibald found the right applicants, he talked to them about transferring to Pennsylvania.

Advertisement
Londonderry Journal
March – 1784

Arrival – Ship *Stewart* – from Providence, Rhode Island

The 300-ton ship *Stewart* has arrived accompanied by the owner, Mr. Archibald Stewart, merchant of Providence and native of Ballintoy, will sell on Wednesdays and Saturdays. The sales to begin at 1 o'clock each of said days on the Ship Quay, for terms for cash or good bills on London at thirty-one days sight – a cargo of flaxseed, white oak barrel staves, wheel timber, and American pot and pearl ash of the first quality. All interested parties should report to the dock at Ship Quay where the auction of flaxseed and other provisions will commence on each market day until the entire contents are sold.

Many years before, the wall surrounding Londonderry offered protection to the residents inside. Four gates provided access to the town. A walk to the diamond in the center of town was but a short stroll through the Ship-Quay gate, up Ship-Quay Street to the intersection of Ferry-Quay Street and Butchers Street.

Ship-Quay Street contained red-bricked Georgian-style buildings, all attached, some with exterior windows covering four stories, and others with the roof slanted to accommodate three levels. A number of the buildings were residences of prominent people of Londonderry society. Other buildings, constructed with large glass windows suitable for merchants displaying their goods and wares, faced the street.

All four of the streets led to the center of town, ending at the diamond. The market days of Wednesday and Saturday were the center of attraction for many people, those conducting business, others procuring the necessities, and a place where socializing abounded.

Stores lining the streets were places to conduct business, and everyone was there. One found a painter, a baker, a farrier, horse dealers, and a chandler (dealer in equipment and supplies for a ship). Walk further and you pass the shoemaker, cheesemonger, breadmaker, gardener, and lamplighter. Continue further and there is an upholsterer, carpenter, coal merchant, coachman, newsman, wheelwright, a saddler, who makes and repairs saddlery, a tailor, fishmonger, linen draper, bricklayer, coach-master, physician, auctioneer, wine merchant, and coach maker.

John Moore, a Londonderry physician, lived at Clerger Street, Charles Elliott, an auctioneer, maintained an office on Bond Street, Barth Arlett, coach-master, was also on Bond. Clement Watts provided engraving services, William Wheatley made coaches at North Audleys Street, and the ladies patronized John Drummond, the perfumer on Hanover Street.

Chief agents, acting on behalf of more than one hundred passenger vessels, manned offices at Londonderry, Portrush, Belfast, Newry, and Larne. Farmers and artisans navigated the hinterlands in their efforts to reach the ports. The hinterland was designated by a line joining Dunfanaghy in County Donegal to Castlederg and the Clogher Valley in County Tyrone to the lower sections of the Bann Valley.

Each chief agent would hire out-agents and place them at locations where potential emigrants would seek information to assist them with making the passage to foreign ports. Agents servicing the port of Londonderry focused on obtaining passengers from eastern Donegal, most of Tyrone, and the entirety of Londonderry. They were near the Loughs Foyle and Swilly, and the valleys of the Foyle and Strule inhabited by a concentration of Protestants, those more likely to have money.

There were instances where the captains of ships made unadvertised visits to towns and villages on market days to meet people. Charles McKenzie, Master of the ship *Peace & Plenty*, visited Ballynahinch, Lisburn, and Ballymena, advertising for passage from Belfast to New York and Philadelphia. Potential emigrants learned to ask questions to discern truth from fiction. Master McKenzie spoke of opportunity in America, describing the land as good, cheap, absent of taxation by the church, with little or no rent. Ulstermen approached the decision of a lifetime, uprooting an entire family, and therefore were justified in scrutinizing everything told. The phrase "Look before you leap" was repeated often in the marketplace, cautioning anyone to examine what they were told by merchants, chief agents and out-agents, captains, and land speculators.

Londonderry grew into an active shipping port and for a variety of reasons. Transporting people was one of them. Local merchants owned passenger vessels named *Diane, Hamilton Galley, City of Derry, Hopewell, Willey, Jupiter, Admiral Hawke, Henry, Alexander, Hellen, Mary, Minerva,* and *Betty.* There were numerous other vessels with ownership interest vested by Londonderry merchants. Names such as *King George, Phoenix, Marquis of Granby, Rose, Hibernia, Walworth, Prince of Wales,* and *Hannah* were among them.

The port of Londonderry received many emigrants through the services of the out-agents. There were five located at Coleraine, four at Maghera, both in County Londonderry, Ballygawley, County Tyrone, and Rathmelton, County Donegal. Also, the port of Belfast maintained three out-agents: two at Omagh and one at Strabane, County Tyrone. Other out-agents worked at Garrison, County Fermanagh, Caledon, Carntiel, Eskra, County Tyrone, Castledoe, Convoy, Fahan, Letterkenny, and Raphoe, County Donegal, then Richhill, County Armagh, Downpatrick, County Down, and Ballymoney, in County Antrim.

Side streets including Rosemary Lane, Eddes Lane, and Castle Lane contained buildings occupied by more merchants, including many who were shipowners, possessing shares in a vessel outfitted for passenger trade. The names of some shipowners included Robert Alexander, Thomas Beesley, Ninian Boggs, Ephraim Campbell, Samuel Curry, Abraham McCausland, James Miller, James Mitchell, Thomas Moore, and James Stirling of Walworth.

The town directory included all. It was common for James Harvey, Abraham McCausland, James Mitchell, James Stirling, and others to seek Samuel Carsan and his partners for securing passenger trade. Fourteen years prior, in 1770, Samuel Carsan opened a branch in Baltimore to expand his merchant business. He was also active in providing information to residents of Ulster, assisting them to relocate to Donegal Springs in south-central Pennsylvania. Carsan Barclay & Mitchell was deemed the most important firm dealing in flaxseed and merchant trade. Merchant R. Caldwell sold flax and spirits such as rum and brandy, along with soap, indigo, steel, almonds, tea, porter, and even tar and gunpowder.

∞

The harbormaster at Londonderry records the details of ships arriving and departing the port. During the 1780s, some of his records included specifics for the following vessels.

Walworth – 250 tons – Master Connolly McCausland – Agent, Abraham McCausland, James Mitchell, James Stirling

Jupiter – 300 tons – Master Alexander Ewing – Agent, Andrew Gregg, James Mitchell & owners

Admiral Hawke – 300 tons – Master McCadden – Agent, Caldwell, Vance & Caldwell

Marquis of Granby – 300 tons – Master Archibald McIlwaine – Agent, John Maulevery, Thomas Beesley, Dickson Cunningham

Henry – 350 tons – Master Samuel Hunter – Agent, Alexander, & owner

Phenix – 300 tons – Master James Mitchell – Agent, Caldwell, Vance & Caldwell – Owner James Stirling

Rebecca – 150 tons – Captain Marcus McCausland

Rose – 300 tons – Master William Dysart – Agent, James Harvey, Thomas Moore, Samuel Curry, William Hope

Minerva – 400 tons – Master Francis Fearis – Agent, Caldwell, Vance & Caldwell

Prince of Wales – 300 tons – Master Thomas Morrison, Agent, James Thompson

Betty – 200 tons – Master James McCay – Agent, Abraham McCausland, Robert Houston, Maxwell Kennedy

Hannah – 400 tons – Master James Mitchell – Agent, James Stirling, James Harvey

Nancy – 300 tons –Master Norman Cheevers – Agent, William Caldwell, John Caldwell

Hellen – 200 tons – Master James Ramage – Agent, Dickson, Conyngham, Abraham McCausland

Mary – 350 tons – Master Robert George – Agent, William Hope, William Glen, Thomas Chambers, Abraham McCausland – Owners, Joseph Adams, John Alexander, Andrew Cochrane

∞

Archibald Stewart and Abraham McCausland met at Mrs. Millers on Brewery Lane nearby the Ferry Quay. The reason for the meeting, suspected by Archibald, was imminent to Abraham – he wished to purchase his ship, *Stewart*. Abraham, from Limavady, was well connected in the market towns from Coleraine to Londonderry. He built several investment partnerships with other merchants in multiple trade ships. A savvy man, Abraham saw an opportunity and wasn't about to pass on this one. Some other merchants will seize it if he doesn't do so first. Archibald Stewart trusted him and Abraham gave him no cause for distrust. The McCausland family was well-known, landlords holding a significant acreage with tenants residing for many years about thirty miles distance west of Ballintoy, the place of Stewart's upbringing.

"Your ship has fine lines, and she's a new vessel," Abraham opened.

"Had her built last year in Philadelphia – this was her maiden voyage."

Abraham surveyed the vessel. "Who laid the timbers?"

"Built by Manuel Eyre and his two brothers at Kensington. Perhaps you have heard of them in your travels. The Eyres, Manuel, Jehu, and Benjamin, at one point, set aside their business to join the American Revolution."

The McCauslands were loyal to King George III – they found leaving the homeland objectionable. However, there was an empathetic bond with those leaving, and there was money to be made. Archibald's character and beliefs formed within the Presbyterian community; Abraham joined the Church of Ireland, which presented a difference.

"My brother Connolly may know of the brothers."

"I'm sure he has," Archibald replied. His home was in Providence and he was a citizen of the United States. Abraham, while trustworthy, was also shrewd, an astute businessman, a proven negotiator.

Archibald added, "The ship was designed to be a fast sailer and appointed for the passenger trade. The English and French can be troublesome on the high seas, but you know that, Abraham. The Eyres built her to outrun them if they prove to be trouble."

"Archibald – would you consider the sale of your ship?"

Archibald, armed with foreknowledge, knew many American-built sail ships rarely crossed the Atlantic more than two times before they were bought – snapped up by foreign merchants and investors. He knew of some newly built sail ships loaded with a cargo of masts and spars, freight in demand, and set sail for a promising market. Upon reaching their destination the cargo would be unloaded, new cargo loaded, and they set a course for England where the ship would be sold upon arrival. The crew would secure passage in another ship to return home or engage in another sail. Shipbuilders in America also found work in building frigates and sloops of war for the British Royal Navy.

"Abraham, I intended to employ the ship in the merchant trade for some time," he shrewdly responded.

"We desire to add a ship to our fleet – we will consider terms to make it profitable," Abraham added. He knew Archibald built the ship in America for less money than the same ship built in European ports. Why not capitalize and purchase a new vessel at a cost below what he would pay for a vessel constructed in Belfast, for example.

"Abraham – I consider your interest to be serious – I might entertain a sale, but I must advise – it would require a combination of payment of cash and a reputable note for me to consider parting with a ship of this quality. You see, I am placing an ad in the Journal, seeking passengers to accompany our return voyage to New Castle and Providence, and soon," he responded.

"I am fully aware of your plans." Abraham unfolded a page from the Londonderry Journal and laid it on the table in front of Mr. Stewart.

FOR NEWCASTLE AND RHODE ISLAND
The Ship *STEWART*
Burthen 300 tons
Jos. Haynes, Master

Will be clear to sail for the above Ports the 15th of May next. This vessel was built last Year, sails remarkably fast, and is in every respect well calculated for the Passenger Trade. For Freight or Passage apply to Mr. A. Stewart at Mrs. H. Millers next the Ferry Quay, or the Master on Board said Vessel.

A few good Coopers (a maker of casks and barrels) and House Carpenters may meet with advantageous Offers, by applying to said Mr. Stewart, who is a native of Ireland, born in the County of Antrim, near Ballintoy, but hath been in America these 22 Years last past; and as he intends returning in said Ship to his Family in America, he will take particular Care upon the Voyage, that all Passengers shall be treated with Tenderness and Humanity, and that Provisions of every Kind shall Be amply laid in, and of the best Quality. – Londonderry, 22nd March 1784.

∞

"Archibald – should you desire to sell your ship, know that my brother, Captain Connolly McCausland, of Streeve Hill, Limavady, is interested in an ownership position also. We would entertain a proposal from you to purchase the ship and take ownership ourselves, however, should you desire to maintain partial ownership we could discuss the details of your requirements." Abraham desired to purchase the ship for himself, but he would settle for an interest in a partnership if he and his partner held a majority interest.

Archibald studied the merchant's facial expression and measured his words, responding, "I'll give serious thought to your proposal. Joseph Haynes, Master of *Stewart*, also maintains an ownership position, and together, we will discuss your interest and respond."

Archibald poured over McCausland's interest in securing ownership in *Stewart* and brought the offer before Captain Haynes. The captain encouraged Archibald to consider a fair price, sufficient to provide them with a fair profit. Captain Haynes believed one captain owning an interest in the ship was enough. The new partnership bought his interest. Archibald considered a price sufficient to provide them the desired profit. Abraham eagerly agreed. In April 1784, the ship *Stewart*, the name changed to *Faithful Steward*, was sold. A new partnership of Abraham and Connolly McCausland, owning two-thirds interest, joined Archibald Stewart, retaining one-third ownership.

Londonderry Journal, Tuesday, April 20, 1784
And April 27, May 4, May 11, and May 18

FOR NEWCASTLE, DELAWARE, AND RHODE ISLAND
THE SHIP *FAITHFUL STEWARD*
Burthen 300 Tons
Jos. Haynes, Master

Will be clear to sail for the above Ports the 15th of May next. This vessel was built last Year, sails remarkably fast, and is in every Respect well calculated for the Passenger Trade. For Freight or Passage apply to Mr. A. Stewart, at Mrs. Millers next the Ferry Quay, or the Captain on Board said vessel.

As Abraham McCausland, Merchant, and Connolly McCausland have purchased two-thirds of the Ship *Faithful Steward*, they Pledge themselves to every Person that would wish to take their Passage in said Ship, to have the greatest Plenty of Provisions laid in, so that they may have a pleasant and agreeable Voyage. Connolly McCausland goes out Master of said Ship (with Jos. Haynes, Master), who is well-known to have made many fortunate voyages to America. Any Passenger that would choose to go in said Ship will have two free Houses at each Side of Culmore Point until said Ship sails, and any Passengers coming from the County of Antrim will have also free Stores at Coleraine or Portrush, by applying to Robert McCausland, Esquire, Custom House, Coleraine, who will give every Encouragement necessary.

All Passengers that intend going in the above Ship are requested to come to Londonderry by the 20th of May, which Day they will be taken on board, and proceed immediately.

On Tuesday, May 11, the Londonderry Journal published an advertisement notifying all potential passengers *Faithful Steward* would sail on May 20th next. Two weeks later, Tuesday, the 25th, Master McCausland requested all passengers to attend at Culmore located four miles downstream where the river joins Lough Foyle, positively this week, as all will be taken on board and sail without delay.

People continued to make way for Londonderry, expecting to sail on *Faithful Steward*; therefore, the increase in interested passengers precipitated a delay in departure. The Journal, on Tuesday, June 15th, ran an ad, "Cleared for Newcastle, *Faithful Steward*, McCausland." The Tuesday edition of the Journal on June 22nd ran a follow-up. "Since our last, the ships *St. Patrick* and *Faithful Steward* sailed for America, having nearly one thousand passengers on board.

The McCauslands owned partnerships in other vessels aside from their newly purchased shares in *Faithful Steward*. A brig, *Culmore Packet*, was an example. The Londonderry Journal ran another ad in their June 22nd edition.

FOR NEWCASTLE AND PHILADELPHIA
THE REMARKABLE STOUT NEW BRIG
CULMORE PACKET – Burthen 300 tons

Micah Campbell, Master – Will be clear to sail from this Port, the 1st day of August next. Passengers, Redemptioners, and Servants, that wish to go in the completest Brig ever leaving Derry are desired to apply to Abm. McCausland, Merchant, Connolly McCausland, Master, Streeve Hill, or Mr. Rob. McCausland, Coleraine. Beef and the best Provisions will be put on Board, and Water in Abundance. Free houses will be at Culmore, and no Passenger shall be at a Penny Expense in going in and out. Capt. Campbell has had as much Experience in the Passenger Line as any other out of this Port. Whoever wishes to be at Sea, I beg they will make no Delay, but give their Earnest the right of way. A. McCausland.

Given the number of vessels owned by Londonderry merchants sailing to American ports, it was common for one vessel to pass one another, and many sail ships were from Irish and British ports. Captains of each ship engaged each other on the seas, weather conditions permitting. In so doing, they reported sightings, relaying news at their destination. Current news was printed in the papers for the benefit of family, friends, business associates, and other interested readers.

On Tuesday, October 12th, the Journal received news from the brigantine *Peggy*, Master G. Stewart, arriving in Londonderry after a passage of thirty days from Philadelphia. "By this vessel, we have an account of the safe arrival of the ships *St. Patrick* and *Faithful Steward*, and also the brigs *Buckskin* and *Jenny*, all from this port." The captain delivered several newspapers, including a copy of the Pennsylvania Gazette, to the Journal.

7

Wharves of Philadelphia C. 1785

Merchants used the term, carrying trade – financing a sail ship at lower rates and using the ship as an asset to generate trade overseas. By the 1780s, trade was expanding between the colonies and the West India Islands, which meant a lucrative business existence for the merchants of Philadelphia. Residents near the Delaware River were treated with views of an assortment of vessels, small sailboats to large brigs and ships, all arriving and departing the wharves by the riverfront. Colonial merchants amassed pork, beef, flour, apples, onions, butter, and lard, exporting their goods to the islands. They loaded their ships with sugar, rum, coffee, oranges, lemons, and pineapples on the return voyage.

People near the wharves heard cannon booms nearly five miles downriver, signaling another safe arrival of a merchant ship. Men, young and old, boys too, walked to the docks to watch the ship make the turn at the bend in the Delaware River. If one were standing at the Water Street wharf by Callowhill, they saw a grouping of dirty yellow frame structures. Boarding houses, places to lodge, and *groggeries* occupied the area. Many a seller of provisions conducted business along the street, and sometimes hucksters auctioned their unsold property to would-be purchasers.

Britton's Wharf occupied a significant section along the river for shipbuilding. Taylor's Dock provided a respite for one seeking a bath and revival of the muscles. And West's Wharf received imported salt. The river on the upper side of Vine Street was a muddy branch, the dock dirty, but smaller craft and *shallops*, a light sailboat used for coastal fishing, were moored there.

Water Street, aptly named for its convenient location, consisted of an assortment of wharves lined in a row. On the opposite side, one found the business locations of a variety of merchants. Wood Wharf, rightly named, was built behind John Bretton's boatyard, and Vine Street Wharf was nearby. Lumber was loaded for export at this location as Eyre and Massey sent their ship *Portia*, carrying lumber as far away as Madeira, an archipelago of islands southwest of Portugal. Harvey & Davis, a ship *chandlery* – seller of sailing equipment and supplies, was located in the middle of the pier by a group of buildings called the red stores. It was common to watch silver – Spanish dollars, changing hands to complete trade transactions. Nearby, Arch Street Wharf smelled of alcohol seeping from the cut lumber of hickory, oak, pine, maple, and gum, all stored in anticipation of being exported by the merchants owning the stock.

William Newbold, a partner in Montgomery & Newbold, formed a counting-house. Pennsylvania farmers, growers located in Chester and Lancaster Counties planted flaxseed for consumption. Merchants bought excess harvests and shipped them to Ireland. Flour and bread were primary exports; however, flaxseed ranked third. As trade associations formed, counting houses were employed to tabulate all import and export shipments. A hogshead was the measurement for seven bushels of seed, and exports shipped from Philadelphia totaled 70,000 bushels.

Residents enclosed their yards with wooden fences. After passing the offices of Montgomery & Newbold, a narrow passage led to Clifford's Wharf. One merchant, Stephen Girard, owned the length of a dock of such breadth to accommodate the largest of his sail ships. At the northeast corner of his wharf, the dock sunk to a low water mark at high tide, providing a convenient place (broken-wharf) for swimming. It was common to see Stephen, constantly rising near dawn, making his way down to the wharf's edge, hoping to see the latest ship arrival turning the bend. He was shrewd, employing intellect and instinctive bargaining to obtain what he was after. His goal was to generate wealth, do good deeds, and increase his wealth that much more. In society, the man was imbued with an overwhelming sense of doing what was right, coming to aid fellow men, assisting the poor, and those in need.

A story once circulated of a man, struggling economically, who approached Girard, asking for alms or a means of work. Stephen pointed to a large pile of bricks, requesting he move the bricks to the other side along his property line. He would pay him for his efforts. The man moved each brick, piling and stacking them as instructed, then knocked on his door. Stephen asked him to move the bricks and place them on the opposite side to the place where they once lay. The man did so, completed the task, and knocked on his door, the job done as instructed. He paid him for his work and asked once more – please move the bricks across the property to the spot where he first laid them. The man refused. Mr. Girard replied – you do not want to work.

Jacob Dunton harbored small sailboats, and William Bethel operated another ship chandlery at Bickley's Wharf. By the corner at Bickley's, the ferry house used to transport people and goods across the Delaware River to Camden, was purchased by Stephen Girard.

Residents living on the eastern side of Philadelphia walked to Market Street Wharf to frequent the fish market operated at the entrance. Once winter arrived, children and the young at heart used the hills next to the wharf for sledding. A transportation terminal used to harbor the *packets* from Wilmington-New Castle materialized the next block below.

Traveling further south, one found a series of piers where trade from fascinating places around the world transpired. The area from Chestnut through Walnut Streets was named the India Wharf, 170 feet in width, owned by merchant and financier Robert Morris. He made provision for the Burlington packets, ocean-going sail ships carrying mail, to moor at his wharf. After Commodore John Barry finished his command of the famed frigate, *Alliance*, Mr. Morris bought the vessel and re-fitted it for the East India trade. The *Alliance*, 724 tons burthen, made a voyage to China under Thomas Reed, Master, Commodore Dale, First Mate, and George Harrison, Supercargo.

Merchants wishing to export and import goods to Liverpool waited for notifications for available shipping dates at Cope's Wharf. Next door to India Wharf, the 160-foot-long dock was administered by Thomas Cope. The next wharf down was Boss's Wharf, also 160 feet wide, harbored brigs and small sail-craft.

Morton's Wharf led to Morris Wharf, which led to once Scottish lawyer Andrew Hamilton's Wharf, and at the corner was James Yard, another merchant specializing in shipping goods to St. Croix in the Caribbean. Some of the ships docked at Yard's Wharf sailed to Spain, Havana, and Europe.

On the south side of Dock Street, the Joseph Stamper family-owned and operated Stamper's Wharf. Stampers was the same wharf where Connolly McCausland docked his ship, *Faithful Steward*, a year earlier, after sailing into the Delaware Bay and securing the service of a riverboat pilot from nearby Lewestown, to sail to New Castle and northward to Philadelphia safely. Touring the rows of wharves wasn't complete until one visited the Spruce Street Wharf – the oysterman's wharf, where oyster boats harvested the seafood delicacy from the nearby Egg Harbor or the Chesapeake Bay.

8

Currency in the Colonies

There was none – at least there was no official currency. George III, King of England and Ireland during the War of Independence forbade currency minting thereby controlling colonial fiscal policy. Post-war, copper currency and silver or gold were in apparent short supply, and the quantity fluctuated with the economic conditions of the individual states. Merchants carried coins when they sailed from Londonderry or Belfast, and passengers coming to Nova Scotia and the thirteen states packed their life savings stored in trunks and chests.

Coinage was necessary for the payment of goods and supplies. Currency was transferred to the pockets of merchants sailing back to Ulster for payment for additional trade. Clearly, cash was required, and the provisioning of cash was mismanaged since there was insufficient coinage to facilitate commerce. People deferred to bartering, employing their craft or skills for another's benefit, to obtain goods or services they required in exchange.

Voids were filled when merchants devised a system of credit, issuing notes or bills of exchange. A note became a bill of credit – redeemable in coin when presented for payment. The practice was accepted as a viable form of payment for trade contracts, but it never became widely accepted. The danger of inflation of the cost of merchandise was of primary concern, and the pressure for a systematized currency grew. Before the revolution, Robert Morris, the financier, was frustrated by refusals from the king to permit coinage of currency, colonial currency, since a medium of exchange to enhance commerce for everyday life was missing.

Meanwhile, Stephen Girard's wealth grew exponentially due to his trading and investment activities. His employment of sail ships voyaging to ports in Europe and the West Indies provided the funds to increase ownership in more vessels. He had few equals if one measured intellect combined with a shrewdness to capitalize on opportunities.

Coins appeared in Philadelphia as a result of trade with the islands. The Spanish dollar became the unofficial and most popular medium of currency exchange. A Spanish dollar, constructed of silver, displayed a distinctive design and was a trusted medium for exchange. Many Philadelphia shipbuilders quoted the price for one of their finely made vessels in Spanish milled dollars.

Word spread through supercargoes working on sail ships of nearly two dozen mines located in Mexico and South America, and they struck or pressed the milled dollars, quantifying them as *reales*, meaning royal. Fractional equivalents of the coin were divided into sections – one-half, one, two, and four reales. If the four reale was divided in half, merchants referred to the "*pieces of eight*" to define the eight reale.

Reales remained scarce. Colonists experimented with minting coins in Massachusetts, and this spread to other states. Coiners, acting independently, struck their coins defined as pattern coins, with the hope of striking one that would be favored and adopted by the Continental Congress.

Robert Morris, understanding the need for a mint, initiated a process in 1783. His first coin, the *Nova Constellantis*, never received the approval of congress. John Chalmers, a silversmith from Maryland, struck three-pence, six-pence, and shillings. Others followed suit, aspiring for their coin to favor congress to be adopted as official currency.

The Articles of Confederation

Eight years before, in 1777, the Continental Congress drafted the first constitution to organize and guide the governance of the thirteen colonies into independent states. Of paramount concern was a provision to preserve the independence and sovereignty of the individual states.

Although the British Army surrendered at Yorktown, the war was not entirely over. There would come a day when this new ill-advised form of government would fail – and fail miserably. Temporarily there was a military defeat, but economics – the lack of money supply and a means of facilitating commerce would contribute to their downfall. Or so the king planned for this event.

The Articles became a legal document devised to conduct business. Governmental business affairs were established for the independent states to be organized into these United States of America. The Articles were examined and ratified in 1781.

The first president of this newly formed congress, Richard Henry "Lighthorse Harry" Lee, III from Virginia, was voted to lead the new governmental body. Years before Lighthorse Harry called for the colonies to unite and write a resolution, and declare their independence from their mother country.

For a time, Congress could not act to formulate a federal mint, or if not, to engage in contracts with independent coiners to provide a recognized national currency. Thomas Jefferson, a visionary, met with Alexander Hamilton to pursue the possibility of introducing a coinage act to congress. Jefferson devised the decimal system realizing the Spanish dollar was so widely accepted. The dollar or silver coin, mathematically, would be divided into tenths, and his plan would require coins to be struck based on one-half, five, twenty, twenty-five, and fifty cents.

The Critical Period

That's what they called it. A year before, in 1784, with independence secured and the economy dismal, merchant exports of goods were reduced, credit was expensive to obtain, and hard money – currency was limited; therefore, the bartering system prevailed.

Virginia half-pence copper coins, now legal, were struck as early as 1773 but were not circulated widely. Foreign gold, Spanish *doubloons*, coins minted in Spain and Mexico, and *pistoles*, gold coins circulating in Europe were exchanged in the states. And English gold guineas from 1766 lined the pockets of merchants and those considered wealthy.

Copper coins known as *regales,* minted in England, made up the greater portion of small change. Unfulfilled demand for a stable federal currency was exploited by illegal trade. Counterfeit Irish coppers brought in through merchants and often unknowingly, by immigrants, circulated in multiple states in the 1780s.

9

Trial of the Pyx

Gustavus and Thomas Colhoun dined at a wooden table close to the fire being stoked by the innkeeper. Dampness infiltrated the room but the warmth from the nearby fireplace reduced the chill penetrating to the bones this winter eve. City Tavern, the same place where General Washington met on occasion with the Marquis de Lafayette, was deeded to seven wealthy citizens of Philadelphia.

The younger, a merchant and financier, and the eldest, a seasoned mariner, brought a business plan across the Atlantic. Hugh, a partner and third brother, and a merchant remained at home in County Tyrone. Economic opportunity was the topic, and the mission, fulfill a need and create wealth. Family ties in Ulster produced connections advancing wealth, enough for the two brothers to journey to the north of Pennsylvania near Lackawanna. They secured warrants containing rights to purchase acres of land as they became readily available.

Tonight, the brothers dined with an established reputable citizen of Philadelphia. One they were informed would be interested in their idea. His hair was dark and cut short – balding in the forehead, and his frame was of medium build. Citizens nearby the waterfront recognized this merchant as a very wealthy one. His office, located at 37 N. Water Street near the docks, fit in with many other merchants, artisans, and businessmen. Everyone knew him as one of the wharves bore his last name. He pushed his chair back, stood erect with purpose, extending a greeting to the Colhouns. Introductory pleasantries dispensed, Gustavus handed him a letter of introduction – hoping the content would open a door for the benefit of their enterprise.

Stephen Girard, now thirty-four years of age, was born in 1750 at Bordeaux, France, to Pierre and Ann Marie Girard. Pierre, a naval figure, loved the sea and made it his occupation for a while. King Louis XV bestowed upon Pierre a knighthood, and a gold medal was struck for his service, acknowledging with gratitude Pierre's bravery demonstrated in a naval battle with England. The year of his service to the king was 1744.

Stephen spoke directly, inquiring of the brothers, all while measuring character, integrity, and potential perseverance, traits he would exact from himself had he been seated at the other side of the table. He was curious about the scars upon Thomas's face; however, he would reserve those questions for later. The Colhouns watched intently as their new acquaintance read the letter slowly. Hampered by limited eyesight, he wore a black felt patch over one eye.

"I owe it to youth and foolishness — something I cast aside many years ago." His new acquaintances were curious; therefore, he addressed their curiosity. "I was eight and I amused myself by casting wet oyster shells into a bonfire. The heat from the fire caused a shell to crack and a fragment flew into my eye, blinding me permanently and producing the visible scar covered by the eye patch."

The incident left a physical and emotional mark that he would endure for the rest of his life.

"My life changed dramatically," Stephen reflected.

"In what manner?" asked Gustavus.

Stephen leaned back in his chair, looked at the two, and drew in a breath, and continued. "My father carefully drilled me in all categories of studies and at the earliest appropriate time." He picked up a glass of Madeira and sipped. "My mother died when I was very young — my father in time remarried — my step-mother and I didn't see life eye to eye."

Gustavus listened, eager to hear more of his story. Thomas, the impatient one, preferred to get to the point, their point for a visit. Stephen continued. "My life outdoors became more exciting and important to me — my brothers and sister were different than myself." He paused as someone brushed by with an armful of cut logs. The aroma of cherry wood filled the air.

"My application for study drifted, and my father's propensity to force me to study, something I lacked a desire to do, grew to the point of disinterest. My siblings became his focus and interest." Pausing, he sipped from his glass.

"And you seized upon your interest in a mariner's life?" Thomas responded, reaching for his mug filled with ale.

Stephen observed everything and at a very young age. He possessed a brilliant mind — his ability to remember everything was his strong suit.

"My stepmother was determined that I would acquire self-control. Being assertive by my very nature, I displayed a temper, one at times that was domineering, even to the point of upon being challenged could result in my tendency toward violence."

"So, you left home for a life at sea?" Thomas inferred.

"A heated argument with my stepmother ignited the flame that sent me to sail upon the sea." Stephen captured the brother's attention. "Father issued an ultimatum – apologize to my stepmother in front of my siblings – and be sure to choose my words carefully and solemnly."

"Or…," Gustavus joined in.

"Or leave," Stephen emphasized. "With my back stiffened against my father's admonishment – I chose the latter – I left. That was in 1764 – I was fourteen."

"What happened next?" Thomas inquired.

"My father being one with connections arranged passage for me on the brig, *Pelerin*, captained by Jean Courteau, a shipmaster. We left France sailing for Santo Domingo. My father sent me away with my personal belongings, including coin, everything I had amounted to £3,000."

Two of the three men attended the meeting for specific reasons – but developing a business connection leading to future opportunities became the main focus. And the Colhouns had a plan, something they would divulge at the right time.

Thomas, curious about what happened next, sipped from his mug. "Did you enjoy life at sea?"

"Yes – I sailed for the next ten months. It was my father's plan, and I think he hoped that the reality and rigor of life at sea would change his headstrong son and return him to home. His plan was partially successful. I returned home – but I enjoyed life at sea, so I sought multiple voyages and returned home several times." Thomas could relate to that feeling.

"Furthermore, my first voyage was profitable, and for the first time in my life I learned how to engage in merchant trade for gain."

Stephen continued his story – assessing the character, fortitude, and intellect of the brothers he would consider engaging in business.

"Life upon a sail ship intrigued me – especially the challenge of navigation – I endeavored to study the subject to perfection. I began as a cabin boy, but after my sixth voyage, I was granted a license as a master. The year was 1773." He concluded, reminiscing – "I haven't returned to France since. On another voyage, 1774, I was on the ship *La Julie* with Captain Mouroux, sailing to St. Marc's on Santo Domingo. This time we left the island and made way for New York – my first time in North America. I think it was the month of July."

Upon arriving in New York, Stephen was introduced to Thomas Randall, a prosperous merchant. Randall became interested in Stephen after assessing his business acumen and shrewdness. He was twenty-five at the time. Randall traded goods to New Orleans, Port au Prince, and the West Indies, and he offered Stephen a position as the first officer under the command of Captain Maloherd. After his first voyage, he purchased an interest in the ship, and the captain and he continued shipping and freighting to New Orleans and the West Indies.

"Both of you traveled a long distance. You must have an important plan for merchant trade," Stephen inserted.

Gustavus and Thomas nodded.

"Your letter of introduction is impressive. Tell me about the Colhoun family."

"We have a third brother who partners with us," Thomas responded. "Hugh remains at home in Ireland conducting business."

Both brothers spoke of their ancestral roots stemming from Scotland, followed by their family's migration to Ulster. Their father, William, embarked upon a long career in the merchant trade, working as a cargo handler and mariner.

Hatching a Plan

"Captains of merchant ships bring newspaper articles with news of events here in your country," Gustavus began. "Merchants trading cargoes of flaxseed and passengers between Londonderry and ports along the east coast deliver news as well. Letters of correspondence from Ulster merchants and others, having left for Philadelphia, describe the current monetary conditions."

"Who are the others?" Stephen asked.

"Many are Scots-Irish – descendants of people who left the lowland region of Scotland for Ulster years ago. Some are merchants, and in migrating to the colonies, they joined their brothers and sisters, participating in your quest for independence."

Stephen listened intently, reminiscing about his struggle and the adversity he experienced at a very young age. His interest peaked upon hearing the brothers describe life stories in Ulster – famine, religious persecution, lack of economic opportunity, a desire to own and farm the land, and freedom and the opportunity to improve their lives.

"And what is your opportunity?" Stephen queried.

Gustavus reached inside his coat and pulled out a brown leather packet tucked inside his breast pocket, laying it on the table.

"King George III is furious they lost the war. The British Empire – ever-expanding, capitalizing on their naval power has been crippled dramatically. Not long ago, the war ended – do you think he believes these United States will survive?" His question was rhetorical. "There is no federal monetary supply – none that supersedes the individual efforts of states who intend to create their currency. The United States must secure economic stability by providing a stable currency. And the king believes your quest for self-governance will fail for lack of it."

Stephen was still and quiet, eyes gazing upon Gustavus. The burning logs in the fireplace crackled, emitting a pleasant cherry aroma. "And you, by yourself or with the assistance of contacts, other merchants perhaps, have hatched a plan to mitigate this risk?"

Gustavus continued. "Linen markets are suppressed as we speak – annual exports are declining throughout Ulster. Merchants with an ownership interest in ships are looking for a new opportunity. For years they have relied on transporting passengers and linens to Philadelphia. In return, they carry flaxseed and American-made wares and goods imported from the West Indies, returning to Ireland. We know there is a demand for coinage – local merchants in Philadelphia and those in the other states are struggling with a currency to facilitate trade."

Thomas interrupted at this point. "You know coins are scarce, and copper coins are in demand. The available supply is migrating to locations that need them the most. And what they need is a mint and a supply chain of raw material to support an official supply of the currency."

Stephen knew all of the patriots, men of the caliber of John Maxwell Nesbitt, Alexander Hamilton, and others who were experimenting and promoting the concept of a national currency, even to the extent of laying plans to build a mint. It was a matter of time.

Still a bit skeptical, he questioned the ability of the two. "And you have a source of copper or coins?"

Thomas opened the flap of the brown leather folder, reached inside and unfolded a large piece of paper, a document, and handed it to Stephen.

IRISH HALFPENCE MINTED FOR THE KINGDOM OF IRELAND

For Account of the Irish Halfpence stored and delivered out of his Majesty's mint in the Tower of London by the Honourable Charles Sloan Cadogan (now Lord Cadogan) Master and Maker of the said Mint, between the 30th June 1773 and the 13th November 1782 taken out of their Dye Box and dyed at the Mint Office this 13th day of May 1784, before William Milford, Esquire, pursuant to an order from the Right Honourable the Lords Commissioners of his Majesty's Treasury directing him to make Trial of the Copper Pyx at this mint, dated 8th May 1784.

Date		Species	Quantity
1775	30 June	Halfpence	5 tons
	31 August	"	5
	6 October	"	5
	18 December	"	10
1776	20 February	"	5
	12 March	"	5
	2 May	"	5
	4 July	"	5
	21 September	"	5
1781	5 December	"	5
1782	7 January	"	5
	5 February	"	5
	19 March	"	5
	26 April	"	5
	14 June	"	5
	6 August	"	5
	12 October	"	5
	27 "	"	5
	13 November	"	5
No. of Shipments 19			100

To the Right Honourable the Lords Commissioners of his Majesty's Treasury. May it please your Lordships.

In obedience to your Lordship's commands, I have this day attended the Trial of the Pyx of Copper in monies coined within the Tower of London by the Honourable Charles Sloan Cadogen (now Lord Cadogan) late Master and Maker of his Majesty's Mint, particularly specified in the account hereunto annexed, and find that the Halfpence made of fine British copper for the Kingdom of Ireland will when heated and hot, spread thin under the Hammer without cracking.

That 52 Halfpence are coined for Ireland of such a *ligne* as to make a pound weight avoirdupois and do not exceed in .... Above the 30th part of the whole weight.

I therefore humbly report to your Lordships that the copper monies above mentioned, have been made by the said Master and Maker, according to the directions in the respective Royal Sign Manuals in that behalf, bearing date the 8th December 1774 and 18th July 1781.

William Milford

Mint office 13th May 1784

Stephen read the entire report, studying each section, evaluating the content, contemplating his next move. Unfamiliar with this aspect of English procedure and law, he laid the paper on the table.

"Where did you get this document?"

Gustavus sipped from his glass of Madeira. "We have our sources. The document you hold is a copy of an official report from the *Trial of the Pyx*."

Thomas hastened to finish the discussion to arrive at a decision. Was Stephen Girard, one of the wealthiest merchants in these new United States, ready to buy into their plan? He commented, "Congruent with English law, after an official minting, there is a ceremony of the Trial of the Pyx, and the report is given to the ruling monarch."

Stephen was engaged. "Tell me about the Trial of the Pyx."

Trial of the Pyx

The king or queen of Britain issued an order for the minting of the coin, and the order was concisely carried out. The issuance of the order was more than five hundred years old, dating back to the thirteenth century. The minting of the coin was a process, and when completed, a scheduled official ceremony was attended by a select group. The ceremony was an event, and it took the form of a judicial proceeding with a judge and a jury comprised of metallurgical assayers.

Newly minted coins were stored in a boxwood chest called a Pyx, before they were presented to the jury of assayers. The judge presiding over the trial was known to be the king's or queen's *remembrancer*, depending upon who was the reigning monarch at the time. The remembrancer fulfilled their obligation to make sure the trial was held according to law. They would present a written report to his or her Majesty's Treasury. A representative of the treasury determined the timing and location of the trial. One point was clear. There would be a trial in any given year when the Royal Mint issued coins.

The assayers were to draw coins from samplings because they were responsible for testing each coin. The Master of the Mint would, throughout the year, select many samples, thousands, and he kept them for the trial procedure. They determined a system designed to pick several samples as well. For every batch of 5,000 coins struck and issued, one was set aside. If the coin was silver the ratio increased to one for every 150. Each assayer examined their lot of coins to test the metallic composition, the diameter, and confirm the coin's weight met specific criteria.

∞

The treasury for the Kingdom of Great Britain issued a decree – there would be a minting of Irish half-pence for the benefit of Ireland. The minting of the coinage would commence in 1773, extending a length of time determined to be sufficient to strike one hundred tons of coinage. The process was initiated at the mint in the Tower of London, and the Master of the Mint was responsible for recording specific criteria. The criteria included the minting date with the year stamped on each coin, the date of the month and year for minting, and the number of coins minted specified in tons.

The Master of the Mint, Lord Cadogan, was appointed to the position in 1769 and would oversee the process, including the upcoming trial. Charles Sloan Cadogan was fifty-six years of age in 1784 at the time of the Trial of the Pyx. Educated at Magdalen College, Oxford, he was a British peer and a Whig politician. Before undertaking the current responsibility, he was a member of parliament representing Cambridge from 1749-1755. Upon leaving parliament, Lord Cadogan accepted an appointment as *Keeper of the*

Privy Purse – treasurer to the king or queen. In this role, he was responsible for maintaining all of the finances for the royal household.

In 1784, with the minting process of the coinage complete, Lord Cadogan orchestrated the details for holding The Trial of the Pyx. Upon completion of the trial, the issuance of the report before William Milford, Esquire, followed.

Stephen completed his review of the copy of the original report, lifting his head to look at the Colhoun brothers. Their letter of introduction combined with their documentation secured his attention, raising the interest of one of, if not the wealthiest man in Pennsylvania, perhaps the thirteen colonies, now states.

"Very interesting report – what is your plan?"

"Precisely," Gustavus responded.

"Think about the profit motive," he began. "We think the British half-pence circulating in the thirteen states outnumber Irish half-pence 3 to 1, and depending upon location may be as high as 20 to 1. The scarcity of the Irish coin should increase the value. We think the Irish coin is worth nine percent more than the English half-pence. And we all know there is plenty of demand for copper here."

Thomas interrupted. "The coins will be loaded in a ship at London and unloaded in Dublin. Our brother Hugh contacted the treasury in Ireland to negotiate a purchase of coins. They will be secured, guarded, and held at the dock until we arrive."

"As many coins as possible – how many?" Stephen inquired.

"That will be determined – we need funds, your capital. This is what you can bring to the plan if you are inclined to join us," Gustavus boldly announced.

Stephen didn't hesitate. "What percentage of investment will you require?"

Gustavus was ready to conclude the meeting and walk out with the money. "We are requesting seventy-five percent."

"And the implication is I will underwrite the greater portion of the risk." Stephen placed his hand upon his chin. "And what if your ship encounters privateers along the way?"

"We will be manned and armed," Thomas replied. "Better yet – we intend to mask our cargo by disguising it."

"And how do you propose to do that?"

"People – they continue to migrate through the port of Londonderry. The key is passengers – we load the coins on a passenger ship."

Stephen, contemplating, "And what comes next?"

"Gustavus and I return to Londonderry. We coordinate the plan, transmit payment for the cargo, assume the role of cargo handlers, supervise all the detail and accompany the cargo to Girard's Wharf."

"You're both young. What are your ages?"

"Twenty-four," Thomas replied. "And my brother is nineteen."

"And do both of you have cargo carrying experience?"

"We do – our father taught us – and we apprenticed with his contacts," Gustavus replied.

"Then both of you realize the danger you are about to undertake?"

Thomas turned in his chair toward the merchant and pointed to a scar on the back of his head. "I've undertaken risk before." Turning again, he added, "I've got multiple scars to prove it."

Stephen surveyed the multiple marks on his head and face. "How did the other man fare?"

"He went overboard."

Satisfied, Stephen avoided further detail. "Have you selected your ship and master?"

Thomas chose to respond. "Certainly – a 300-ton ship – recently built, the registration name is *Faithful Steward*. She won't sink, sir – no wormwood holes in this vessel, too new."

"And who is the captain?"

Thomas and Hugh gave this subject much thought and reasoned it must be a master they know and one to be trusted.

Thomas responded. "Connolly McCausland, sir. He has plenty of experience – he sailed the Atlantic many times. He and his brother Abraham purchased two-third ownership in the vessel. The captain is from Limavady, his brother, Culmore Point nearby Londonderry."

Stephen leaned forward in his chair, reasoning. A chill in the tavern air developed as the fire required stoking and rekindling. "I am willing to take the risk and participate in your venture. There is one condition."

Gustavus leaned forward in his chair. "What would that be?"

"You cannot leverage your twenty-five percent through a third-party investor. I want you to have a stake in the investment personally."

Gustavus was the business figurehead for the Colhouns. All financial decisions were finalized with his agreement. "I can assure you our twenty-five percent comes from our family – that includes the three of us."

"There is another condition. Your plan is worth the risk. I'll secure an insurance policy for the cargo's value. You will provide the funds to cover the cost. Upon delivery and satisfactory inspection of the cargo here in Philadelphia, I'll reimburse you for the cost of the policy."

Both brothers nodded affirmatively.

"Have the two of you a longer-range plan? What are your intentions if you are successful in this undertaking?"

Gustavus, while younger, assumed the role of family spokesman for business matters. "We plan to return to Londonderry, however, in time I intend to settle in Philadelphia to embark on new business opportunities."

"What about Hugh?"

"He intends to remain in Ireland – in a few years, he will move here."

Stephen glanced at Thomas. "And you?"

"I love the sea – cargo handling – that is my life, sir."

Stephen closed. "After this mission is complete, let's meet again. I could use all three of you in my business. I own the premises at #27 Water Street. It would be an advantageous location for you and Hugh to set up a business."

10

Supercargoes

A shipment of copper half-pence was transported from the Tower of London to the shipping dock per instructions; and loaded on the *HMS Formidable*, a 177-foot long three-mast frigate armed with 98 guns. The first leg of the sail was 350 miles to the southeastern coast of England; then the captain would sail north by northwest a distance of 300 miles to the port of Dublin in the Kingdom of Ireland.

Minting dates for the stored copper half-pence ranged from 1775-1782 per the certification of William Milford on May 13, 1784. In June 1775, the dye masters struck a total of twenty-five tons of copper half-pence for the remainder of that year, averaging nearly five tons per month. During 1776 they resumed in February and through September struck another twenty-five tons averaging three and three-fifths tons per month. Minting didn't continue until 1781 when five tons were struck in December. And in 1782, forty-five tons of coppers were minted at an average of more than four tons per month, beginning in January and ending in November. Samples taken from each minting were thoroughly examined and tested for proper weight and appearance, all per the specifications and rules per the centuries-old ceremony – Trial of the Pyx.

Gustavus and Thomas traveled by horseback to Dublin. Upon arrival, they planned to consummate the financial transaction with the government of Ireland, deliver payment supplied by their investor, and secure possession of tons of copper half-pence. Transporting goods of value presented risk, therefore, to manage risk, it was wise to have Thomas, a brawny mariner with a fiery temper, accompany the younger Gustavus, a muscular but lean book learner with a wise head for business.

King George III forbade the transporting of gold and silver coins to the newly formed United States. There was no restriction in the Kingdom of Ireland for selling and transporting coppers across the Atlantic, especially when Ireland was over-supplied, and the coppers were dumped on them by Britain. During 1719-1775, there was a continual exporting of British coppers to former British America. Coppers, limited in supply in the colonies, traded at a premium, a price per coin over their stated value.

Upon arriving at Dublin Quay, the Colhouns found the coins stored in 400 individual white oak barrels with no identifying name stamped on the exterior, all following protocol for the British currency. There was no reason to advertise the content in each barrel. Counterfeiters, some in Ireland and certainly one in Birmingham, located one hundred miles northwest of London, were secretly producing counterfeit coppers.

Counterfeits were transported to British America from the 1740s through the 1750s. The assembly of the colony of New York grew increasingly intolerant of the passing of counterfeits. It approved a law setting a fine of £100 for anyone convicted of importing illegal coppers. They also imposed a fine of ten times the value of the copper coins on anyone who knowingly passed a counterfeit currency.

Thomas relied upon Captain McCausland's referral to secure a reliable and trustworthy captain to transport the coins from Dublin to Londonderry, a distance of more than 300 miles. The two brothers would conceal and guard the cargo while waiting for their transport from Londonderry to Philadelphia.

∞

Pirates sailed the seas throughout the seventeenth century before privateers received their letters. A letter of marquee gave a private citizen official authorization from their country, allowing them to raid ships flying the flag of other specified countries. During the latter 1700s, some pirates were former privateers, and they came from various countries, including England, Scotland, Ireland, and Wales. Some had links to Liverpool, Bristol, and Plymouth. There were pirates from France, Portugal, Holland, Belgium, Denmark, and Sweden. At one time, nearly one quarter was spawned in the West Indies and North America. A few were women, and others were slaves having escaped their unruly masters.

One thing was sure, privateers came from the lowest class of society, and pirating was their pathway for an opportunity. Their goals were quite simple – ignore existing social rules, ignore the law of established countries, and obtain wealth – the more the better. They were the opposite of an organized social world that embodied mercantilism and order. And they sought to wreak havoc on that society by attacking it from the sea. Piracy was illegal, and if caught you swung from the rope. They were as young as fourteen and as old as fifty. Nearly one-half were in their twenties, with nearly one-fifth of their rank less than twenty. Age or gender didn't matter if you were caught and brought to justice – you hung anyway.

Many a merchant questioned the motive of pirates, however, in time, it became clear. Some were disgruntled seamen. Close to one-third of ship mutineers became pirates. For those, it was difficult submitting to the authority of a demanding, sometimes demeaning captain, who barked orders at you all day every day. And some pirates were former privateers. They found the life of raiding another's ship adventurous and productive – making money – they continued the lifestyle after their letter of marquee expired. They didn't turn over the bounty to their country in their new life – they kept it. The shipowner shared it with his (or her) crew and kept the greater portion for them-self. It was an equitable system in their eyes. If caught, why hang for a smaller cut of the profit.

Other pirates were seized and taken off a captured merchant ship against their will. Still, others would volunteer to join if taken hostage, thinking there was little difference between what they did and what they were asked to do as a pirate. And there was another group of society that readily joined the ranks because they were out of options. This described the indentured servant. Some of these people were criminals – referred to as fourteen-year indenture for committing a crime in England. Sentenced to a fourteen-year contract, they were cast off from society and transported to the colony of Georgia, in the southern part of America. After the War of Independence, this practice stopped.

Pirates employed tactics, and they thrived using the element of surprise once they spotted prey. Their ship was often a sloop, and sometimes, if lucky, a captured fully rigged *pinnace* as they were larger yet easy to maneuver. Their primary mode of attack was intimidation instead of outright violence, but they would resort to physical violence if required or if backed into a corner. Their weaponry consisted of pistoles – sometimes tucked inside their belt on each side of their waist. Other pirates carried a pistole and knives, and some drew a *cutlass* sheathed inside a leather belt.

∞

Edward Less determined to sail his sloop far off the stern of the *HMS Formidable*, far enough to remain undetected as the ship's captain tacked toward the Dublin Bay. After the barrels of copper coins were loaded to another ship, they would attack, raid, and plunder. He planned to sail past the lighthouse on the Howth Peninsula. The lighthouse, built at Baily on the far eastern coast of the peninsula, was in operation for over one hundred years. A coal fire supplies the power to light a beacon, and the light penetrates the Irish Sea. The area surrounding the peninsula claimed many ships and wrecked them over as many years. After passing the lighthouse, Captain Less would sail nearly ten miles to the northwest side of Lambay Island, drop anchor, and wait for his prey to pass.

Captain Walsh, Commander of the *Forsa* (Gaelic for force), would set sail east from Dublin a distance of seven miles out to the Irish Sea. He would tack into the wind around the peninsula, and turn northwest for ten miles passing Lambay on the Howth Peninsula. Lambay is the largest island, two and one-half square miles lying off the east coast of Ireland. The rocky landscape is the highest point rising over four hundred feet above the Irish Sea. Cliffs are located on the north, south, and eastern side of the island. It's a perfect place for a shallow drafting sloop to surprise a schooner. Edward Less could drop anchor, hide, and wait on the eastern side of the island, then slip out and surprise the *Forsa* off their stern as they tack north, passing to the west side.

And that was the plan – Edward Less hid his sloop on the west side of Lambay in the Dublin Bay, waiting and watching for the *Forsa* to pass to the northeast side of the peninsula. At that point, he would raise sail, overtake the *Forsa*, and attack off the port bow of the schooner. If all goes according to plan, they could intimidate their prey, force the ship further into the Irish Sea, and transfer the copper coins. And if the captain and cargo handlers fight – they would respond, and secure the cargo, and sink the vessel.

∞

Gustavus and Thomas found Dublin, the second-largest city in Ireland, a bustling community with news of change stirring in varying ways. In addition to Gaelic and English, people commonly spoke French and Norse languages in the marketplace. Always interested in money and banking, Gustavus' first stop was to visit the College Green to inspect the Bank of Ireland, founded two years before by the decree of a Royal Charter issued by King George III.

Parliament House, home to the House of Lords and Commons, was nearby. The Royal Exchange (city hall) was completed in 1779 following a

72

ten-year process. Education and cultural changes were ever-present. News spread of the founding of the Royal College of Surgeons a year before, and the Royal Irish Academy, designed to advance studies in the sciences and humanities, was born.

Ireland, courting political change was also filled with considerable unrest in religious circles. William Pitt, at the young age of twenty-four, was appointed prime minister in 1783. His recent attempt to unify some commercial interests of Ireland with Britain failed. There were too many obstacles set forth by British merchants together with the demands issued by the Irish. Fortunately, Prime Minister Pitt successfully secured the passage of laws designed to reduce many grievances of the Irish. One example – Irish judges were granted the same tenure as those in Britain.

The brothers planned to remain invisible and hastily made way to the Royal Exchange to complete paperwork, assume ownership of their cargo, and leave for the docklands. River Liffey flows into the Irish Sea, and the coins were stored by the piers and docks located on each side of the river. Captain William Walsh hired laborers to load the cargo.

Captain Walsh was of medium height, a stocky, muscular frame, black hair, and sun-beaten weathered face. The only time he removed the clay pipe from his mouth was when he slept, and sometimes not even then. He was said to be short with a conversation, serious-minded, and always timely, bent on leaving port early the following day. His primary income came from cargo runs along the entire Irish coast, but years before, he had his fill of trans-Atlantic voyages to the Caribbean. He could change to a nasty rough man if cornered by the wrong person. The coppers were loaded after the sunset. Gustavus and Thomas, pistoles nearby, remained on the *Forsa* and bedded down in their berth for the night.

By the dawn of the following day, Captain Walsh and three of his crew scurried about the schooner. Preparation began to set sail to guide the *Forsa* from the river into the Irish Sea. The day was cloudy and cool. Thomas climbed the ladder atop the deck, his flintlock dueling pistols manufactured by Wogdon & Barton in London tucked inside his leather belt. Gustavus woke earlier than his brother and was atop the deck, nervously pacing. He sheathed his pistole inside his belt, not because he wanted to, but because Thomas gave him one of his, instructing him to prepare. Gustavus was a thinker, a planner, a visionary, and one with intellect who took advantage of opportunities. Thomas was an adventurer, not known to back away from a brawl, and he wore the scars about his head to prove his badge of courage.

Six and one-half miles out, Captain Walsh ordered the braces turned to tack with the wind flowing off the eastern side of the Howth Peninsula. Before the hour, they would pass to the east side of Lambay Island, continuing north, a distance of seven miles. Upon passing the island, *Forsa* neared the Skerries Islands and tacked northeast more than fifty miles, passing between the Isle of Man and the port of Newcastle followed by Ardglass.

The Colhouns, young cargo handlers, believed they were ready to assume the responsibility at hand. Stephen Girard entered into his decision to employ them based upon their letter of recommendation and replies to his questions. He considered them forthright, assertive, and Gustavus displayed advanced insight and wisdom in merchant affairs. And Thomas was fearless, a helpful attribute given the risk they were undertaking. Besides, he was enthralled with the opportunity to sail and transport coinage; the more the better.

The act of cargo handling at sea was relatively new to Gustavus, however, Thomas had more experience. The sights of coastal Ireland, the sounds of the gulls, the shearwater and black guillemot, and the aroma of the salt air were a constant refreshing reminder of a life few realize. Lambay Island lay to the southeast as the *Forsa* sailed with the Skerries coming into view. John Berry, the helmsman, pointed to a distant sloop tacking in the same direction far off the stern. Within time the sloop drew closer. John asked one of the crew to inform Captain Walsh, below deck. There was no observance of the sloop since leaving the Dublin docks, therefore, the vessel must have hidden near the eastern coast of Lambay Island. Why was this ship sailing between Lambay and the east coast?

Captain Walsh observed the movement of the sloop, noting the suspicious tack in the same direction as the *Forsa*, and closing distance between the two vessels. Curiosity was replaced by heightened alertness because the sloop continued to follow, drawing closer. If there was malicious intent, he was unable to lengthen the distance between those in pursuit. Captain Walsh knew there was minimal ballast to throw overboard, and he didn't want to do that, therefore, they would learn the intent of their pursuer soon.

Within the hour, the unidentified sloop closed on the port side. Captain Walsh, his crew, and the Colhouns stood by the gunwales anticipating the worst. They could see Captain Less and the faces of his crew. They hurled angry obscenities at the crew of the *Forsa*. And how many were positioned below deck out of sight, waiting to spring the element of surprise? One of them hoisted the black flag – SURRENDER – was the clear message.

Intimidation reigned. Thomas, standing by the gunwale, became unhinged. He screamed, taunted, and begged the first bastard to come aboard. Having been in battle before, Thomas was furious, and he had accumulated the wounds to prove it. Placing his foot on the side of the gunwale, he climbed over the top. Captain Walsh grabbed the back of his coat and yanked him back onto the deck.

"Stay calm mate – let them come to us."

A metal grappling hook dug into the side of the *Forsa*. Thomas tried to pry it loose; however, the weight of a pirate climbing the rope made it impossible to dislodge to toss overboard.

Thomas, excited to fight, pushed aside one of the crew – waiting for the aggressor to jump to the ship. Unwilling to draw his flintlock, he called to Gustavus to pull his gun in the event the situation grew worse. A second grappling hook lodged in the gunwale on the same side. One of the pirates lunged at Thomas. Gustavus sheathed his pistole and ran to the gunwale to grab the hook. It was weighted down by a second pirate climbing the rope, and it was impossible to free the hook. Thomas chose not to fire a warning shot. If he did, he would disadvantage himself with no time to reload. His adrenaline spiking, he prepared for the inevitable brawl.

Thomas snarled and reached for the pirate, now bounding over top of the gunwale. A cutlass was in the pirate's right hand, so Thomas grabbed him by the collar and yanked him onto the deck. The scoundrel was lighter than he, and he rolled and sprung to his feet quickly. Brandishing his cutlass, he swung it toward Thomas, but he was met with a right-hand jab to the jaw and went sprawling backward. Thomas, screaming intimidating obscenities, raised the scoundrel off the deck, punched him in the gut with his left, and countered again with his right, landing a crushing blow to his jaw, and threw him overboard into the sea.

Gustavus spun around, catching a fist from another who climbed the rope on the same side. Reeling backward, he stumbled over a rope and fell, hitting his head on the deck. Captain Walsh rushed toward the perpetrator to protect Gustavus, lying unconscious on the deck. Thomas, leaping in the air, collided with Captain Walsh as they both descended upon the pirate. The captain struggled to stand. Thomas quickly threw a series of three punches, landing blows, and sending him back against the gunwale. The two of them tossed him overboard into the sea.

With the attack foiled, Thomas turned his brother onto his back and helped him to his feet. Gustavus' head ached, and he was bruised and bleeding from a split lip. Within the half-hour, Captain Walsh ordered the crew to set sail northward to Londonderry.

11

Londonderry 1785

With the onset of June, Captain McCaulsland anticipated he would secure his tally of passengers, including concealed cargo, and obtain the required clearance to depart Culmore Point for New Castle and Philadelphia, the second trans-Atlantic crossing for *Faithful Steward*. James Lee I, in his seventy-eighth year and patriarch of the Lees, and Simon Elliott, a patriarch too, met with their combined kinfolk at the quay to discuss details of their voyage.

The extended families, combined, numbered more than sixty passengers, all having prepared to leave for Pennsylvania. The elder Lee pointed to an article published in the June 15th edition of the Londonderry Journal.

Londonderry Races – 1785

On Tuesday the 28th of June, his Majesty's Plate of One Hundred Guineas, by Irish bred horses, and weight for age, viz. Four-year-old carrying 7 ft. five-year-old 8 ft. 2 lb. six-year-old 8 ft. 10 lb. and aged 9 ft. 3-mile heats.

On Wednesday, 50 l. (lengths) by any six-year-old, and aged horses, six-year-old carrying 8 ft. 7 lb. aged 9 ft. 4-mile heats.

On Thursday, 50 l. by any five-year-old, and carrying 8 ft. 7 lb. 3-mile heats.

The running to be according to the King's Plate Articles and; all the rules (which are mentioned at length in the handbills) of the last running to be observed. John Clark, Clerk of the Court – Ordinaries and Assemblies as usual.

> Right Hon. T. Connolly
> Sir Hugh Hill
> Jas. Alexander, Esq.
> Stewards

Members of the Lee and Elliott families gathered around the two patriarchs, listening to their discussion, hoping the ship's departure was delayed until the races were concluded. An annual event, the race generated much excitement and enthusiasm, combining sport with a venue for social gatherings. The race, advertised in the Belfast Newsletter over seventy miles distant, would bring many more attendees.

Patronage of the county landed gentry sponsored the various plates and stakes. James Lee III, grandson of one of the patriarchs and an aspiring young man of twenty-six, heard rumors the event would be attended by fair young ladies from nearby places. A crowd of nearly 10,000 souls was expected.

∞

The editor of the Londonderry Journal received word from Abraham McCausland, merchant and part-owner of *Faithful Steward* to advertise the ship was cleared for sail. The edition for the 28th of June advised all passengers to make final arrangements with the merchant or the captain aboard the ship, and make way to the quay to prepare for departure on July 1st, pending continuing favorable winds.

Another vessel, the *William*, a 200-ton brig, was scheduled to depart for New Castle and Philadelphia on July 10th. One month previous, *Alexander* and *Pinkerton* sailed for Philadelphia accompanied by the *Buckskin*. The Journal reported *Alexander* and *Buckskin* were carrying an estimated 800 passengers.

Captain William Gafney, Master of *Earl of Inchiquin*, 250 tons burthen, loaded Irish wares to be delivered to New Castle and Philadelphia. He was also transporting 100 tradesmen from Cork and Waterford. The editor at the Belfast Newsletter received word of the fate of the brig *Liberty*, having set sail for Baltimore from Dublin with passengers, however, the ship was lost in the Chesapeake Bay. Thirty people perished while nearly one hundred others were rescued.

Emigrants filled Mrs. Miller's boarding home at Culmore Point, waiting for word of departure. A similar situation occurred at nearby Limavady, where Abraham McCausland provided housing to passengers. Many who secured passage through an agent of the merchant working the outlying regions of Londonderry, and unable to secure temporary quarters were packed and traveling from varying distances and nearby towns, all anticipating beginning a new life far across the breadth of the Atlantic.

∞

A partially covered sun rose over the eastern sky at daybreak, July 9th, and many would-be passengers, over two hundred and counting, made way to the quay at Culmore Point. She stood gracefully yet silently in a calm harbor on the River Foyle. The length of the McCausland's newest ship was 150 feet, and the ship's weight was advertised as 300 tons burthen. A method to calculate tonnage was derived in England years before. The measurement of the length and beam of the vessel were the key components used to calculate the total tons a ship could carry – burthen or burden (loaded) in transit.

She was a wooden ship, a real beauty, and indeed a fine one, constructed by the three Eyre brothers, successors to Richard Wright, noted shipbuilder at Kensington – Philadelphia. Each of the three masts was painted with yellow ochre, and the foremast and mainmast being the tallest, rose sixty-one and sixty-six feet above the deck. Together with the mizzenmast, the two masts were fashioned from black oak harvested from Pennsylvania forests. The top half of the hull was painted in black ochre extending below the gunwale halfway down the ship's side. The bottom half of the hull was decorated in red ochre. The paint on the ship's rails circumventing the vessel's perimeter matched the yellow ochre on the masts, and the taffrail at the ship's stern was outlined in the same yellow.

Rigging and the accompanying sails defined the ship. All of the sails were bound to the spars. Under sail, a taller gaff mainsail and a square topsail would unfold from the spars. The topgallant was configured to harness much wind once set to the pole mast. The Eyres designed their ships to sail successfully, navigating coastal and deep-sea areas, and they were conducive for loading and unloading trade at smaller ports due to their smaller size.

Abraham McCausland advertised his new ship to be a fast sailer. His claim was based upon his brother's experience after sailing across the Atlantic on the second voyage. Regardless, the papers often advertised ships to be fast sailers, a ploy to attract passenger business.

A mere four years had passed since Lieutenant General Charles Cornwallis surrendered his army to General George Washington's Continental Army, assisted by French troops in 1781 at Yorktown. Since the cessation of the revolution, there were acts of piracy upon the Atlantic.

English and French ships continued to engage in hostilities with one another. America's merchantmen, some previously engaged under Letters of Marque, and now with a government independent of England, had to evade the possibility of being fired upon due to mistaken identity.

Ship's Crew Agreement

An official document maintained by the captain listed each of the crew, place of origin, if known, and their official position, was signed by all.

Connolly McCausland, Master, shipowner, Limavady
Mr. Stanfield, First Mate, Londonderry
Mr. Gwyn, Second Mate, Donegal
Mr. Linn, Ireland
Samuel Irwin, Carpenter, Londonderry
John Quigley, Helmsman, Worcester, Massachusetts
Patrick Mourn, Ireland
Edward McCaffrey, Boatswain
John Brown, Sailmaker, Londonderry
William Dalrymple, Ireland
Robert Kelley, Ireland
Pelig Hudson, Steward, Newport, Rhode Island
Owen Phillips, Londonderry

The McIntire family, James I, his wife Rebecca, James II, a sister Rebecca, one brother, a brother-in-law, and nephew, and eight sisters gathered together, waiting to board the ship. Onlookers gathered, some curious, others coming to bid their family and friends farewell, realizing this would be the last time they would spend together.

Having left Ardara and Killybegs days prior, the Lee family was shepherded by James Lee I, his wife Isabella, and a significant portion of their relations walked the pathway to the quay. All were excited. Hugh Lee, forty-five years of age and older brother to James Lee II, and Hugh's wife, Mary Elliott Lee, and five sons and three daughters, stood on the quay waving goodbye to their family. The Thomas Lee family joined them. All of them, having arrived at Londonderry later than anticipated were unable to secure passage, and would wait to board the next ship for Philadelphia. Most of the passengers boarding this day had never been more than five miles from home, or the town square where everyone met on market day, or the farm they leased and worked and knew as home.

Pelig Hudson avoided recording passenger names at the gangplank. Many were people of respectable means, some carrying wealth of measure. Others brought what little they had, and some may have avoided the law or an unfulfilled contractual agreement. With payment for passage secured, Pelig asked no questions.

Passengers – *Faithful Steward*
July 9, 1785
(Partial List)

James Lee I & Isabella – Ardara, Donegal
James Lee II & Mary Hamilton Lee – Killybegs, Donegal
Simon Lee
Thomas Lee
Isabella Lee
Mary (Polly) Lee
James Lee III
Mary Lee (sister-in-law to James III)
James McIntire I & Rebecca – Ardstraw Bridge, County Tyrone
James McIntire II
Rebecca McIntire – daughter to James I & 7 sisters, one brother
McIntire son-in-law, his wife, daughter to James I, and son
Samuel Hepburn & Mrs. – Donegal
John & Mary Elliott Hepburn
Janet Hepburn
Hugh and Mary Stewart Espey – Tobermore, County Londonderry
James Espey
John Espey
Mary Espey
Robert Espey
Thomas Blair – Donegal *
James Dougherty – Donegal
James Marshall – Donegal
John O'Neill – County Tyrone
John York – Roscommon
Thomas Baskin – Donegal
James Beaty – County Tyrone
Matthew Caldwell – County Fermanagh
James Gregg – Mr. and Mrs. – Donegal
Sarah Campbell – County Tyrone
John Davis – Londonderry
James Devin – County Tyrone
Simon Elliott I & Sarah D. Lee Elliott – Donegal
William Elliott

John Elliott
Simon Elliott II
Elizabeth Elliott
Ann Elliott
Jane Elliott
Mary Maginnis – Leitrim
William McClintock – Donegal
Hugh McClean – Armagh
Doctor James McDougal – Londonderry
John McIllhinney – County Londonderry
John McMullan – County Tyrone
John McNab – County Antrim
Charles McWilliams – County Tyrone
Alexander Moore – Donegal
Samuel Moore – Donegal
Thomas Moore – Donegal
John Scott – Donegal
John Shaw – Londonderry
James Smyth – Cavan
Andrew Watt – County Tyrone
Samuel Watt – County Tyrone
Edward Cooke & Mrs. – Fermanagh
Cooke family brothers and sisters – 10

*The location of those with surnames appearing after the Espeys, except for the Elliott family, are used with poetic license based upon educated guesses after examining the frequency of those surnames, and their geographic location appearing in a list of linen weavers dated 1795. The passenger count of 249 has been reported as 149 men and 100 women and children.

Pelig Hudson, a Rhode Islander, was a strikingly handsome man with dark wavy hair, gray eyes, and a lean muscular build. As the steward, he would instruct passengers about the accommodations and appropriate conduct. Mary Lee, a single woman, and daughter to James I, stood nearby. Pelig's mouth dropped when he saw her – he tried to close it – and he clumsily tangled his foot in the rope wrapped in a circle lying on the deck. Pelig gawked, staring into the most beautiful blue eyes he had ever seen. Her hair was thick and black, with curls falling underneath the hood of her cloak. Of fair skin tone, she was captivating. His head turned as he continued to stare in disbelief as she brushed by. He thought to himself – it will be interesting to observe the captain's face the first time he lays eyes upon one so beautiful. James Lee II, Mary's brother, and his wife and family stared at him as they followed her.

Except for the Greggs, Doctor McDougal, and the Cooke family, many passengers farmed and grew flaxseed or were involved with linen production. There was, however, a contingent of merchants who gave their names to Pelig at the time of boarding. Thomas Colhoun walked by Pelig, attempting to conceal the double pistols holstered in a belt around his breeches underneath his unbuttoned frock.

Pelig announced he would hold a selection process for president, a representative for the group. The person chosen should have leadership capabilities to organize and plan. He would need a president to assign the responsibilities for chores, including cooking, cleanup, deck washing, and deck and ship cleanliness.

Hugh Espey of Tobermore, chosen to be president, accompanied Pelig below deck to work out the detail for assigning berths to everyone in steerage. The size of each berth was five-feet-six inches wide, and the height between the lower and upper berths was four-feet-six inches. Each passenger was free to explore below on the second and third deck in steerage, and secure personal belongings in their assigned location, as their berth would serve as sleeping quarters and storage for miscellaneous small items not packed in a trunk.

Ten cabins – individual compartmentalized rooms with a privacy door, lined the port and starboard side of the ship, forward from steerage on the second deck. Those passengers who afforded the extra cost for cabin accommodation were usually merchants, a family of notable society, or people with sufficient wealth, such as *landed gentry* who desired privacy for the trans-Atlantic voyage. Nearly two months at sea would be arduous for anyone, even in a cabin.

Each cabin contained a small hollowed wooden basin for washing and a hammock or two hung from the deck beams. A wooden berth for additional sleeping arrangements was fixed to the wall. Pelig attached small individualized signs to each cabin door, listing the surnames Blair, Colhoun, Dougherty, Hepburn, Laurence, Marshall, McCallister, O'Neill, and York.

Each berth in steerage was prioritized – first by family, then individual, separating single males and females. Stories abounded of captains that ignored standards of decency, thereby not providing for separation by gender. Sometimes unmarried men and women were forced to share a berth designed for four, and on occasion, a married couple occupied the same berth. If uncontrolled, the forced mingling could be a nightmare. Younger women, at times, chose to spend the night sitting on a box slumped against a post, as opposed to being forced to crawl into a berth with an unknown male.

Some passengers signing for passage investigated two priorities before committing to sail. First, they reviewed Captain McCausland's credentials by speaking with previous passengers and those who knew him, and second, a specified few met with the captain to lay down their requirements for the treatment of the passengers, especially women. This was not always the prerequisite for sails under other captains.

Those designated as cooks would be responsible for handling shifts and maintaining a safe fire. Others volunteered to attend to anyone who became sick or for the needs of the older population. The remaining passengers were assigned duties on a rotating basis, sweeping the ship's decks daily, and washing them once per week.

Crewmen constantly moved about the main deck, checking lines, maintaining sails and rigging, and attending to all matters relevant before casting the ropes, setting sail, and departing from the quay. John Brown, hammer in hand, swung out over the *prow* (forward of the ship) scraping and chipping, removing accumulated rust on the anchor. Robert Kelley inspected the ropes, collecting *oakum,* a loose fiber used for caulking the joints between the sideboards of the ship.

Samuel Irwin, ship's carpenter, was busy carving a series of new belaying pins. The constant friction of the rope lines rubbing against the pins wore them down, and replacements were routine.

"Mr. Stanfield – all passengers have boarded – my count including those in cabin and steerage is 249," Pelig loudly announced.

Edward McCaffrey, Boatswain, responsible for the loading, positioning, and safe storage of many trunks and chests, signaled the ship was properly ballasted and prepared for the sail. As boatswain, he was required to supervise the realigning of the stored items to improve ballast, before they sailed into heavy seas.

Mr. Stanfield, First Mate, nodded to helmsman Quigley and proceeded down the ladder to knock on the door of the captain's quarters at the stern of the ship.

"Captain McCausland – Mr. Hudson reports all passengers are accounted for and boarded – prepare to make way."

Captain McCausland ascended to the quarterdeck. An agreeable sort with the ability to charm, his initial appearance on a passenger sail was to create visibility, display leadership, and promote stability and authority.

"Mr. Stanfield – cast away the lines," shouted the captain.

Sailors were a well-drilled crew, they had to be. Mistakes were kept to a minimum – they could be costly. Some passengers wanted to watch them, moving about the ship's deck, climbing the rigging, yards, and braces, all with efficiency and ease. The crew's expectations were simple, and they received command in stride, performing their tasks flawlessly. Chanty songs were common-place, and it provided the crew an opportunity to show off their voices, singing in unison as the work of sailing the ship progressed. Passengers were unaware their songs were understood by seamen all over the world.

With inspection complete and clearance obtained, *Faithful Steward* sailed away from the quay with the passengers crowding the starboard gunwale, pressing against each other, waving goodbye to relatives and friends. Tears were streaming down the faces of most of the women. Those of the stronger lot stifled the tendency to cry.

"Mr. Stanfield – set the topgallants on the foremast and mainmast," cried the captain. "Two points to port," he ordered the helmsman. Six of the crew stood on the braces, three were spread to the right, three to the left, and loosed the *buntlines*. The canvas sails rumbled as they fell in unison toward the deck.

Mr. Stanfield was responsible for the sails secured to the bowsprit, the foremast, mainmast, mizzenmast, and the rigging. The sails and canvas stowed in the lower hold of the ship were his responsibility too. People watched with curiosity as the Second Mate – Mr. Gwyn climbed the ratlines to the crow's nest on the mainmast. It was his responsibility to check for wear and tear and damage, and he would also assist the crew when commands to change course were announced.

As First Mate, Mr. Stanfield was young and muscular, in his late twenties. He retained responsibility for all of the merchant and passenger-cargo, everything except for the coins hidden in the 400 barrels. They were hidden in the lower hold with passenger's trunks and chests piled systematically around the barrels. Under the watchful eyes of the passengers, the storage of the rest of the cargo was supervised by the first mate.

The safe navigation of the ship fell upon the shoulders of the captain. The chronometer and sextant were his tools for determining the ship's position and direction of sail. He alone was responsible for daily entries in the ship's log, describing any important maritime events. Mr. Stanfield was required to use the instrumentation to assist the captain if he became ill or was unable to command the ship.

John Brown – a sailmaker of nearly fifty years of age, was usually a pleasant temperate man. He could change quickly, displaying stubbornness when problems with the sails developed. As a sailmaker, he fabricated new sails to replace worn-out ones and maintained the surplus supply of canvas stowed in the ship's lower hold.

With goodbyes from family and friends behind, the men chose to remain topside, engaging in maritime and other banter of sorts. *Faithful Steward*, forced to delay departure to take on more passengers, was now sailing north, up the River Foyle toward the narrow channel between Greencastle and *Ard Mhic Giollagain* (Magilligan Point), a large peninsula located in northwest County Londonderry. The lush green Mourne Mountains provided a picturesque landscape as the ship passed through the Lough Foyle, an estuary of the river between Greencastle and Magilligan Point.

The brig *Ann* and the ship *Congress*, filled with passengers, linen, and trade goods, departed at Culmore Point shortly before *Faithful Steward*. James Ramage, Master, commanded *Ann*, 300 tons burthen and six months old. The shipowners were Sam and John Curry and William Walker. The *Congress* was owned and operating under Blair M'Clenachan, formerly from Ireland, now living in Philadelphia and a veteran and privateer of the American Revolutionary War.

James McIntire I, approached his son, standing alone near the bowsprit with the billowing stunsails capturing air.

"What are your thoughts?"

James II continued to peruse the fading coastline.

"Father, I have a mixture of new feelings – I'm leaving my homeland forever."

His father put his arm on his son's shoulder.

James continued, "Yes – you, mother, my brother, and his wife, a nephew, and my sisters are in my company. I am not mourning the absence of any kindred. And now, at twenty-two, I am emerging into manhood and active adult life. I'm a suitable person to seek the wilds of America."

"But you're leaving Ireland forever," his father interjected.

James paused, "This is what I see – In my imagination beyond the bright expanse of water, there lies a country where heroes live, where genius expands to full perfection, where every good is possessed. I see, or at least I think I see, another paradise, a new and flowery land, such as mortals can never see, such as mortals can never enjoy." *

∞

Faithful Steward passed the northwest side of Tory Island, a small remote stretch of land off the Donegal coast. More than one hundred miles later, and with the sun setting in the western sky, many women and children

88

descended to steerage for storytelling and socializing. Most of the men and their sons stood atop the deck, some smoking their clay pipes, some engrossed in conversation with fellow passengers. The day's events were the main topic, coupled with minimizing potential fear, especially from the women, as the sun would soon disappear, leaving the sight of land behind while sailing into the deep dark Atlantic.

Captain McCausland, below deck in the privacy of his quarters, wrote his first entry of a new voyage in the ship's log.

9th July 1785 – Departed Londonderry, passing Tory Island, more than 125 miles passed, into the North Atlantic. All well.

The days ahead would bring lively discussion – stories of people, some driven by events. Others will be stories about relatives or friends of passengers who left for Nova Scotia or British America, many years before.

*Taken from the personal account of James McIntire II

12

At Sea

Pelig Hudson struck the ship's bell two times (5:00 a.m.) in the morning watch of the following day. The sky was dark, the air was dry, and the westerlies blew across the surface of the Atlantic. Mr. Quigley reappeared at the ship's wheel after being spelled to get some sleep, and Mr. Gwyn led his crew in the long drag – "Haul on the bowline." The men sang in unison as they untied the lines from the belaying pins to turn the braces and adjust sails.

Isabella Lee awakened and shook her husband's shoulder.

"Listen, James – listen – what an eerie sound." At this hour in the early morn, below deck in complete darkness, other women aroused their sleeping husbands to listen to the eerie deep-pitched droning sound of the crew's voices as they sang.

Haul on the Bowline

Haul on the bowline, homeward we are going
haul on the bowlin', the bowlin' haul!
Haul on the bowline, before she start a-rolling
haul on the bowlin', the bowlin' haul!
Haul on the bowline, the captain is a-growling
haul on the bowlin', the bowlin' haul!
Haul on the bowline, so early in the morning
haul on the bowlin', the bowlin' haul!
Haul on the bowline, Philadelphia we are going
haul on the bowlin,' the bowlin' haul!
Haul on the bowline, Kitty is my darling
haul on the bowlin', the bowlin' haul!
Haul on the bowline, Kitty comes from Coleraine
haul on the bowlin', the bowlin' haul!
Haul on the bowline, it's a far cry to payday
Haul on the bowlin', the bowlin' haul!

The cook struck the ship's bell eight times – 8:00 a.m. Captain McCausland stood stationary on the quarterdeck, inhaling the fresh salt air, and observing the adjusting of sails. He was of average size, muscular but thin, with dark eyes, fair complexion, his nose a bit long and pointed. Word in the trade routes from those that knew the captain described him as a humane civil person, and they used that description when advertising for passengers in the Londonderry Journal.

His uniform was similar to the one he wore while serving King George III. His frock coat, woven from brilliant fibers of wool dyed medium red, displayed eight brass buttons top to bottom. His pants, a subdued white, covered white silk stockings tucked into knee-high black leather boots. His dark brown hat made of beaver fur, pinned to form two corners, was worn with the sides jutting outward from each ear. The perimeter of his hat was stained with sweat as it was pressed tightly on his brow to avoid being blown by strong sea-breezes.

Two of the patriarchs, James Lee I and Simon Elliott I, ascended the ladder to the main deck, turning toward the quarterdeck. A wooden railing with a built-in gate separated the quarterdeck from the main deck. This area was the captain's workplace, and only he, the ship's officers, and the helmsman occupied this territory.

A brown wheel made of oak was attached to the wheelhouse, inside the quarterdeck. The deck, elevated from the main deck, provided the captain and mates visibility to the fore, starboard, and port side of the ship.

Pelig informed the passengers of the unwritten rule – strictly observed – no passenger ever opened the gate and stepped onto the quarterdeck without the captain's permission. And it was extremely rare for the captain to invite anyone into his domain. This was his command post – he was the law upon the ship – he gave the orders, and they would be obeyed, by all, and depending upon who captained a sail ship, it would be best to wait for the captain to address you first.

"Good morning, gentlemen," Captain McCausland greeted the patriarchs. "Enjoyed last evening atop deck – I hope."

James Lee and Simon Elliott nodded their heads, returning the captain's greeting respectfully.

"Captain – it was a fine evening," James offered. "Was it a late evening for you, sir?"

"Yes Mr. Lee, – many of them are."

Late evening hours hastened the return of passengers to their berths, including the women and their noisy children. It was the favorite time of day for many captains commanding a passenger vessel.

"Clear skies – fair winds – calm sea," Captain McCausland continued. "First time for you to observe the plough (big dipper) from the darkened night sky while at sea?"

"Yes, a divine display – a beautiful sight – one of your navigational beacons, I suppose."

"Agreed, Mr. Lee – have you any experience as a seaman?"

"I have none, sir – our first sail, but I do have questions. Would you indulge…"

Captain McCausland interrupted – "Both of you should meet me in my cabin this afternoon. We'll talk then." The patriarchs nodded in agreement.

Later That Day

Mr. Stanfield, on watch on the quarterdeck, permitted the two patriarchs, James Lee I and Simon Elliott I, to walk through the gate, ascend onto the deck, and down the ladder to the captain's quarters. After a knock, Captain McCausland opened the painted pine door. Located aft of the ship, the cabin was fitted with pine on each side. A ship carpenter built some shelves into the port wall, so his books were stored neatly in a row. His cabin, illuminated by six glass-paned windows inserted directly above the stern, provided plenty of light in an otherwise dark space. An oak table with four wooden chairs sat in the middle. A comfortable sleeping bunk, starboard side, completed the cabin's interior. It was an impressive habitat, designed by Manuel Eyre's carpenter.

"Where is home, Mr. Lee?" The captain continued following their morning inquiry.

"Ardara in Donegal – our new home – the wilds of western Pennsylvania."

"And what about the Elliott family?"

"Left Donegal – we plan to follow the same path, captain."

"You have thought this through – and what information have you evaluated to support this decision?"

"Information provided by my son," responded Simon. "He sailed on the Lazy Mary and scouted the land below Pittsburgh. Irish organized Strabane Township a few years prior. This is where we plan to homestead captain."

Captain McCausland, always curious, was interested in their plan. "How did he describe the land?"

"Rolling hills – the elevation reminiscent of Donegal – fertile soil, good for farming," Simon responded again. "Captain – do you have information about the land in western Pennsylvania – they call it the frontier?"

"I have made multiple crossings to Philadelphia – my stays between sails were limited to the immediate region. No – I have never visited the area you seek, sir – but word passed by others – yes, it is frontier, the presence of settlers increasing, and you may encounter remnants of the Lenape, sir. You will encounter the Iroquois," he added.

James Lee listened intently. "Captain, we have brought a large family between us. We recognize there will be a risk, and there is reason to believe we have made the right decision. What other information do you have for our benefit?"

"I have heard stories – the Lenape have a reputation for trading – and it is known William Penn befriended them. He benefitted from his respectful treatment of them."

"And what of the Iroquois?" inquired Simon.

"Two very different tribal communities, Mr. Elliott."

"How are they different, captain?"

"They speak different languages. The Lenape descend from the Algonquian, a tribe originating in Canada. The Iroquois are part of the Six Nations. Lenape migrate from Canada based on the season and return. Possessing title to land is not part of their culture – there is no title by deed. Instead, they work and live on the land, believing it is endowed to them by the spirit."

James inquired, "Captain – why are the Lenape leaving western Pennsylvania?"

"Mr. Lee – they are peaceful traders, but the Iroquois think of them as weak; they try to intimidate them. And the Iroquois are war-like, so between advancing settlement and warring tribes they face being driven from their homeland."

Captain McCausland stood to secure another bottle of Madeira. Switching the subject, he continued. "This morning, you spoke of questions regarding navigation. Any concerns?"

"No, captain…there are no concerns…well, my wife is nervous, but yes, I have questions."

"And what are they?"

James Lee I leaned back in his chair, drawing a breath of air, while Simon leaned in, interested in the conversation to follow. James continued. "We overheard the first and second mate talk about navigating the stream. Is there anything of concern? What does this mean?"

"They were referring to the Gulf Stream – and no, there are no concerns, at least not now."

"What is the Gulf Stream?" asked Simon Elliott I.

Captain McCausland loved to talk about navigation and sailing the seas. "The story is an interesting one – a tale that, if heard, is told by the people who discovered the Gulf Stream. And they would be Benjamin Franklin and his cousin, Timothy Folger."

The patriarchs, eyes fixated upon the captain, listened intently.

"I can convey what I heard from Captain Blair McClenachan, commander of the ship *Congress*. He met Franklin after he migrated to Philadelphia. And this is the story he told me."

∞

A dimly lit room in the corner of the tavern and a few rays of light shone through a window onto the table. A Man Full of Trouble Tavern nearby the docks on Spruce Street, Philadelphia, was frequented by laborers, dock workers, shipwrights, carpenters, and shipbuilders.

Benjamin Franklin pulled an oak chair away from the table and sat to talk with his cousin. Franklin was twenty-six years older than his younger relative, Timothy Folger, a whaler and native of Nantucket, a thirty-mile-long island situated off Massachusetts. Franklin's cousin, a young man, was well steeped in navigation and understanding the sea. His love was whaling, and he captained his crew on a whaling ship off the island of Nantucket.

Franklin was puzzled. "Something confounds me, Timothy – I need your input about navigation." Benjamin peered over the top of his spectacles.

The subject fascinated him.

"And what confounds my scientific – inventor cousin?"

Benjamin, pondering: "In my crossings over the Atlantic to England – there are changes in the current." Benjamin, reflecting, "What baffles me is the return trip – sailing west to the colonies. It takes much longer, sometimes two weeks longer to complete the sail."

Timothy swallowed a sip from his mug. "This is what I have observed – what I have learned after talking with other whalers. There exists a powerful current off Nantucket. We whalers know the flow of water, and it is constant, the direction changes little."

"Tell me about the direction of the flow."

"Southwest by northeast when we sail out to sea," Timothy offered.

"Why – what is the source of its existence? There has to be a reason." Franklin was curious by nature.

Timothy thought of his discussions with many New England merchants. "Of course – certainly there is a reason: captains on merchant ships believe there is a great current beneath the Atlantic – an immeasurable force producing a flow of water. We sail into it – we sail out of it – yes, it exists – and your point?"

"The cause Timothy – if we find the cause, we find the answer to why it takes much longer to sail on a return trip from England. I think this current is one of the results of the rotation of the earth – that's my theory."

"It's never been mapped Benjamin – there are no captains who possess a chart illustrating the current. But we whalers know what we experience – and what we experience we use as our guide."

Benjamin, steeped in thought, responded. "And what do you whalers experience? Be specific."

"This we have observed. We encounter whales nearest the edge of the water flow – and the men call it a gigantic stream. Some of the captains measure the ocean temperature – it's warmer during July through September. They observe the speed of the current and the surface air bubbles," Timothy added.

Benjamin, considering his cousin's comments, responded. "I'm thinking of the London *mail packets* (sail ships) as they have to navigate the current with each return delivery. Up to two weeks delivery time is added, Timothy. If we can chart the stream, we can add notes assisting ship captains. They can shorten their journey by learning how to navigate the stream."

His cousin sat in silence, thinking of the prospects. "We can map it,

Timothy – I think we can produce a chart for merchant sea captains navigating the Atlantic, leaving ports in England and Ireland."

"You have a good idea, cousin."

Benjamin, still thinking: "Once we complete our chart, we can ask John Dunlap to print copies – we can publicize it. I think of those leaving Ireland for Pennsylvania. We are experiencing increased migration, particularly from Ulster."

Timothy suspected his cousin had a brilliant idea. "It could be valuable. English ship captains would benefit from a chart. They do not understand and navigate the stream as we New England whalers do."

∞

James Lee I was tall, measuring nearly six feet. Given his age, his hair retained most of its original dark color intermixed with strains of silver. He was a gentleman having a quiet demeanor. Those who knew him described him as possessing determination, an exacting man, certainly prompt because he faithfully discharged all personal obligations. He displayed empathy for the needs of others, and his word was sacred. When he attended market-day at Ardara, people took notice. They saw a man with a natural presence. His eyes were rich blue, his nose prominent and broad. When he spoke, it was after he gave thought to his message.

He traced his English ancestry to the picturesque cliffs of Cornwall. Isabella and two of their four sons, James and Simon, and daughters Mary and Isabella joined them on the voyage. Their eldest son Hugh and his wife Mary Elliott Lee would migrate from Londonderry in time. Another son, Thomas, and his family were forced to delay departure due to the crowded ship. Each of the Lee, Elliott, Stewart and Espey families had the blood of English and Scottish ancestry from across the channel. Isabella Lee, the matriarch of the family, grieved within. They were leaving some of their family behind in Donegal.

James I, born in 1708 and at seventy-seven years, was the eldest passenger onboard *Faithful Steward*. He earned the title patriarch due to his years, experience, and accumulated wisdom. Isabella (her baptized name in 1715, Arabella) was the daughter of Lord Hugh Boscawen (1660 – 1751) and Charlotte Godfrey (1662 – 1754). Isabella was born at Albermarle, Westminster, London – one of nine children, having four brothers and four sisters.

Lord Boscawen was 1st Viscount Falmouth, and in 1720, he received the title Baron Boscawen Rose. He was instrumental in representing Tregony, Cornwall, Truro, and Penryn in the British Parliament. Hugh Boscawen married Charlotte Godfrey in 1700 at Henry VII's chapel at Westminster Abbey. Charlotte's father was Colonel Charles Godfrey, Master of the Jewel Office, and her mother was Arabella Churchill. Her father held a position in the Royal Households of England, as he was responsible for managing the Jewel House, which houses the Crown Jewels.

Admiral Honorable Edward Boscawen (born 1711) was an older brother to Isabella. He was charged with the command of a ship for the Royal Navy in the French and Indian War (1754 – 1763), one of a series of wars between the British and the French.

James told the story of Admiral Boscawen and how he became entangled in an engagement, the Siege of Louisbourg, in 1758. Louisbourg consisted of a French fortress built on Isle Royale, Nova Scotia. A joint naval and military force, the largest attack devised by Great Britain was deployed against the military at the fort. Admiral Boscawen commanded a fleet of ships for the Royal Navy. Participating in the naval battle was Captain Joshua Loring, commander of the *HMS Boscawen*. The vessel was built in British America by shipwrights under the direction of the Royal Navy. The rigging was that of a sloop, and the shipwright armed the *Boscawen* with sixteen guns. The keel and frame constructed of white oak stretched sixty-five feet in length. The tonnage was one hundred fifteen. Unfortunately, *HMS Boscawen* met her fate and sunk off Fort Ticonderoga, New York, in the 1760s.

13

Atlantic Crossings

Children standing on the main deck watched the crew loosen sails and pull on the halyards to change the direction of the braces. Each topgallant collapsed and sunk loosely. Once the braces were repositioned and the sails raised, they filled with air, snapped, and resounded with a loud noise. Mr. Brown was spotted climbing the ratlines, inspecting the topgallants for signs of wear on the yards holding the sails. Danger was ever-present upon a sail ship, and it came in a variety of forms. Had one snapped loose, it could carry a crewmember with it, plunging them into the sea and certain death by drowning.

Pelig Hudson designated two locations where passengers were welcome and permitted to occupy. They were atop the main deck from the bow to the quarterdeck but never onto the quarterdeck. And below deck, in steerage, there was a sight to behold. Berths provided sleeping and accommodated relaxation. The long tables served as a place to sit and eat, and to gather for conversation and drink. Some sat at the long tables or on a nearby bench, or lay in their berth recording events in their journal.

A series of three thick oak masts supported the main deck, positioned in the middle of the long tables with benches paralleling each side. Food, placed in carved round wooden bowls, was consumed by the passengers at regular dining intervals. Randomly placed mugs and smaller wooden bowls were spread about the table. And benches, built-in front of the berths, lined the port and starboard sides of the passenger's deck. People congregated, a mug filled with a drink in hand, conversing about all sorts of matters.

Mothers, sometimes relieved by single women, took turns reading stories to children, anything to pass time to shorten the mental strain of being at sea. Atop the deck, although not discussed, the scene was a reminder the captain and crew were the only ones standing between them, their family, and the potential of peril.

Isabella Lee called to her daughter, "Mary – the women are asking if you would teach the children to dance."

Upon hearing the invitation, some of the mothers joined in and cajoled Mary to teach the children to step-dance. She learned various dances at the feis (local festival), or from the dancing master. He traveled among the townlands and villages, teaching anyone a series of three of the most popular routines. Any number of participants could learn the step-dance, therefore most, if not all of the children were involved. Dancing was entertaining, requiring the participant to expend much energy, and it was the preferred method to relieve boredom and pass the time at sea.

"Mary – would you fetch your fiddle and play while I teach the steps?" Mary Maginnis retrieved her fiddle encased in a black cloth case from storage. And Mary Lee pulled two of the McIntire sisters and two of the daughters from the Cooke family aside, explaining she would teach them several dances, and they, in turn, could lead the children in dancing for the remainder of the voyage. Historically speaking, the step-dance was learned and performed in very tight spaces. Small pubs and barn dances were often the venues for Irish dancing; therefore, given a crowded area, dancers had little room for movement. Arms were positioned parallel to ones' body. The wooden deck provided an excellent surface for the resonating tapping sound emanating from their shoes. And Mary's beauty was matched by her charming personality. It wasn't only the children that wished to watch her dance this afternoon.

Thoughts from the Steward

The ship's Steward, Pelig Hudson, was the only crewmember most available to the passengers. His responsibility was to educate them about a world they knew nothing of – life during an Atlantic crossing. If he did his job, he could avoid the potential of people getting in the way of the crew while they went about their work.

Men gathered about the long tables to listen to Pelig's stories, but on this particular day, some of the women congregated nearby, fascinated by what they might hear. A Massachusetts man and sailor, Pelig familiarized them with life at sea, and he knew about life in the land where they hoped to settle.

Pelig looked about. Given the crowd was growing, he took a seat at the head of the long table.

"Decades ago – 1749 – the Pennsylvania Assembly passed a law designed to protect immigrant families. Built upon a new principle, the new law required passengers must be suitably accommodated."

Hugh Espey, being president, inquired. "Explain what you mean."

"The law addressed limits on passengers per berth and the number of passengers per registered tonnage of the vessel."

"Did it help?" Hugh asked.

"The law could not stop abuses inflicted on passengers by captains or crew who ignored the law, but it did prohibit captains from approaching the port of Philadelphia with an overcrowded ship. After the ship was inspected, a common occurrence, a fine was assessed if the law was violated, and the captain paid the fine on the spot."

James Lee I and William Elliott sat nearby with their sons.

"What about our parliament – what was their position?" James inquired.

Pelig knew the history and broadened the subject to include the Continental Congress. "Parliament, as was the case with the Continental Congress, was reluctant to meddle with the affairs of the commercial shipping trade. When they did enact a law, the captain complied or simply ignored the law. Port inspectors, such as the one at Londonderry, when assigned, were responsible for overseeing the condition of the ships, clearing them for departure and receiving those arriving vessels." Pelig paused. "And if favorable winds arose or depending upon the size of the port, the captain sometimes chose to set sail, leaving without ship inspections."

William Elliott inquired about health. "We heard stories of spreading disease – how bad is it?"

"Maintaining health standards for passengers didn't exist on some ships, and overcrowded conditions created stench and filth. Remnants of leftover food, broken biscuits, bones, soiled rags, refuse of all kinds of description, even maggots, were discovered on some vessels."

At this point, the women understood why Pelig pestered them to keep living areas as clean as possible.

Thomas Colhoun, used to multiple ship passages aboard older sail ships, interrupted. "Tell them about the smells on some of those old ships."

Pelig grimaced and thought some more. "The smell was sometimes worse than the dirt. There are normal smells on a ship and its' cargo, both previous and existing, and aging wood, plus the condition of the bilge, and a perpetually rotting hull were a few." Pelig didn't stop. "Toilets, if atop the main deck, are out of reach from passengers during storms. Disease or the threat of it is my worry."

Bad weather forced passengers to remain below, either resting in their berths or socializing at the long tables. Weather conditions would dictate if one could remain seated at the tables due to the upheaval of the ocean and the constant pitching of the ship. Passengers sang songs to pass the time. One could often hear the weeping of a woman, thinking of her loved ones left behind. And they rejoiced upon the birth of a baby and wept when another departed this life. Children helped their mothers upon their beck and call. Some played on the wooden floor, and others amused themselves playing on the benches lining the long tables.

News of Passages

Linen manufacturing declined in 1772, causing migration to increase during the next two years. With news transmitted by word of mouth, the Londonderry Journal and Belfast Newsletter printed stories of people, entire families, leaving their farms. Marketplaces were cradles of perpetual communication. Farmers and linen workers shared stories of adversity faced by family and friends, seeking avenues to alleviate their misery.

A decade passes, and on January 27th, 1784, the news was received in Belfast of Captain Tarrens of the *Philadelphia Packet*. High winds produced from a storm drove his sail ship ashore twenty miles south of the Delaware Bay at Cape Henlopen. News of calamity was infrequent, however, when it did occur, the report served as a sobering reminder of the risk undertaken with migration. All 250 of Captain Tarren's passengers got ashore safely, however, seventy of the survivors hired a schooner to take them to Philadelphia, but the schooner sank, and everyone aboard died.

Bad news – the type of news describing the reality of disaster, courting risk associated with peril at sea was not enough to deter those departing Ulster ports. Persistence prevailed, and the desire to experience life in a new land was worth taking the risk. On May 4th of the same year, the brig *Liberty*, departing Dublin, was lost in the Chesapeake Bay en route to Baltimore. There were 100 souls saved however, thirty were not rescued and perished in the disaster.

Sixteen years prior, December 1768, Captain Ferguson commanding the *Earl of Donegal* departed Belfast for Philadelphia and reported sailing near the Delaware Capes. His vessel was embroiled in a nor'easter and the wind's strength laid his ship on her beams end. He ordered the mizzenmast cut down to get the ship to right itself. In his judgment, he determined to sail with the wind for safety reasons and reached the island of Antigua a month later on January 7th, 1769. Captain Ferguson had his sail ship repaired and sailed away, heading back to their intended port of Philadelphia. All passengers on board reached their destination in February, all reporting to be well.

Rumors, along with true stories of abused passengers, were heard in the marketplaces. The Pennsylvania Assembly spoke yet again – years before they passed the Pennsylvania Act of 1765. The German Society of Pennsylvania experienced much illness after leaving the Palatine due to overcrowding ship conditions. The new law required each vessel to carry one doctor, and their services were to be made available free of charge.

Trans-Atlantic crossings involved boredom, and passengers reported uncomfortable conditions on uneventful passages. Agents advertised the promise of comfortable accommodations; however, the reality was the opposite of the anticipated. The diet of the passenger was usually meager and unappetizing. People brought provisions with them – had they not, they would have starved, and by the voyage end, they had a want for fresh meat. Stormy conditions rendered it impossible for passengers to prepare food in the *camhouse* on the main deck. During these times their diet was relegated to bread, butter, and grog, a mixture of water with a dash of spice to prevent scurvy, and rum.

Those sailing on *Faithful Steward* were fortunate compared to others departing from distant ports. Passengers routinely brought provisions without the fear of inviting molestation from the ship's officers or crew. Londonderry merchants made it their priority to secure this right for their passengers, using their influence with the captain or the shipowner. A sad, familiar scene of emigrants standing on the deck of their ship, in tears, waving to relatives and friends at the dock was a regular occurrence at Ulster ports. Passengers longed for news of family and events occurring at their planned destination. Sometimes the news came from relatives or friends who made the voyage previously, and often they chose to settle in Pennsylvania.

Information was transmitted between passing sail ships. Weather conditions, in particular high winds, drove seas to choppy conditions creating monstrous waves. Passengers remained below deck while the crew dealt with the risk associated with navigating rough seas. Other times the westerlies died down, producing a very smooth ocean. While these sailing conditions were easier on one's stomach, the increase in the length of the voyage added to discouragement.

People hurried to gather atop deck when word spread of sails spotted near the horizon. Captains piloted passenger vessels known as slow sailers. This description depended upon cargo weight and the number of passengers. More importantly, the term was applied to the construction of the hull and the design of the rigging. Faster sailing ships, sometimes smaller with less weight and improved rigging and hull design, created increased speed overtaking another merchant ship. People embraced the opportunity to exchange communication of news from back home when this happened.

Depending upon the person, it could be critical to occupy one's time during a trans-Atlantic voyage. Mothers read stories to children below deck. Men played card games, congregating around the long tables. Daybreak, early morning, and the sunset brought the best time for fulfillment, enjoying Mother Nature's spectacle in the atmosphere. People flocked atop deck to view the sunrise or the setting sun. The rays produced an array of colors, including a burnished gold reflecting on the swells of the deep.

An advertisement dated June 25th, 1784, declared the *Congress* 600 tons burthen, and the captain, Francis Knox, a Derryman, would depart for New Castle and Philadelphia on June 1st. Blair M'Clenachan, a resident of Philadelphia for twenty-five years, a Revolutionary War hero, and a former privateer acting for the Continental Congress invited the people of Derry to a dance on his ship. Those attending praised his vessel, fashioned of the best oak including live oak by Kensington shipbuilder, Manuel Eyre.

Mr. Neal M'Colgan and his wife Grizey, from Hanover Township, Pennsylvania, sent a letter dated 1784 to Grizey's parents, brothers, and sisters in Belfast. Grizey left Ulster before the American War of Independence, and her letter contained a word of warning for her relatives. If you can – come to America, but do not come as servants – come if you can pay the passage.

Passengers were composed of a mixture of humanity. Some were young, more middle-aged, and some old. They congregated around the long tables and swopped stories of home and their intended destination. Others sang songs; some laughed, others cried. Men performed personal hygiene in the open. They had to shave – still others sought cover for washing and dressing. Many were married, and some were single. Most adhered to religion, and others were indifferent to practicing a guiding faith in a superior being.

Securing migrants for passenger sail ships departing Ulster ports was very competitive. Shipowners, masters and their crew were often comprised of local people. Communities built around tightly knit enclaves knew of migration details through word of mouth, before advertising for passage spread throughout the marketplaces. Vessels bearing good reputations were recognized by name. And if you sailed, it was common for the passenger with trade skills to lend a hand with ship repairs. Some assisted the crew with routine operations; others such as carpenters lent a hand with maintenance assignments. Shipmasters and stewards periodically visited passengers on the emigrant deck seeking assistance.

∞

Frequent passing swells caused the ship to pitch slowly. Captain McCausland watched from the quarterdeck as the southern Irish coast disappeared off the stern. His ship was tacking through the Atlantic drift of the Gulf Stream. Tacking became a science combined with experience, therefore increasing an officer's knowledge. *Faithful Steward* was sailing through the northeasterly drift against the westerlies blowing across the Atlantic from the coast of North America.

Children of the Cooke and McIntire families watched Mr. Stanfield measure the ship's speed with a logline. Mr. Mourn took the rope made of hemp tied to a block of wood in hand. Knots were tied in the rope forty-eight feet apart. He extended the line over the ship's stern, continually leaving out more rope to float in the ocean. A large sandglass hung from a hook nearby the helmsman. By suspending the sandglass, the device remained perpendicular to the ocean when the ship pitched and rolled with the sea. Mr. Stanfield watched the sandglass, measuring a period of elapsed time. Each knot tied in the rope was counted as Mr. Mourn let the rope run out from the stern. It was the responsibility of the first mate to measure the ship's speed by counting the knots against the elapsed time from the sandglass. And thus, four knots extended indicated the rate of speed of the ship.

Faithful Steward, built two years prior, provided safety for the passengers. The oldest ships were being eaten away by worms embedded in the wood. Over the years, many vessels succumbed to foundering due to wormholes bored into the hull. Most women feared shipwreck, but it was prudent to keep those fears hidden inside, not to be verbalized and spoken for others to hear. Nonetheless, it was a burden put aside when turning in at night and hopefully forgotten when daybreak came.

The Derry Journal and the Belfast Newsletter reported incidents, mishaps, often close to the coastline, of unfortunate ships and the passengers aboard. A few of the older adults remembered the news of the *Edinburgh,* carrying forty passengers from Newry to Philadelphia. The ship ran aground near Cape May, New Jersey, close to the mouth of the Delaware Bay. Fortunately, local rescuers saved the passengers from harm, even death. In 1773 two brigs, *Phoebe* and *Peggy* departed from Newry to Philadelphia with 400 emigrants but courted disaster. The master of the *Hopewell* reported they lost all of their sails on a voyage from New York to Newry.

Characteristics of Ships

A ship and a brig carried two longboats or one longboat and a *yawl*. These rescue boats accommodated nearly sixteen people. The thought was crude, but the rule of thumb inferred the boats were for the safety of the captain and crew. Passengers were freight. Captains were privy to details of stories from other shipwrecks, otherwise unknown to the transported passengers. Should a disaster occur, the greater the crowd, the slimmer the chance of survival. People on board the *Providence* watched in shock and horror when their captain and crew took to the boat, leaving those remaining to fend for themselves.

Many merchant ships were constructed nearby eastern seaports when the United States was British America. England was losing its forests and the colonies were ripe with timber, hardwoods that would endure harsh elements, and punishment from the sea. Live oak was transported from the Carolinas to Philadelphia shipbuilders. Natural bends in the wood were sought-after for main timbers because they resisted rotting for many years. Shipwrights steamed scrap wood using it as fuel to heat the planking for binding and filling cracks. White oak, cedar, chestnut, and black oak were for underwater planking. Once the framing was finished, pine pitch mixed with fibrous material such as hemp was applied as caulking. Still another source for caulking was gum, a sap from wounds inflicted on living pine trees. The planking and decking were built from yellow pine and red cedar, when available.

Stalls built of wood were located amidships on the main deck starboard side. Two longboats, tightly secured, sat on top of the stalls. Some pigs, cows, and sheep were fed and housed inside the stalls. A sturdy iron grommet fastened into the deck secured a thick chain that slipped through the hole. One of the crew looped the opposite end of the chain around the head of the animal, while another chain, attached to a second grommet, secured the legs. A crewman held the chain taught while a butcher slaughtered and dressed the animal. Another carried the meat to the galley where the cook salted it for preservation, with separate portions divided for consumption by the passengers.

The process of feeding the abundance of people was daunting but organized – it had to be. Families, grouped with others, took turns feeding everyone, employing shifts. Once the last shift was fed, tables were cleared and freed for anyone to gather, break a deck of cards to play *maw*, read, or drink and engage in conversation.

Crowded conditions implied people were everywhere atop the deck, taking in the sights and inhaling refreshing salt air, or below deck in steerage, helping with the duties assigned by the president, and reading or playing games with the children. In some instances, able-bodied passengers asked by Mr. Gwyn, Second Mate, assisted the crew, adjusting sails, performing carpentry repair, and maintenance of the ship.

There were many with idle time, passengers engaged in conversation with others for the first time, and they recognized there were those who spoke a dialect different from their own. Some were tradesmen and crafters, but many were farmers. And in addition to being farmers, they became linen weavers, *bleachers*, or those employed by the *drapers*. As former tenants, they were obligated to a landlord for the lease of a *ballyboe*.

∞

With the long tables cleaned and wares removed and stored, James Lee I spoke to those surrounding the long tables.

"Fellow Irish – we have chosen our lot and will be on this ship for weeks awaiting arrival to a new land. A land where we will seek new opportunities with freedom to buy land and to worship without fear. We can explore and build for the future. But for now, we occupy the closest of living accommodations, and we have much time to learn who we are and where we came from before we embark upon who we will become. I propose we occupy some of the time with stories which describe many places in Ireland that we left behind. And let's use the next weeks to reflect upon our past and learn about our future." And the stories began.

14

The Province of Ulster

Together they became the fabric of Ulster, a land occupied by the forerunners of the native Irish more than a thousand years before. And since the early 1600s, those from England and Scotland joined the Irish in the Plantation of Ulster. Family records, histories, and recorded critical historical events buried in trunks and chests were stowed in the ship's hold. And years before, a family member memorized and recited these events from family history for all to hear.

The Nine Years War (1594-1603), fought in the countryside of Ireland was concentrated in Ulster. The tribal rule of *Gaelic* chieftains Hugh O'Neill and Hugh O'Donnell and their allies joined against the English Army was brought to a bloody end.

Tyrconnell Tyrone and Cuconnaught Maguire of Fermanagh, two examples of earls ruling Ulster, were forced to flee their homeland, the empire they occupied. The impending defeat of Gaelic chiefs led to the Flight of the Earls – an evacuation of nearly one hundred tribal rulers. They set sail from Donegal for Europe by 1607 and the rebellion of Sir Cahir O'Doherty was put down in 1608.

People in the Province of Ulster, now purged of tribal rule, prepared for a new plan of colonization. A large influx of those from lowland Scotland, and others with social standing and influence in southwest England, stood at the doorstep to participate in a major settlement. Events about to unfold would forever change the ownership of land, agriculture, society, and their history.

∞

Land in the six counties of Antrim, Down, Londonderry, Armagh, Tyrone, and Fermanagh, was divided into individual parcels. Hugh Espey of Tobermore, the elected president, announced he would moderate and lead in organizing those who would speak, representing their county.

"Who among us is from County Antrim?" he began.

John McNab, sitting to his left with some of his family, raised his hand.

"To the front of the long table, John, you will be first."

County Antrim

John walked to the head of the table, lurched because the ship pitched, regained his balance, and sat in a wooden chair.

"Let me first tell each of you where we McNabs came from before our family settled in Antrim. Killen is a village located at the western end of Loch Tay, a freshwater lake in the highlands of Scotland. It was believed many years ago, Clan McNab ruled the highlands nearby Killen. There is an ancient burial ground at Inchbuie, nearby the River Dochart."

People stopped talking with one another and began to listen to John. Unless you were a merchant used to traveling overseas for trade or throughout the counties of Ulster, there was a likelihood you knew little of the counties about to be discussed. Many of the passengers never traveled more than five to ten miles from their farm.

John, a Scottish farmer, was five feet – six inches tall and built of a sturdy frame. His hair was very dark, his eyes too, and a scar on the left side of his face served as a reminder after his horse kicked him.

"I'll do my best to describe County Antrim for those of you who have never been there. Cushendun is a small village, the name derived from the Gaelic, *Cois Abhann Duinne*, interpreted beside the River Dun. The village is a sheltered harbor lying at the river's mouth adjoining Glendun, one of nine *glens* of County Antrim."

John paused. He wanted to tell the people how Scots became familiar with Antrim. "The *Mull of Kintyre* is at the southwestern tip of Kintyre, a large island of the Inner Hebrides, and it protrudes from the west coast of Scotland, a sixteen-mile sail across the North Channel, separating County Antrim from Scotland. Antrim represented the gateway to a land inhabited by others in *pre-Norman* times, later to become territories of Irish dynasties lasting for many years."

John continued. "Long ago, a ferry provided transportation for people and goods from the small village, Dunaverty, Scotland. Rathlin Island, approximately seven miles long by one and one-half miles wide, is located nearby the coast of County Antrim and is visible to the west when one crosses by ferry from Dunaverty. A customs house and passport office maintained at the harbor at Cushendun, required clearance for those crossing the channel. When the weather clears and the sun brings blue skies, one can stand on the cliffs at Cushendun and the nation of the Scots will appear before their eyes."

Hugh Espey placed a mug filled with water next to John as he continued his story.

"County Antrim (*Aontroim*) means lone ridge. The county, located on the northeast shore of the *Lough Neagh*, is the largest freshwater lake in the Isles of Britain. The glens of Antrim are one of nine valleys known to radiate an abundant beautiful spectacle of green grasses. Mountainous scenery abounds from the Antrim plateau as far as the eye can see to the coast."

"Tell us about Portrush – we know passenger ships depart often," James Espey interjected.

John, enjoying the spotlight, continued. "Portrush is a land of footprints. The history of prior inhabitants can be traced thousands of years. This small village is known for fishing, and there are sandy beaches along the northern coast. Portrush is thirty miles west of neighboring Cushendun. In Country Antrim, the lay of the land is hilly toward the east. The mountains increase in size from 1,600 to 1,800 feet. Along the northern shore, the mountains descend in an abrupt pattern joining the shoreline, providing a landscape of spectacular coastal scenery. Ancients could stand at the edge of miles of *basaltic* (a dark magnesium-rich rock) cliffs and gaze downward to earthen colored columns, all arranged in a line, leading to mossy laden cliffs dropping off to the sea."

John continued, changing his topic to Larne. "*Latharna* is a Gaelic term for Larne, an eastern coastal seaport located thirty miles southeast of Cushendun. The area was inhabited for more than one thousand years, one of the earliest settlements in Ireland. The River Inver flows through Larne, forming a pathway connecting with the North Channel. And one can stand on the shore of Larne and distinguish coastal Scotland on the opposite side of the channel. The early population of Larne was traced to a settlement of people from Scotland – the inhabitants engaged in trade along the shores of the North Channel, even venturing across the body of water to settlements along with coastal Scotland."

He sipped from his mug, looked around the table, noticing all eyes were upon him and continued his story.

"Years later, many lowland Scots migrated from the land of their forefathers and left the existence they had for land in the north of Ireland.

Settlements occurred as early as 1605, continuing through the year 1697. The uprooting of Scots transitioned into an organized settlement process, initiated and decreed by King James I in 1606. A new breath of life swept over Antrim because people of Scottish descent were encouraged to cross the North Channel and establish settlements. King James I entered into agreements with nobles and multiple London-based companies, and they received land grants entitling them to enter into tenant leases with farmers, those willing to work and cultivate small tracts – *ballyboes* of leased land."

"Is there more?" Hugh asked.

John took another sip – "Almost done," and continued. "During the pre-plantation period, the countryside was inhabited by Irish. Fertile lands, a portion of which were part of the central Ulster basin, were located west and south of Lough Neagh. A *ballybetagh,* a territorial unit, was under the control of a *sept* – or clan. And the ballyboe was a small farm that was cultivated by one to several families. I suspect all lands located in Ulster were under the control of septs, made up of groups of small land units."

John finished his remarks talking about something he knew much about. Farmers living in pre-plantation Ulster concentrated on cattle grazing and the cultivation of leased land, all performed by hand using a wooden spade wrapped with an iron shoe or fitting. And in more fortunate instances, they used teams of horses to cultivate the soil for planting and growing oats, wheat, and barley. When the harvest was near, the crops were cut by hand using a wooden sickle, and the labor was long and back-breaking.

Farmers required the services of a *cooper* as there were limited means for the storage of harvested crops. The cooper made a *ruskin* or small wooden container by scooping out the interior portion of a tree and used it for the storage of harvested crops. Lastly, Danish-designed mills ground large quantities of threshed oats.

County Down

"Is anyone from County Down?" Hugh inquired.

No one raised their hand. The reason, a resident from Down could leave Ireland at the port of Belfast because it straddled Antrim and Down.

Gustavus Colhoun spoke up. "My family is not from County Down, however, I have visited Belfast for merchanting reasons. I could comment."

"Take the chair," invited Hugh.

Gustavus, standing in the back of the crowd, strode to the front of the long table, his pistole tucked inside a belt underneath his brown frock.

"County Down covers a large fertile landmass, and over the years, the linen trade has prospered, producing many wealthy merchants investing in trade and trade ships. South of Belfast lies the Mourne Mountains with granite peaks near 2,800 feet. They create a beautiful scene descending nearby the Irish Sea."

"Why was County Down left out of the plantation plan?" Hugh asked.

Gustavus responded – "Many years before the plan, Down received an influx of English and Scottish settlers, with the Scots being greater in concentration. In the north of the county are many Presbyterian settlements."

Gustavus continued with his description. "County Down is near the southeast shore of Lough Neagh and Newry, an old village established on the western border." And then he asked a question. "Do you know Newry was to grow as a market town because of jewelry production in the 1700s?"

A few of the merchants on board the ship nodded in the affirmative, and he concluded with his narrative. "The settlement, divided by the twelve-mile-long River Clanyre, empties into the Carlingford Lough. Newry is located in the valley between the Mourne Mountains rising to the east, and the River Guelin to the southwest, all providing a backdrop for land with outstanding beauty."

County Armagh

Gustavus rose from the seat at the head of the long table to be replaced by Hugh McClean from Armagh. Clan McClean, with family roots traceable to the eleventh century, was one of the oldest clans in Scotland.

Hugh's appearance was striking. A man of medium height, his lean muscular build was accented by flaming red hair and green eyes.

"Our family storyteller is in Pennsylvania awaiting our arrival. Many years before our clan settled the Inner Hebrides, islands populated with many seals and seabirds, and the western highlands, before crossing the channel and settling in Armagh."

"Would you describe County Armagh?" Hugh Espey asked.

"The Gaelic word for the county is *Ard Mhacha*. County Armagh is a rich fertile land in the southernmost of the six counties in Ulster. Our forefathers were granted land leases to cultivate the soil, grow crops, and plant fruit trees – the apple tree being very popular."

Hugh continued. "Farmers constructed homes consisting of two rooms, possibly three, and heated by a prepared turf fire. Some homes were coupled, and the roof was thatched, supported by A-shaped timbers with rafter trusses. The roof was hipped, and the walls were thick, using earth and wood post construction techniques. The center of the house contained an open hearth."

"What about your utensils and furnishings," Hugh inquired.

"People cooked with red glazed crockery. Only a few had metal pots. Furniture constructed of wood was basic in appearance. Our diet was always a challenge – it was also simple, at times at a subsistence level. We grew oats and potatoes, ate some beef, and depending on location, fish included with the diet."

The men wanted to lament about farm equipment, therefore Hugh changed the subject. "Farm equipment was crude and of poor quality. We used wooden plows and spades, and the work was backbreaking. Animal manure and lime were our main sources of fertilizer." He added, "Farm communities expanded over time and eventually attracted merchants, setting up village markets and developing trade channels."

∞

Nearly one hundred years before, James I of England created the Royal School to provide for teaching the sons of local Protestant merchants and farmers. With the passage of years, an educational center grew. Sister schools sprang up in Dungannon, County Tyrone, and another in Enniskillen, County Fermanagh. The planting of educational seeds facilitated the cultivation of the settler's faith, and the Roman Catholic Church and the Church of Ireland established roots in Armagh.

Development of the plantation in seventeenth-century Ulster could be segmented timewise. During 1610 – 1615 colonization was slow except in County Down. From 1615 – 1620 migration increased. Throughout the decade 1620 – 1630, internal mobility increased. From 1630 – 1641, migrating Scots to Ulster took center stage. Then came 1641 – 1654 when many Protestants were killed during a rebellion, and from 1654 – 1670, English migration increased beyond their Scottish counterpart due to the restoration under Oliver Cromwell.

The logical person to take the chair was the patriarch of the Lee family, so James Lee I took the seat. If a passenger didn't know him, they knew him by appearance. He was one of the taller men on board the ship, with dark hair streaked with gray, and handsome.

"*Dun na nGall,*" he began, "Is interpreted – fort of the foreigners, and it lies west in the Province of Ulster bordering the Atlantic Ocean. Years before, Donegal was under the control of the *Clan Dalaigh*, a powerful ruling family. The topography is mountainous with valleys, some lush, especially surrounding the River Finn and Foyle Valley. The most elevated mountainous regions include Errigal – 2,463 feet and the Blue Stack Mountains – 2,213 feet."

James Lee continued his narrative. "The Lees migrated to Donegal from Cornwall years ago. There are fertile valleys suitable for farming in the baronies of Kilmacranan and Innishowen, a peninsula bounded on the east and west by the gulfs of Lough Foyle and Lough Swilly. And many small lakes suitable for fishing populate Donegal. In the north, we have breathtaking views of the ocean filled with abundant wildlife at the point of Innishowen and the Malin Head Islands. *Loch n Eachach*, or *Eachaidl's* Lake, known as Lough Neagh, is the largest of all the freshwater lakes in the British Isles. Inflowing water from the upper part of the River Bann winds its way to the lower River Bann and the River Blackwater."

Hugh asked James to share history handed down about the time of the plantation.

James paused for a moment, "At the time of the plantation, English and Scottish settlers followed those given land grants intending to enter into leases and settle the region. Together they occupied the land, living nearby the Irish after the departure of the clan chieftains. During the early days of settlement, numerous English settlers traveled to the Foyle Basin in the northwestern portion of Ulster. And the area surrounding Londonderry and Strabane grew."

"Tell us about the *Laggan* area," asked James McIntire I.

"It's located in East Donegal and spreads into the Finn Valley east to the River Foyle. And in that valley is very fertile soil – well suited for farming and favored by those migrating from Scotland."

"How was the land divided at the time of the plantation?" James inquired again.

"The land was parceled into twelve divisions of one thousand acres. And there was a provision included that the undertakers would settle the parcels with English and Scottish families."

James Lee continued. "Five boroughs – Ballyshannon, Killybegs, Donegal, Lifford, and St. Johnstown were developed as part of the plan of resettlement. By the mid-1600s, County Donegal had nearly 12,000 inhabitants – approximately 3,400 descended from Scottish and English ancestry, and the remainder, about 8,600, were native Irish. Years afterward, the eastern portion of Donegal, maintaining a strong streak of independence, was inhabited predominantly by migrating Presbyterians, many being Covenanters." The Espeys and the Hepburns, identifying with Covenanters, nodded their heads in agreement.

County Tyrone

Hugh Espey didn't bother to ask who wanted to describe the county. The logical choice was James McIntire I so he took the seat at the long table. At fifty-seven years of age, he possessed a God-given intellect, and his word choice was often with purposeful intent. He and his wife Rebecca focused on one thing. It was to move their large brood of daughters together with their sons to Pennsylvania. Robert, a nephew, was waiting in Lancaster County. James' hair was gray, thin on top, and flowed to the top of his ears. Gray eyes hiding behind wire spectacles portrayed an aura of seriousness. He was thin and muscular, nearly six feet tall.

Those surrounding the long table experienced an invisible energy field as if a wise schoolteacher entered their presence. James began. "Ardstraw is the smallest of villages, but many years ago, members of the early clans would meet by the bridge and hold talks. For example, the O'Donnells and the O'Neills met at the bridge to discuss peace. But this was preceded by many years of warring clans," he continued. "We have a local Presbyterian Church. It sits upon a hill overlooking the River Derg. It was founded in the 1650s, and a short time ago our family bid goodbye to Reverend Robert Clarke. He lives nearby at Tullydortans in the barony of Lower Strabane." James changed to agriculture. "Farmers living in the surrounding area cultivate the rich land, and of course we harvest flaxseed to make linen."

"Tell us about the land, paint me a picture," someone at the end of the table requested.

"Certainly. An artist painting a landscape within the border of Tyrone would brush impressive views of heather-filled meadows graduating up to the peaks of the Sperrin (meaning little pinnacle) Mountains, above the 2,000-foot level." James II nodded as his father spoke. "The mountains spread across the center of Tyrone into the eastern portion of the county penetrating County Londonderry. And the land stretches to the shore of Lough Neagh and northward to Limavady. Flat peatlands and bogs dominate the eastern section, consisting of harsh, wet, nutrient-poor environments."

James transitioned to describing the region's history. "*Tir Eoghain*, the Irish Gaelic describing the land of *Eoghan*, was a conqueror of northwestern lands in Ulster. He controlled the countryside of Tyrone, Londonderry, and Innishowen before the 1600s. Many years later, the rise of the Gaelic Kingdom increased under the power of the O'Neill dynasty."

And then he changed the subject back to geography. "Ardstraw is interpreted hill or height, specifying a location. An ancient bridge built to span River Derg is the only one for a long distance. Water from the River Derg moves with such force, the rapids sound like music as it flows underneath the bridge." James could mesmerize people with his words, and he chose them wisely, painting a picture while he spoke. "The land encompassing the area is filled with lush green fields and fertile rolling farmland. And a very old road covers the distance from Dublin, passing over Ardstraw Bridge to Londonderry."

He finished by combining geography and history. "Omagh, a town destined to grow into a central county role lies where the Rivers Drumragh and Camowen meet, and together they form the River Struhle." And he added, "The Franciscans arrived during the mid-fifteenth century and developed a friary at Omagh."

County Fermanagh

Matthew Caldwell, born in Ireland in 1757, was nineteen when he served as an ensign in the Pennsylvania (troop) State Militia during the War of Independence. Edward Cooke took a seat next to him at the long table.

Hugh Espey addressed the crowd. "We have two on board this ship – one served in the American War of Independence – the other has brothers who served on both sides. What an uncommon occurrence this is."

James McIntire II, stirred by Hugh's comments, drew closer to pay attention. Two men sat before him, and they possessed stories to tell. One was in the heat of battle – the other had family members on opposing sides. Was it likely one of the Cookes knew and served with General Washington? James thrived on these stories – after all, they were sailing toward the land where his heroes live.

Edward had two brothers, Lieutenant Colonel Charles Cooke and Major Robert Cooke that joined the British Army. A third brother, Jacob, settled in Lancaster County, Pennsylvania. The other, Colonel William Cooke, joined the 12th Regiment Continental Line from Northumberland, Pennsylvania.

"My brother," Edward began, "Colonel William Cooke, fought in the 12th alongside General Washington at the Battle of Brandywine in New Jersey. It was the only battle where the general met General Howe on the same battlefield. Colonel Cooke fought at Germantown and at Brandywine in Pennsylvania where an estimated 29,000 British and Colonial forces clashed, and another battle at Monmouth, New Jersey. The Battle at Brandywine, Pennsylvania was an open field and spread out over many acres of land. Due to an intelligence mistake, General Washington was outflanked by the British and had to cut and run. On the other hand, Germantown was fought following a hard march through difficult terrain to get to the battle site. My brother will remember Germantown for a long time – it was a fierce bayonet charge against the British, hunkered down in an old brick building. A British sharpshooter, after the shooting ceased, informed his commanding officer he had a Continental officer in his sight and was ready to pull the trigger. He didn't, because military protocol forbade shooting a high-ranking officer if possible. His commanding officer asked his sharpshooter to describe the officer. Upon hearing the officer wore a yellow sash, he told his sharpshooter you had General Washington in your sight."

Together, Matthew Caldwell and Edward Cooke described Fermanagh as a patchwork of outstanding natural beauty, with nearly a third of the area covered by lakes and waterways. Three highland areas are known as the West Fermanagh *Scarplands, Sliabh Beagh,* and the county's *Breifne* Mountain range.

Matthew added, "Many hundreds of years ago, the *Manapii* were the only known Celtic tribe dwelling in the area. And after those years, people inhabiting the land were referred to as *Fir Manach* or man of Manach, resulting in the name attributed to Fermanagh."

Edward Cooke intervened. "By the fourteenth century, with tribal rule now in the hands of the Maguire chieftains, their original stronghold originated at Knockninny. The Maguires constructed the massive stone castle at Enniskillen by the River Erne. King James I ordered the English army to invade Fermanagh as part of a greater war, and those rebelling against his authority were killed or driven out of the land. The ancient Gaelic law formulated by a society known as the *Britheamh,* (anglicized as Brehon) an educated class of people, was done away with and replaced by a new administrative law."

15

The Ulster Plantation
Baronies, Undertakers, Servitors, and Companies

Ulster, derived from an Irish word, *Cuige Uladh*, means the province of the *Ulaid*, or a group of tribes living in the land. The concept of escheating land was approved by King James VI, son of Mary Stuart, Queen of Scotland, the only surviving daughter of King James V. Escheatment, passed by parliament, declared property, land specifically, abandoned or without an owner. Therefore, the land could be confiscated subject to a higher authority, and this power determined the future of the property. Escheatment, now law on the eve of a plantation, initiated a plan to develop a plantation. And this is why the prerequisite for the plantation required the completion of surveys of acres of land within areas designated to grantees.

Land in Ulster, territory controlled by Gaelic Lords, was no longer under their control following the flight of the Earls. Hugh O'Neill left his native County Tyrone and Rory O'Donnell, the Earl of Tyroconnell left County Donegal, and Cuconnaught Maguire witnessed land in County Fermanagh taken from his control.

Legislation authorizing the plantation provided for a new name, one decreed for the purpose behind the plantation. And the king's decree was officially recognized as, The Society of the Governor and Assistants, London, of the New Plantation of Ulster, within the Realm of Ireland. Thousands of acres destined for new ownership would require numerous divisions applied to new entities taking title to the land. The primary forces behind the plantation concept were developing agriculture and promoting social change.

The plantation was multi-faceted – land was apportioned to multiple groups for different reasons. New colonists, English-speaking Protestants, brought loyalty to the king. Lands not previously mapped, particularly in western Ulster, would undergo the mapping process before any distribution could be decreed by the authority.

Baronies

Ireland's counties, divided into areas labeled baronies, became subdivisions of a county. Thousands of acres, now seized by England's Parliament became integrated into an organized system of redistribution. A designation of individual baronies throughout the counties of Ulster ensued, and a prerequisite for the Plantation of Ulster included completing surveys with designated grantees identified as follows.

Baronies by County

County Londonderry
Coleraine
N.E. Liberties of Coleraine
Keenaght
Tirkeeran
Loughinsholin
N.W. Liberties of Londonderry

County Tyrone
Strabane
(James Hamilton, Earl of Abercorn, Sir Claude Hamilton, Knight, Sir George Hamilton, Knight, George Hamilton, Gentleman)
Dungannon
Omagh
Clogher

County Armagh
ONeilland
Tiranny
Armagh
Fews
Orio

County Donegal
Kilmacrenan
Innishowen
Raphoe

(Duke of Lennox, Sir Walter Stewart, Knight and Laird of Minto, John Conyngham of Crawfield, William Stewart, Laird of Dundorff, James Conyngham, Laird of Glen Garnocke, Cuthbert Conyngham, James Conyngham, Esq., John Stewart, Esq.)

Boylagh

(Sir Robert MacLellan, Laird of Bombay, George Murray, Laird of Broughton, Sir Patrick Mackee of Laerg, Knight)

Banagh

Tirhugh

County Fermanagh
Lurg

Magheraboy

(Robert Hamilton, Sir John Hume, Knight, Alexander Hume)

Tirkennedy

Clanawly

Knockninny

(Thomas Moneypenny, Laird of Kinkell, Michael Balfour and son, Lord Burley)

Coole

Maghera Stephena

ClanKelley

County Cavan
Loughtee

Tullygarvey

Clankee

Castlerahan

Tullymunco

Tullyhaw

Clanmahon

List of Counties and Baronies
Not Part of the Plantation of Ulster by County

The following counties including baronies were excluded in the Plantation of Ulster. Migrants from Scotland settled these areas before the plantation.

County Antrim
Cary
Dunluce
N.E. Liberties of Coleraine
Kilconway
Glenarm
Antrim
Toome
Belfast
Massereene

County Down
Iveagh
Castlereagh
Aards
Kinlarty
Lecale
Dufferin
Mourne
Newry

County Monaghan
Farney
Cremorne
Dartree
Monaghan
Trough

Undertakers
English Undertakers

The quantity of land one owned for lease defined Ulster's social structure. Rental income from tenants was a substantial portion of the undertaker's revenue. And leases to tenants were based on profit; therefore, undertakers did not always grant leases by following the rules laid by plantation commissioners.

Englishmen with financial backing took control of seven baronies. As undertakers, their directive and mission involved building defensive structures to support the planting of English settlers. Undertaker's estates ranged from 1,000 up to 2,000 acres. A total of fifty-one estates received aggregate grants of 81,500 acres.

Every undertaker paid an annual sum to the king equal to £5, 6s, 8d for every 1,000 acres owned. An average annual income for an English undertaker was £150 to £300.

Scottish Undertakers

The Cunninghams were among the most important Scottish undertakers with land granted in County Donegal. Others included the Achesons, with land granted in County Armagh, the Humes, taking title to acreage in County Fermanagh, and the Stewarts in County Tyrone.

Scottish undertakers received a quantity of land above their English counterparts. There was a total of fifty-nine estates designated within nine baronies. Differences between English and Scottish estates were determined by size. Scottish estates were smaller with less acreage. It was reasoned smaller estates owned by Scots were a result of the lower incomes of the undertakers. Many of the undertakers, English or Scottish, were people of moderate financial means. Annual incomes quantified by an application process were near £150 for Scottish undertakers. They migrated regardless, and some of the settlers from the border areas of southeast Scotland bore surnames of Armstrong, Beatty, Elliott, Graham, and Johnston.

Servitors

Servitors, defined as those providing services to others, particularly the king, were military or governmental officiates and were divided into three classes of individuals qualifying them for grants of land, the total reaching nearly 55,000 acres. Most servitors were granted 1,000 to 2,000 acres, with some receiving as few as 200 acres. When acting in the capacity of a landlord, servitors leased land to native Irish and British tenants in accordance with law.

Servitors were required to pay an identical amount to the king as did the undertakers, provided the servitor leased to the English. If their tenants were Irish, the servitor was required to increase his annual payment to £8 to the king.

The first group consisted of Councilors of State, the second group was thirty-nine captains and nine lieutenants of military commands already in Ulster. The third was English freeholders, those previously owning estates within the boundary of the confiscated lands.

The concept of councilors receiving land grants stemmed from leading figures in English administrative positions in Ireland. An example was Sir Thomas Ridgeway, granted land in County Tyrone. Sir Arthur Chichester, Lord Deputy of Ireland, originally from Devon, England, received title to land in the Barony of Dungannon, County Tyrone. Chichester also received a grant of the entire barony of Innishowen, County Donegal, plus land in southeast Antrim close to Belfast and Carrickfergus.

Gaelic Chiefs

King James I complicated the process by re-granting land taken from Gaelic chiefs O'Neill and O'Donnell to fulfill negotiation for their surrender. Twenty-six "important Gaelic Lords" came by grants of 1,000 acres or more. Connor Roe Maguire acquired 5,980 acres in the barony of Maghera Stephena, County Fermanagh, and Sir Turlough McHenry McNeill amassed 9,900 acres through a grant. English servitors considered the re-granting of land to Gaelic chiefs in western Ulster a betrayal of their service rendered to the king.

∞

Immigrants exploring opportunities to farm on these estates fell under the categories of leaseholders, cottagers, and under-tenants. One could question, why did they leave Scotland and England to become a tenant to another. The answer is fourfold: (1) To pursue a new, improved life (2) Secure an opportunity to acquire an estate creating income (3) For farmers, larger or better farms, and (4) For those laborers who owned no land, an opportunity to possess their farm.

Undertakers and servitors bore responsibilities to be fulfilled, but undertakers had more demands to meet. Servitors were obligated to remit a yearly rent payable to his majesty for eight pounds per 1,000 acres and ten shillings for sixty-acre parcels if leased to Irish tenants. Rent changed to five pounds, six shillings, and eightpence for every 1,000 acres if leased to English and Scottish tenants.

Undertakers built castles, houses, and bawns, and they were to dwell on their land within two years. And they brought a good store of arms to protect their estate. Commodities could be transported provided they subscribed to the "Oath of Supremacy," committing to conform to religious practice. Anyone not willing to take the oath was eliminated from entering into a lease for the land.

Companies

Land Grants to London Companies

Grants of land filled a variety of development prerequisites, all aimed at ensuring successful colonization. An allotment of acreage of land was apportioned by the delineation of trade groups within a barony.

London-based entities were responsible for forming joint-stock companies comparable to the Virginia Company, an entity formed to plant a colony across the Atlantic Ocean in Virginia. It was similar to the East India Company and its responsibility to colonize India.

Colonization and development would require capital, wealth, and the source for much of the wealth would come from merchants living in England. The importance of accumulating a network of merchants to form companies for investment purposes would be of primary concern in developing Londonderry and Coleraine, two areas with ports for trade and shipping, and designated to be valuable for the future growth of the region.

The total acreage set aside for London Companies was 38,520. A portion of the tracts was inevitably divided by vocation and populated with English settlers. Examples included cloth workers, drapers, fishmongers, goldsmiths, grocers, haberdashers, ironmongers, tailors, salters, skinners, vintners, and merchants.

*Trade Group	Acreage	Barony
Clothworkers	3,210	Coleraine
Drapers	3,210	Loughlinsholin
Fishmongers	3,210	Keenaght
Goldsmiths	3,210	Tirkeeran
Grocers	3,210	Tirkeeran
Haberdashers	3,210	Keenaght

Ironmongers	3,210	Coleraine
Mercers	3,210	Coleraine
Merchant Taylors	3,210	Coleraine
Salters	3,210	Loughlinsholin
Skinners	3,210	Keenaght
Vintners	3,210	Loughlinsholin
	38,510	

Implementing the Plan

The plantation was advertised, orchestrated, and carried out per the plan to populate Ulster. Some were hand-picked men and women, those with skills and societal standing. A total of 162,500 acres previously surveyed and mapped were granted to and administered by English and Scottish undertakers.

Everyone would populate their land based on a minimum of twenty-four adult males from England or those leaving the lowland region of Scotland for every 1,000 acres included in the grant. Twenty-four males were required to represent at least ten families in the process of plantation. Per computations, English undertakers would generate 3,900 adult males and the London Companies 925 males. A total of 4,825 males moved to Ulster over a transition period of several years.

*Articles of Plantation
Distribution of Land for Rent
Estates of 1,000 Acres

Undertakers – retained 300 acres for personal use
Freeholders – two of them allotted 120 acres each
Leaseholders – three of them allotted 100 acres each
Cottagers, *husbandmen,* and *artificers* – the remaining 160 acres were divided and leased to this group.

Summarizing – Britain planted ten families on each 1,000 – acre parcel.

Building Requirements
For Each Plantation Grantee of 2,000 Acres +

A castle built within the bawn must be a fortified stone dwelling or an unfortified manor house. The bawn must be created for estates of 1,000 acres and include a small single-story thatched cottage.

The architectural style of the castle or fortified dwelling mirrored the nationality of the undertaker or servitor, be they English or Scottish. Over time castles of Scottish appearance dotted the Ulster landscape. English undertakers and servitors, built lime or clay mortared stone houses with large glazed windows at each level. The size of the houses varied from eighteen to twenty-five feet or twenty to twenty-four feet in length. Wealthier landowners increased the size of their dwelling to forty to sixty feet in length.

∞

Churches, an integral part of their society, received grants per the Ulster Plantation. A total of 48,158 acres was set aside as *termon*, derived from the Irish word tearmann, defining the land as a place of sanctuary and exempt from taxation. Acreage, defined as termon, came under the control of the bishops of the church.

Trinity College, formed in 1592 and located in Dublin, received an extensive landmass, 6,000 acres in the Barony of Armagh. They also received a grant of 4,000 acres in County Donegal, part of the *Tirhugh* barony, and another 2,400 acres in County Fermanagh.

Designers of the plantation required each grantee of 2,000 acres to build a castle to be located within a *bawn*. The bawn was a cattle fort constructed of earthen material and bark, including timber or clay mortar.

Tower houses designed for defense appeared on the Irish and Scottish landscape in the Middle Ages. Each undertaker was required to build a tower house of one form or another. Some were literal towers; others, built a stone house with a mixture of clay and lime, mortar, and timber, all based on English design.

Thatched roof houses could be identified as Irish. Most dwellings were approximately eighteen to twenty-five feet front to back, or possibly twenty to twenty-four feet, with some larger and rectangular in design and shape. The freemasons of English descent, wealth being greater, built larger houses in Londonderry, Dungannon, Lurgan, and Coleraine.

Sir Francis Bacon developed an idea to locate a castle, positioning the structure to draw the farms circumventing the castle into it. Villages and hamlets began to appear on the scene, and in time, a corporate town was born, supplementing development and drawing tradespeople and *artificers* – skilled craftsmen and inventors. Necessity required their presence to provide the settlers with implements to farm, producing trade, and increasing their livelihood and security.

Scots and English, desirous of a new start in life, were attracted to an elaborately fabricated plan. Sir Arthur Chichester, a man with cunning foresight, wanted the existing element of native Irish to join in with dwelling in the villages. The fulfillment of his idea generated services for the inhabitants and provided for defense. And who did they fear? The possibility of the return of the earls that fled from Rathmullan, Donegal, for Spain. Driven off course by a storm, they landed in France. The earls planned to return with a foreign military force to reclaim dispossessed land. Barring an invasion that never materialized, the villages metamorphosed into towns, appearing as nucleated settlements.

Scottish farmers concentrated on cultivating oats, barley, and wheat. Craftsmen built mills to harness water to power and process their crops. Malthouses and kilns followed together with sawmills, glasshouses, and smiths. London Companies hired Irish horseman using carts and pack horses to move lumber, stone, and lime to build inland roads and passageways over bogs to link towns with coastal ports.

Undertakers brought English cows, bulls, and sheep. The terrain was ideal for grazing and sheep-farming, resulting in woolen refinement and production. *Tuckmills*, invented for *fulling* wool were built. This required water used in the process of fulling – beating the woolen cloth with a wooden hammer – and fulling stock, a process required for cloth-making. A cam was attached to a shaft connected to the waterwheel to drive the tuckmill furthering the woolen production process.

Villages were transformed into agricultural settlements consisting of small farms, family-run, but leased. Laborers known as cottagers lived nearby the *bawn*, the grassy land outside the tower house. Established law required townlands to incorporate. As they grew, the need for more services increased. Examples included the erection of a church, a school, an inn for travelers, or a taphouse. It was critical to facilitate a marketplace. A weekly event, it became an important social structure where artisans and farmers exchanged goods and services. Communication with the greater area of Ulster was received and transmitted, and news from the world filtered through.

Approximately two-thirds chose to live in rural areas, content on arable farming, and located away from planned villages. Some land leases contained a provision for settlers to remain on the land, restricting travel significantly. Marketplaces provided farmers a place to trade their produce and secure services from artisans required to carry on their trade.

At the center of each marketplace was the *diamond,* and it was as close as possible. Hopefully no more than four to eight miles travel per day. Per plans, a market cross became a characteristic highlighting each diamond. Many displays were shaped in cruciform (having the shape of a cross). Others were not.

*Summary of Land Grants for
the Plantation of Ulster

Grantee	Acres	Townlands	Combined Acres
English undertakers	81,500	1,267	418,110
Scottish undertakers	1,500	1,232	406,560
London companies	38,520	572	188,760
Servitors	54,632	994	328,020
Church (Termon)	74,852	1,338	441,540
Irish	94,013	1,301	429,330
College	12,400	157	51.810
Schools, towns, forts	15,193	266	87,780
Irish Society	7,000	151	49,830
	———	———	———
Totals	459,110	7,278	2,401,740
Unidentified townland		3,938	1,288,974
		———	———
Totals		11,216	3,690,714

* Philip S. Robinson, author of "The Plantation of Ulster – British Settlement in an Irish Landscape, 1600-1670."

16

Colonizing the Plantation

With Gaelic lords driven from their homeland, people came to Ulster for settlement. Beautiful mountain scenery, lush green fields, and marshland with bogs and moors; woodlands, loughs, rivers, and magnificent basaltic cliffs descended to the seas. They inhabited and viewed Ulster, a land surrounded by the sea on the east, west, and north, now at the doorstep of integration with the Irish by people from England and Scotland.

Multiple factors facilitated competition, driving the movement of people entering Ulster's ports. And sometimes they settled a short distance from their port of entry, after evaluating the physical and economic environment. Though not readily available to everyone, *Muster rolls* dated back to the 1600s, identifying the location of groups of people. Traveling by sea, it was common to exchange information, and stories about specific estates in various baronies. Tenants contacted landowners quickly, and decisions to locate to a particular estate followed.

Colonization brought groups of people and families to a new environment. Scots and English sometimes settled outside their society, implying Scots did not choose land leases with Scottish undertakers all the time. Likewise, English sometimes entered land leases outside their society. From a geographic perspective, a higher concentration of English settled across the southern half of Ulster. They embraced the liturgy of the Church of England (Anglican). Scottish settlement unfolded differently. Scots dominated the north of County Down, the south of County Antrim, and northeast County Londonderry. And sometimes proven to be more adaptable to farming, the Scots occupied the *Laggan* area (Gaelic for low-lying fertile valley) of the Foyle Basin in the northeast of County Donegal and northwest County Tyrone.

Decades later, settlers spoke different English dialects, evidenced by the Ulster-Scots dialect and Ulster Anglo-Gaelic. The Ulster-Scots dialect and a mid-Ulster dialect originated from seventeenth-century speech patterns found in southwest Scotland and the northwest midlands of England.

As people migrated through the seaports and spread across Ulster, there was a concentration of cottagers and under-tenants among the Scots. However, more of the English were leaseholders and *freeholders* – signifying they had an ownership in the title to buildings on their land, all subject to the plantation law. Scottish migrants outnumbered their English counterparts by a margin estimated near twenty to one.

Authorities investigated the progress of the plantation grantees and their requirements to fulfill specific obligations. The undertakers and servitors were obligated to build houses and bawns (cattle forts), and those with larger estates erected houses or castles constructed of stone or brick. An owner of an estate of 6,000 acres or more was required to provide for the defense of their bawn. The size and design of the bawns varied according to wealth and if built by Scottish or English estate holders. Some bawns were square or circular, however, rectangular shapes were more common. The size was near sixty by one hundred feet in width and length, with walls built to a height between eight to fourteen feet.

In the early days of the plantation, the supply of timber was plentiful, however, it diminished over time. The wooded area of Glen Conkeyne and Killetra, part of the Barony of Loughinsholin in the southern portion of County Londonderry, was filled with oak, ash, and elm.

Fired clay products such as bricks and roof tiles were produced by the trade for building material. Thatched roofs were common, wood shingles covered many houses, and slate roofs were sighted around Londonderry. Brick houses, crafted by the English, sprung up in the lowland bay areas in the Laggan Valley, the northern section of Armagh nearby the Erne basin, and in the central area of Cavan, northwest of Lough Neagh.

Mills sprang forth – tenants used corn mills built by undertakers and servitors due to clauses in leases binding them to use their mill. Many were powered by water, and a few were powered by wind. Each county in the plantation used a tuck mill for the fulling of woolen cloth. Migrants built kilns, saw-mills, glasshouses, and malt houses.

Repression

Many years later, the Plantation Act of 1699 excluded wool from the export markets. Commerce grew due to prosperity in the linen trade. Two other acts, the Union with Scotland Act of 1706 passed by the Parliament of England, and the Union with England Act passed in 1707 by the Parliament of Scotland created the Treaty of Union. The law - both English and Scottish law - prevented the people of Ulster from exporting woolen products to mainland Britain. A law passed to protect the British woolen trade benefitted Irish linen, helping this industry to become the most important in the counties of Ulster. On the other hand, limiting the processing and production of wool implied Ireland was destined to trade wool within. This stifled trade outside the country and reduced wealth.

As the seventeenth century folded into the eighteenth, nearly 50,000 Scottish immigrants occupied counties in the north of Ireland. They migrated due to the availability and low cost of farms, with increasing opportunities for trade. Years followed, and the English woolen trade declined. Those in the trade determined it was competition from the Irish that lead to their plight.

People in Ireland, now firmly entrenched due to the implementation of the plantation, became a mixture of native Irish, some Roman Catholic, some Church of Ireland, Scottish Presbyterians, and the English, steeped in the history of the Church of England.

The Acts of Union, be they related to commerce and trade, brought religious persecution – and the passage of penal laws produced strife during the reign of Queen Anne (1702 – 1707). Catholics were forbidden to worship publicly – the penalties for doing so were harsh and merciless. Laws impacting Presbyterians were less strict. Nevertheless, they were frustrating and infuriating when applied to men.

The vilest of law is not effective without a name, and the Test Act of 1715 fulfilled the intent by which it became law. People inhabiting the entirety of Ireland were subject to tests – investigations – leading to assessments and impacting the foundation of their lives. Those practicing Anglicanism were granted an element of protection for their speech, and the right to engage in dissent, thus resulting in a form of liberty.

Women did not possess political rights – therefore, they could not own land, and were banned from entering into bonds for the lease of land. Upon the passing of their father, they could not inherit his land. Some women were poor, many came from middle wealth, with no exercise of law, but all maintained a persevering stock. They were dependent upon their father's business, perhaps working on their farm as a laborer, or in the absence of business, relegated to farming another's land. Some were laundry workers and kitchen aids, and others were forced to steal if destitute. Most were dependent upon their brother (s), if they had one, for support, or marrying when of age, relying upon their husband for economic care and position in society.

The Test Act required all men serving in a governmental capacity to participate in the communion of the established church. Town councils in Ulster now lacked in participation with anyone who was Presbyterian. Actions have consequences, and the Test Act broke the back of the inhabitants of Ireland, plunging people into broken-heartedness, stifling agriculture, and producing a scarcity of food, bringing famine for future generations.

17

Covenanters

A covenant is not to be taken lightly, and a covenant may be sacred. It's an agreement – a promise, a contract, oral or written, a pledge to perform, and the Scottish Presbyterians were serious about the covenant.

In 1581, Scottish minister John Craig devised a covenant based upon his interpretation of scripture. The resulting covenant breathed life into a movement initiated among Presbyterians. This movement played an essential role in the developing history of Scotland and to a lesser role in England and Ireland.

Covenanters entered into a solemn agreement between themselves, the church, and God. Two branches materialized, and important covenants were established for Scottish Presbyterians to follow. The first could be described as the "National Covenant," and the second, the "The Solemn League and Covenant." The covenants followed the actions taken by King Charles I of England who ruled from 1625 – 1649. At this time, he formulated an attempt together with William Laud, the Archbishop of Canterbury, to force the Scottish Church to conform to English liturgical practice and church governance.

A group of Scottish churchmen assembled at Greyfriar's churchyard at Candlemaker Row, Edinburgh, in 1638, and they adopted the National Covenant. Upon taking the oath, a member acknowledged they were bound to maintain the Presbyterian doctrine and policy as their only form of religious faith and practice. In 1643, The Solemn League and Covenant was adopted as a treaty between the Parliament of England and its Scottish counterpart. The intent was to preserve the reformed religion in Scotland.

Most covenanters were not among the societal elite. They were farmers and craftsmen and flourished as linen producers and merchant traders. After migrating to Ulster, they established dwellings in the eastern part of County Antrim and County Down. Most of them escaped poverty and persecution, seeking the lure of fortune and an improved life.

Samuel Hepburn, from Donegal, was a covenanter as were his sons, John, Simon, William, and James. Included in that group were Hugh Espey and his sons, Hugh, William, James, and John. And other covenanters sailed on the ship. Both families traced their forefathers to the area of South Lanarkshire near the River Clyde in Scotland. Samuel claimed he was a distant relative of Patrick Hepburn, Third Lord Hailes, and First Earl of Bothwell, a descendent of Reverend John Hepburn from Keith.

The Hepburns came from a family of high standing, having a good education with experience in the mercantile trade. Married in Glasgow, Samuel and Janet (Sinclair) Hepburn were forced to move because Samuel's views as a covenanter were unpopular. The elder Hepburn paid for two sons, James and William, to sail from Londonderry to Philadelphia in 1773. Upon arrival, their mission was to travel west to the Susquehanna Valley to investigate the surrounding fertile land and report to their father. James traveled to Sunbury in Northumberland County, formed in 1772, and successfully purchased warrants, a contract to buy land, and then returned to Philadelphia. After a while, he traveled west again, purchased more warrants, and returned to Philadelphia. Brother William chose to settle near Sunbury, and in a short time, volunteered for the local militia due to an Indian uprising. Years passed, and in 1778, he was placed in command of a company at Fort Muncy and later commanded a garrison.

In returning to the mid-1700s, migration from Scotland and England to Ulster changed. No one had to convince lowlanders and border Scots to chance the opportunity to leave their homeland. Poverty abounded, impoverishment was everywhere, and these conditions forced some to resort to marauding, stealing, and horse thievery, all contrived in the Scottish countryside. They had to persevere as farmers accustomed to existing in miserable conditions. Many produced a minimum for the survival of their family. An estimated forty-thousand Scots crossed the North Channel, settling in Ulster.

Not all were covenanters, but those who shared a common bond, fearing religious persecution and dispossessed of land, were sometimes led by a fearless clergy.

18

The Linen Region

With the plantation process a century behind, Ulster was populated with a new persevering stock of people. Inter-marriage between the offspring of those previously considered migrants existed for years. The enumerators counted residents of English descent living on English estates. Their education was not neglected. By 1700 ninety-five percent who signed a document did so by writing their name, with the remainder making a mark.

Market towns expanded, encouraging the increase of crops for export in addition to feeding local populations. And others engaged in manufacturing necessities to be consumed by locals with the excess offered for export trade. A group of entrepreneurs, bleachers of linen cloth, developed in County Armagh and the small town of Lurgan, (Irish, *An Lorgain*), meaning shin-shaped hill. Lurgan was located along the southern shore of Lough Neagh, situated in the northeast corner of County Armagh. Roads in Lurgan were straight, with room for cottage rows to occupy the sides.

The knowledge of linen manufacturing was brought to the inhabitants by Thomas Turner, James Bradshaw, John Nicholson, and John Christy, all familiar with linen bleaching and all introducing their services to Ulster townlands during the 1700s. Artisans built weaving looms and many people learned spinning or weaving fiber. The knowledge of linen bleaching techniques grew in importance, and early developers brought business contacts to manage the increase in the manufacture and trade of the products. Their connection with members of parliament at Dublin and London enabled the improvement of linen production sold in the marketplace.

In 1711 the Irish Parliament approved the Board of Trustees of the Linen and Hempden Manufactures of Ireland. And this development would promote the manufacture of linen across the entirety of Ireland. The industry grew in the earlier stages, and employment opportunities increased in County Antrim, Armagh, Down, Londonderry, and Tyrone. With the concentration and increase of linen production, more income followed. Family households engaged all members in linen production. Approximately three-quarters of the planters were tenant farmers and farm laborers and they grew and processed farm produce. Scottish farmers gained an edge because the English were not prepared to endure the rigors associated with farming. Villages dotted the landscape with towns following. Opportunistic tradesmen filled the required roles of carpenters, sawyers, bricklayers, tilemakers, plasterers, masons, slaters, and lime burners.

Growing Flaxseed

Seed could be grown on local farms or purchased at a market town. The source was produced from another farmer or imported by merchants with business ties in Pennsylvania. Seed was sown in April. By early June, flax grew in thick medium green clusters roughly six inches high. Within two weeks, the clusters reached twelve inches, and in early July, the plant was near twenty-four inches tall.

As August neared the plant was ready to be harvested. Bunches were pulled from the ground and tied together in bundles. Rope-like strands stood upright to air. After airing, the bundles were soaked in water and spread on the ground to dry.

By September, the flax was medium yellow to light brown in color and straw-like in appearance. Within two weeks, the color changed to pale yellow. In mid-September, the flax was bundled and stood upright to air and dry.

Scutching, Heckling, and Beetling

Farmers found linen processing lengthy, and the cost to obtain the equipment was modest. They dedicated a portion of their land to growing flaxseed for their economic survival. If the production of flaxseed was insufficient to cover their weaving requirements, they would visit the nearest market town to buy additional seed from the traveling yarn jobber.

Flax, harvested in a raw form, had to be *scutched*. Workers separated the woody portions from the fibrous part of the plant and then *heckled* – meaning the fibers are combed from the plant and prepared for spinning into yarn. Much of the spinning was performed by women and children, however, men would join in the process. Weavers bleached then washed and dried the fibers, and wound them around wooden spools. Next, the same weavers wove the fibers into cloth using a handloom – the process performed in the weaver's home. Summertime was used for the bleaching process, saving the winter and spring for weaving fibers into the fabric.

Linen drapers frequented the brown linen markets systematically. Drapers purchased the linen for cash since weavers lacked a method to extend credit. Those same linen drapers, either bleachers or agents for other bleachers, put the linen through another bleaching using a potash solution to remove impurities. Afterward, the drapers loaded the cloth upon a horse-drawn wagon to bleach-greens (grass fields) where it was laid in rows, watered, then dried in the sun. The effect of the sun shining and warming the cloth produced the desired whitening in the linen. The final production stage involved a finishing process called *beetling* – pounding the linen with a heavy wooden instrument to give the cloth a smooth texture.

Marketing linen involved a *factor* – a merchant responsible for accessing credit and facilitating financial transactions. Weavers and bleachers lacked access to credit, and could not generate enough cash for trade. Drapers borrowed money from factors and pledged the linen for security. Workers packed the linen in boxes and shipped the cloth to the Linen Hall at Dublin. There the merchant factoring the goods received the product including payment from the draper to pay off the loan.

Dublin, Ireland

Farming Flax

Farmers divided their land to grow the crops necessary to survive. Flaxseed was sewn in the leftover land portions after vegetables were planted for consumption by the family. As years passed, the population grew, and with this, the number of families growing flax increased. Land became in short supply and farmers turned to purchasing flax at the marketplace. A flax market flourished in County Donegal whereas linen markets were concentrated in the counties of Antrim, Armagh, Tyrone, Down, and Londonderry.

As linen markets matured, higher production was concentrated in County Antrim, followed by Armagh, Tyrone, Londonderry, and Down. The bestselling linen markets metamorphosed into a line running from Belfast to the town of Armagh, including Lisburn, Lurgan, and Tandragee. Banbridge and Newry markets contained the simpler and also fine linen cloths. This notoriety produced higher prices for their products, called lawns, to make handkerchiefs, children's clothing, and diapers. Merchants seeking the famed three-quarter wide and seven-eighths linens frequented the market areas of northwestern Ulster and Counties Tyrone and Londonderry. Linens were referred to as Tyrones and Coleraines. And one-yard wide Armaghs, course brown linens, became the specialty in the south of Armagh.

Linen Markets and Economic Cycles

The processing and bleaching of linens became entrenched in Ulster society. Those visiting the marketplaces sold and bought multiple sizes, textures, and colors. During February and March, the farmer, now a weaver, was kept extremely busy. And the weaver turned into a husbandman from August through October as seed was sewn and later harvested.

Material sources used in the bleaching process consisted of *kelp*, *cassub*, *barilla*, *potash*, and *pearlash*. Western isles located off coastal Ireland and Scotland became sources to harvest, heat, and burn seaweed to produce a substance – alkali or iodine. Locations in the southern portion of County Antrim and the southwestern region of County Donegal processed the kelp to ash. These by-products were necessary for use in the textile industry, including soap-making and glass. Kilns were constructed together with drying walls and storehouses. Belfast merchants found barilla, a substance made from the ash of a Mediterranean shore plant, and imported it using their trade connections.

Local town merchants purchased brown or unbleached linen for exportation. Coarse linen was traded to Liverpool and the finest of linen was sold in various places. White linen, for instance, was sent to Dublin and sold in local markets. Another option was to ship the white linen to Liverpool and London, where the product was consigned to factors to assist with dispersing the product. Growers and processors would keep a portion of their product for home use as needed.

Overseas commerce increased, and Londonderry, no longer a settlement by the river, grew into an important port for exporting textiles, specifically linen. The list of bleachers operating within the province of Ulster increased, and nearly 250,000 pieces were bleached annually. The individual production of a bleacher was measured and found to be capable of producing about 5,000 pieces each year.

The Emergence of a Cotton Industry

Cotton, popular in Europe was late in coming to Ulster. Larger employers added cotton manufacturing and imported the raw material. The Linen Board distributed grants to encourage manufacturing cotton, and Belfast produced one of the first spinning machines. The Linen Board financed the first Irish mill in Whitehouse located between Belfast and Carrickfergus. Linen processing remained as Ulster's primary industry throughout the eighteenth century, however, mechanized technology brought the promise of a cotton industry.

Lancashire, England, led the development in spinning cotton, however, the surrounding area of Glasgow, Scotland wasn't far behind. Years later, the Irish made advances in cotton but lagged in new production compared to neighboring Scotland and England.

A growing presence of Belfast artisans and the surrounding areas of Larne and Carrickfergus pursued spinning cotton and weaving. In northwestern Ulster, yarn was taken to the Londonderry market from Innishowen and mountain districts. And yarn was sold to merchants for exportation to Liverpool and Manchester. Sales of coarse yarn thrived at Londonderry while the finest sold well at Coleraine or Newtown. Irish and Ulster Scots remained content with linen production, a less mechanized industry. And through their dedication and persistence, the annual tally of linen production increased in Ireland.

Linen Markets of Ulster

The Plantation of Ulster succeeded in many ways, lacking in others. Scots, exhibiting patience and endurance, now firmly entrenched, improved farming knowledge and animal husbandry, including the beef market, and vegetables, all required for sustenance.

English employed their craftsmanship and business expertise as Ulster grew as a collective society of farmers, crop growers, linen weavers, and bleachers. They were known as marketers, merchants, producers of linen, capable of distributing their products throughout England, Scotland, and overseas. Trade expanded as they sought commerce with British America and this association grew to Ireland's second-largest export market.

The cost to produce linen in British America was higher than in Ireland, and therefore the manufacture of linen was discouraged. During the decades 1750-70, linen exports doubled, increasing to 4,400,000 yards per year. In the 1770s, nearly twenty percent of exports were destined for a new market, the West Indies, as plantation owners needed supplies to clothe laborers. Philadelphia was known for exporting Irish linen because Ulster merchants moved there and established businesses in the preceding decades. And expeditions promoting more trade opened secondary markets at the southern ports of Charlestown and Savannah.

County Antrim

The Linen Board of Trade designated six villages and towns as marketplaces for the distribution of linen. Lisburn conducted their weekly market day on Tuesday, Belfast's market was Friday, and Ballymena each Saturday, drew the highest number of linen sellers. Ballymoney's market opened each Thursday, Ahoghill on Friday, and Portglenone, visited by the second-highest number of sellers opened on Tuesday.

Linen production was tabulated for the six locations in County Antrim by the Linen Board of Trade. The number of linen sellers exceeded 3,000 in the six markets. Selling is not complete without buyers, and the number of buyers in the six markets was near 275. Total merchants attending the multiple market locations were 150 unless they arranged to send a commissioner in their absence.

Securing capital – money, became a critical component if a person succeeded as a linen merchant. Most merchants accumulated a minimum of £1,000 before entering transactions, and a merchant desiring to persevere in linen trade required £3,000 to £4,000.

Linen sales, tabulated regularly, were measured by the number of webs sold in the marketplace. If the total sales for the six market locations were combined for County Antrim, near 12,000 to 13,000 webs were sold. During one week the prices ranged from £1.7 to £4 per web.

Ballycastle merchants included George Fullerton and Hector Boyd. They broadened their business by setting up a store importing linens and dry goods at Walnut Street in Philadelphia. Fullerton parlayed profits into purchasing trade ships such as *Prince George* and *Catherine*.

With roots from the village of Glenarm in County Antrim, Randle Mitchell sold quality linens in his store at Water Street, Philadelphia. Merchants seized opportunities by partnering with others, thereby spreading the investment risk, a sizeable undertaking in owning ships. Thomas and Robert Montgomery, in Philadelphia, owned the vessel, *Mary*, in a partnership with Fullerton, John Campbell, and John Gregg from Belfast. Another ship, *Pennsylvania Farmer*, was jointly owned by William and Andrew Caldwell, James Blair, and George Fullerton.

County Armagh

Four towns and villages dotted the countryside of County Armagh, offering linen markets located at Tandragee each Wednesday, the town of Armagh on Tuesday, Lurgan on Friday, and Portadown on Saturday. Each week the four locations produced 900 to 1,000 linen sellers and nearly 250 buyers, split between 210 merchants and 40 commissioners.

Lurgan's marketplace, meeting each Friday, drew the highest number of sellers estimated at 350, and Tandragee and Armagh, very close in comparison, drew an estimated 275 sellers each. The marketplace at Portadown, held each Saturday, was a relatively small market with 40 to 50 sellers. The town of Armagh generated the largest number of webs of linen sold on a given day, nearly 2,500, but the price per web was closer to £1.4.

County Tyrone

Every Thursday, sellers met at the marketplace of Dungannon, offering linen to interested merchants. Of the twenty-eight marketplaces, Dungannon supplied the greater amount of linen, and the Board of Trade chose this location to gather statistics. Approximately 1,000 sellers made the journey to market with nearly 1,700 to 1,900 webs of linen products.

There were seven other marketplaces spread throughout County Tyrone in addition to Dungannon. Ranked by the highest to lowest number of sellers, they were the Tuesday market at Strabane, the Saturday market at Omagh, and a Friday market at Fintona. Lower tier markets were Cookstown, operating on Saturday, and three other markets nearly equal in size. Ballygawley was on Friday, Stewartstown on Wednesday, and Newtownstewart meeting on Monday. Each of the latter three markets drew 150 to 175 sellers.

Upon measuring the number of merchants, Dungannon drew close to 100 with commissioners near 60. Sellers trading at Strabane was near 500, with the number of buyers near 50, split evenly between merchants and their representatives, the commissioners. The market at Fintona drew about 350 to 400 sellers weekly. Strabane's market drew a higher price at £3.3 per web, while Dungannon's price per web was closer to £2.2. The markets at Fintona and Cookstown drew roughly £2.6 to £2.7 per web, and the remaining three lower volume markets were bringing in prices from £2 to £3.

County Londonderry

Londonderry's history pre-dates the Ulster Plantation. One section of the wall was built beside the River Foyle. A wooden quay, a platform used for loading and unloading brigs, was erected with bulwarks and gates. The town, formed using English design, required the alignment of the streets in a grid pattern within the fortified walls.

In the 1750s, Philadelphia received about thirty sail ships from Irish destinations each year. Londonderry merchants, eager to set up trade connections, apprenticed with relatives or friends, sending them to Philadelphia to operate business ventures in British America.

The tax assessment roll for 1756 in Philadelphia listed 170 merchants and 88 shopkeepers. Thirty-five of the eighty-eight shopkeepers were women. Many merchants migrated from Ulster however, a considerable number of shopkeepers and merchants were English Quakers. Profits from trade converted to real cash, and it was common for a merchant to accumulate wealth, double the amount of the shopkeeper. Thomas Campbell, in Philadelphia, dealt in dry goods and with linen bleachers. John Bleakley invested in sail ships trading with Ireland.

By 1775 commerce increased in Londonderry due to the convenient access to shipping and trade. English settlers accommodated numerous craftsmen, traders, and merchants. Assorted linens lined store shelves, tools were sold, and farmers supplied grain, butter, hides, and sometimes cattle, purchased by merchants for export. Other merchants with connections in Scotland, British America, and places distant sold imported household wares, clothing, tools, food products, iron products, and hardware.

The diamond was the central meeting place within the protective walls of the Londonderry marketplace. The town crier stood at the market-cross where he announced proclamations to the community.

Many years before, the London Company received a grant of 4,000 acres adjacent to the County Donegal side of the Foyle. Originally, fifty-five London Companies received invites to finance the venture, and eighteen of them accepted land grants. Londonderry, a corporate town, acquired the power to send burgesses – representatives to parliament.

Settlement spilled outside the town gates near the bogs across the River Foyle. Land suitable for development was split into estates and set aside for churches, schools, and Irish freehold land. A freeholder took title to the land for the duration of one's life. The Society of the Governor and Assistants, London, of the New Plantation of Ulster, within the Realm of Ireland, was responsible to administer local governmental law.

1775

"Come along girls," beckoned Sarah Moore to her three daughters as they made way through the fields and bogs toward Waterside, a community located on the east bank of the River Foyle. They could see the spire from St. Columb's Cathedral rising above other buildings from the river bank. Wednesday was market day, the busiest day of the week. "Hurry Ann, walk faster, move quickly, we must hurry to the diamond because the ferryman won't wait," she called. Ann, the youngest, was a daydreamer and a dawdler. Elizabeth, the oldest of the sisters, grabbed her by the hand to move her along.

The ferry, situated on the east side of Londonderry, transported people bringing trade goods across the river. After they passed through the Ferry Quay Gate, they walked to the diamond filled with linen weavers, farmers bringing produce, and manufacturers of housewares and farm implements.

Ann stumbled on the path once again. "Elizabeth – look at those big beautiful ships." The Londonderry Journal listed the names of three sail ships docked at Ferry Quay, two arriving from British America and the third from the Caribbean. Most of the goods would be sold at the diamond. Other merchants chose to auction their stores and wares from the deck of the vessel.

The Moores were among 300 or more sellers of linen today. They anticipated upward of 50 to 70 buyers, some merchants, with the remainder consisting of commissioners, those capable of entering into transactions on behalf of the merchants, all seeking and purchasing webs of linen. Sarah was hoping to strike a price near £2.5 to £3 per web.

People traveled up to ten miles by foot and horse-drawn cart from Ardlough to Londonderry. The constant wear from travel reduced primitive paths to worn dirt roads. Timber was laid on top of the bogs to enable the passerby to navigate their journey. On market day these roads supported the carts of farmers destined to deliver surplus agricultural products, including cattle, beef, hides, sheepskins, tallow, and butter and cheese.

Trade goods increased because people attended from as far away as Raphoe and Letterkenny, together with those living nearby creeks by the eastern side of County Donegal. Those traveling from the western side of the town entered through Bishop's Gate or Butcher's Gate.

Coleraine in County Londonderry, near the northeast coast and on the River Bann, was less than thirty miles from Londonderry. The two towns had the most input in plan design compared to other towns. Planners used a centrally located diamond with a gridiron street pattern. Their marketplace, smaller than neighboring Londonderry, met every Saturday drawing between 200 to 250 sellers and perhaps two dozen merchants or their commissioners.

Coleraine had less traffic and reduced volume of linen sales, about 200 or higher webs sold weekly. John Rowley, an agent associated with the City of London, erected Coleraine's first market-cross. Instead of placing the cross in the diamond, it was located outside the town. He chose to locate it on the other side of the River Bann (Irish – Bhanna – for goddess), the longest river in Ulster.

There were seven marketplaces at the towns of Banbridge, open each Monday, Newry on Thursday, Downpatrick was a Saturday market, Kilkeel each Wednesday, Rathfriland met on Wednesday, Ballinahinch met each Thursday, and Hillsborough met on Wednesday.

The largest group of linen sellers gathered at Downpatrick, numbering near 400, with nearly twenty-five merchants or up to ten commissioners, inspecting the webs of linen brought for sale. Markets at Newry, Kilkeel, and Banbridge, plus the remaining four markets, drew twenty-five to fifty sellers with a smaller number of linen merchants.

20

People, Parliament, and Currency

During the mid to latter 1700s, Ireland's religious and economic history played a crucial role, impacting and forming the lives of the descendants of those who participated in the plantation. Given their backgrounds, some areas of Ulster grew as a Protestant stronghold. Fertile land obtained through ownership by grant, purchase, or lease was passed down to surviving generations of English and Scottish settlers.

Native Irish, descendants of those under the control of the earls, occupied territory in the mountainous regions. They also inhabited many areas beyond the limits of land apportioned to the church, or the undertakers, servitors, and Irish grantees. And there was a significant amount of Irish living on the estates. When traveling in Ulster, one noted the further they were from a market town, the more likely they would find Irish that did not assimilate into the culture.

One's religious foundation would play a forceful role in future affairs. Some were adventure seekers, others looking for a better life, a number thought they were escaping poverty, and a remnant led scandalous lives. Scottish presence increased, and the descendants of the covenanters remained faithful to the tenants of Presbyterianism.

Londonderry and Portrush, situated near the border of County Londonderry and County Antrim, and Larne, on the east coast of Antrim and Belfast, were strongholds occupied by Scottish Presbyterians. The evolving sociologic structure produced tightly knit communities in each of the named counties. This influence spread into the eastern side of County Donegal and the northern portion of County Down.

There was a time – years prior – where the parliament of England acted to ban the importation of livestock and related products. Still, they continued to allow wool to be traded within their markets. The Ulster society engaged in trade with British America, distributing their linen products and avoiding England. Many engaging in wool manufacturing and the woolen trade were Protestant planters, having learned their expertise in England.

Parliament moved to curtail the woolen trade from Ireland, and the new law produced an intensified distaste toward England. While the woolen market traded within Ireland, the exportation of linen was near one-half their trade value. At one point over 35,000 people invested in the linen market with 10,000 employed in the home. Small to more significant manufacturing industries were impacted. By 1741 linen exports were valued near £500,000. Thirty years later – 1771 – the total increased to near £1,700,000.

British Currency Denominations – 18th Century

Two farthings = One half-penny
Four farthings = One penny (d)
Twelve pennies = One shilling (s)
Five shillings = One crown
Four crowns = One pound (£)
Twenty-one shillings = One guinea

Linen weavers earned about one (s) shilling to one (s) shilling and 4 (d) pennies, and a farm laborer earned about 8 (d) pennies for their efforts of a day's labor. Farthings, half-pennies, and pennies were minted in copper. Shillings and crowns were struck in silver and the guineas in gold.

Linen trade flourished, and cotton grew steadily. Land values rose to a level negatively impacting the farming communities. More acreage was relegated to growing staples, decreasing the supply available to grow flax. In some locations, rents escalated and terms for leases shortened. Fewer acres were farmed, and famine increased. Flax was spun at the level of three to four *hanks* – a measurement for the length per unit of yarn available for sale at the market.

Flax imports increased from New York and Boston, and a growing farming community in Pennsylvania and Newfoundland provided flax for Ulster's linen communities. British American seed ranged between fifteen to twenty shillings, while seed from Holland and Riga, in Russia, drew a price between twenty to twenty-five shillings per bushel. The price of each source of seed was predicated upon the quantity found at each port, and the demand or vigor of yarn and linen sales.

21

Sylvania

Colonists navigating the wilds of British America used the *Warrior's Path* at their peril. It was a great system of well-traveled routes – pathways extending through thick woods for hundreds of miles carved by members of the Six Nations, and the paths meandered through gaps in mountains to places further south known as the Catawba country. People of the Six Nations were tribal groups within the Iroquois society. The six members included the Mohawk, Onondaga, Oneida, Cayuga, the Seneca, and the Tuscarora. The tribal communities originated from the Iroquois League of Nations in Canada, and over many years gravitated southward.

The Warrior's Path cut through New Netherland, named in 1609 by Dutch settlers. Trails penetrated further south through the heartland of the Susquehanna and Juniata Valleys, with dense woodland, many streams, great rivers, and abundant wildlife, bending westward toward the Allegheny Mountains.

A *Shawnee* word – *Ath-ia-mi-owee* – was used to reference the trails in the pathway – and the word meant "path of the armed ones." The Warrior's Path was built by wear and tear, the constant grinding of the earth's vegetation to a level where animals and men used the route for travel. The pathway stretched outward in many directions, and the system of trails existed for hundreds of years, well before Europeans explored continental North America. The athiamiowee was used extensively for war and hunting game because nomadic herds of buffalo and elk used the trails for migration. And the Warrior's Path could be a place of danger for the *Lenape* (Le-nah-pay), the Shawnee, or a tribe within the Six Nations.

The Shawnee descended from the *Algonquians*, a people located to the north of eastern North America. Algonquians were unrelated to the tribal Iroquois, and they warred with one another. The languages of the Iroquois and Algonquians were very different. Each of these communities spawned many tribal divisions that migrated throughout the Warrior's Path and inhabited the great woods.

The Lenape, descending from the Algonquians, divided into several tribal subsets and migrated into heavily wooded areas, settling near or alongside the two great rivers, Delaware and the *Schuylkill*, both flowing through the eastern section of the great woods. The *Munsee*, the *Unami*, and the *Unalatchtigo* were English words used to describe three common tribal communities of Lenapes, dwelling between the two great rivers extending eastward to the Atlantic Ocean.

∞

He was a man of great distinction, capable of accumulating wealth, and he employed a significant portion of his wealth by loaning a sum to King Charles II of England. Admiral Sir William Penn was English and an ardent Anglican, a member of the Church of England in the seventeenth century. His son, William Penn, born in 1644, was educated at the Chigwell School in Essex and later graduated from Christ Church, an integral school of the University of Oxford. Upon reaching age twenty-two, his religious thinking was influenced by a friend, George Fox, a devout and founding member of the Religious Society of Friends – *Quakers*. William Penn believed an inner light rested within man, and it was this light that was responsible for the guidance of one's conscience.

England fell into times of turmoil, and members of the Religious Society of Friends became targets – some of their beliefs and practices differed from the established Church of England. The Society – referred to as Quakers – believed if the inner light was foremost in purpose and deed, then a man should not bow before another man, be they king or otherwise. Oaths swearing allegiance to someone or something should be avoided. The resulting change in beliefs, behavior, and practices placed William Penn at great odds with his father. These divisions led to times of persecution.

On September 1, 1677, prominent members of the Quakers, Penn being one, left Downes, England for Philadelphia on the ship *Welcome*. By October 24, they entered the Capes of Delaware. Unfortunately, someone brought smallpox on board the ship at Deal, England, and thirty of the one hundred passengers died at sea. Penn, along with the survivors, reached New Castle, Delaware, on October 27.

King Charles II granted a colony, West New Jersey, to be settled by approximately two hundred people. They left behind the settlements of Chorleywood and Rickmansworth located in the county of Hertfordshire and other places in the county of Buckinghamshire. By 1681 and upon the king's death, he canceled his debt to Admiral Sir William Penn by granting a substantial parcel of land in British America. Thousands of wooded acres located in West New Jersey were titled in the name of Penn's father.

Sir Admiral Penn determined his son would be better suited to employ his administrative skills by colonizing the newly acquired tract of land. Penn named the vast area Sylvania – Latin for woods. And the work of distributing land parcels, grants, and sales of tracts of land fell upon him and his selected administrative assistants.

His first task involved drafting a charter described as a Charter of Liberties, used to guide people settling Sylvania. Built into the charter were four principles believed to be the foundation for a new colony. People were to benefit from; (1) A free and fair trial by a jury, (2) Freedom of religion, (3) Freedom from unjust imprisonment, something not experienced in their motherland, and (4) Free elections.

The first county established by Penn was Bucks, named after Buckinghamshire, the previous homeland for some in their number. In the following years, word spread of the new settlement with migration possibilities and merchant trade was at the forefront. People from other nations took an interest in leaving for Penn's new experiment, a new colony bringing promise. Many were enticed upon hearing of the principle of freedom of religion.

A great river, Delaware, divided the settlement of West New Jersey and Sylvania. It was the same word used by European settlers to describe the many tribes of the Lenape, those occupying lands on the shores of the large bay emptying into the Atlantic Ocean.

Penn enticed other English to set sail for the distant port of Philadelphia. In 1681 and 1682, twenty-two sail ships embarked from the docks at Deal and sailed to Philadelphia. The contingent on the vessel traveled to Upland, a small settlement nearby Chester Creek south of Philadelphia. Penn made his last trip to Sylvania in 1699 and returned to England for the remainder of his life. Meanwhile, migrants from Wales, Sweden, and German farmers, religious sects described as Mennonites, Amish, and Lutherans sailed for Philadelphia. Dutch Quakers set sail together with Huguenots from France, all desiring to obtain land and settle in Sylvania.

An Overseer of Philadelphia

King Charles II, years before, was advised that Admiral Sir William

Penn's son named the expansive grant of land New Wales, however, a Welsh friend persuaded Penn to change it, and so he did, to Sylvania. The king, having distaste for William's choice of names, decreed to insert Penn before Sylvania, and by this order, the land would forever be Pennsylvania – Penn's woods. The admiral was embarrassed, thinking his friends would fear his ego so big he had to name this tract after himself.

Patrick Logan studied judiciously, becoming a scholar and receiving a degree from the University of Edinburgh. Initially, he became an Anglican clergyman but later chose to follow the teachings of the Quakers. Patrick left Scotland for Ulster, and his son James was born in 1674 near the Lough Neagh in Lurgan, County Armagh. At age thirteen, James apprenticed with Edward Webb, a linen draper in Dublin. Years later, Patrick moved his family to Bristol, England, and it was at the Friar Meetinghouse School where James Logan and William Penn became tightly knit friends.

Years later, Logan, now an eligible young bachelor, married William's sister, and together they departed for Philadelphia. By the turn of the eighteenth century, upon visiting Pennsylvania for the last time, William appointed his personal friend and brother-in-law, James Logan, to administer responsibilities in Pennsylvania.

James assumed the role of Chief Steward for the settlement. Penn wished him to hold the responsibility for recording and recordkeeping of all land transactions, conveyances of title, and the collection of any proprietary income generated through these business interests. In time, William approved additional appointments resulting in Logan's increase in responsibilities. He assumed the title of Commissioner of Property, followed by Receiver General, and later became a Provincial Council member, followed by Mayor of Philadelphia. By the mid-1700s, Logan, having acquired experience in Philadelphia County law, advanced to filling a position on the Pennsylvania Supreme Court.

22

Passengers Talk

The long tables were unoccupied after mothers finished feeding children their morning meal. Stories designed to teach and educate the little ones were suspended. All went atop the main deck, inhaling fresh air from the salt-laden breeze while keeping a watchful eye for approaching ships. Some of the crew prepared them for the likely event, realizing they were sailing the broad expanse of the North Atlantic.

Margaret Kincade, traveling with her father and mother and a young brother, was the first child to spot a sail ship on the horizon. Within minutes not one, but three vessels approaching *Faithful Steward* dotted the blue sea. As the vessels passed nearby, Mr. Stanfield announced, "Brig *Hannah* is to the port side." Minutes passed, and he barked, "Another ship – port side – *Prince of Wales*." It was common practice for ships sailing east to encounter other ships sailing west on a return voyage to England or Ireland. Many of the ships bore a forename, sometimes one from a prominent person. Children, assisted by Pelig Hudson, identified the brigs *Betty, Alexander, Minerva, George, Jenny, Ann,* and *Rose.*

Simon Elliott I, one of the patriarchs, unfolded a letter and laid it before him. Two of his four sons, James, age twenty-four, and Simon, twenty, accompanied their father at the table. His wife and five daughters remained atop the main deck. A fourth son, also John, penned the letter months ago. John and his brother William were living in Pennsylvania.

James Lee I, accompanied by his son and grandson, all bearing identical names, sat nearby discussing family matters. Male members of the Espey and Stewart families joined the group, all related to the other members at the gathering. Hugh and Mary (Stewart) Espey and three of their five children joined their relatives in the voyage to Philadelphia. Hugh sent two older sons, Hugh Jr. and William to Pennsylvania years before to research the possibilities to buy farmland.

James Lee asked Simon to read the letter aloud. One of the merchant ships delivered his son's correspondence from Philadelphia months before. His fourth son left Ulster in 1784. John was a young man, now twenty-three, full of promise, and a gifted man with a bright future. Given the ages of his brothers, all were vulnerable to being pressed into service in the British Army. They were Presbyterian and impacted by the laws passed by parliament, therefore, joining in service to the king was to be avoided. Their father devised a plan to move his family from County Donegal. He planned to ensure James and Simon escaped King George III's grasp and to relocate his entire family to Pennsylvania. The risk of detainment of his sons in Londonderry was a possibility. His objective, travel to the western frontier of Pennsylvania and settle in this region. He was to follow his father's directive and inform him if their family was to leave Elliottstown.

Mindful that letters transported from the colonies, now states, could be intercepted and read by the king's agents, Simon instructed his son to insert a coded message within his letter. If his son assessed the land to be promising for settlement and they should leave, he must include a signal. And the sign would be in the form of a request, suggesting his father perform a task – an unreasonable task. Simon continued with the reading of his son's letter. In the third paragraph, John commented he could not build proper housing and asked his father to disassemble their dwelling and ship it to Philadelphia. The moment his father understood the sign, he knew it was time – time to liquidate their real estate, sell all assets not transportable by sea, and bring the family to Pennsylvania.

Together with sons John and Samuel Jr., Samuel Hepburn sat alongside Hugh Espey and his son John. Hugh's wife Jean, and their daughter Mary accompanied Janet Hepburn, Samuel's wife of thirty-nine years, and their daughter Mary atop deck with other women and children. It was common to reminisce and speak of family, particularly ancestors while passing the time and reducing boredom at sea. Samuel devised the Hepburn migration plan differently from their counterpart, the Elliotts. Two of Samuel's sons, James, twenty-six years of age, and William, eighteen, set sail from Londonderry twelve years prior in 1773. James and William devised a plan to explore the western boundary of the Susquehanna River, known as the wilds of America. Reports received by the senior Hepburn suggested the tribes of the Six Nations were driven from the territory, however, some remained, occupying the western frontier into the Ohio territory. Twelve years later, the elder Hepburn drew closer to reuniting with his sons, bringing the remainder of their family together.

It wasn't natural for these passengers to leave their country. There is a connection to home and family, the love of all they know, and distrust which can create fear for something new. The tendency would be for them to reside close to their known home. The level of their distress caused them to sell possessions, say goodbye to friends and family, and leave, acting upon that which is unnatural.

Parliament passed additional Penal Laws, imposing them on the people in the Kingdom of Ireland. It was an attempt to coerce a Catholic or Protestant dissenter to embrace doctrine defined by the English State Anglican Church, and adhered to by members of the Irish State. A great struggle occurred within the heart and soul of these people. Together with a lack of opportunity to the point of starvation, the possibility of leaving for another country was confirmed. Dissenters, with no economic opportunity, couldn't advance materially. Progress was always distant, never within reach. An inability to provide materially combined with religious persecution unleashed a potent force.

Matthew Caldwell joined the Lee, Elliott, Espey, and Stewart clans at the long table. A product of a family with a merchant background, he identified with the plight of those in Ulster.

"Not many years prior, there were more than 500 of our kindred who set sail for Nova Scotia," Matthew interrupted. "They stated their reasons for leaving – 300 responded they desired a better livelihood – the remainder complained of excessive rents."

Those around the long table murmured, nodding. There was a significant number on the ship with sufficient means to begin a new life in one of the thirteen states. Others appeared to have limited means to fund the cost of their voyage. One with as little as £10 capital would find it very difficult to survive the first year until their first harvest. The monetary equivalent in Ireland was equal to one year of wages. This element of uncertainty produced the redemptioner, an individual who signed a contract, an indenture to the shipmaster, or his assigns for payment of passage.

Many men congregated around the long tables. Everyone was familiar with stories of the American Revolution that ended two years prior. James McIntire II, possessing a keen interest in events, was excited to hear Hugh Espey's stories, who desperately wanted to reunite with William and Hugh Jr., now living in Pennsylvania. These passengers heard about liberty; now they craved for it, a commodity embraced by and fought for by patriots, and James knew this well. Ten years prior, William and Hugh Espey Jr. joined the Pennsylvania militia and marched and fought for the patriots.

A packet of correspondence with dates from 1778 to 1783 lay on the table before Samuel Hepburn. Each of the letters had been penned by son

William, describing his experiences during the war.

"Mr. Hepburn – please tell us more of the service of William," asked Hugh Espey. A covenanter, Hugh knew by his question he entered a territory taken very seriously by Mr. Hepburn.

"In a letter dated 1778, William wrote he served as a captain in the 4th Battalion of the Northumberland Militia. He was in command of forty-five men in the 5th Company," Samuel explained. "What I found to be very interesting is his connection with Jacob Rush."

James McIntire II was always eager to discuss and learn more about those who participated in the revolution. He added to his list of heroes each time he became involved in a new discussion. "In what manner – describe more about William's connection."

"Jacob Rush was born into a family from New Jersey. In 1776 he volunteered for a short service in the New Jersey Line. Jacob had multiple sisters, and a brother, Benjamin."

James II wanted to know more. "Who is Benjamin Rush?"

"At the beginning of the American Revolution, he was Dr. Benjamin Rush," interjected Samuel.

James II didn't recognize the name, and if others around the long table knew of Dr. Rush, no one spoke up.

Mr. Hepburn continued. "He was a medical doctor, but more importantly, he was a political statesman and very close friend of John Adams from Massachusetts. At the onset of the revolution – and over many years, John, and come to think of it, Abigail Adams, a close advisor to her husband, put a lot of faith and trust in Dr. Rush's opinions."

Mr. Hepburn had command of the younger McIntire's attention at this point. Surprised, but more importantly, desiring to know more, "So your son William served alongside Jacob Rush – brother to Benjamin – advisor to John Adams. Fascinating."

Hugh Espey, often a visionary, turned his head and glanced at James II. "You may be a farmer and linen weaver, but I have a prediction."

"What is your prediction?" asked James' father.

"Once your family gets settled in Pennsylvania – I think James II will be a teacher."

"Perhaps," James II responded. "But I do want to know more about William Hepburn and Jacob Rush."

"You are fortunate, James." Mr. Hepburn opened another letter and unfolded it on the table. "William describes the following. Jacob is four years younger than my son, born in 1757 at Lamington, Somerset County, New Jersey. He began his service enlisting for five months in June 1776 under the command of Captain Nathan Lewis in the New Jersey Line. He marched with his unit crossing the North River at Powles Hook, landing in New York on July 4, 1776. All of the troops estimated between 10,000 to 15,000 took their hats off and gave three loud huzzahs because the Declaration of Independence was read publicly."

"I hope you have more," offered Hugh Espey.

Mr. Hepburn did. These were the type of stories that commanded the interest of the men surrounding the long tables. Momentarily, most of them forgot they were in the hold of a ship on top of the vast Atlantic.

"Jacob was nearly killed when a musket ball grazed the side of his head," announced Mr. Hepburn.

James McIntire II sat at the edge of his seat. "How did this happen?"

"His unit marched to Long Island and then reversed, ending up at Flatbush where they battled the British. Blood was running down the side of his body to his legs. He was detained about two hours."

"One of the lucky ones," James muttered.

Mr. Hepburn folded the letter. "Yes, the ball made two holes in his hat – one entering, one leaving, but not before it tore alongside his skull and ripped the flesh to the bone."

"Is there more?"

Mr. Hepburn retrieved another letter. "Jacob returned home for a time and enlisted for more service. This time – the fall of 1778, they captured and imprisoned him for two and one-half months at Bottle Hill (New Jersey). He was searched and stripped of his commission and personal papers. Everything was burned." He studied more of the letter. "Jacob escapes – returns to his home for two weeks, and joins up with another militia at Bound-brook, where he meets General Washington."

James II, caught by surprise, "He meets General Washington?"

"Yes, he did – the general scolded him for returning to service and exposing himself, mentioning if the British caught him again, they would kill him."

∞

Each passenger carried a bill of exchange issued by the merchant responsible for arranging the terms of passage with shipowners. John

Maxwell Nesbitt of Conyngham, Nesbitt & Company, a Philadelphia merchant firm, partnered with Abraham and Connolly McCausland to secure the passengers for this voyage.

James II, flanked by his father, initiated the conversation. "Who can tell us more about the merchant Nesbitt?"

His father knew a portion of the history; however, he deferred to Samuel Hepburn. "Nesbitt understands our plight," he began. "He is forty-five, born in 1730 at Loughbrickland, County Down, and he is the son of Jonathan Nesbitt. His mother is a sister to Alexander Lang, a shipping merchant from Philadelphia. They are all tied together in business."

James II studied his face. "Did the rest of his family remain in Ireland?"

"The year was 1747. Master Faulkner commanded a ship from Belfast, and their uncle, Alexander Lang, paid for the entire passage. Two of John Nesbitt's brothers, Jonathan and Alexander, left for Philadelphia, and two additional brothers, James and George, owned land adjoining John in Philadelphia. His sisters Frances, Sarah, Ester, and Elizabeth Ann left Ireland for Pennsylvania."

"What happened to David Conyngham?" inquired James II.

Samuel joined in the conversation. "David Conyngham (from Donegal) was a partner with Gardner and John Nesbitt. He was to apprentice with their firm in the shipping trade. Circumstances changed."

"What changed?" asked Hugh Espey.

"Alexander Lang's health changed, and John Nesbitt stayed with Conyngham and Gardner," Samuel explained. "But in time – nine years later – John Nesbitt formed a partnership with Redmond Conyngham of Letterkenny in County Donegal, David's son."

Many Ulster merchants desired to expand their linen business overseas using trans-Atlantic trade. It was common for a family member or friend to partner with them, and one of them moved to Philadelphia. The vessel that carried linen to the city was loaded with flaxseed and flour and returned to Ulster. As profits grew, some merchants invested money in shipbuilding. After Redmond partnered with John Nesbitt, William Hamilton of Londonderry joined them, and they oversaw the building of their brigs, the *Hamilton Galley* and *Prince of William*, 100 tons each, nearby the port of Philadelphia. Later these merchants were joined by Londonderry merchants Robert Alexander and John Knox, who contracted to build the *Culloden*.

Hugh Espey, with sons John and James, grew increasingly interested in business and making money. And patriarch Simon Elliott I, with gold guineas stowed in bags in a trunk, joined in.

"John Nesbitt made a lot of money, but he also increased in prominence as he became involved in managing the affairs of Philadelphia," offered Samuel Hepburn. "Years ago, Nesbitt gave a welcome address to John Penn, then Governor of Pennsylvania and William's son."

Conyngham and Nesbitt established their firm as one of the most influential in Philadelphia. Upon the dawn of the revolution, John Nesbitt was appointed a member of the Committee of Correspondence in 1774. It was the committee's responsibility to inform each of the thirteen colonies when a new development occurred with trade and taxes imposed by the king. When war broke out, Nesbitt was appointed Paymaster of the Pennsylvania State Navy, and in time he assumed the position of Treasurer of the Council of Safety.

"What about the printer from Strabane?" Simon Elliott II called out.

One of the men appeared puzzled.

"My son's referring to John Dunlap – he's the printer – came from Meetinghouse Street, Strabane," Simon inferred.

Not all of the male passengers were connected to the current events shaping the future of the new America, but some were. Samuel Hepburn, relying on his son's letters, was one of them.

"Strabane is the home of Gray's Printery," he mentioned. "And the town has grown into a very active publishing center. Young Dunlap left his home at age ten for Philadelphia."

James Lee III mentioned, "A very young age to leave home for a foreign land."

Samuel thought some more. "His uncle, William Dunlap, married a distant relation to Benjamin Franklin. The two paid for his passage and arranged for an apprenticeship for the young Dunlap. He was working for his uncle, however, his uncle enrolled in divinity school and the boy took another apprenticeship."

"There's a lot more to the story," Simon II inferred.

James McIntire II commented, "Tell us about it."

Samuel peered around the table. Everyone was engaged. They loved to hear stories – especially when they involved the Irish who left Ulster for British America. And Samuel Hepburn knew the rest of the story.

"By the time young Dunlap reached twenty, he was in full control of the printing business. That was in 1766, and after five years passed, Dunlap established a newspaper, the Pennsylvania Packet."

"It all ties together," said James II, "Some of the ships bring copies of the Packet when they return from Philadelphia."

James was right. People would wait with anticipation for the arrival of news when a ship from Philadelphia docked at the quay. The captain delivered a copy of the paper to the Journal, and they reprinted relevant articles if they thought them newsworthy. A recent copy of the Journal was displayed at the diamond in some of the marketplaces.

"Does the story stop there?" asked James II.

"No, it doesn't," Samuel said. "There is a lot more to it. Four years later, John Dunlap enlisted in the Continental Army. As the story goes, John assisted General Washington at Philadelphia."

James II listened to every word of Samuel Hepburn's narrative. "What else can you tell us of his military history?"

Samuel pulled gently at his gray beard, thinking. "His initial appointment was a *cornet*, however, in time he became a lieutenant. One of my sons mentioned in a letter that Dunlap founded the 1st Troop of Philadelphia City Cavalry."

"Was he injured in battle?" Hugh Espey wanted to know.

"I don't recall, Dunlap served in an arena of high risk since he was with General Washington at the Battles of Princeton and Trenton. He was promoted to captain toward the end of his service."

Everyone could tell Samuel was intent on providing all of the details of the printer from Strabane. He continued, "He had to be fearless, reliable, and trustworthy. He and the 1st Troop Philadelphia City Cavalry acted as General Washington's bodyguards."

James II, along with the Elliott and Espey sons, focused on the details of what was said. Samuel sipped from his mug filled with Madeira wine. "And there is more to the life of our printer turned militiaman. The Commonwealth of Pennsylvania appointed John as their printer. In time the Continental Congress followed," Samuel added. "John Dunlap was given the task to print two hundred broadsides (large one-sided copies) of Thomas Jefferson's Declaration of Independence by John Hancock."

Hugh Espey wanted to know. "What happened following the printing of the Declaration?"

Samuel thought some more. "Another Virginian entered the picture at that point."

"And who was that?" inquired James II.

"His name was Richard Henry Lee – but the patriots called him Lighthorse Lee. He was the one selected to read the Declaration of Independence to the Continental Congress. And after that, John Dunlap's situation grew worse."

"In what way?" inquired James II.

"The year was 1777, and the British Army took control of Philadelphia. That event forced Dunlap to move his newspaper business to Lancaster in Pennsylvania." Samuel paused, "I should add, many sacrificed financially by donating from their wealth for the war effort. A couple of years later, Dunlap contributed the sum of £4,000 to the army."

As the afternoon advanced, women atop deck were waiting for the men to conclude their discussions. Below deck at the long tables, there was an interesting discussion – all occurring as the crew atop deck changed the braces, adjusted the sails, and tacked in a direction toward coastal North America. Men loved the stories – those about people with roots in Ulster – people that left Ireland leaving everything behind to cross the Atlantic to join the patriots.

23

Women Making the Passage

By noon the air warmed by the sun, rose, causing dense cooler air to drop from above and sweep over the ship's deck. The topgallants, square-rigged sails set at the top of the fore and mainmasts, billowed. Mr. Kelley, at the helm, inhaled the fresh sea-breeze, his ship slicing through the sea with the westerlies blowing across the Atlantic. Weather conditions remained fair and the seas relatively calm for the past two weeks. Captain McCausland, below deck in his captain's quarters, wrote in the ship's log.

Thursday, August 11, 1785
Seas calm, estimate halfway to Newfoundland, encountered two ships following, passed one sailing to the Baltic.

The men moved to the main deck together with the children. Enjoyable sights eased boredom and discomfort from crowded conditions while watching the horizon for passing ships. Crewmembers assisted with identifying each vessel, by pointing out sizes and shapes of the hull, placement of masts, and changes in the rigging.

Women took their turn congregating around the long tables, partaking in food and drink, and discussing what their lives would be like, and how they would change after the ship docked at Stampers Wharf. About one-third of the passengers on any given voyage to North America was comprised of women.

Mr. Quigley, atop in the crow's nest on the mainmast, yelled loudly – "A whale breaches!" Pointing to the bowsprit and starboard side, he yelled again: "Look, a whale breaches!" Mr. Quigley couldn't hide the jubilation and opportunity to appear important to those below. In his former occupation as a whaler and harpoons-man, he joined other Gloucestermen off the coast of Massachusetts on many harvesting trips. Perhaps it was an act of providence that he was fifty feet above the deck. If he were assigned deck duty, he would have ceased working to tell everyone of his knowledge of whaling. The beginning of his story would be romantic and filled with adventure, describing the hunt of the grey whale. By the time he finished his depiction of reigning in the bowline of the whaleboat, piercing the mammal's flesh with additional harpoons, blood spewing everywhere, and the inevitable demise of a gigantic creature, the women would be green in the gills, rushing to get their heads over the gunwales.

Passengers pushed toward the starboard side, leaning against the gunwale to get a glimpse of the attraction. Mr. Stanfield watched as people pushed and rushed, creating disorder in the process. As the ship drew closer to the pod of North Atlantic Grey Whales, Mr. Stanfield ordered the helmsman to turn the wheel two points starboard, so those on deck had an improved view. The pod circled and was no more than one hundred yards from the ship. The temporary excitement of experiencing whales gave the children a memory to talk about for a long time to come.

∞

News in the Belfast Newsletter and Londonderry Journal advertised the busy, bustling places of Philadelphia, New York, and Charlestown. The Commonwealth of Pennsylvania contained more land than the entirety of Ireland. And if one were to extend the boundaries beyond the thirteen states, there was a vast wilderness, a land occupied by scores of tribal societies, one under exploration by frontiersmen.

Many women were encouraged to seek a new home in America. Some acted on letters of influence received from family and friends who migrated before. They spoke of property, land suitable for farming in Pennsylvania, New Jersey, Delaware, and Maryland. Settlers endured laborious work to clear and cultivate the land, but it would be worth it. Obtain your funds for passage and come.

There were warnings in correspondence too. The political rights and freedom sought by many were not equal, and some laws didn't apply to women. Regardless, remaining in Ulster was more challenging. Women were not permitted to vote in the United States, and they couldn't by law take title to land. They were dependent upon their husband in this instance, and if unmarried, their father or if they had none, a brother. Since they were ineligible to inherit land from their father, it was bequeathed to a son instead.

Crossing the Atlantic took a long time, and it became physically and emotionally unpleasant for many women. They left rural farmland, endured lengthy journeys, traveled on foot or horse and cart to busy ports, and each stage involved delays and sometimes danger.

Pelig Hudson was in charge of the stores for everyone. Hugh Espey was responsible for meeting with Mr. Hudson to distribute food supplies for each group. His primary concern included the equitable distribution with appropriate portions, considering the length of the voyage.

There were occasions when captains delayed leaving port to secure additional passengers. Such was the case with Captain McCausland's ship. This tactic could be detrimental to everyone if the steward did not plan for enough stores given the number of passengers. A voyage lasting longer than anticipated meant the captain risked starving his passengers until they arrived at the port.

Rumors were common. Many of them described captains acting inappropriately, reducing the daily allowance of food per passenger, limiting each to one and one-half biscuits and three small potatoes, two ounces of salt beef, and six spoons of pea soup. A nasty captain could order loud complainers bound in irons or lashed to the shrouds and flogged by the bosun. Fortunately, Connolly McCausland was deemed a better captain. Adequate food and reasonable living space were the common complaints, no matter the ship boarded for passage.

Too many passengers could be crowded into the ship's hold. Surprisingly, the mortality of passengers wasn't higher. Before committing for passage, Hugh Espey discovered it was typical for the tally of passengers to be close to a number equal to the ship's tonnage. Using this comparison, Hugh anticipated the passenger count should be near 350, but whatever was in those barrels in the hold took up much space. Therefore, the passenger count didn't exceed 250. Passengers with financial means secured cabin accommodations, and single berths were usually rare. Before this ship's departure, the Belfast Newsletter noted twelve people occupied seven cabins.

∞

James placed his hand upon Isabella's shoulder, offering comfort as she sat at the long table in tears. Uncertainty prevailed – how would their extended family of relations, forty-eight in number, survive settling in a new and wild land. The longevity of the voyage coupled with her advanced years caused anxiety and emotional fatigue.

"Everything will be as we planned, Isabella."

Gustavus Colhoun stood nearby. "Mrs. Lee, may I paint you a picture – one that may help to relieve your distress?"

Isabella lifted her head to look into his face. "You may, Mr. Colhoun."

"Close your eyes – think of your first glimpse of America – what will it look like?"

"Have you been there?" she asked.

"Yes – I have. Close your eyes – breathe slowly – picture a scene – you are standing atop the deck. The sun is shining in your face, the ocean air is cool, fresh, and you breathe in the sweet smell of the salt air as it fills your lungs. Captain McCausland orders his helmsman – two points to starboard as he prepares to guide *Faithful Steward* into the mouth of the Delaware Bay. Can you visualize this?"

"Yes, I can."

"Look to the port side of the ship. In the distance, you can see the shoreline of Cape Henlopen. Beyond the shoreline in the distance is the settlement at Lewestown. Turn your head to the opposite side, and you see the coast of New Jersey. Time passes, our ship is sailing into the Delaware River and approaches New Castle, where the ship docks to let passengers disembark. The sandy banks along the coast narrow, drawing closer to the ship. Your senses tell you the voyage is nearing an end and the anticipation of arriving in Philadelphia brings excitement." Isabella drew slow deep breaths. "More time passes – ships and boats of varying sizes are all around you. We sail to Stamper's Wharf. You hear a loud boom from a cannon. Our ship rounds a bend in the river, the arrival of *Faithful Steward* has been announced. Buildings appear in the distance – you're approaching the wharves. Open your eyes."

Isabella opened her eyes. "What will the city look like, Mr. Colhoun?"

"The docks accommodate many merchants and their wharves line the banks of the Pennsylvania side of the river. Your family will leave the ship at the center of the city near Vine Street."

Other passengers, all making the crossing for the first time, ceased talking and listened to Gustavus describe their anticipated arrival.

"William Penn designed the streets in a grid pattern. The pattern is unlike any you have experienced in Ulster. Those owning lots subdivided them into smaller parcels, and they created alleyways to the rear of their homes. You will find the red-bricked homes built in a row tightly packed together."

"And how many people live in the city of Philadelphia?" inquired James McIntire II.

Gustavus knew the facts, and he was anxious to deliver their cargo to Stephen Girard. "About twenty-five thousand – the city is near seven times larger than Londonderry and three times larger than Belfast."

∞

Threats were standard onboard a ship. Danger, sometimes from an unruly crew, one that would intimidate and steal from a passenger occurred. An unprincipled shipmaster would purposely delay the departure of his ship. The delay caused some passengers to use funds intended for settlement in the colonies to cover food and housing costs. On occasion, the margin was so thin some people were forced to enter into indentured servitude. The alternative was to go home without money. Poor treatment from a captain couldn't be mitigated unless they found safety under a good captain.

Hardship came from boredom and discomfort while at sea. A worse scenario was the risk of terror, even death. Storms brought danger; some were violent, causing waves to sink a ship. Men inflicted other hardships. The meanness of a master was one, the potential for encountering a privateer was another, and there was the risk of running short of food or water. Overcrowding could bring disease and sickness, and mental despair was common.

The owner of the *Britannia* carefully listed in his advertisement – provisions per week – six pounds of good beef, six pounds of oatmeal, one pound butter or a pint of molasses, and fourteen quarts of water. The shipowner of *Nancy*, on a run from Belfast to Charlestown, promised passengers seven pounds of beef, seven pounds of bread, one pound of butter, and fourteen quarts of water every week. One-half of the passengers were between the ages of two to twelve and received half of the allotment. Rum sold on board the ship for three shillings, nine and one-half six-pence per gallon.

People knew the average passage time from Londonderry to Philadelphia could run eight to ten weeks. Captains completed some crossings in six to eight weeks with an average near seven. And the season of the year could bring weather that changed the length of the crossing.

Regulations became necessary, limiting the number of passengers and setting requirements for food allotment. Well-intended laws were followed by shipmasters wanting higher fees for passage. And only those of financial means chose cabin accommodations on a passenger ship. The cost increased to fifteen guineas per person. And the cost was reduced to ten guineas for a berth in steerage and eight guineas for those between decks. Women traveling single were accustomed to the wages of a launderer or kitchen assistant, working for one year to earn five to six guineas.

Everyone enjoyed letters from former passengers filled with stories of life in America. Many challenges weren't outlined for the reader to discern. Post-revolutionary Philadelphia meant more people, and the city became dirty, unsanitary, and prone to the spread of disease.

Sometimes the fabric of social connection was the determinant as to whether a woman could prosper. When cash was low, they ran up debt with a brother, if they had one, and if not, would turn to a male acquaintance. The last option was to seek charity, and if desperate, succumb to the sin of prostitution.

Women leaving Ulster in the 1700s were used to the social differences in the provinces of Ireland. People were accustomed to hard work, and they endured and were pioneering in spirit. Their lives were dependent upon fluctuating textile markets. For some women, employment in this industry became their first paying job outside of the home.

That portion of society designated as Ulster-Presbyterian lacked a ruling class with a power base. One path to becoming elite occurred when their father became a successful merchant. Another option was to meet and marry a flaxseed merchant. The alternative was to struggle to survive, obtaining work as a launderer, possibly a kitchen maid, or working on a farm. The Londonderry Journal and the Belfast Newsletter reported occasional articles listing names forced to resort to stealing.

∞

Sarah Elliott, the wife of Simon, took advantage of the discussions at the long table, facilitating a conversation of hope for their new lives. Women of this passage had their own set of priorities, much like the men. Stories of post-revolutionary women were as popular to the women as the stories of the patriots were to the men.

One of the storytellers, Isabella Lee, remembered, "I learned that Elizabeth Griscom was twenty-three at the onset of the Revolutionary War. And she was raised in a large family – the eighth of seventeen children, only nine survived."

Rebecca McIntire was the first to gasp at the thought of raising seventeen children. She had ten of her own with her on the ship.

"Who is she?"

"You will be surprised, Rebecca. Unlike any other on this ship, she was raised in a Quaker family and attended a Quaker school. Her father apprenticed her to an upholsterer."

"She was English," interrupted Mrs. Elliott.

Isabella knew the story. "Miss Griscom's great grandfather left England in 1680, and they joined Christ Church after settling in Philadelphia. She was industrious – an experienced seamstress and dressmaker as well. And during the war, she sewed thousands and thousands of musket cartridges – ammunition for those Pennsylvania long rifles the men speak of."

Janet Hepburn inquired, "She had help, didn't she?"

And this was the goal, passing time, eliminating boredom. Isabella was enjoying the moment, raising everyone's curiosity.

"Yes, she did. Hannah Griffitts, a friend of hers, also a Quaker, helped."

Women, listening to their story were used to long hours and plenty of hard work, however, the thought of sewing ammunition was foreign to them.

There was more to the story. "Elizabeth sewed the flag for the Pennsylvania Navy. And in time she married – those that know of her good deeds in Philadelphia address her as Betsy Ross."

There were other women to speak of, those influencing Philadelphia society during the period of the revolution. Women loved to hear more stories, including the examples of Martha Jefferson, wife to Thomas, Dolly Payne Todd, who married James Madison, and Mrs. Julia Rush, wife of Dr. Benjamin Rush, a physician, social reformer, and confidant to John Adams. Dr. Rush was a respected humanitarian and Surgeon-General of the Continental Army.

Those on board were ill-prepared to grasp the reality of the society they would encounter in Philadelphia. An elite class of craftsmen and artisans, both men and women, flourished. Family names, including the Willings, Powells, Logans, and Shippens, were bandied in local conversation. And stories surrounding the Shippen family always drew an interested crowd. Edward Shippen, favoring loyalty to the king, permitted his daughter, Margaret (Peggy), to marry Benedict Arnold. She was his second wife and ultimately found to be a spy for the British Army.

Thomas Willing formed a partnership with Robert Morris Jr. –

Willing & Morris Company, becoming wealthy merchants, owning ships, and trading in Europe and the West Indies. Robert's grandfather, Andrew Morris, was a mariner in England. Robert's father, a tradesman, originally settled in Maryland with his son. As for Robert Jr., thirty-eight years of age in 1785, he married Mary White, daughter of Thomas White of Maryland. Mary's brother, William White, became the 1st Bishop of the Protestant Episcopal Church in Philadelphia. During the war, William was a member of the Continental Congress. After the war, the Church of England in America was dissolved. In British America, the Church of England was state-sponsored. In the United States, there would be no state-sponsored exercise of religion. A church constituency sailed to England to modify the church governance and reorganize under the Episcopal banner.

∞

In Philadelphia, the assortment of food dishes was always a prized topic for discourse. Those with reasonable financial means chose roast beef or leg of mutton. Ham and cabbage were also prevalent, as were fowl of various sorts. For the men, supper was served with a mug of ale or Madeira provided by merchants Searle or Henry Hill. Another option was a glass of Jamaican Rum with hot water, a beverage of choice.

Affluent colonists purchased damask-covered couches, and their furniture, usually of a plain design, was built from oak or mahogany. Carpeting, traditionally placed in the center of the floor, adorned some of the colonial homes. Furniture, arranged in a pattern surrounded the carpet. If curtains were attached to the windows of the home, it was a sign of wealth. And with the presence of curtains, one would find glasses placed on the mantles and candelabra in the parlor.

Merchants' storefronts and offices lined Water Street near the wharves in Philadelphia. The importation of a variety of goods continued to grow due to strong demand. Most of the merchant homes contained cups and saucers manufactured in England. Tankards were fashioned from silver, as were bowls and waiters. Dishware consisted of pewter plates and tableware if one could afford them, otherwise; bowls and plates fashioned of tin or wood would do. Almost everyone had a punch bowl, even in the home of the Quaker. Dipped candles were costly, therefore illuminating a home once darkness set in was done sparingly. If one had the money, candles were placed in brass candleholders. Beds were constructed of mahogany, if affordable, and

Robert Hargraves introduced the art of interior decorating with wallpaper in 1745.

Residents from Philadelphia south to Wilmington enjoyed amusements. Some of the men engaged in bullbaiting and bearbaiting, while others attended boxing matches. And men of the highest respectability could be found attending cockfighting. Billiards increased in popularity; however, no gambling could be involved. Gambling would be frowned on. Another popular participatory sport was bowls or ten-pins, and there were frequent games of quoit-throwing and shuffleboard.

Men and women enjoyed cultural events and entertainment. Concerts were popular, and everyone desired fireworks on special occasions. Dancing and traveling shows became popular. Dancing masters frequented Wilmington north to Philadelphia, and significant attention was paid to music, especially if it was sacred. Women would prepare invitations to parties or an upcoming ball by writing the invite on the back of a playing card.

The celebration of holidays in the colonies was limited. Philadelphians hadn't learned to celebrate Christmas; however, it took on a new role in Wilmington. People formed parties known as mummers, and they dressed in a variety of disguises. Traveling door to door and house to house, they recited poetry that rhymed, explaining who they disguised themselves to be.

Further north in Philadelphia, celebrating Christmas was defined by one's religious background. Quakers and Presbyterians didn't celebrate holidays. German immigrants dotted the farmlands surrounding the counties nearby Philadelphia. Some adhered to the Reformed faith, being Lutherans, while others were Catholics and still others Anabaptists. Those from German religious societies observed Christmas as a day for family reunions and social gatherings with religious festivities. And they did this by decorating a Christmas tree with trinkets, angelic figures, and lighted candles.

∞

The security of their family was the foremost thought of every woman on board the ship. And with that came the anxiety and reality of life in a new land. Isabella Lee knew more of their plight through informed conversations with her husband.

"We have some history to draw from," she remarked to Sarah Elliott and other relatives and those interested parties nearby. "James speaks of the

Peace Treaty of Paris signed in 1783 between England and the colonists. The treaty represented a document, an agreement between England and the colonists formally ending the Revolutionary War."

Taking title to a deed of land and owning and operating a small farm was a cherished dream for many on the ship. Benjamin Franklin, Thomas Jefferson, and John Adams negotiated the peace treaty, creating a society absent of restrictions of anyone associated with a religious denomination. Within the content of the treaty was a declaration. All land south of Canada, north of Spanish Florida, and east of the Mississippi River were now considered the United States. Within these boundaries, men, women, and their children were free to worship without fear of legal consequences.

Conversation thrived around the long tables. Most felt their passage was timely, and everyone enjoyed the calm sea. Excitement was building to set foot in New Castle or Philadelphia, depending upon their choice of destination. Women were grateful for the time of year of the passage. Since it had to be endured, it was best to make the voyage toward the end of spring and no later than October, before winter. Weather conditions were more favorable. They were warned by Mr. Stanfield, everything movable would move in the event of a storm, and they should hunker down in their cabin or berth in steerage. The ship would heave in unpredictable ways with everyone at the mercy of Neptune.

There were passengers from an entire family, and there were others, such as the Elliotts, who were meeting family members, usually sons, who emigrated before. Aside from families making the voyage, there was a remnant of women who followed their husband's lead, and said goodbye to everything they knew, thinking, hoping, and praying that the news reports from overseas would support their decision. A month at sea, for some, the memory of leaving Londonderry, watching family and friends walking along the shore, left a swell of sadness that could not be erased. The occupation of time spent below deck, talking, dancing, or singing, provided a brief respite from a sickening feeling, one that occupied their mind when their thoughts of home returned.

24

The Long Tables

Men were familiar with stories of the American Revolution that ended two years prior, September 3, 1783. And the covenanters had a vested interest in the outcome. Some of them had family, even sons who left Ireland years before and joined the militias, particularly in Pennsylvania. James and John, sons of Hugh Espey, were examples, together with others who joined the patriots. James McIntire II, one with a keen interest in events, was interested in the stories told by Hugh, who desperately wanted to reunite with his sons in Philadelphia. Passengers craved the concept of liberty, the right to have freedom of choice, embraced by and fought for by the patriots, and James understood this feeling.

"Does anyone know what happened to the troops from Philadelphia once they engaged in battle?" inquired Doctor McDougal, the physician from Londonderry.

James Lee I was the first to answer. "The fighting was hard in 1775 – '76. And the militias from Pennsylvania were involved in many engagements. Colonel Anthony Wayne, from Philadelphia, ordered his regiment to Canada, a long distance from home, and Colonel Edward Hand commanded a regiment in New York. Remember we spoke of John Shee – he became a colonel in charge of a regiment."

"Someone mentioned the merchant, James Mease, in one of our gatherings around the table," added John Elliott. "He saw action on the seas with Commodore John Barry."

"The light horse troops formed in Philadelphia operated under the direct command of General Washington," another voice announced.

"The troops from the light horse will one day become famous," Matthew Caldwell replied. "On December 25th, Christmas of 1776 – they crossed the Delaware River at McConkey's Ferry, ten miles above Trenton. The passage was dangerous due to bad weather, darkness, floating ice, and cold. Men were forced to take to the water before landing, riding their horses between the breaks in the ice."

James Lee joined in once again. "It was the beginning of the planned attack on the British and Hessian soldiers at Trenton."

"How many generals were Irish?" asked James McIntire II.

"Many – there were many," John Elliott responded.

The Continental Army – Military Generals

George Washington – Born 1732, Popes Creek, Virginia

Anthony Wayne – Born 1745, Easttown Township, Pennsylvania

Edward Hand – Born 1744, Clyduff, Ireland

Richard Butler – Born 1743, Dublin, Ireland

William Thompson – Born 1736, Ireland

Henry Knox – Born 1750, Boston, Massachusetts

Stephen Moylan – Born 1737, Cork, Ireland

William Irvine – Born 1741, Enniskillen, Ireland

John Cadwalader – Born 1742, Trenton, New Jersey

Walter Stewart – Born 1756, Ireland

John Shee – Lancaster, Pennsylvania

Thomas Proctor – Born 1739, County Longford, Ireland

John Cochran, Surgeon General – Born 1730, Sadsbury, Pennsylvania

John Peter Muhlenberg – Born 1746, Trappe, Pennsylvania

Samuel Meredith – Born 1741, Philadelphia, Pennsylvania

Callender Irvine – Carlisle, Pennsylvania

The Continental Navy – Officers

Admiral George C. Read – Ireland

Commodore John Barry – County Wexford, Ireland

Commodore Thomas Read – New Castle, Delaware

Commodore Charles Stewart

Captain Henry Geddes – Ireland

Captain John Green

Captain Paul Cox – Ireland

Captain Nathan Boys

Captain John Mitchell

Captain James Montgomery – Ireland

Purser Matthew Mease – Strabane, Ireland

25

The Irish Club

Merchants in Philadelphia, decades prior, set up intricate networks of business relationships. Fathers and sons, cousins, other related family members, including their friends who joined in the process of forming merchant partnerships. William and Richard Caldwell, and Arthur Vance became successful flaxseed merchants and accommodated passengers as well. Meanwhile, William, operating out of Londonderry, joined with his cousin Andrew, setting up a merchant business located in Philadelphia.

Samuel Carsan, of Presbyterian roots, was local to Strabane in County Tyrone circa the 1760s. He relocated to Philadelphia where he prospered in the flaxseed trade and passenger business for nearly thirty years. His Londonderry merchant connections were numerous. In 1763 and 1764 Samuel's cousin, William Mitchell, son of James Mitchell, a mariner and a nephew of Samuel, and Thomas Barclay, also from Strabane and Philadelphia started a new firm, Carsan Barclay and Mitchell.

The Mease family of Strabane was composed of merchants and ministers. Their patriarch, John Mease, departed Strabane in 1736, seeking to trade in flaxseed in Philadelphia. A Presbyterian, John served as an elder in the First Presbyterian Church established in Philadelphia. John tutored his nephews in the flaxseed trade and brought James, John, and Matthew Mease to Philadelphia. After John died, in 1768, the three nephews continued with the business their uncle built.

John Burns Tavern – Philadelphia 1771

A band of merchants of Irish ancestry met informally at the tavern located nearby the docks at the Delaware River. Many with contacts to the merchant firm, Conyngham and Nesbitt, assembled to discuss business, facilitating immigration from their homeland and assisting those with needs now residing in the colonies. After dispensing with business matters, they gathered around the tables engaging in games of backgammon and whist. A card game, they played whist with fifty-two cards in the deck, and each of four players dealt thirteen cards to a hand. A game with English roots, whist stood for quiet, silent, and attentive. Upon concluding the games, supper followed, and the evening closed with a drink enjoyed by all.

By late afternoon on Sunday, March 17, those in attendance gathered to discuss ideas offered by regular attendees.

"Gentlemen – we have met weekly for the past few months, and – I've been thinking – we should add to our cause," announced John Maxwell Nesbitt, an influential person.

Members of the group pulled their oak chairs toward the long table – each with an ear bent toward the speaker.

Benjamin Fuller was one of them. "What are you thinking, John – what do you have on your mind?"

"Formalize our Irish brotherhood – establish regularly scheduled meetings – build attendance – set new goals," John echoed. "I think that should be our next step. What do the rest of you think – suggestions, ideas?"

James Mease, a nephew to the merchant John Mease, was anxious to get started. "Set a day of the week and meet once per week."

"Good idea," added William West, one of the regulars.

"You're speaking of a club, John – organize formally, I'd say," Benjamin replied.

"Yes – meet weekly, prepare an itemized agenda, and build a sense of purpose based upon our beliefs. Identify that which we share in common – perpetuity should be the focus," John Nesbitt responded.

Stephen Moylan, a merchant with Irish roots, joined the cause. "What about money? Who among us thinks membership and dues should be part of John's proposal?"

Everyone nodded in the affirmative, and those possessing canes stamped them on the wooden floor, signifying unity. In the following months, a subscription was raised based on a demonstrated need. A flow of recurring donations provided funds when needs arose.

"This will require elected officials – nominations must be secured," Stephen Moylan explained.

John Nesbitt took to the floor. "Agreed – we have to sharpen our focus and develop a plan to perpetuate the club. There is time to nominate and vote on officers at an upcoming meeting."

James Mease, thinking about names for the club, spoke up – "The Irish Club." All eyes turned toward the energetic member of the Mease & Caldwell merchant firm. "We could adopt the name, The Irish Club."

The men pondered in quiet solitude and reflection. Each of them had something in common. They were either born in Ireland, or one or both of their parents were Irish, and now natives of Philadelphia.

"Gentlemen – it's Saint Patrick's Day," announced John Nixon. "In a short time, we have demonstrated loyalty – and we have engaged in acts of helpfulness. Our club should be remembered for years to come – we should call our club, The Friendly Sons of Saint Patrick."

And those in attendance stamped their canes and voted to provide the breath of life, giving birth to a club. It would be a club for the Irish – Presbyterians, Episcopalians, and Catholics. Before they celebrated their first anniversary officers were elected with each fulfilling a role with duties. Stephen Moylan was elected President, John Maxwell Nesbitt, Vice-President, and William Mitchell, Treasurer and Secretary. By March of 1772, club membership increased to twenty-four, adding honorary members as well. Some of their number revisited the name of their club and determined to make changes that were voted upon.

Members of the society were successful merchants, dealing with the importation and exportation of goods to and from Europe and the West Indies. The merchandising of these goods included teas, silks, wines, and linens from East India and the West Indies.

Pennsylvania was growing and Philadelphia's bustling port became the largest most important city on the eastern seaboard. A new society, the Irish Club, was unknowingly serving as a platform, leading to a new future. A higher power would orchestrate future events, guiding their lives while assisting in formulating decisions and shaping the outcome of future events that would forever impact their brethren in the colonies.

THE SOCIETY OF THE FRIENDLY SONS OF ST. PATRICK FOR THE RELIEF OF IRISH EMIGRANTS
March 17, 1772

REGULAR MEMBERS

Stephen Moylan	merchant
Colonel Turbitt Francis	officer - French & Indian War 1754-63
John Maxwell Nesbitt**	flaxseed – passenger merchant
Benjamin Fuller	shipbroker
William Mitchell *	flaxseed merchant
George Fullerton***	flaxseed merchant – indentured servants

Thomas Barclay**	flaxseed merchant
Ulysses Lynch	merchant
John Boyle	linen merchant
George Meade	merchant
Andrew Caldwell***	flaxseed – passenger merchant
James Mease**	flaxseed merchant
Samuel Caldwell***	flaxseed – passenger merchant
John Mitchell *	merchant
George Campbell	attorney
Randle Mitchell**	flaxseed merchant
George Davis	private gentleman
John Nixon	merchant
Thomas Fitzsimmons	merchant
John Shee	merchant
Tench Francis	merchant
William West	merchant

*The Mitchells were brothers, as were the Caldwells
**Merchant firms represented – Conyngham & Nesbitt, Carsan Barclay, & Mitchell, Mease & Caldwell
***Partner Boyd & Fullerton

HONORARY MEMBERS

Henry Hill	wine merchant – Hill's Madeira
Robert Morris	merchant - financier
James Searle	wine merchant – Searle's Madeira

∞

Seated at the head of the long table, Simon Elliott poured a glass of Madeira. "General Washington was extended an invitation to join the roll of the Society of the Friendly Sons of St. Patrick."

Rebecca McIntire, sister to James II listened to his comment, always enamored by any stories told of the heroics of the general. "How did that occur? He wasn't Irish."

James Lee II glanced at his father because he retold the story to the Lee family. The patriarch, excited, drew in another breath, preparing to tell the story again.

"It was later in the year of 1781 at a meeting of the society. One of their members invited General Washington to dinner, and they planned to add his name to the roll. The general, due to another commitment, was unavailable to attend the dinner. Members of the society adopted a rule limiting the number of Honorary Members, those who were not of Irish birth or ancestry. As the story unfolds, the list of Honorary Members was full. Someone, unhesitatingly made a motion to adopt the general as a member of the society, and so, unanimously they did. A member attending the meeting later recalled, the group made him as much of an Irishman as was in their power."

The patriarch paused momentarily and motioned to the group surrounding the long table. "There is more to the story. The society officers determined they would present him with a medal to be worn on occasion. James Mease offered his medal for the cause, and it was presented to the general and gladly accepted."

Those surrounding the long tables listened intently, smiled, and applauded. Rebecca glanced at her brother, relishing the moment.

26

The Society and the Revolution

All members were required per the rules to pay three guineas, the cost for producing a gold medal to be stamped and worn to each meeting. The design stamped on the medal was distinct. And the description displayed their identity, purpose, and their mission. James Mease secured a set of dyes used for striking the medals. Repayment for the cost of the dyes was £50 and each member was assessed 50 shillings as reimbursement for the cost.

The right side of the medal displayed an insignia, Hibernia, the Latin word for the island of Ireland, and the left side for America, with Liberty occupying the middle space. The Society of the Friendly Sons of Saint Patrick was inscribed in the middle of the front, joining the hands of Hibernia and America. A female figure holding a harp represented Hibernia, and an Indian holding a quiver with a bow depicted America. Below was one word, "Unite." The reverse side of the gold medal depicted St. Patrick dressed in a robe, holding a cross in his hand, and trampling a snake.

Additional people wished to be added to the society's membership roll. By the close of 1772, James Moylan, John Patterson, Robert Glen, and a druggist, Sharp Delany, were inducted. Every member was required to attend meetings, however; merchants, if absent, were listed as – beyond sea. Regardless of their reason for absence, each was assessed a fine of five shillings, and the sum was promptly remitted.

William West was installed as president in 1774, succeeding John Maxwell Nesbitt, who served in the preceding year. Mr. Nesbitt, due to many influential contacts, secured Richard Penn, grandson of William Penn and Governor of the Province of Pennsylvania, to become an Honorary Member. Edward Shippen accepted an invitation to attend the annual meeting as a visitor. Anthony Wayne and Dr. Robert Boyd applied for admission as new members. Turnout for the annual meeting in March 1774 declined, due to increasing political disruption in Philadelphia.

May 20, 1774 – Philadelphia

A meeting of citizens took place at City Tavern, built for the owner,

Thomas Proctor, at 2nd and Walnut Streets. Before the meeting concluded, a significant step was approved; the appointing of an official "Committee of Correspondence." John Maxwell Nesbitt, Thomas Barclay, John Nixon, and John Dickinson, all members of The Society of the Friendly Sons, were selected to serve on the committee. Chosen from a group of nineteen members, their duty included corresponding with the colonies in British America.

June 18, 1774

A follow-up to the May meeting was called by the citizens' group, now increasing to forty-three. John Dickinson, appointed chairman, assumed responsibility to secure a consensus of the people. Ultimately, the intended purpose was to appoint delegates to a general congress.

September 4, 1774 - Philadelphia

Cultural differences existed between people in the colonies. Under the guiding hand of William Penn and his family and friends, being Quakers, Pennsylvania was devoid of a formalized military organization. In the 1740s, volunteers began to assemble, forming military associations. Years following, the Pennsylvania General Assembly recognized them officially, organizing men from a single township into a company naming them Associators. Several townships pooled their Associators into a unit known as a battalion. Their ages ranged from sixteen up to sixty.

The First Continental Congress, a group of influential individuals from ten of the thirteen colonies, organized and met at Carpenter's Hall in Philadelphia. Two months later, the members of the Light Horse of the City of Philadelphia formed. Later, their name changed to the First Troop Philadelphia City Cavalry. A total of twenty-eight men participated in the initial sign-up. Ten were members of The Friendly Sons of Saint Patrick. James and John Mease, Henry Hill, John Boyle, Andrew and Samuel Caldwell, George Fullerton, William West, John Mitchell, and George Campbell joined the troop. John Dunlap, a printer, and Blair McClenachan, owner of the passenger sail ship, *Congress*, joined. The members of the First City Troop increased to eighty-eight with The Friendly Sons of St. Patrick contributing thirty of the total membership.

April 24, 1775

Attendance swelled at the next meeting of The Society of the Friendly Sons of St. Patrick. A few of the newly inducted members included John and Lambert Cadwalader, Richard Bache, married to Benjamin Franklin's daughter, and David Conyngham and Samuel Meredith. Four of the members were absent, listed as beyond sea.

∞

A sundial attached to the side of the building displayed five o'clock in the evening. Great excitement stirred outside City Tavern. A messenger was dispatched from Trenton and rode into the city. He secured passage on the McConkey's and Johnson's Ferry, and crossed the Delaware River ten miles above Trenton in colonial New Jersey, carrying an express dispatch to Philadelphia residents. Arriving with great haste, the horse hoofs dug into dry dirt, kicking up dust as the rider drew the reins toward him. Yelling and making a disturbance, he drew his horse to a halt in front of City Tavern. People ran into the street, crowding around the chestnut stallion. And members attending the meeting of The Friendly Sons of Saint Patrick vacated the tavern, hearing loud shouts of alarm outside.

"SHOTS FIRED AT LEXINGTON," the messenger proclaimed. His stallion circled in the excitement. "THE BRITISH HAVE FIRED UPON OUR COUNTRYMEN," he announced in haste, his eyes wide with alarm.

Stephen Moylan rushed to his side, seeking more detail.

"The militia is in peril – the Province of Massachusetts is under attack," the messenger responded once more.

Stephen, alarmed, "Do you have a report of casualties?"

"Forty-nine Massachusetts men killed, sir."

A loud cry could be heard in the distance. Sounds of shrieks from the women followed.

"We have thirty-nine wounded, sir – they are being cared for as we speak," his voice trailing off.

Stephen recoiled, "What about the British?"

"The British suffered more," the messenger exclaimed. "Seventy-three killed – 174 wounded," he announced, raising his right arm in defiance.

He carried the dispatch a long distance, and it was late in the day for a public response. The following morning – Monday, nearly 8,000 citizens assembled in front of the State House as the news spread rapidly. An enlistment of citizens began with two troops of light horse, two companies of riflemen, and two artillery companies.

Members of The Society of the Friendly Sons of St. Patrick came to the forefront with vigor. Newly appointed Colonel John Dickinson led the First Battalion, and John Cadwalader became a colonel, together with Lieutenant Colonel John Nixon. And the Third Battalion was led by Major Samuel Meredith. Other members of the society, Richard Peters, Tench Francis, Lambert Cadwalader, and John Shee, were appointed captains. By December 1775, the Pennsylvania Navy formed to defend ports by the Delaware River. John Maxwell Nesbitt was appointed paymaster.

Monday - March 18, 1776

Military titles interestingly appeared at the next meeting of The Society of the Friendly Sons of St. Patrick. Anthony Wayne became a colonel, Samuel Meredith, a major, William West, captain, and Andrew Caldwell, a commodore in the Pennsylvania Navy. Alarmingly, the Colony of Pennsylvania was under siege, the British invaded.

Each Associator was required to arm himself with a good firelock, a bayonet with steel ramrod, worm, priming wire, and brush, and a bag capable of holding four pounds of lead ball. Every private of a rifle company had a good rifle, powder horn, charger, bullet screw, twelve flints, and a pouch to hold four pounds of ball.

27

A Merchant, Shipmaster, and Privateer

The McCausland brothers, Abraham and Conolly, often partnered with their cousins, Robert, from Coleraine, and James Stirling of Walworth. There was sufficient opportunity to transport linen products and dry goods, plus passengers with various backgrounds to British America. A merchant's life was one of staying abreast of competition, maintaining the appearance of their ships, and advertising, emphasizing the benefits of humane treatment and accommodations for all passengers willing to venture forth and leave their homeland forever.

Trans-Atlantic merchant trade metamorphosed into a new meaning with the advent of 1777. The brig, *Jane*, owned by a partnership consisting of James Stirling of Walworth, Ballykelley, James Mitchell of Londonderry, and Thomas Barclay of Philadelphia, was captained by another part-owner, Connolly McCausland. But in this year, political winds brought change. *Jane* sailed the Atlantic as part of a convoy of sail ships. And Captain McCausland's new responsibility was to sail the *Jane* as a victualer, supplying British troops and ships with food and supplies. By the close of the year, *Jane* left the Atlantic sailing into the mouth of the Chesapeake Bay, their destination, docking at Hampton Roads along the James River. The *HMS* (His Majesty's Ship) *St. Albans* followed nearby, responsible for protecting *Jane*. The vessel carried butter from Cork, a goodly supply of Irish hams, and a quantity of salted beef, all provisions for British troops.

Patriots found themselves fighting battles in the second year of an eight-year war. Anarchy ruled the Atlantic during this time. British, French, Spanish, and Dutch navies maneuvered many ships at sea, all designed to control colonial ports.

Pennsylvania, with a port at Philadelphia, was forced to establish a navy. The Committee of Safety asked for the assistance of the Delaware Riverboat pilots, located near Lewestown, to assist with tarring and feathering captains who smuggled goods in British ships. Riverboat pilots knew the navigational challenges between the Delaware Bay up the river to Philadelphia. Procedures, drawn by the newly formed committee listed the steps to be taken by riverboat pilots if they spotted a mercantile vessel from

Britain, for example, a tea-ship or a privateer.

The first course of action was to deny the tea-ship access to the Delaware River. If unable to prevent the tea-ship from passing, they gave the committee advance notice of the ship's arrival. Word circulated to the committee that citizens around Lewestown favored the British cause. Riverboat pilots received a warning. If they assist a tea-ship, they will be branded for a treasonous act. There was a penalty and the committee proclaimed, the riverboat pilot would be treated seriously if caught assisting a tea-ship. They would be made a spectacle and listed as a traitorous pilot who allowed the vessel up the river.

Less than a year passed, it was November 1778, and Captain Ham, commanding an American sloop, ordered his helmsman to head south. Leaving Providence, Rhode Island, his intended destination was Philadelphia, a sail of more than three hundred miles. Upon approaching the Delaware Bay near Cape May, New Jersey, the crew of the *Jane*, commanded by Conolly McCausland, confronted Captain Ham and his crew. The surprise came when Captain Ham quickly discovered *Jane* was part of a fifteen-ship convoy destined for New York. Once a peaceful merchant vessel, *Jane* had been retrofitted with sixteen guns, and eight portside were pointed at the captain's sloop.

Captain Ham lowered his gangplank after the *Jane* came broadside and Captain McCausland boarded the sloop. Captain Ham was presented with a document by Captain McCausland, informing him his ship was sailing under an official "Letter of Marque and Reprisal." The document represented a license issued by Britain, and Captain McCausland, a private person, was authorized to act in the capacity of a privateer. His mission was to attack and capture ships and seize the cargo of enemies of Britain, and Captain Ham's sloop was unfortunately one. Within two days after his capture, Captain McCausland did not keep the sloop. Upon being treated humanely, Captain Ham and his crew were provided stores and released with their sloop to finish their journey.

∞

Captain Castle wrote the following in his ship's log.
Ship's Log – *Ashley* – August 1785 - On the first instant spoke with Captain McCausland, *Faithful Steward*, from Londonderry to Philadelphia in latitude 44 N. longitude about 36 E. All well.

Passengers watched as the stern of the *Ashley* sailed over the sea, disappearing beyond the horizon. The captain invited James Lee I to visit in his quarters. The patriarch was the only passenger who received an invite to share a glass of Madeira in the captain's domain. There was more than one occasion where the time passed with the captain sharing his sea-venturing stories, and the patriarch was an ardent listener.

On this particular afternoon, their conversation diverted to a different topic.

"Our merchant business was generating a lot of money before the revolution. My brother, Abraham, and our cousins built a network of contacts to ship goods and transport passengers."

Profits grew by leaps and bounds an expression used since the time of Shakespeare.

"And somehow your business plans were changed," queried the patriarch.

"Yes, the Continental Congress passed a law banning the importation of any goods from Britain. Ireland was excluded from the new law and we were free to conduct trade with the colonies. You see, the colonies were not at war with Ireland."

"You were granted favor."

Captain McCausland sipped from his glass of Madeira. "For a time, yes, but later, the Congress enacted a law prohibiting anyone in the colonies to export colonial goods to Britain, the West Indies, and they added Ireland. Flaxseed trade was stopped – they crippled us."

"And we and our kin were impacted economically." James Lee I was careful to couch his comments by identifying with Ireland, despite the fact he and every ship passenger were days away from setting foot on new soil. They were still subjects of the Kingdom of Ireland.

Captain McCausland had more to say on the matter. "Barclay & Mitchell were one of the merchant firms impacted by the law. And now you have another situation more severe than trade – colonial merchants were forced to choose sides."

"What happened?"

"Thomas Barclay cast his lot with the colonies. Most of them made the same choice."

"How did you, your brother, and cousins respond to the decision?"

"We sought another opportunity. The king was faced with a problem – he needed to transport supplies to his troops if he was going to win the war."

"And therefore, it became accepted practice to issue the Letter of Marquee and Reprisal," responded the patriarch.

"Yes – you might say we provided a valuable service. Therefore, we were issued a letter and set about on a new mission."

Captain McCausland was interested in the roots of the Lee family. The patriarch told of their history in Cornwall. English blood flowed through their veins – but that was many years ago. Their life in Ulster was not as fruitful as anticipated, and it was difficult to overlook the economic instability and persecution forced upon others.

"And the merchants convert to privateers – at least temporarily," concluded the patriarch.

"Of course – it seemed to be a viable alternative. Besides, the king required our help. That was until July 1780."

"Something else happened?"

Calm seas continued with fair winds, and the sails were full. There was no immediate reason for the captain's presence atop the deck. He poured another glass of Madeira for both of them. Obviously, he respected the patriarch, holding him in high regard, and his opinion led to further discussion, otherwise; he would have remained silent about such matters.

"Certainly – we were involved in an incident after we set sail from Cork. *Jane* was full of provisions – 4,000 firkins (small wooden barrels) of butter, plus pork, beef, and a variety of dry goods. We were transporting the value of £15,000 of supplies."

"And someone or something changed your plan?"

"What an understatement," he replied, gesturing with his hands. "My brig was part of a convoy – and that is when I met up with Captain Hopkins."

A Massachusetts man, John Burroughs Hopkins commanded one of the first vessels in the Continental Navy. Captain Hopkins, acting under a Letter of Marque, captained the brig, *Tracey*, armed with eighteen carriage guns to engage in acts of privateering.

"What happened – something catastrophic?"

"Certainly – during the summer of 1780 my ship was raked broadside with rounds from *Tracey's* four and six-pound cannons. And the sound and smoke were devastating. It felt like hell was spewing forth fury."

The patriarch, an ardent listener, remained quiet.

"This was the first time I was involved in a naval battle, and my ship suffered structural damage. It took no more than twenty minutes for the battle to be over."

"There must have been a loss of life. What about the casualties?"

"We were sailing with a crew of fifty-six. Seven were killed. Fourteen more were wounded, some severely."

"Did you fire any rounds at the *Tracey*?"

"We did. We sent a volley of cannon fire and inflicted wounds upon a few of Captain Hopkin's crew."

The patriarch paused, contemplating the severity of the situation. "You've lived through a horrible battle. Did they sink your ship?"

"She was damaged but still afloat. The wind blew the smell of sulfur from gunpowder over our vessel. My lungs were clogged with thick black air. My men staggered about, choking, gasping for clean air. Still navigable, Captain Hopkins ordered me to sail to Boston, where he filed papers to have the ship condemned and sold as a prize of war."

"And what happens to the money after the ship and cargo are sold?"

"The proceeds are distributed among the ship's captors."

"And what happened to you?"

"We became captives – prisoners of war."

Captain McCausland, together with his brother-in-law, William Stewart, the ship's surgeon, and his cousin, Captain Marcus McCausland, and James Campbell, a passenger, became prisoners. The four of them were released on parole and directed to sail on a ship chartered by Robert Temple. He was returning with his family to Ireland but bound for London and flying a flag of truce. The two McCauslands, Stewart, and Campbell were to be exchanged for American Patriots in prisons in England.

Much to the surprise of Captain McCausland, he and his fellow prisoners became victims of a prolonged process with lack of urgency, difficulty with the British law and prisoner exchange, and disinterest in securing their freedom. Without any success in a prisoner exchange, the four were forced to return to New York, where they served a prison term.

On the ninth of November 1780, Captain McCausland penned a letter to Benjamin Franklin in Paris.

His Excellency Benjamin Franklin
    *Sir,

I have your esteemed favour of the 9ᵗʰ and agreeable to your desire applied with Mr. Robert Temple at the Board of Sick and Hurt, who gave for answer that no exchange of prisoners immediately from Boston to England could be admitted, nor would they exchange us by receipt as you expected. I therefore beg to know if we were to go to France and surrender ourselves to your Excellency, whether or not we could be exchanged there, to cancel our parole as getting that affected would give us the greatest pleasure for hard as our case is we are determined to abide by our agreement. We therefore pray your answer on this subject I am for Willm. Stewart, James Campbell, Marcus McCausland, and self.

With respect and esteem.
Your most obed. Very humble servant, Connolly McCausland.

"Did Mr. Franklin receive your letter?" asked the patriarch.

Captain McCausland reached for the bottle of Madeira, filling the patriarch's glass.

"Times changed, and those in London became disinterested in prisoner exchanges."

The patriarch was confused as to the outcome. "How did the four of you obtain your release?"

Captain McCausland, avoiding the question, appeared annoyed. "A certain Irish rascal – Gustavus Conyngham, made life miserable for us and many others. The scoundrel became a major problem for the British."

Stories of the revolution and the struggle between Britain and her renegade child were fascinating topics for many – and this was no different with the patriarch. As a result of this story, the patriarch was able to put events into perspective and gain more insight – why the American Revolution caused nearly everyone to choose sides.

*Contribution of a copy of Captain McCausland's original letter provided by Dr. Mary Wack, Professor, Washington State University.

Listening to the events in the life of Gustavus Conyngham made the voyage all worthwhile for the patriarch. "Between Thomas Barclay, James Mitchell, and Gustavus Conyngham, all of you knew each other and were business associates before the revolution."

"Exactly – we had multiple merchant business dealings with them. That ended with the beginning of the revolution."

Hiding his emotion, the patriarch enjoyed each new revelation. "How did Gustavus Conyngham, now a privateer, become a problem?"

Captain McCausland shrugged and groaned. "Let me begin by telling you who he was. His father was Gustavus of Largyreagh, a gentleman. And his uncle was Reverend William Conyngham of Letterkenny. His uncle sent him to Philadelphia in 1763 at the age of nineteen to apprentice with Redmond Conyngham. Gustavus inflicted more damage on the British fleet except for one other mariner. Captured three times, he escaped every time. Benjamin Franklin was very impressed with his success. Overtaken by his pleasure, he scoured about to find other captains that would merit issuing a commission as a privateer."

"You mentioned another person – one whom I suppose was a major hindrance to the British Navy – more than Conyngham?"

"That would be John Paul Jones, the Scotsman. In his youth, he was involved in an altercation in Scotland and forced to leave, forever."

The patriarch hung on the captain's every word, enjoying the stories one by one.

"Jones was a tenacious seaman – feared by many – no one wished to sail in his path. Did you hear about his declaration to the Board of the Pennsylvania Navy? It occurred at a time when the navy was assigning officers to new ships."

The patriarch, sipping from his glass, paused. "No – I didn't."

"Give me a fast sailer for I intend to sail in harm's way. Those were his words – no wonder he fought with tenacity. And it got worse. He and Gustavus Conyngham sailed together on more than one occasion. Between the two they were fearless, inflicting more damage to the British fleet than most. They were a threatening force."

28

The Society and the Bank of Pennsylvania

Endless morning conversations convened around the long tables, however, there was a change in the topic. Gone were conversations and lamentations of family and friends left behind. New discussions encompassed their favorite subject – who did what – when did they do it – and the impact of what they did. The primary focus covered men and women, a few of them relatives, labeled patriots.

Almost a decade before 1774, the First Continental Congress met in Philadelphia and voted to cut off all trade with England, unless their demand was met. Parliament must repeal the Coercive Act. Parliament responded quickly and decisively, and it wasn't what Congress anticipated. They passed a law restricting the colonies of New England from trading with anyone but England and Ireland. They also refused the fishermen of New England access to the rich fishing banks off of Newfoundland. The result – tensions between the mother country and her colonies increased. Action evolved in 1775. British troops left Boston on a mission to destroy arms and munitions near Concord. Parliament followed up and issued an edict that no colonist could hold an office without their approval. Men of Irish descent, now residing in Pennsylvania, were accustomed to this new tactic.

The Continental Congress responded by issuing more than 600 Letters of Marque to Massachusetts vessels, authorizing privateering. About 20,000 colonists, now patriots, sailed on these vessels. Their number was calculated to be 2,000 more than the total of troops in General Washington's newly raised army.

In September 1777, General Sir William Howe, Commander of the British Army, engaged General Washington's Continental Army. The British beat them back at successive battles at Brandywine, Paoli, and Germantown, with each battle fought in Pennsylvania, forcing the Continental Army to retreat to the bank of the Perkiomen Creek nearby Schwenksville. General Howe succeeded by forcing an evacuation of all of the troops organized years before by the citizen's committee and the influential members of The Society of the Friendly Sons of St. Patrick.

Men gathered around the long tables, and this time, Rebecca McIntire asked to join the group. Members of the Elliott and Espey clans could be counted on for lively discussion.

Simon Elliott, anxious to hear more stories, began. "What happened once the British took control of Philadelphia?"

Gustavus Colhoun, with prior travel experience to Pennsylvania, knew what happened next. "During October and November, summer transitions to autumn in Pennsylvania. The farmers finish harvesting crops and they prepare for the advent of winter. General Washington's army was despondent – they lost three important battles – and they were driven out of their capitol, Philadelphia."

Winter at Valley Forge

General Washington chose to move his entire army, 12,000 soldiers, including the 2nd Canadian Regiment and the Iroquois, tribal Oneida, and Tuscarora warriors, to nearby Valley Forge. There they wintered until April and the advent of spring. Twenty miles outside Philadelphia, the territory sat on a high plateau, filled with plentiful hardwood trees. They could watch for the movement of General Howe's troops if there be any winter maneuvers. General Washington deemed it a strategic location. Valley Forge was surrounded by a series of hills, improving the detection of the British and providing security for the Continental Army.

Cold weather set in during December, and the general's army realized their new headquarters would become a cold and dreary place. Many in the army suffered from exhaustion and lacked adequate clothing to protect them from dampness, cold, and snow. Some of the troops suffered from typhus and smallpox. Others marched without adequate foot covering, leaving bloody red spots on the trail. Food supplies consisting of twenty-five barrels of flour and a limited supply of salted pork were what remained to feed his army. Two generals ordered scouts to search the countryside for food for their army to survive through the winter.

With knowledge of surveying and construction, General Washington designed an encampment and issued orders to build log huts fashioned from harvested trees. Each cabin would be constructed fourteen by sixteen feet, with walls measuring six and one-half feet packed tight with clay and a roof sloping to each side. The fireplace and chimney were positioned at the rear of the structure and packed with more clay. Troops obeyed orders to scatter into nearby fields and secure hay to provide additional warmth. Ownership of the crop was not debated. It was confiscated for the army's survival.

General Washington secured quarters at a farmhouse located on the perimeter of the encampment. His mission, by December, was redirected from military tactical planning to supervising the construction of the encampment, finding sources for logistical supplies of food and medical aid, and equally important, providing encouragement and leadership for his army. Congress lacked resolve in addressing multiple letters, requesting help. Financial assistance required to supply his army, a force rapidly depleting of physical and mental stamina, appeared inadequate.

Once the Marquis de Lafayette, a Frenchman with military experience offered his help, he was appointed major general, and the event lifted the general's spirits. After the New Year passed, Baron Friedrich von Steuben arrived at the encampment, promising his allegiance and willingness to assist with the Continental Army cause.

Through the turmoil, congress increased pressure to mount a mid-winter attack on the British in Philadelphia. General Washington, displaying foresight and resolve, was determined to rest his army and revive their health, spirit, and dedication before advancing upon the British at Monmouth, New Jersey, come springtime.

Baron von Steuben was assigned an unofficial position of inspector general, as he was a veteran of the Prussian army, having seen action in the Seven Years War. Upon assessing the army's weaknesses, the baron prepared a plan to educate and drill them in combat maneuvers designed to defeat the British army.

Valley Forge National Park – Chester County – Pennsylvania
Recreation of cabins at the Winter Encampment

∞

The meetings of the society ceased from June 1776 to September 1778. James McIntire II questioned, "What happened to the members of the society after the British occupied Philadelphia?"

"We know they spoke defiantly, in action and deed," replied James Lee I. "They provided supplies, gave of their wealth, and fought for liberty."

Hugh Espey broke into the discussion. "My son William sent me a letter of his first encounter with a company from the Massachusetts Militia."

James inquired again, "Do you have it – what did he write?"

Hugh retrieved a leather pouch and sat at the table. "This letter provides some insight – an understanding of these people and what motivated them. William Espey was a scout under the command of General Knox. While on patrol in dense woodlands in New York, he stumbled upon a militia from Massachusetts. A young boy was carrying a white flag with a green pine tree sewn onto the cloth. The words – An Appeal to Heaven – were sewn above the tree." Hugh continued, "The message seems obvious, but there must be a deeper explanation."

It was James Lee who understood the source. "This is a phrase from John Locke – the flag of the Massachusetts militia bore his quote."

"Who was he?" inquired Hugh.

Many men looked to the patriarch for the answer. "A member of the English parliament – he lived decades before us. His thoughts and opinion were published in his work, *Second Treatise of Government.*"

"What was this treatise about?" Hugh wanted to know.

"There was a conflict between parliament and the crown. Locke's thoughts were visionary." The patriarch surveyed the faces of the men. "Locke believed when people think their rights are under a power which takes away their rights, and if they have no other appeal on earth, they have a liberty to appeal to heaven."

The men were quiet, contemplating; a few murmured to another.

"The Society of the Friendly Sons of St. Patrick contributed four battalions for the Pennsylvania militia," mentioned Simon Elliott II. "They were commanded by Colonels John Shee, Anthony Wayne, Lambert Cadwalader, and Francis Johnston – all appointed Lieutenant Colonels."

Alexander Nesbitt, brother of John Maxwell Nesbitt, joined the society in 1778 together with Commodore John Barry. A call for funds issued in June of 1780 raised a total of £315,000, payable in gold or silver. The sum of £103,500 came from the wealth of twenty-seven members of the society, with Robert Morris contributing £10,000 and John Maxwell Nesbitt, £5,000.

Gustavus Colhoun commented, "They organized the Bank of Pennsylvania to fund the war effort."

"They did," confirmed John Elliott. "Out of the five inspectors appointed to oversee the bank – three were members of the society."

"Who were they?" inquired James McIntire II.

"Robert Morris – an Englishman, John Maxwell Nesbitt, originally from Loughbrickland, and Blair McClenachan, a Derry merchant turned privateer."

∞

On June 17th, 1780 a subscription was drafted, signed, and supported by ninety-three individuals and firms from Philadelphia. The document outlined in its purpose the love of and patriotism toward their country. In this document, the signers expressed the willingness to support the subscription to fund the Bank of Pennsylvania. One month later, on July 17th at Front Street, the bank opened two doors below Walnut Street. And it was the society's response to waging a successful war against Britain. Together they pledged their property and credit to support the bank's efforts in supplying provisions for the Continental Army.

The Society of the Friendly Sons of St. Patrick
For the Relief of Irish Emigrants
Subscriptions Measured in Pounds

Robert Morris	10,000	John Mease	4,000
Blair McClenachan	10,000	Brunner, Murray & Co.	6,000
William Bingham	5,000	John Patton	2,000
J.M. Nesbitt & Co.	5,000	Benjamin Fuller	2,000
Richard Peters	5,000	George Meade & Co.	2,000
Samuel Meredith	5,000	John Donaldson	2,000
James Mease	5,000	Henry Hill	5,000
Thomas Barclay	5,000	Kean & Nicholls	4,000
Dr. Hugh Shiell	5,000	James Caldwell	2,000
John Dunlap	4,000	Samuel Caldwell	1,000

John Nixon	5,000	John Shee	1,000
George Campbell	2,000	Sharp Delaney	1,000
Tench Francis	5,500	Total	103,500

It was impossible to stop with one story. Men love stories, and those surrounding the long tables were no exception.

Simon Elliott declared, "What about the Continental Navy?"

"Their first ship to be deployed was the *Lexington*," mentioned the patriarch. "And Commodore John Barry was the first to put to sea – the year was 1775."

Matthew Caldwell stood nearby, mug in hand, listening to their comments. "Andrew Caldwell was a Commodore in the Pennsylvania Navy. And he was in command when the British sent two brigs, the *Liverpool* and the *Roebuck*, up the Delaware River to attack Philadelphia. Before they received orders to engage the Pennsylvania Navy, they hid in the Broadkill River near Lewestown, Delaware attempting to remain undetected."

∞

Lewestown

Lewestown, established as an English settlement near the Delaware Bay in the 1600s, contained more than fifty families occupying the village. Their first doctor arrived from Waterford, Ireland, circa 1725. His destination was Philadelphia; however, his passenger ship anchored at Lewestown. He went ashore for temporary recreation, fell in love with the surroundings, and sent for his wife, who remained at home. William Penn asked him to reside in Philadelphia but the doctor refused.

The *Siconese*, a sub-group of the Lenape and early inhabitants of Delaware, shared their knowledge of medicinal plants with settlers. Horehound, a flowering plant with gray leaves and white flowers, grew from the mint family. The plant improved respiratory ailments, sore throats, and poor digestion. Boneset, from the sunflower family, reduced fever. Pennyroyal, a mint plant used in cooking, smelled fragrant upon crushing the leaves. And the leaves from the sassafras tree when ground together and rubbed onto an open wound, promoted healing.

Buildings constructed by the settlers were made of wood and covered with shingles to protect them from storm-driven wind and rain. By 1763, two hundred acres were surveyed under the direction of Governor John Penn. Four years later, the British built an octagonal lighthouse seven stories high and attached a dwelling for the keeper at nearby Cape Henlopen. A subscription was raised to maintain the light and buoys at the entrance to the Delaware Bay.

Nearby timber was available for the shipbuilding industry. A significant number of riverboat pilots made their home at Lewestown by the mid-1700s. Bailey Art, David Johnson, and Henry Fisher were a few of them. During the Revolutionary War, Lewestown Creek offered a protective channel for the navigation of small sloops and schooners. Lewestown was a hotbed for Tory activity, and captains sought assistance from sympathizing riverboat pilots to navigate their vessels through dangerous obstructions in the Delaware River.

∞

"What happened to the British brigs, *Liverpool* and *Roebuck*?" asked James McIntire II.

Andrew Caldwell knew the end of the story. "The Pennsylvania Navy repelled the brigs."

Those surrounding the long tables were engaged – listening, and thinking about each story told.

Andrew recollected the tale of the Eyres. "The three brothers – Manuel, Benjamin, and Jehu were shipbuilders along the Delaware River above Philadelphia."

One by one, each apprenticed with Richard Wright. After a while, Manuel, with the assistance of Jehu and later Benjamin, took over the business and became the leading shipbuilder in Philadelphia. Manuel joined the Pennsylvania Navy Board when the revolution began. Each of the brothers believed the war to be necessary, even righteous. The Eyres built the first gunboats ordered by the Committee of Safety for Pennsylvania, and in 1775 Congress launched the *Bull-Dog*, the *Franklin*, and the *Congress*. In time Manuel became a delegate to the Provincial Convention of Pennsylvania.

Jehu was a person of considerable energy and determination. He was also generous, a hospitable man, and one who loved his country. His associates saw in him a man willing to sacrifice. A disciplinarian, he joined the Continental Army as a private – in time becoming the captain of Jehu Eyre's

Artillery Company. He organized his carpenters, workmen, and apprentices to form a military company of fifty-two, and served under the command of General John Cadwalader in the Pennsylvania Militia.

Andrew recalled the plight of Jehu Eyre. "After the British captured Philadelphia, they occupied Jehu's home, including his shipbuilding business. And they secured a brig under construction and stole all of his timber, planks, boards, his tools, and took his furniture in his home."

Brother Benjamin joined the cause, rising to Lieutenant Colonel commanding the Second Battalion of the Pennsylvania Militia. Trusted by General Washington, Benjamin received an appointment as a personal assistant.

Born in 1747 at Kirkcudbrightshire, Scotland, John Paul Jones sought an apprenticeship that led to commanding English merchant ships as a young man. He got in an entanglement with a crew member and ran him through with his sword. He had no choice but to flee to the colony of Virginia in 1775. At the age of twenty-nine, he accepted a command in the Continental Navy, serving off the coast of France and later taking the fight to the English coast.

By 1782, Jones relinquished command of the thirty-six-gun frigate to Captain John Barry, an Irish immigrant residing in Philadelphia. The *Alliance* was built five years prior in Massachusetts by William and James Hackett. The builders launched the ship, named *Hancock* in 1778, however, the name was changed to *Alliance* in recognition of a newly formed treaty between the colonies and France. Captain Barry, sailing near the West Indies, operated under a Letter of Marquee. During 1782 and 1783, they captured *Kingston*, *Brittania*, *Anna*, and *Commerce*, all British vessels.

Thomas Barclay, fulfilling the role of American Consul in France, distributed the prize money raised from captured ships. The *Brittania* and *Anna* transported coffee, longwood, sugar, and rum. The four sail ships were escorted to France by Captain Barry with the men under his command, and Barclay ordered the vessels sold at public auction in France.

By April 1783, five months before the war ended, the final count of the auction proceeds was made known. The *Brittania* and cargo raised £83,087, the *Anna* £136,488, the *Kingston* £144,446, and *Commerce* £198,597, for a total of £562,618. The crew of the *Alliance* received a distribution of £107,091, with each crew member receiving £350. The Surgeons Mate received £1,275, and the midshipmen received £1,350. Lieutenants and Marines received £2,580. Those receiving distributions served in the following capacity. Among them were seamen, landsmen, steward, marines, quartermaster, carpenter's crew, gunner's crew, midshipmen, armorer, boatswain mate, and chaplain. The Continental Congress received the remainder of the prize money.

American privateers acted valiantly in their efforts, navigating across the Atlantic to the English Channel and entering the North Channel, capturing an estimated 800 British vessels. The element of personal sacrifice was evident during the days of the revolution. Those backing the formation of the Bank of Pennsylvania invested heavily in personal wealth, demonstrating ingenuity, foresight, brave patriotism, and sacrifice.

No Tories – British sympathizers, existed among the members of The Society of the Friendly Sons of St. Patrick for the Relief of Irish Emigrants. Each member took a stand – and stand they did, donating wealth, forming troops, and risking life. They volunteered and fought in state militias, the Continental Army, and the Pennsylvania Navy, diverting from merchant business to performing daily drills as soldiers, preparing for the inevitable, a battle with a professional army and navy, and they cast their lot and fate with other patriots.

29

Jamaica
August 26, 1785

Sail ships navigating off the coasts of New Jersey and Delaware risked capsizing and foundering from the brunt of storms. Seasonal storms heighten during June through September because the sun heats humid air creating powerful storms bringing strong winds and heavy rain. They form far west of the Susquehanna River, raking through the forests and fields heading eastward through Pennsylvania before passing over New Jersey and Delaware and blowing off the coast into the sea.

Far greater storms in the South Atlantic spawn over days as they gather warm moist tropical air forming offshore near Central to South Africa. The mixture of warm air and moisture provide ideal conditions to generate storms the sailors call hurricanes. The storms propel through the vast waters of the South Atlantic with rotating air currents spinning across the ocean for thousands of miles. The storms travel unpredictable paths, sometimes veering toward the islands of the West Indies. After passing over the islands in the Caribbean, they turn northward, heading into Spanish Florida and blow through the coast of North America, passing over the Carolinas, Virginia, Maryland, Delaware, and even New Jersey.

Dangerous seas spawned by Mother Nature present obstacles for many a mariner. Inlets are subject to erosion, exposing sandbars. Heavy seas create swells, and dangerous waves increase the risk of sailing coastal New Jersey and Delaware, including the mouth of the Delaware Bay. Many ships, driven dangerously close to the coastline, succumb to the wreckage forming the graveyard of the Atlantic.

Jamaica lies 1,400 miles south of the Indian River Inlet, Delaware, and it's one of the largest islands under British rule. The topography consists of mountains, rainforests, and reef-lined beaches. Many merchant ships frequent multiple harbors transporting the island's primary export, sugar. By 1785 English merchants systematically built a network of business partnerships employing credit advances, all designed to facilitate and grow an exporting economy. Many merchants invested in full ownership or a partnership interest in sail ships engaged in the sugar trade.

Merchant trade evidenced by increased shipping was very active on the eve of the twenty-fifth day of August. Thirty-one vessels were about to feel the fury of a violent hurricane moving across the Atlantic toward the Caribbean. The storm increased in intensity after inhaling the warm moist atmosphere from the sea. By the dawn of the twenty-sixth, ship's captains battled ferocious wind-driven rain passing over Jamaica.

Eighteen merchant vessels were heaved by ocean swells and driven ashore on the island. The names of the ships were *Adventure*, *Alexander*, *Amity's Production*, *Dispatch*, *Fame*, and *Favourite*. Another vessel, the *Holland*, commanded by Captain Erman, was driven to the shore by the storm's force. The *Hornet*, *Minerva*, *Molly*, and *Philadelphia* suffered damage from the storm.

A ship named *Neptune* couldn't escape the wrath from the king by the same name, as he inflicted damage on the helpless ship, driving her upon the shoreline. The *Sally*, commanded by Captain Patterson, succumbed to the same fate as the others. More vessels, the *Swallow*, a second named *Swallow Packet*, *Triton*, and *Washington* sustained damage. Salvagers refloated *Triton* following the storm.

East of Jamaica, Thatch Island, beaten by the hurricane saw the vessel *Constantine*, en route from Dominica to Bristol, wrecked by the shore. Islanders rescued the crew from impending peril. More damage to other sail ships ensued and the toll increased. The captain and crew of *Endeavour* lost their bearing in the storm near Castle Fort, Jamaica. The vessel, *General Campbell*, was reported wrecked, as was the *Henry*, *Hope*, and the sail ship *Jamaica*, the latter shipwrecked at sea.

The storm landed at Bull Bay, where the vessel *Industry* was driven to shore and wrecked. On the northeastern side of Jamaica, *Mary Ann* foundered in Annato Bay, a location with an active trading port. *Savileand*, and *Success* suffered damage, lost in the storm. The *Swift* sank on the twenty-sixth, and *Rover* was damaged and wrecked at Bush Quay.

Ship damage was severe, and loss reports abounded. Thirty vessels, all British-owned, suffered varying fates. The hurricane's path was unpredictable, sometimes moving slow, stagnating, and deluging an area with large amounts of rain. Other times these storms move fast, generating increasing wind speeds. This storm passed over Jamaica and turned westward, pummeling the territory of Spanish Florida, then turned north following a path up coastal North America.

30

Pandemonium

A dangerous wave pummeled the port side of *Faithful Steward*. Many passengers, steeped in darkness, were thrown from their berths and tossed on the deck. Women screeched in horror. Edward Cooke and his wife lifted themselves from among tangled bodies and legs. Hit by flailing arms, they cried in desperation, reaching and grasping to save their ten children.

Mr. Mourn, thrown from his berth in the foc's'le, hit his head on a wooden beam as he fell to the deck. Stunned, with his head bloodied, he got up and stumbled to the ladder leading to the main deck. A wave crashing over the bow drenched him after he bounded to the last stair landing on the deck. Crewmen, trying their best to secure loosed sails, spread themselves across the spars. Aghast, with his senses surrounded by darkness, Mr. Mourn turned to scurry down the ladder to announce to everyone, they were in trouble.

Captain McCausland, in shock, screamed into the wind. "Mr. Stanfield, gather some crew – put some men on the foremast halyards – we'll turn the sails starboard to move her out toward the sea. Move – fast – we'll sail her off the bar!" He was furious and fearful of their predicament – not a minute could be spared for self-deprecation. Crewmen were screaming, cursing, moving about in the darkness, fruitlessly attempting to redirect sails in the hope the ship would respond.

Below deck, people struggled to their feet, hearing shrieks from women echoing off the wooden hull. Children were crying and shaking uncontrollably, and moving about trying to locate their father or mother, alone in the darkness. Fear and terror enveloped the passengers from the ship's hull to the fore near the galley. Men called for their spouses and flailed about, trying to gather children. Others pushed and pulled and punched at dark figures, those daring to get in their way while finding the ladder, attempting to ascend to the deck to inhale the salt air and relieve their state of panic.

Mr. Quigley remained at the helm, horrified by what he saw unfolding before his eyes. He watched the crew attempting to reduce the impact of the wind upon the leeward sails by re-positioning the spars. They hoped to create buoyancy and sail the ship away from shallow waters to a path of safety.

Pandemonium ruled below deck in the darkness. Southeast winds slammed into loose sails, causing sounds akin to gun reports. Meanwhile, the sounds of horror and shrieks of madness settled in below. Passengers making way to the ladder leading to the deck found themselves stepping on or over bodies lying beneath their feet.

Pelig Hudson pushed his way through the galley and up the ladder into the dark nighttime sky. Others followed behind him to get out of the cramped hostile quarters below deck. Atop deck, fighting fierce wind pressure, the crew attempted to turn the ship out to sea.

Matthew Caldwell screamed to Simon Elliott, standing on the ladder leading to the main deck. "Stay here – form a chain – tell the one behind you to do the same. We need to form a human chain, a path so others will follow to get to the deck. We need to guide everyone to safety."

Simon followed the command. Within minutes they formed a chain of human flesh, assisting others, hoping this would reduce the blockage of bodies and the level of hysteria of those attempting to get to safety. Mr. Quigley watched, as passengers, one by one, stumbled and fell to the deck after making their way along the human chain up the ladder.

The sails on the foremast were furled with some tied and secured, and the staysails were flapping uncontrollably. Captain McCausland, rallying his crew around the mainmast, contemplated his next decision. Waves creating swells and the force of wind upon the mainmast sails caused the ship to budge forward, the hull leaning to the leeward side of the ship. But the shift was brief – the hull lurched forward, emitting a grinding, screeching sound, digging once again into the seabed of sand below.

Captain McCausland hoped for a reprieve from a stranding, however, his ship dug into the bottom. "Mr. Stanfield – get the axe; we'll cut her down. We'll cut the mainmast – we have to lighten the vessel amidship – get her to float off the bar – cut her down."

A breaking wave crashed into the port side of the ship. The impact jarred Mr. Stanfield as he recovered the axe. His leg caught in an entanglement of rope, and it twisted as he fell backward. His head hit the deck and something snapped.

Passengers spilled onto the ladder leading to the deck. Water penetrated through the seams on the hull's port side, flooding the lowest level of the ship. Untold bodies, men, women, and children, a few lifeless, others writhing in pain, badly bruised, lay on the deck in steerage. The ship's bell no longer sounded its hourly ring. Mr. Stanfield lay still, in pain – his leg broken, and unable to move.

Captain McCausland beckoned. "Mr. Linn – chop here – cut the mainmast here – we'll bring it down and lighten the ship." The mast, twenty-one inches in diameter and cut from solid white oak, towered above the main deck. Darkness continued to cover Neptune's seascape. Storm-driven wind crossing the ocean tilted *Faithful Steward* to starboard. The crew could not take any assessment or bearing of location but suspected they were close to the shoreline. Where – no one knew.

There was no hiding the look of terror on each of the crew's faces. Confusion and panic spread among the passengers in the dark of the early morn. Indescribable utterings were common – and bone-chilling shrieks emitted from women unable to find their children. No one was left alone in suffering – the tragedy impacting everyone's emotions. Some of the men appeared dazed – a few stunned – others unable to speak. Amidst the turmoil and mayhem, others displayed steadfastness and resolve – fortitude. Dr. McDougal responded to Mr. Stanfield's cry for help, by loosening the ropes wrapped around his leg and dragging him to a safe place where he wouldn't be trampled.

"Mr. Mourn, spell Mr. Linn – get the mast cut down," commanded the captain.

Urgency prevailed, and the captain, albeit in a state of panic, knew the single most important event was to remove the mast from the main deck and get his ship to float. Patrick Mourn took the axe from his hands and began striking blows at the base of the mainmast.

"Faster, Mr. Mourn – faster – cut the mast down quickly mate – chop it down."

People packed themselves shoulder to shoulder from the bow to the quarterdeck. The unthinkable, passengers standing upon the captain's bridge, became a temporary refuge for some. Others, attempting to avoid hysteria, heard the cries of children calling for their mothers, unable to move from their station, and mothers called for their sons and daughters. Fathers pushed bodies aside in a desperate attempt to locate their families. One wave following another crashed into the wooden hull of their only source of refuge for the past fifty-three days, somewhere on the Atlantic Ocean, many miles from Ulster – a land distant and far from present memory.

31

Daybreak

Dark stormy clouds blocked the view of the heavens above Neptune's seascape. The ship's bell, silent since three bells of the first watch the night before, never rang six times (6 a.m.) during the morning watch. Passengers spent the entire evening on board a wooden ship, unrelieved from their nightmare. Derangement of mind onboard a ship at sea in darkness, grounded in stormy weather, lacking knowledge of their predicament, was reaping a toll among many. As the dim light of day provided the first glimpse of their whereabouts, a new reality, one no better than the darkness of night, prevailed at the first blushes of light.

The ship refloated and moved during the cutting down of the masts, only to ground once again on a shallow ocean floor. Unrelenting wind produced a billowing sea surrounding their temporary abode. Neptune's Atlantic color, usually a greenish hue, was dark and murky in appearance. Wind from the hurricane passing over Jamaica days before was now reduced to a storm. Moving northward through a corridor, the path of the storm hovered over the Delaware coastline. Passengers standing on the quarterdeck through the nighttime ordeal had the best view of the shoreline in the distance. Humanity, many existing in a state of mind too difficult to describe, packed together in clumps. Some families remained together while others, crying incessantly, attempted to locate a lost loved one.

Mr. Kelley swung the axe hitting the final blow to the mizzenmast, the third mast cut causing it to come crashing down, bringing with it sails still attached to spars and halyards entwined in rope rigging, spilling over the stern of the ship into the sea. Captain McCausland and Mr. Linn peered over the stern to assess the difficulty in cutting the rigging from the masts and the ship. Multiple bodies, drowning victims, some with faces staring into the sky, were enmeshed with feet and arms wrapped in the rigging. A wave jarred the port side of the ship. Unless *Faithful Steward* frees itself with the oncoming high tide, manning the two longboats would be imminent.

"CAPTAIN," screamed Mr. Irwin. "Someone cut one of the longboats from the deck – it's gone!"

Captain McCausland pushed aside passengers to get to the gunwale to observe the obvious. "Damn – damn." Their situation had worsened exponentially.

Mr. McCaffrey, assessing the nightmare, stood nearby. "Captain – some of the passengers cut the lines in the dark of night and attempted to lower the boat – the sea swept it from their grasp! The boat floated to the shore – it's onshore."

Time was slipping away. Options for rescue diminished. Captains and their crew never spoke of this fact – longboats were for their rescue – passengers are cargo. Crewmen John Quigley, William Dalrymple, Pelig Hudson, and Patrick Mourn prepared to climb onto the mainmast, floating on top of the ocean, to jump into the swells and swim to shore and safety. Pelig tied one end of a rope together in sections and wrapped it around his waist with the knot positioned at the small of his back. He was the first to jump into the ocean. Captain McCausland and Mr. Gwyn watched, as one by one, spanning two-minute intervals, they plunged into the murky sea, floated to the surface, and began to stroke with their arms, systematically swimming toward shore.

Passengers, those capable of maintaining a semblance of mental stability, watched and cheered as the crew began an epic, heroic swim to shore. Many minutes passed – time suspended as they followed each of the four crewmen's progress. The force of the wind and the strength of the current swept the crewmen downwind from the wrecked ship. Pelig, barely visible, swam within reach of the shore. He was lean and muscular, a veteran seaman, and he stroked and struggled, wading through the surf to stand on the shoreline. Pelig proved to be the strongest swimmer. He waded into the surf to assist John Quigley, exhausted, thrashing about in the last breaker before reaching the beach. Mr. Mourn and Mr. Dalrymple followed, reaching the shoreline within minutes of each other.

The sand on the beach was medium brown. Small bushes of sassafras and wild berries grew in clumps between scrub-brush, all lining the edge of the sand more than one hundred yards from the surf. A desolate wind-beaten scape, the area appeared absent of human life, no buildings, no evidence of habitation, only sand, and sea. Where were they? Crew members were not trained in navigation, be it celestial or by instrumentation. The captain and first mate bore the responsibility to maintain a fix of position at all times. What mattered was the urgency of retrieving the longboat.

Crewmen ran to the longboat, drifting nearly two hundred yards downwind from the wrecked ship. The keel dug into the sand with each passing wave pressing on the stern. Pelig reached the rescue boat and promptly untied the rope from his waist, tying an anchor bend knot to the metal ring on the bow. Mr. Dalrymple stood by the stern and grabbed the side. Mr. Mourn and Mr. Quigley grabbed along the sides while Pelig tugged at the rope at the bow. Together they maneuvered the longboat through the surf, knee-deep, paralleling the beach until they reached the point where *Faithful Steward* lay opposite them. Pelig waved to the officers on board the ship, signaling to haul the longboat through the rough surf back to the ship.

Mr. Gwyn and Mr. McCaffrey, the bosun, together with Mr. Irwin and Mr. Phillips, grabbed hold of the opposite end of the rope pulling the longboat through the heavy surf toward their ship. Many of the Lee family lined alongside the ship, arms propped on the gunwale, watched and cheered as the longboat cut through each passing wave, coming closer to the battered vessel. Passengers frantically pressed to the starboard side and began to push and crowd against each other, all struggling to be the first to escape the wreck.

Except for Rebecca, the entirety of the McIntire family stood next to the gunwale, filled with fear and anxiety, hoping they would be part of the first passengers rescued and rowed to shore.

James II looked about in alarm. "Father, where is Rebecca?" Panicked and in a state of urgency, he called again, "Father – Rebecca is gone – what happened to her – where is she?"

The ship's bow heaved as a passing wave crested then broke beyond the longboat, flattening it in the trough of the wave. Men seized the slack in the line pulling the boat closer to the ship. The strength of the current and the weight of the wooden longboat created a heavy drag on the line. Mr. Kelley, Mr. Brown, and Mr. McCaffrey replaced those holding the rope, giving them time to rest aching arms. Passengers screamed in panic as they pressed upon each other, watching the longboat drawn to within reach of rescue, yards from *Faithful Steward*.

Another wave crashed into the side of the ship, causing passengers and crew to fall to the deck. People were stepped on, kicked, and bruised. Others, in a state of panic, struggled to their feet to board the longboat. The strength of the wave heaved the longboat upward then backward, causing the rope to tighten, snapping the knot tied to join the two ends together. Everyone shrieked and gasped as the rescue boat disappeared beyond the wave, then reappeared briefly in the surf, capsized, and moments later, disappeared beneath Neptune's seascape. Cries of men – a moaning sound issued in desperation emanated from deep within. Voices of mothers awaiting the rescue of their children screeched with unintelligible sounds, realizing all hope of a rescue by boat slipped away.

People screamed, "Where is the second longboat – where is it?" Unfortunately, during the dark of night, a group of passengers cut it down and cast it over the gunwale, only to have the ferocious sea tear the rope from their grip, and the boat drifted away, never seen again. In the ensuing moments' voices could be heard, passing the bad news from one to another. The longboat is gone – both are lost - hope has drained away.

Passengers acting in a panicked state hemmed in James Lee I and Isabella, together with some of their family at the starboard side of the ship. Many with hope for rescue and fear of impending doom creeping inward to the soul, remained motionless, frozen, pleading to God for a miracle. James McIntire I, Rebecca, and their family found themselves in the same predicament. James II left their side and pushed through the crowd of passengers, calling for his sister, making way to the ladder leading to the mid-deck and steerage.

People emptied trunks filled with possessions and scrounged for splintered wood from the cut-down masts and the ship's interior, anything thought to float, to be tossed into the sea. Minutes, seeming to be hours passed, and James, unable to navigate the disorder and mayhem, returned to his family unable to locate Rebecca.

Passengers acting out of panic and despair threw chests overboard and jumped into the ocean, clinging to temporary floatation devices, begging God for mercy, and hoping to drift to shore. Hinges to wooden chests broke open, clothing and personal belongings floated to the surface.

"Not now – don't do it – not now – don't jump," cried James II, a strong swimmer.

His friend, Dr. Campbell, a polished youth, climbed over the gunwale and plunged into the ocean, hoping to swim to shore. The tide, aided by the wind, was now ebbing and running in the opposite direction from the beach. Anyone caught in the current of outward flow would be fighting against the wind and flow of water. James watched in a state of alarm as Dr. Campbell surfaced, thrashing, moving his arms to swim to shore. In a matter of minutes, his dear friend, bobbing helplessly, drifted away from the ship toward the sea.

Mrs. McIntire shrieked, covered her eyes, and turned to bury her head in her husband's chest. They spotted Dr. Campbell drifting away from shore and out of reach from the ship. Alone, his friend struggled by himself, holding onto life until he could see him no more, disappearing underneath the sea.

A reprieve from the helplessness enveloping the ship was non-existent. People were faced with choices to survive. It was time to think strategically, to increase their chance to make it to shore – or drown. People continued to stumble and fall, pressing upon each other as waves hammered the ship, causing the hull to continue to list. Each mast, cut away by the blow of the axe, fell leeward and lay in the ocean, still attached to the ship by a tangled mess of rigging fixed to the top-mast and topgallants.

Captain McCausland's voice and those of the remaining crew were barely audible. Calls for help, injured passengers, others reacting in fear and hysteria, created a horrific scene for a few who began to gather on the shoreline.

"Stop – don't climb out there – wait – now is not the time!" commanded Captain McCausland. "Mr. Gwyn, restrain them."

Younger male passengers, all single, decided it was time to climb onto the mainmast, and navigate the tangled rigging to the end of the mast, resting on the water. A few of the crew grabbed hold of stragglers, dragging them back to the deck.

Mr. McCaffrey climbed out on the mast. "Now is the wrong time, mate – the tide is at an ebb; wait for the tide to turn!"

Passengers and crew watched as a few stood on the mainmast and one by one plunged into the sea. The ocean temperature in early September was usually mild, but the storm was churning colder water from the bottom, replacing the warmer surface water. One of the men cleared the rigging and surfaced, kicking his legs while forming a breaststroke with his arms. A second followed suit – the third caught a leg in the rigging as he fell into the sea. Submerged, one of his mates clung to the rigging, attempting to free him from the entanglement. The force of the ocean proved too great. He had to free himself and swim away from the rigging lest he be caught in the same predicament. Passengers watched as the young man slipped below the surface beneath the mast and the lines. More followed, jumping from the mast into the sea. They ignored the calls from the captain and mates to wait for a change in the tide. People watched as one by one, the heads of those brave enough to jump, disappeared beyond each passing wave. A few floated, flailing their arms, drifting parallel to the beach. Others closed the distance to the shoreline.

Casualties mounted. Hugh Espey knelt by his wife below deck, bruised, battered, and lifeless. A beam shifted, striking her head after the ship grounded the night before. Families discovered some of their members below deck, smothered after being trampled. Water inundated the bilge, filling the lower deck, and penetrating steerage. Bodies, the children from the Cooke family succumbed to suffocation, floating in saltwater. A guttural manifestation, one impossible to describe, resonated from those in pain on the main deck after hearing the plight of their loved ones and friends below.

Mr. Gwyn screamed, "Sail ship off the stern – sail ship on the horizon." He remained on the mast to discourage others from jumping prematurely into the ocean. Afar in the distance, another ship was in peril.

Masts and sails, faintly visible in the distance appeared over the stern of *Faithful Steward*. Captain McCausland raised his long glass, spotting the stranded ship. Another vessel, one flying the flag of France, was stranded and unable to make headway under sail.

32

Mid-afternoon

The morning passed – and the tide, now incoming, pulled the ocean toward shore. Mrs. McIntire watched Thomas Blair, James Dougherty, Neil and Sarah McKinnon, and George Munro jump from the mainmast, plunging into the sea. She cupped her hand over her mouth, gasping as Mr. Campbell, an aged parent, and his daughter, Sarah, climbed up on the taffrail and jumped from the stern. Sarah, adorned in a bright blue dress, followed her father, plunging into the ocean. Mr. Campbell flailed about, attempting to stabilize himself to swim to shore. He was in trouble and unable to keep his head above the water. Perhaps he jumped, realizing his impending plight but did so to bring Sarah to a state of courage, knowing she would never have jumped by herself.

Rebecca watched in shock and horror as the sea tossed the girl's father. She screamed aloud when she saw him rise to the surface once again.

"Mr. Campbell, swim – swim for your life!"

He arose twice, arms flailing, his body now facing away from shore. With panic on his face, he struggled to keep himself above the ocean. Another passing swell picked him up and dashed him against the stern of the ship. His body submerged underneath the hull. Rebecca never saw him again. Moments later, she spotted Sarah, reaching to lay ahold of a passing floating timber.

"Kick your feet, Sarah, kick your feet. Kick your feet," Rebecca shouted again and again. "Rest, then kick some more. Live, you must live Sarah!"

Rebecca beckoned to Sarah again when a passing wave carried the girl toward shore. Tears filled her eyes as she repeatedly called to her. The passing minutes filled with anxiety and agony. She continued to keep her eye on her friend's plight. Sarah held the timber tight against her chest and kicked with her feet as often as possible, allowing the current to bring her closer toward shore. As time passed, the swells in the sea blocked Rebecca's sight of Sarah, and she couldn't determine if she arrived safely onshore.

Mr. and Mrs. Gregg stood near the bow watching Sarah Campbell's struggle for survival.

"Look, you saw that didn't you. What can we do – what should we do – I can't think," cried Mrs. Gregg frantically.

One year before, they were greeting guests at their wedding in Ireland, and one year later, they faced doom, maybe death, and the possibility their lives together would be brief, very brief.

"You heard the captain – try – we must try – we will make it to shore, and we will survive," implored Mr. Gregg.

Timbers were scarce; none were in sight. People sat and cried, hope draining away. Others displayed varying stages of anxiety and fear. Mr. Gregg decided the time to abandon the ship arrived.

"Yes, it's time; we must go now," he spoke, looking into his wife's brown eyes. She was frail and he knew this would be difficult.

Mrs. Gregg, petrified, couldn't answer. Her husband took her hand, and together, they navigated a few steps out on the mast. Without hesitating, he grabbed hold of her waist and jumped, pulling both of them into the sea. Thomas and Gustavus Colhoun observed their plight from the gunwale above. Mrs. Gregg, arms floundering, struggled. Thomas, watching the turmoil below, secured a timber and called to Mr. Gregg, throwing the board far out in front of them into the ocean. Together the Colhouns observed the couple swim to the timber, wrapping their arms around it, attempting to float.

Captain McCausland turned his long glass toward the stranded French brigantine off the stern of *Faithful Steward*. The ship, now grounded, was leaning toward the leeward side. The wind ripped through the sails, tearing the seams and rendering them useless. Meanwhile, the crew occupied their lifeboats.

The Captain, Mr. Gwyn, and Mr. Linn knew the moment had come. It was time to abandon their ship and swim to shore. It was time to address the passengers, at least those with a presence of mind capable of understanding directions. It was time to give them instruction, useless as it may be, to provide those that could, a chance to survive and make it to shore. Mr. Gwyn and Mr. Linn secured the axe; each taking turns chopping a few spars to make floatation devices. Mr. Stanfield, a broken leg and unable to stand, would be floated to shore.

Captain McCausland stood on the fallen foremast at the ship's bow. "Everyone – hear my words loudly and plainly," he warned above the noise and chaos. "We have met with a most unfortunate and dire situation. The tide has changed – it's now incoming – the afternoon will end and evening will come. It's time to abandon ship. The crew of the stranded brig off the stern of our ship has taken to their lifeboats. We do not know of their present state or if they made it to shore. There is no hope of rescue – rely upon yourselves. God save you and your families."

Those who heard the captain were faced with a new reality. Captain McCausland spoke again, holding the axe in hand. "My crew will cut pieces of timber – use what you can for support – tie guineas to your waist, fill your pockets if you will." He drew in another breath. "Mr. Stanfield is severely wounded – we will take him to shore. May God have mercy on all of us and the rescue we are about to undertake."

Mr. Linn swung the axe and dug into the side of *Faithful Steward*, prying away pieces of oak timber. Owen Phillips and John Brown rigged a sling from a staysail, and Samuel Irwin and Edward McCaffrey picked up Mr. Stanfield. He shouted in anguish as pain coursed through the broken leg. The sling was placed under an arm, around his chest, and slipped underneath the other arm, and tied in a knot behind his back. A rope was tied to the sling, and they hoisted him over the starboard gunwale, lowering him over the side to float him to shore.

Captain McCausland, followed by Mr. Phillips, Mr. Irwin, Mr. McCaffrey, and Mr. Gwyn, jumped into the ocean, clinging to oak planks for flotation. They pushed away from the rigging toward John Brown and Mr. Stanfield, and together they proceeded to swim away, clinging to the wood, leaving the anguished crowd toward shore.

Edward McCaffrey, together with Robert Kelley, remained aboard the ship, determined to cut what timber they could to assist with the rescue of the passengers. The sight of the captain, his mates, and crew leaving the clutches of the ship, caused a disruption of anxiety and cries of desperation among the passengers. Pieces of timber were handed to women and children by Mr. Kelley, hoping this would increase their chance of surviving the perilous situation.

Thomas Colhoun, the experienced mariner, made a way through the crowd of passengers to go below deck to assess the condition of the hull. Water seeping into the bilge was now flowing into the mid-deck. Pushing floating bodies aside, he returned to the ladder to ascend to the main deck. Gustavus, born with a heart for people, attempted to assist the injured and those lacking the courage to leave the ship.

Mr. and Mrs. Kincade, their baby, and fourteen-year-old daughter, Margaret, waited for scraps of wood. Thomas grabbed the next available board and handed it to Mr. Kincade.

"Can either of you swim?"

He searched the paralyzed eyes of the parents. Shaking, Mr. Kincade responded, "Little – very little." Whimpering, Mrs. Kincade, holding her baby, nodded no.

Thomas looked at young Margaret, summoning her to his side. "Turn around Margaret."

She turned as instructed. Thomas took the timber and positioned it underneath each arm across her chest, attaching it to her body by securing it with strips of cloth. Mr. Kincade, hands shaking, took his son from his wife, wrapped him in a garment, and handed the boy to Thomas. Together they placed him on Margaret's back and tied him in place, securing him as best they could with torn strips of clothing.

Thomas glanced at Mr. Kincade. His wife was sobbing and in pain – young Margaret was petrified. "Are you prepared for this – the next step?"

The Kincades nodded in agreement, reacting while in a state of panic. Thomas secured another board from the bosun's hand and walked the Kincade family to the mainmast, outstretched over the ocean. Tears streamed down Margaret's face as she clung to her mother's side. Together the parents stood poised on the mast, preparing to leap into the sea.

"Mother – I'm so scared – I …." Mrs. Kincade took hold of her daughter, stooped to kneel, and looked into Margaret's eyes. Fear, coupled with streams of tears, flowed down each of their cheeks.

"Margaret – LIVE – child, you can do this." She placed her hands on her daughter's cheeks. "Margaret, LIVE – YOU LIVE – your father and I will follow behind you."

Thomas cut a section of rope from the rigging and wrapped it around Margaret's arms from behind her back. He guided the young girl along the mast and lowered her slowly into the ocean. Mr. and Mrs. Kincade placed their piece of timber underneath their arms, steadied themselves, and lept.

Mr. Linn returned from an inspection of the lower hold of the ship. Water poured through the mid-deck, and the danger of the ship breaking to pieces was imminent.

"It's time we leave – let's make the swim to shore."

Mr. Kelley refused. The desire to linger to continue to assist with the rescue was overwhelming.

"Mr. Kelley – the time is now – the tide will change – stay at your peril – I'm leaving," warned Mr. Linn.

Thomas Colhoun, standing within earshot of Mr. Linn, requested the axe. The two remaining crew looked toward the stern where the ship's flag flapped in the breeze. Passengers, one by one, panicked and fearful, stood on the taffrail leaping into the sea.

Simon Elliott I, his spouse, their five daughters, and sons Simon and James stood by the ship's railing, waiting their turn. There were those passengers who jumped from the ship's taffrail, haphazardly, determined to make it to shore. Other passengers studied the efforts of those who abandoned the ship, determined to learn from their mistakes to survive. The Elliotts secured a few of their many chests, emptied them of clothing and other contents, hoping, praying they would float and support their rescue. Many chests remained, filled with personal articles, fine clothing, and a wealth of coins to be swallowed by Neptune's sea.

Hugh Espey stayed below deck, holding his wife in his arms. Dreams of a new life shattered before his eyes. His sons, James and John, together with their sister, Mary, stood by the taffrail. A crowd of people blocking their way crammed near the mizzenmast stretching out over the water.

James turned to glance over his shoulder. "The time has come – we have to jump – now!"

John nodded in agreement and took a tight hold of Mary's hand. James leaped first and splashed into the sea. John watched as he began to stroke away from the ship. "It's now, let's jump." He held onto his sister's hand, pulling her over the stern, plunging into the murky water. James continued to stroke away from the hull, away from danger. Mary collided with John, landing on top of him as they submerged into the ocean. He felt a blow to his skull after he submerged into the sea. His vision blurred, his senses darkened, he felt Mary's hand separate from his. John bobbed in the water, attempting to regain his senses. The current pushed him underneath the hull of the ship. Panic set in, and he struggled to stroke away from the hull as he felt his leg twist and jerk, catching an object underneath.

A remnant of the Lee family, unable to locate some other members during the morning mayhem, found most of them during the early afternoon hours. Huddled together, scared and wet, they struggled to process the dilemma unfolding before their eyes. Their immediate family surrounded the patriarch from Donegal and his wife Isabella, grandparents to a portion of the contingency. Included in the remnant was their daughter, Mary, son James II, his wife, and their six children, a sister-in-law to James II, and a sister-in-law to James III, a total of thirteen Lees. Of the remaining thirty-five members, more than two-thirds jumped from the ship, hoping to float or swim to shore.

Horror, infiltrating to the very core, struck many of the Lee family. They witnessed the demise of most of their kin into the murky Atlantic. A few who managed to escape and swim or float beyond the breakers slipped out of sight. No one knew if any in the group made it to shore.

James II, together with his son, James III, scurried about searching for remaining boards or cut timber, or an unclaimed chest to be used for flotation for the family women. Past the age of three score and ten, the patriarch and Isabella remained on the deck, standing in water. Isabella, flocked by her grandchildren, in shock, watched as her family prepared to abandon the ship.

Departing words were challenging, virtually impossible to speak; all overcome with fear and emotion. The patriarch and his wife, desiring to go, would hear no urging from the others or argumentation that they must join the group. Neither would place their family at risk, thinking some would have to come to their aid, risking peril and drowning themselves. They would wait longer, hoping God would cause the wind to lessen and the sea to calm. Perhaps together, they could find a board from *Faithful Steward* to cling to and float for as long as they could, before the ship broke apart. James III, the last one in their family of thirteen, climbed out onto the mast. He turned to face his grandparents, tears running down his cheeks, stretched his arm to wave, then turned to face the Atlantic, and jumped.

By three that afternoon the McIntire family gathered together. Bound by their love for each other, but filled with anxiety and fear, doubt began to erode their hope they would rally in a spirit of thankfulness upon the shore. James II previously advised not to attempt the swim at ebbtide, now stood on the mainmast surveying the possibility of making it to the shore alive. A number proceeded before him, yet he watched in anguish as they failed and drowned before his eyes.

"Mr. Hepburn – can you swim?" He called as he climbed over the rigging on the mast.

"A little, I am determined to make it to shore."

Samuel Hepburn, minutes before, watched his two sons jump into the sea. Unknown to him at the time, one struggled and drowned. John, the elder, a strong swimmer, made it to the shoreline. John had hold of his brother but lost his grip after a crashing wave separated the two.

"Mr. Hepburn, wait – wait, let me find you a timber, a piece of wood," called James II.

He crawled over the rigging toward the deck, found a piece hanging from the side, broke it off, and returned to the mainmast.

"Mr. Hepburn – Mr. Hepburn," he screamed in alarm. His elder friend leaped from the mast, and the flap of his coat was the last thing he saw as he entered the sea.

James II lay upon the mast, watching for any sign of his friend. Mr. Hepburn surfaced, he sank, and he surfaced again, arms flailing; he sank once more. James leaned over the mast, stretched, and reached into the ocean, grabbing Mr. Hepburn by the hair. He pulled his head above the surface. The mindset of his friend was frenzied and acting irrationally, as moments before he witnessed a son in peril. James grabbed a board floating nearby and pulled his friend by the arm toward it, hoping he would maneuver himself to drift. He did, and pushed away from the mast, determined to follow his eldest son.

James stood and turned to go back to the deck, knowing the time was now if he was to save himself. Thoughts of self-preservation appeared selfish, not supportable by logic. How could he leave his father and mother, and all of his family, including a young nephew? None of his friends had gone before him, but they privately urged him to depart, and often. He was overwhelmed by a mixture of emotions penetrating his inner core.

"James, you can swim. You must go now – save yourself – the afternoon is advancing, the evening is coming," warned one of his sisters.

The infiltration of water covered the mid-deck, spilling onto the main deck. *Faithful Steward* was helplessly stranded, pitching to one side. James felt a pressing weight. He approached his father and mother, seeking their blessing, one extended to him on previous occasions. Agonizing, he began to speak to his mother.

Rebecca McIntire, crying, spoke in a trembling voice. He would hear his mother's cries years later. "Son – you must go – now."

James embraced his family one by one and reached down, placing his hand under the chin of his nephew. They wept with the bitterest of anguish. They lurched forward, surrounded him, and clung to him. He felt the weight of his father's hand upon his shoulder.

"Go James – God is with you, my dear son."

He returned to the mainmast and walked toward the end, then turned for a final glance at his family. Standing on the deck, they waded in saltwater, and he walked back to them. They were barely visible through the tears covering his eyes. A second time he returned to the mainmast, and a second time, he returned to his family, thinking he heard their screams above all the others, unable to carry out the deed to save his life. His mother, standing in water nearly waist-deep, watched as he approached.

"James," she implored with tears streaming down her cheeks. "Son, you must go – go my son – and may God preserve you."

He turned and climbed through the mass of rigging attached to the end of the mainmast for the last time. Traumatized, he felt as if there was a separation of his body from his soul. His family watched as he sprung from the mast into the sea. He rose to the surface; he swam, one stroke after another, he swam. The wind and tide continued producing swells in the ocean. He rode each surge turning his head to watch for a breaking wave, then timed the break, caught the crest, and rode the wave. Rough churning water surrounded him. His eyes took in the vastness of the ocean before him. He floated briefly, then stroked with each arm rhythmically, gaining upon the sea, noticing the shoreline. On one occasion, his body submerged in the ocean, and his legs dangled. He touched the sandy bottom. He continued to stroke, hitting the sandy bottom a couple of times. Tiring, he continued to raise a limp arm to gain upon the sea, approaching nearer the shore. Arms aching, he struggled to stay afloat, however, he was in trouble, his strength was near gone.

John Brown swam to shore that morning and stayed to assist others struggling in the surf. He watched as a wave crested and heaved James in the air, sending him crashing to the sandy bottom. He dove into the ocean, swimming quickly to save him. James clung to the crewman frantically, to the point of pushing him down beneath the ocean's surface. John pushed at James and tore himself away, a distance of mere yards from the shore.

"Will you drown us both," he angrily yelled at him and turned to swim to shore.

James began to sink once more. The crewman, realizing he was in trouble, serious trouble, waded into the ocean up to his neck, struggling to keep his head above water, grabbed him, and pulled him toward shore.

Horrific events, those seldom experienced by humanity, unfolded the remainder of the afternoon into the evening. The day began to close without the slightest appearance of the sun in the western sky. One by one, each passenger, father, mother, son or daughter, brother and sister, a few grandparents, uncles, aunts, and cousins; all would remember Friday, September 1, 1785. Every survivor was traumatized, destined to endure a lifelong memory, the day *Faithful Steward* wrecked. Each would remember the reality of the past and find hope for the future, as they struggled with the emotional upheaval dwelling within.

Darkness descended on the shoreline of a country unknown to most onboard the ship. The foundering French brig provided a clue of their proximity to the mouth of the Delaware Bay. The survivors knew nothing about the sand-strewn beach they now inhabited.

Young Margaret Kincade washed ashore upon the dark wet sand. The incoming tide, depositing her on land, began its slow descent ebbing into Neptune's domain. Dazed, she lifted her head, noticing a distant fire. Too exhausted to move, she laid her head on the sand, drifting away from reality. After waking, she saw the fire glowing in the distance. People surrounding the fire were cooking in the dark of night. Struggling to her feet, she regained her senses. Her baby brother was dead; her parents were gone. Margaret untied the knots to the rope holding fast the wooden board to her chest and stumbled along the windswept sand to join the strangers inhabiting her new-found world.

33

Morning Shoreline
Friday – September 2

A yellow sun burst forth over the eastern horizon, and warm gentle breezes blew over quiet bodies strewn over the shoreline. Neptune's tide, beginning another descent into the sea, scattered them along the surf's edge. Clothing, chests of varying sizes – some with lids closed, some pried open – wooden boards – splinters – the fragments of what was once a beautiful stately three-mast ship washed up on the beach. Unlucky victims – there were men's and women's bodies, including their children, people with names, each a member of a family. Survivors knew their identities, formerly possessing occupations – people of meager to middling wealth – and a few with significant means lay along the surf's edge, some barely alive or others deprived of life, drowned.

James McIntire II woke to the morning sun beating upon his face. Lifting his head, he saw the remains of *Faithful Steward*, badly damaged, stranded offshore. He would, in time, learn the ship ran aground a short distance from the Indian River Inlet. The Atlantic Ocean flows into the channel at the southern end of Delaware. During the advent of high tide, the inlet receives a strong flow of water from the ocean, and this flow of saltwater fills the Rehoboth Bay, and the bay funnels the excess flow into the Indian River Bay.

Weakened and deprived of food and fresh water, James stood, surveyed his surrounding, and began to patrol the beach, searching for the whereabouts of his family and friends. People, multiples of unknown people, were combing through the debris from the wreckage scattered along the shoreline.

Captain McCausland's vessel lay broadside, far beyond the breaking surf. She was badly beaten, mortally wounded, water seeping throughout what remained of her hull. On the night of the thirty-first, she hit a bank and ruptured her hull. Some of the passengers thought she broke free of the sandbar. She did, but in a short distance, her hull struck again, and that was the fatal blow.

James II encountered passengers requiring multiple kinds of aid and medical assistance. His knowledge to heal was limited, his attempt feeble, but he did what he could to ease the suffering. Painted in his mind was a picture, a horrible picture, formed by brush strokes from what he saw in the survivor's faces. The farmer and weaver, an intelligent one at that, would remember glimpses of the mural the remainder of his life.

Local inhabitants spotted the wreck on the first of September. Around dawn, some observed the cutting down of the mizzenmast from the second floor of nearby inland dwellings. They lived in small, modest habitats constructed of wood, and rode a horse, hitched one to their wagon, or walked to the shore. Farmers and watermen traveled from sparsely dotted inland areas – Muddy Neck, Cedar Neck, the small community of Middlesex, and various places surrounding the bay areas. Lewestown, a small community of nearly fifty houses, was located near the mouth of the Delaware Bay, next to Cape Henlopen, approximately twenty miles north of the Indian River Inlet.

The coastal inhabitants worked on small nearby farms. Some were watermen, and others were seamen. Another element – scavengers, wreckers – the latter describing people with no conscience, systematically combed the beaches for anything they could find. Wreckers, displaying false signals such as tying a lantern to a mule or horse, lured unsuspecting captains to an intentional stranding, and often the helpless crew ran from the ship as it was relieved of the cargo.

Today on the beach, scavengers came, the dreaded wreckers too, looking for anything of value for their gain. Others employed Christian charity, distributing water to survivors, starting fires on the beach, and cooking food to restore badly beaten people, alone, helpless, some dying on the shore of an unknown land.

James continued his search for his lost parents and his family and friends. Several people assembled and were combing the beach at the water's edge. Others attended to the half-drowned physical and emotional needs, performing acts of kindness while attempting to assist many sufferers. His heart sank as he watched a wrecker strip the clothing from a dead body, and upon leaving the defiled naked person lying on the beach, threw the clothes on a pile with other valuables in a wagon. The spectacle invoked a mixture of frustration, anger, and helplessness.

James Espey began a shoreline search for water and food, anything to revive his body due to a forced fast for many hours. Brother John laid on the sand, battered and bruised, his leg broken. James pulled him from the surf the preceding evening. John retrieved his sister after being pinned underneath the ship's hull. Together they floated, reaching the shore safely; however, the scene being too traumatic and the swim to shore so draining, Mary died of fright and exposure.

Gustavus and Thomas Colhoun awoke, having fallen asleep by the dunes, a short walk from the surf's edge. Collecting themselves, they initiated the same journey James II began, minutes before.

"Look – it's Mrs. Gregg," Thomas raced to the surf to rescue her. Lying face up, she appeared lifeless. Mr. Gregg was nowhere in sight. An unknown man kneeling beside her extracted coins from her pockets and began unbuttoning her dress. It was a beautiful garment, and whether she is dead or not, he was about to rob her of decency. Someone could use it – he would sell it for gain. Thomas ran toward the man and pushed him over, knocking him backward into the wet sand. The wrecker rose to his feet, gained a foothold, and swung his right arm across toward his face. Thomas ducked, the punch missed, and he countered with his right arm landing squarely on the jaw of the thief. The force from his punch knocked him backward, off his feet. He stood up for what Thomas thought was another round; however, he turned and fled upon seeing his scarred face.

Sarah Campbell lay underneath a sassafras bush, a short walk away from the ocean, having fallen asleep attempting to regain lost strength from the swim to shore. She woke, and after regaining her senses, began to cry uncontrollably, her mind focused on finding her missing father. In a depressed state of mind with anxiety controlling her ability to reason, she turned northward, walking along the shoreline. In time she found his corpse, lying upon a sandy bed, motionless, lifeless.

"God is this possible – my father!" She cried aloud, noticing a passerby. Sarah was alone, shipwrecked on a far distant shore, a region unknown, and wanton of money.

"To whom shall I apply for help?" Sarah exclaimed.

In misery, she reached into her father's pockets and removed three guineas. Thinking she found payment for passage to Philadelphia and a means to feed herself, she saw the shadow of one standing over her shoulder. Kneeling beside her drowned father, she turned, the sun shining into her eyes, struggling to see a stranger's face. Relief had come – another heard her cries and willingly would assist. The stranger's voice demanded the coins and proceeded to remove the clothes from her father's back. Displaying a callous attitude toward her plight, he walked off, never to be seen by her again.

James II witnessed similar incidences where wreckers stripped the bodies of drowned victims of their clothes and searched their pockets for coins and valuables. He watched in shock at the look on the face of one man. After scouring through the pockets of a male passenger, he found but a couple of coins and walked away with a disappointed look on his face. James continued his search and came upon what appeared to be the body of one of his relatives. Mistaken identity, he continued, suffering in emotional pain too deep and difficult to comprehend.

Forty-four members, including the extended Lee family, cast themselves into the sea the afternoon before. James Lee I and Isabella, Simon Elliott and his wife, and James I and Rebecca McIntire were among the last to leave the ship as the ocean rendered it impossible to stay.

James Lee III, beaten by the surf, hungry and thirsty, wandered the shoreline. The Colhouns witnessed his cries, unimaginable suffering, sounds of sorrow emanating from within, as he uncovered one body after another, relatives, loved ones he would see no more. In a short distance, he found Mary, no longer the Irish beauty, her body twisted, lifeless, face buried in the wet sand, drowned. The Colhouns ran to his side. James' knees buckled, and he dropped to the sand, crying in anguish over his aunt's demise.

James II continued his march along the shoreline. Confusion reigned – ship passengers, survivors, walked back and forth searching for lost loved ones. People with bleeding feet and torn clothes displayed faces beaten by wind and water and were filled with sorrow and void of hope. Fathers stooped over their children, crying in deep sorrow and despair. Husbands stumbled along the beach, searching for their wives. A few children, standing together and all alone, apparent orphans, cried for their mothers.

Further up the beach, James II spotted an aged man lying near the water. He approached what looked like a corpse, recognizing his father. He was soaking wet, covered in sand, lifeless. James raised his head and spoke to his father, breathing words of revival into him. There was no response as his father continued in a state of unconsciousness. He stayed with him for a time, beaten and tired, resting. James prayed to God, pleading with him to save his father. During his rest, he overheard people uttering painful sounds as they passed by. Some were passengers still arriving onshore, and others were crying, appealing to the heavens for assistance.

Two male passengers, one carrying a young woman in his outstretched arms, approached him. A young woman, limping, leaned on the shoulder of the other for support. He laid the young girl down on the sand next to James.

James looked at her face and exclaimed with joy, "My sister – my sister Rebecca – thank God it's Rebecca!"

"We found her clinging to a plank with her friend," one of the young men replied.

The girl, one of Rebecca's acquaintances from the voyage, relayed their plight, leaping from the ship, floating on the ocean, and getting bruised and wounded after colliding with the ship's timber. There was no sign of the McIntire's mother, sisters, brother, sister-in-law, or their young nephew. Other relatives and friends were nowhere in sight, most likely lost to the sea.

Afternoon advanced into evening, and the September sun began its descent in the western sky. Warm ocean breezes cooled as the setting sun cast a shadow over *Faithful Steward*, beaten to pieces, laying broadside upon the ocean. James II and Rebecca, left with no alternative, prepared for nightfall, lying beside their father, hoping he would regain consciousness. It was a very long night – one filled with pain – one filled with sorrow and gloom, and if one lacked the strength to continue, one filled with loss of hope, even despair.

34

Dawn, Sunday – September 3

Dawn arrived, and the sun sprung forth, separating clouds and spraying rays of blue, yellow, and pink across the sky. Warm, soft southerly breezes fanned the shoreline on a receding tide. Days before, many hoped to celebrate upon arriving in Pennsylvania. It was a day to be filled with hope for a new future. The impending festivities, now unwillingly cancelled due to a disaster, one caused by human error, and aided by Mother Nature. Today, wreck survivors possess hopelessness, with no motivation to continue the journey. Neptune continues to deposit bodies at the surf's edge. The last of the patriarchs, James McIntire I, lay unconscious, flanked by his son and daughter.

"Rebecca, I have to leave you and father momentarily. I must search for mother, for our sisters and the rest of the family." Rebecca, tired, hungry, and thirsty, nodded in agreement.

James turned southward, walking along the beach. *Faithful Steward*, mortally wounded by the surge from the recent storm, lay on her side, the hull filled with water and sand. He walked for a seemingly long time. The small body of a young child lay upon the sand near the water's edge. James stooped, then stared into the lifeless face of his nephew, and proceeded to let the remaining grief pour out from inside. None came forth – it had been spent – he looked upon his nephew, and thought of the life he would miss. Gathering him in his arms, James breathed in silent anguish, and exhaled deep sorrow. Turning away from the ocean, he carried him toward a line of sand-dunes many yards from the surf's edge. There he found a discarded board left from the wreckage, dug a hole, and buried his nephew in the sand.

Drained of what strength was within, he returned to Rebecca, hoping he would find his father conscious. Captain McCausland appeared to both of them. The momentary silence between the three presented an awkward moment.

"How is Mr. Stanfield?" inquired James.

"He didn't survive."

"What is the status of your crew?"

Captain McCausland appeared troubled and disturbed. "Mr. Gwyn has a broken leg and severe wounds – he could die. The remainder survived."

Their patriarch laid unconscious, presumed dead. James II glanced at Rebecca, willing to accept his father was gone, but Rebecca begged him to leave him rest, insisting her father would wake up. Determined to find their mother and sisters, he left for another march northward this time. During his second excursion, he diverted to assist others burying the dead. Passengers still strewn along the beach, bodies picked over, stripped of jewelry, pockets once filled with coins now emptied. The departing tide left more victims drowned and partially covered in sand.

James Lee III, his nephew Samuel Lee, and cousins James and Simon Elliott joined James II. One by one, they carried each body away from the surf toward the immense stretch of dunes. The Colhouns and Espeys assisted the Lees, Elliotts, and James II, digging a mass grave and pausing to pray over them. James counted thirty men, women, and children.

He turned to walk back to Rebecca, hoping to find his father had regained consciousness. James came upon a man carrying a familiar-looking chest. Stopping him, he could see the initials JM carved upon the lid.

"Who are you?" James indignantly inquired.

"Gordon," the startled man replied.

"You're holding my father's chest. Those initials – JM – belong to my father."

Gordon, unwilling to relinquish the chest, recoiled, "How do I know you have any right to this? I found it."

James described some of the contents he knew would be inside his father's chest. Gordon pried the lid open and found the contents accurately described, and he placed the box on the sand and walked away. James, dumfounded, continued his search for any remains of his family. During his absence, Gordon returned and took his father's chest and hid it.

Rebecca sat on the sand next to her father, holding his limp hand in hers, momentarily gazing out to *Faithful Steward* and beyond. Visibly shaken and absent of hope, she broke down in tears at the sight of her brother.

"Captain McCausland said father must be dead – you should bury him," as she broke down and cried.

James stood over his father, looked upon his face, paused, and looked heavenward. "Perhaps he's right – I'm going back to the dunes to search for a suitable place. It can't be any place – this is our father."

"No – you can't bury him – I refuse to believe he is dead – no, not now," Rebecca implored, staring at her brother.

"But Rebecca."

"I think he has a faint heartbeat – no – I said no!"

He acquiesced to his sister's demand. Perplexed and lacking any survival plan, he knelt by his father's side, looking for a glimmer of life, contemplating what to do next. Anxiety filled his exhausted mind as he thought to himself. My father is in the same deplorable condition as that ship. Without hope, I stand on this beach, the sea before me, the sky as my cover, without guidance, alone on a shore of a distant land.

Rebecca's wounds were too painful for her to walk. Her father, lying next to his daughter, awaited the inevitable. James turned, surveying up and down the shoreline. Many people – suffering – too many to receive the necessary attention lined the shore.

"There goes that man again," Rebecca declared. "The one you were speaking with not long ago."

James pursued him. "Mr. Gordon – Mr. Gordon!" He turned to face James.

"Mr. Gordon – my sister and father and I find ourselves in a deplorable state. We need assistance – help us."

"Look about you – there are many in the same predicament," he coldly replied.

"Mr. Gordon – I implore you to help us – we are in a destitute state." Mr. Gordon, unflinching, addressed the situation once more. "Storms are common – shipwrecks too. Do you think you are the first to wreck upon this shore? Sad as your miserable plight is, am I to offer assistance every time a ship is driven to shore?" He turned and walked away.

James, refusing to be denied, ran after him. "My father is dying – the three of us have been fasting for two and one-half days. I beg you this last time. Exercise Christian charity – help us! I have some coin to offer," he begged as he reached in his pocket, pulling out a few guineas.

Mr. Gordon peered sternly into James' eyes, reluctantly responding, "I'll bring my wagon down to your family."

Together they picked up his father and placed him in the back of the pine board wagon. They lifted Rebecca and put her next to him. Calling to his horses, Mr. Gordon transported the remnant of the McIntire family off the beach toward his farm. Upon leaving the surf's edge, James glanced at the horrific scene, relieved he was leaving that frightful experience. His mother, sisters, and brother, their whereabouts unknown, his young nephew, beneath the sand in a grave, conjured up emotions for which his senses could not process. Tired, drained, and without hope, he walked alongside the wagon to the farm.

Mr. Gordon spoke not a word. He was content to look at the back end of his Narragansetts.

"Do you farm, Mr. Gordon?"

"I do."

"Tell me about farming – what is the variety of crops planted in this region?"

Mr. Gordon's responses were to the point. "Wheat, corn, flax, tobacco."

"Flax is the primary crop grown where I came from," James interjected.

Mr. Gordon looked to his left and spit. "Hmm."

James, the inquisitor, wasn't about to give up. "How far is your farm?"

"Far."

"How far will I have to walk?"

The Narragansetts were stepping slowly, plodding along narrow bush strew paths. "Two hours."

With the sun rising high in the west, James knew he was walking north. "Where is your farm, Mr. Gordon?"

Mr. Gordon spit again, "Up the road – Lewestown, Rehoboth Hundred."

James understood counties, townlands, baronies, and parishes, but lacked understanding of his address. "We spoke of Lewestown on the ship – what is a hundred?"

"We have ten of them."

"Ten – ten what?"

Mr. Gordon, for the first time, spoke briefly. "You are walking in one of the hundreds in Sussex County. There are ten subdivisions – they are hundreds – been that way for a hundred years. We estimate one hundred people live in an area divided by the creeks and nearby lands."

"Your description of where you live is different – certainly different, Mr. Gordon. I can tell you how land is divided where we came from."

Mr. Gordon spit again and sighed, "Hmm." James decided it was useless to continue.

Miles later, the McIntires arrived at Mr. Gordon's small farm. During the trip, their father displayed periodic signs of life. Rebecca beckoned to her brother, hoped had returned – the patriarch or their family was alive.

Mrs. Gordon, the opposite of her husband, prepared food and provided their guests' refreshments, attempting to nourish them to restore their health. She consented for the McIntires to stay with them for a brief respite.

On Sunday morning, September 4, James I regained consciousness. Rebecca and James explained the reason for the cause of the disaster. Their father was unable to recall any particulars of the shipwreck, and he lacked any knowledge of the death of his wife.

"Father – listen, please. James was unable to find mother," Rebecca repeated softly.

He stared at her, puzzled and confused, for the moment unable to comprehend her statement.

"Father – James made many marches along the shoreline. She's gone, father – dear mother didn't survive," Rebecca repeated.

Her father shook his head in disbelief. "No – no, that can't be. Your mother is alive; I heard her at the shoreline calling my name."

James attempted to convince his father of their unfortunate situation, however, he refused to accept the facts. He insisted they must return to the coast, locate their mother, assist anyone in need, and return within a reasonable time. They left their father in Mrs. Gordon's care and departed for the coast, on foot, by themselves. Strengthened, Rebecca was able to walk the distance they measured to be near nine miles to the site. The picture of the wreckage lodged in their mind was as they left it days before. *Faithful Steward* remained in the same position, leaning toward shore. A few personal remnants, letters, small articles of clothing, possessions owned by the passengers washed ashore. Particles of the ship, boards, and debris were scattered about. Fresh mounds of sand far from the ocean's edge covered those who perished.

Rebecca surveyed the dunes recalling her father's plight, and turned toward her brother. "James – what if – what if someone buried mother alive? The captain thought our father was dead," she whimpered.

James, mentally exhausted, looked at his sister. "Do not say that – do not repeat that, Rebecca. God forbid our mother met that fate." James responded forcefully. "I made many marches up and down the beach. I looked, I hoped, I prayed. I couldn't find her, Rebecca. I never saw her. I never saw our brother, brother-in-law, nor could I find our sisters." Emotion once again poured forth. "We must return to the Gordons, break the news to father, and make plans to find Robert in Pennsylvania."

The single surviving patriarch woke from his rest when his children opened the door to the room. The look on their faces was enough for him to acquiesce, to accept reality. His lifelong friend would not be by his side again. She would never see Pennsylvania with her beloved family. His son and his daughter watched and listened as their father broke down in spirit. He emitted a guttural sound, a sound from deep within, a sound beyond groaning. Comfort for the moment was impossible for a husband and father in deep, wretched, emotional pain.

35

Lewestown

On Monday morning, Mr. Gordon hitched the horses to the wagon. James, Rebecca, and their father boarded the wagon for the ride to Lewestown. Settled by the Dutch in the early 1600s, Lewestown was located close to the mouth of the Delaware Bay, the portal to New Castle and Philadelphia.

Other survivors from the shipwreck arrived at the small town. Schooners sailed routine trips up the Delaware bay and river to New Castle and Philadelphia. A Church of England, now an Episcopal congregation established in 1681, and a Presbyterian Church, stood nearby the courthouse. Hopefully, they would provide relief for the sufferers until they could regain strength, or get help from relatives and friends awaiting their arrival at Stamper's Wharf.

Mr. Gordon flicked the leather reins and clucked twice. Two old Narragansett Pacers locked in step down the dirt-packed sandy trail. Upon leaving his farm, they turned onto a hard-packed sand and dirt road, heading toward Lewestown. Gone were their possessions. Wreckers, scavengers, and the ocean claimed their chests containing the linens and supplies for the start of a mercantile exchange. What remained was the few guineas in their pockets and no other valuables but the clothes they wore. Mr. Gordon removed their father's chest from underneath the buckboard seat and put it in his barn. They passed narrow creeks, small tributaries leading into Rehoboth Bay, low lying trees, pines, and various bushes and brush, including the sassafras and wild berries. Their new destination was a brief ride up the road.

James, anxious to relocate his father and Rebecca to Lewistown, had no affection for Mr. Gordon. His wife was nervous, had little to say but did offer meals and rest. Her husband was annoying, seemed aloof, and intimated their unfortunate circumstance disrupted his life.

∞

More than one hundred years before, Lewestown was known for

whaling and a trading village, the first settlement in the colony of Delaware. The area was frequented by many a sailor, navigating the coastline entering the Delaware Bay, or seeking shelter nearby the Delaware Capes, escaping a coastal storm.

As time passed coastal Delaware inhabitants became emboldened, and involved in hostile actions. King James II ordered a fleet sent to enforce laws. In 1687, William Penn received a letter from the king complaining of free looters. Two years later, a sloop with fifty men, brandishing arms, sacked and stole from nearly every home in Lewestown. Born in Scotland and an avowed privateer, William Kidd visited Delaware and foraged and attacked the colonists, including those near Lewestown. These actions forced William Penn to call a meeting of the assembly to take protective action.

Years followed, and Thomas Fisher, a wealthy merchant together with his wife Margery, settled in Lewestown. Thomas was a son to John and Margaret Fisher from Clitheroe, Lancashire, England. Colonel David Hall, a lawyer, and former soldier and now judge, occupied a home nearby. Colonel Hall fought alongside General Washington, commanding the Delaware Line. Despite the ties of Colonel Hall to the revolution, many of the residents sided with the Tories.

Three years prior, in the early evening of December 20, the residents of Lewestown stood outside, listening to the cannon fire from the Battle of the Delaware Capes. The HMS *Diomede*, the HMS *Quebec*, and the HMS *Astrea*, all frigates, patrolled and ran a blockade of the Delaware Bay in the Cape May Channel. Captain Benjamin Broadhurst, a privateer with the American schooner, *Seagrove*, armed with six guns, was informed of the blockade. Captain Broadhurst joined a convoy for protection, led by Captain John Joyner of the South Carolina Navy, commanding the forty-gun frigate, *South Carolina*. His vessel was one of the most heavily armed colonial vessels at the time. The ten-gun brig *Hope*, commanded by John Prole, a privateer, and the brig *Constance*, Commander Jesse Harding, joined the *South Carolina* for protection.

The British spotted the American convoy, attempting to run through the blockage on the Lewestown side of the bay. Three British frigates gave chase, and a battle ensued over the next eighteen hours. Captain Joyner of the *South Carolina*, realized his frigate was outmaneuvered and outgunned, so he struck the colors and lowered his flag, indicating surrender. The 466-member crew of *South Carolina* suffered six killed and eight wounded. The *Hope*, crew of forty-two, and the *Constance*, with a crew of thirty, joined in the surrender.

Captain Broadhurst, together with his crew of the *Seagrove*, escaped while the battle raged.

∞

Mr. Gordon's pacers pulled his wagon past the Ryves Holt House at Second and Mulberry Streets, an inn suitable for travelers. The McIntires watched as townspeople entered the inn as they passed by, continuing to the courthouse steps. There they inquired of local assistance and to determine when they could board a schooner for New Castle. James I, tired and worn out, was assisted off the wagon by his son. Together the three of them bade farewell to Mr. Gordon, thanking him for the assistance extended by him and his wife. James was relieved to watch the buckboard disappear around the corner.

Other survivors occupied the courthouse. All available space at the churches was taken, so they would have to make themselves comfortable in this building during their short stay. Sleeping on a blanket on the wooden floor was an improvement, compared to the wooden berth in the emigrant's deck of *Faithful Steward*. The motion from the never-ending pitch and roll of the ship ceased. The constant beating of waves against the hull causing instability, and the tossing of objects to and fro stopped. And the memory of sickness and occasional vomiting from sea-sickness was gone.

Gustavus and Thomas Colhoun were among the early arrivals, boarding a schooner at Lewes Creek, sailing to the Broadkill River and the Delaware Bay, bound for Philadelphia. Their meeting with Mr. Girard would be uncomfortable, ending in obvious disappointment. A carefully planned and orchestrated mission as supercargoes had failed. Many barrels of coppers settled in the damaged hull of the ship, underneath the Atlantic. Captain McCausland and a remnant of the crew slipped away to Philadelphia.

Other survivors made their way to the dock to secure a schooner for transport to Philadelphia. The McIntires planned to sail to New Castle, and from there, walk to the Great Wagon Road and turn west, the distance near fifty miles to Lancaster, rest for a while, and locate Robert at Maytown near the Susquehanna River.

James secured passage on a schooner bound for New Castle. An anonymous benefactor paid the entire fare for his family. On his return to the courthouse, he noticed a man walking along the street, wearing a vest he was sure belonged to his drowned brother-in-law. He picked up his pace, caught up with the man, and confronted him.

"The vest you are wearing – this is not your vest – how did you get this vest?"

"Beg your pardon – this is my vest."

James raised his voice indignantly and quickly. "That vest is not yours – it belongs to a member of my family."

The man, unwilling to surrender the vest, stepped around him.

"Move aside; you are mistaken."

"This is not your vest – relinquish it now," James demanded.

Voices elevated, and an argument ensued. James grabbed at the vest to tear it off his back, but he refused to give it up. Their fists clenched and they exchanged punches. James ducked but caught one glancing off his left shoulder. He countered with a right and caught the man squarely on his left jaw, sending him reeling backward. Two men standing nearby approached the two, yelling to break it up.

"Men – please – lower your voices. What is the cause of your argument?" the Justice of the Peace snapped.

James straightened his shirt and dusted his trousers. "This man possesses a vest taken from my brother-in-law."

"Why is he not here to claim his vest?" the justice responded.

"Because he is dead, drowned, all of them, they're gone."

James launched into an explanation. "Eight of my sisters were passengers, victims of a shipwreck several days ago. My brother-in-law and nephew drowned. I lost my mother and all of my sisters, save one, Rebecca. She, my father, and I are the only survivors. He has my brother-in-law's vest," James cried with emotion.

They followed the Justice of the Peace to his office. James was placed under oath and asked questions attesting to his claim. After the conclusion of the inquiry, the man surrendered the article of clothing as ordered. James left the justice's office, vest in hand, and walked a short distance down Second Street, past the Rodney residence, entering the courthouse to break the news.

The following morning the three McIntires would meet others at the dock and board the schooner to New Castle. During his absence, women from the Episcopal Church delivered biscuits and hardtack, a mixture of flour, water, and salt, and poured mugs of coffee for the survivors.

36

The Courthouse

Two men entered the building, paused, and surveyed the group of survivors hovering around the oak table filled with biscuits and drinks. James recognized the Justice of the Peace. The younger of the two walked with a limp as they approached the McIntire family.

"Mr. McIntire," the justice spoke, looking at James II.

"Yes – thank you again, sir – for returning my brother-in-law's vest."

The justice nodded, "My apologies for your inconvenience given the dreadfulness of the shipwreck and your current state of affairs."

James surveyed the younger of the two. His face was weathered and worn, making him appear older than his current age of thirty-three. James' father and Rebecca sat motionless, looking at the younger one. His appearance portrayed a rugged man, educated, possessing character chiseled from the trials acquired through facing adversity.

"This is my father, James McIntire I, and my sister Rebecca."

"May we sit," the justice asked.

James nodded. "Certainly – what is your business?"

The younger man spoke first, "Your welfare and that of your family."

James assumed the role of spokesman for the family, his father physically and emotionally drained. "My father lost his wife – his love – his companion of many years. My sister and I lost our mother – I buried my young nephew in a sandy grave. All of our sisters are gone. One of our brothers and our brother-in-law is dead. This is our unfortunate plight. How does one repair our welfare?"

Rebecca, shaking, broke down and began to cry. James placed his arm on his sister's shoulder.

"We never recovered the remains of our family, nor could we find our friends from the ship." James sighed, taking a deep breath and a long pause.

Each of the men sat in respectful silence. James continued to lament. "I found my little nephew washed ashore – his smile absent, his youth gone. I dug a grave far back from the surf's edge and buried him."

"What was the name of your sail ship?" The younger one sought to divert the subject from the topic of family.

"*Faithful Steward* – we weighed anchor on the ninth of July last – left the port of Londonderry."

"Do you know the passenger count?"

"There were many – 249 by some report."

The younger one continued with another question. "Any update on the captain and his crew?"

"He survived in good condition. His crew numbered twelve – the first mate was badly injured. He made it to shore – he died since."

The younger pressed forward, gently, "How many passengers survived?"

"We don't know – perhaps fifty, maybe more. I heard estimates – not enough." James exhaled with another sigh.

The younger one examined James's father. "You people have endured much loss and suffered an insurmountable amount of pain."

James replied in anguish, "The night of the wreck was horrifying – the scenes of panic, maddening. Multitudes of people washed ashore. My father was a robust man when we left Ireland. He has been silent since the wreck, speaking little after our mother's death."

"Of course – both of us are very sorry for your loss. We will endeavor to remember with utmost compassion what we are witnessing at this moment." He turned to look at Rebecca, evaluating the impact of emotional damage inflicted upon the young lady. "Do you have family here?"

Rebecca responded, "Our cousin Robert lives near Lancaster. Our next journey is to Pennsylvania – he farms near Maytown, not far from the Susquehanna River."

"I know the territory – good fertile soil, prime farmland."

James inquired, "You mentioned our welfare – what is your concern? My father, sister, and I have been at sea for over fifty days. Several days before, my father was considered dead. Captain McCausland advised us to bury him."

The Justice of the Peace intervened, "I cannot find the words to convey how I feel about your harrowing experience."

James' body ached, he was in pain, and he was emotionally numb.

"Onboard the ship, we shared many stories – stories received from family and friends who left years before us. They told us about life in Pennsylvania. What will we find at Lancaster?"

The younger man paused for a moment. "Rolling farmland – fertile soil – farmers with families, immigrants like you, all of them embracing an opportunity. Many of them came from Germany – Lutherans, Amish, and Mennonites, people looking for religious freedom and seeking an opportunity to own land." The younger man glanced toward their father. "There are people of Scots-Irish descent who settled there as well. They establish Presbyterian churches in a line from the Octorara Creek west to the Susquehanna River and beyond."

The Justice of the Peace interrupted. "You spoke of stories on board the ship – what kind of stories?"

"The men loved to talk about the revolution," Rebecca responded. "They spoke of men – many names – people who left Ireland, and they told stories of these people. They called them patriots. After a while, I realized they were the revolution. The Espey family, for instance, has a son who joined the Pennsylvania Militia."

"Can you describe what they said?"

"They spoke of people who envisioned a new future – a land with opportunity free of persecution, one where the people elected government representatives. These men were brave – brave leaders." Rebecca paused and began to cry again. "My brother believed we were coming to a land where heroes live." Rebecca's passion visibly moved the younger man.

"And now you have reason to doubt those stories heard on your passage?"

There was silence – no one spoke. Other survivors sat nearby in the corner of the courthouse, listening.

"I believe in General Washington," Rebecca, breaking the silence offered.

The younger one commented gently. "You picked a fine example, Rebecca."

"You know him?" Rebecca inquired, lifting her head.

"Yes – I do – I was privileged to serve under his command."

James, surprised, broke into the conversation. "You were in his Continental Army?"

"I led a regiment from Delaware."

The justice broke into the conversation. "My son is Colonel David Hall."

"Your son – tell us more," their father begged.

Colonel Hall began. "We fought together in the Battle of Germantown, October of 1777." Colonel Hall paused, looking at James II.

"Anyone involved will remember the battle for as long as they live."

James returned to the days when he engrossed himself in stories of the revolution. One of the heroes was standing before him. "Colonel Hall, why will they remember this battle?"

"James – it was a bayonet charge – fought close and ugly. You could see the eyes of the British soldiers. I've got a wound and a limp to prove I was there. My regiment – a band of brave men was known as the Delaware Line."

"What happened after the battle?" Rebecca wanted to know.

"The British inflicted wounds on our army at Germantown. General Washington ordered a withdrawal to regather. We moved our troops next to the bank of the Perkiomen Creek nearby Schwenksville, Pennsylvania; buried our dead in a mass grave nearby Skippack Pike, and then marched to winter with General Washington at Valley Forge."

Rebecca, fascinated with his story, stopped crying. "Is it true he rode upon a white horse?"

Colonel Hall grinned. "Blueskin was a fine horse – a bit nervous in battle – but despite his name, you would be correct to say his coat was white. He was a gift to General Washington – half-Arabian – but as a colt, his coat was blue-gray in appearance. When these horses mature, their color can turn white."

Colonel Hall stood. "I must take leave, but before I do, we need to address your welfare."

"You already have," Rebecca implied.

Colonel Hall responded with a nod of his head. "When do you leave for New Castle?"

"Tomorrow."

"When you get settled at Maytown, write a letter. Reference your shipwreck and *Faithful Steward*. Be specific; describe your plight."

Rebecca questioned, "And to whom should we address this letter?"

"To – The Society of the Friendly Sons of Saint Patrick – Philadelphia, attention John Maxwell Nesbitt," offered the colonel.

"He is a Scots-Irish merchant – a partner in the firm arranging everyone's passage – we have heard of his name," their father mentioned.

"And what is the purpose for our letter?"

"He will arrange for you and your family to receive a sum – a contribution to assist with becoming established now that you are here."

The McIntires couldn't hide the surprise from their faces.

"The Society of the Friendly Sons of Saint Patrick," James muttered audibly. "I remember details of the organization from our talks around the long table."

Rebecca inquisitively asked, "Who are these people?"

Colonel Hall turned to address Rebecca. "Merchants – shipowners and shipbuilders – craftsmen and artisans – people of commerce – many are former militia – others joined our navies – citizens of Pennsylvania, Delaware, and beyond. They are the heroes, the valiant ones – they are the bold and fearless Scots-Irish. They are the people your friends on the *Faithful Steward* spoke of during your passage." Colonel Hall paused, looking into the eyes of each of the McIntires, and softly responded, "they are you!"

EPILOGUE
Part I

The Lees
Philadelphia
1846

"Are you certain he is staying at this establishment?" inquired the silver-haired distinguished-looking gentleman.

"I am sir – registered him myself yesterday – the same name as yours. I will take a written oath validating this truth, sir."

His guest grinned and responded, "Your word is good enough."

He turned, glanced around the lobby, and looked once again at the desk clerk. "Describe him, please."

"Certainly, sir – look for a young man wearing a uniform. He is dressed as a captain – the United States Army."

That Evening

(Judge) Robert Lee, visiting from Ohio, exited the lobby into the dining area of the hotel. Surveying the room, he noticed one man sitting at a table by himself. His military uniform was neatly pressed, he presented a striking picture, one worth an artist painting.

"Captain, may I introduce myself? You are Robert Lee?"

"Yes sir, you may. And yes, I am Robert Edward Lee. And who would you be, sir?"

"Robert Lee…Judge Robert Lee, from Bucyrus, Crawford County, Ohio."

Captain Lee, surprised, extended his right hand to greet the judge. "This is an honor … please sit."

Judge Lee pulled an oak chair from beneath the table. Introductions dispensed, each began to query the other, exploring their backgrounds and the possibilities, if any, explaining their common names.

Captain Lee, born at Stratford Hall, Virginia in 1807, was thirty-nine years of age. His schooling at the United States Military Academy was completed in 1829; Lee fulfilled multiple duties in the Army Corps of

Engineers, supervising and inspecting the construction of the nation's coastal defenses.

"Captain Lee – your father – who was he?"

"His name was Henry Lee ... began life as a military man. A Virginian, his counterparts referred to him as "Light-Horse Harry" ... Henry, (Light-Horse Harry) Lee III. And he was a menace to the British Army. His rank during the American Revolutionary War was Lieutenant Colonel, Continental Army. And he signed the Declaration of Independence."

Judge Lee, puzzled and excited, began to think about any commonality the two Lees may share. "My father's name was Robert."

Captain Lee drew a sip from a pewter mug. "And was he born and raised in Ohio?"

"Yes ... but before that, my family came from Ireland many years ago."

Captain Lee inquired, "How many years ago – and where in Ireland?"

Judge Lee paused, pondering the answer to the captain's question. "This would be a story my grandfather should tell – if he were alive. I'll tell you what I remember. He came from a large family – there were forty-eight, and many decided to leave Ireland."

"What happened?"

"A shipwreck – the year was 1785, sixty-one years ago in Delaware. The captain and his mates thought they should be near the mouth to the Delaware Bay. It was late at night."

Captain Lee, surprised, announced, "The shipwreck of *Faithful Steward.*"

"How ... by what means could you learn of that name?" The judge echoed in surprise.

"Details of the people and the shipwreck were passed down through my father's lineage," the captain reflected. "At one time, there could have been a storyteller."

"A storyteller," Judge Lee repeated. "Tell me more."

"Hundreds of years ago, people were unable to read and write, yet they possessed an intellect and desired to record history, their history." Judge Lee focused on every word. "Someone in the family would memorize family history, genealogy, and important events. And they would repeat these details through rhyme or song. And thus, the storyteller was born."

Judge Lee listened, reflecting upon each word in the captain's narrative.

252

"My suspicion is there was a storyteller somewhere in your lineage."

Judge Lee appeared distant to the captain, his mind drifting far away to a time when he was a young boy. "I remember something."

"What do you remember?"

Judge Lee began. "My grandfather, Thomas Lee, spoke of his family. Arriving dockside in Londonderry, they discovered *Faithful Steward* filled. An agent boarded his family nearby, and they secured passage on another ship, only a few days after the departure of *Faithful Steward*."

"What else – is there more?"

"I was a young boy. One day my father was visited by a man – his identity to this day I cannot recollect. Some of my family gathered around. He survived the shipwreck, and he knew the Lees."

"Very interesting," Captain Lee hoped there would be more.

"He told us his story – there were three men, unrelated to the Lees. The tide was changing to an in-going tide. Each of them stripped themselves of their clothes and placed a few guineas in their mouth. And they swam to shore. The man visiting my father was one of the three."

"What else did he describe?"

"Our guest spoke of his feelings after swimming to shore safely; he was in a distant land presumed to be America. Alone, he was naked, devoid of friends, in an unknown land. I remember a crying scene among my family as he described what happened."

It proved to be a fascinating evening – Captain Lee was immersed in the judge's narrative of family stories. And Judge Lee's memory was stimulated by the suggestion of a storyteller.

"Is there more detail about your grandfather?"

"He was born into a large family, and they leased many acres in County Donegal. It was a wild area with many mountains, plenty of lakes and rivers, and some land suitable for farming. He had a brother, Hugh, a sister, Isabella, named after her mother, and another brother, James II, and a sister, Mary."

Captain Lee paused, knowing the subject of his next question.

"Yes, of course," exclaimed the judge. "It was Mary – I never realized until now – Mary was the storyteller, but by then, her family could read and write very well."

Captain Lee, a sociable individual, smiled. "Your father's sister – you think she's the one."

"I think so – my grandfather referred to her as the Irish beauty. Mary was dark-haired and blue-eyed, a young woman with striking attractiveness. Grandfather described her as a gifted person with a beautiful voice – she could sing eloquently. Grandfather remembered her as a woman of accomplishment. And she recited family genealogy."

"What else can you remember about your story, Judge Lee?"

"I think," he continued, "James Lee I and Isabella (Boscawen) Lee, my grandfather's parents, years before left England for Donegal." Judge Lee looked at the captain, adding, "Some of the Lees lived in Cornwall."

Captain Lee interjected, "Judge Lee, we are descended from a distant but related greater family of Lees."

The captain, a storyteller, recalled his narrative of the genealogy of his side of the Lee family. The judge listened intently, learning of a people impacted by war, revolution, and other disturbances, causing a branch of them to leave England for Ireland. Over the years some of their descendants migrated to the United States, at the time British America.

Captain Lee concluded, "All descended from a common ancestry."

With the hour late, Captain Lee stood and pushed his chair away from the table. "I must take leave, Judge Lee – tomorrow I depart from Philadelphia."

"You have a new assignment, captain?"

"Yes, sir – the Mexican War awaits – many troops are gathering. My order is to join General Winfield Scott as an aide. My suspicion is an amphibious assault will occur along coastal Mexico."

*In 1885, Judge Robert Lee wrote a letter to his nephew, Homer Lee, an engraver who fifteen years before left Bucyrus, seeking work in Philadelphia. In his letter, the judge recounted the day he met Robert E. Lee. Coincidentally, the judge's letter was received by his nephew on the 100th anniversary following the shipwreck of *Faithful Steward*.

Part II

The McIntire Farm
East Fallowfield
Crawford County, Pennsylvania
October 15, 1880

He was nearly six-feet-tall, built of a stocky, muscular frame, and his dark wavy hair, gray around the temples, was brushed back over the top of his head. A black coat covered a waistcoat and a neatly pressed white shirt. His mustache, neatly trimmed, met his beard at each corner of the mouth and flowed downward, far enough to hide most of a neatly tied black bowtie.

Robert A. McIntyre, son of James Dickson McIntire, now sixty years of age, strode to take his place before a crowd numbering near 300 attendees at the McIntyre – Mason family reunion. With the day's events near an end, the sun descended over the western sky. Everyone watched as Robert stood still, reaching into his breast pocket for pieces of paper. He had but one final responsibility – to read his grandfather's (James McIntire II) account of the shipwreck of *Faithful Steward*.

Four years prior, Robert, named after his grandfather's older brother, journeyed by horseback a distance near four hundred miles to the Indian River Inlet in Delaware. Overcome with indescribable emotion, Robert was the first McIntire ancestor to visit the site of the wreck of *Faithful Steward*, one hundred and one years following that fateful day when his grandfather, James II, together with Rebecca, walked a great distance to locate the remains of their mother.

As the crowd became silent, Robert cleared his throat, drew in a deep breath, and began. No one could have recognized the fact that his voice – the pitch and quality and tone, mirrored that of his grandfather, James II.

"In an early day, as old settlers would say, when all around where we are now so comfortably situated, was one vast unbroken wilderness. The wild and savage beast, disturbed in his lair, only by the scarcely less wild and savage Indian, a family from Ireland by the name of McIntyre, originally from Scotland, came to Pennsylvania. They were lured by the glowing accounts that reached them from across the briny deep from time to time. The land was described as a land of liberty. A land where the wicked landlord ceased from

255

troubling, and the weary tenant might till his soil, and rest and worship under his vine and fig tree. A land where no one dared to molest him by demanding the lion's share of the proceeds of his toil; or make him afraid by tearing down his humble cot from over the heads of his defenseless wife and little ones. All of this if his crops failed, causing him to default in meeting his rent bills. The McIntires gathered together their earthly stores and embarked for America."

Robert paused and lifted his head, perusing a sea of relatives, fixated on each spoken word.

"This they did," he continued, "However, not without fearful forebodings of impending evil. One of the survivors, James McIntire II, whose blood courses in the veins of children, grandchildren, great and great-great-grandchildren, now within the sound of my voice, was interviewed by Rev. McMichael regarding this disaster. Nearly fifty years ago, Andrew Jackson was serving his first term as President of the United States. The year of the account of the wreck was 1831, my grandfather was sixty-eight years old, and I was eleven. The paper is so demoralized and tender – with your permission I will read it."

Robert proceeded to read the entirety of his grandfather's account of the shipwreck of the *Faithful Steward*. During his reading he would pause, take a breath, and lift his head to determine if his relatives were engaged. The words of his grandfather's account were near 5,000 – and his usage of words to describe what happened, and how he, his family, and what the rest of the passengers and crew experienced left his relatives speechless. They watched, they listened, some bowed their heads in their hands – women wept.

Robert choked back a few tears of his own after finishing his reading of his grandfather's account of the shipwreck.

"I remember grandfather well and might mention some personal reminiscences that would be interesting to the younger branches of the family tree. Allow me to remind you that from this one man, James McIntire, has issued an offspring now counted by the hundred – nearly three hundred all told. They are a plain-spoken people and few, if any of them, can consistently be charged with ever having kissed the blarney stone. Whatever may be said of them individually or collectively, no one can name a single case of marital desertion, divorce, suicide, or a felon's cell or drunkard's grave, filled by one who had a drop of this our ancestor's blood in his veins. And now, let me on this most fitting occasion, suggest we each, here and now firmly resolve, if we can do nothing to brighten, that we will at least do nothing to tarnish the

McIntire escutcheon; so that it always, as truthfully as now, can be said, there is not a drunkard, a gambler or a felon among them all."

*The McIntire prologue was prepared using a combination of the author's thoughts and words and the actual words recorded and extracted from the personal account of James McIntire II, either paraphrased or quoted verbatim, of the shipwreck published in the Meadville Courier 1881.

HISTORICAL EXTRACTS

The L:Derry Journal, Tuesday 15 November 1785

The following account was published on page 4 column 2
[This news had reached Derry after passage of 5 weeks from Philadelphia in the papers brought by the ship Friendship, Captain Miller]

LONDONDERRY: From American papers: Philadelphia, September 14

A brief account of the unfortunate Disaster which befel the Ship Faithful Steward, Connolly McCausland, Master, from Londonderry, bound to the Port; taken from a Gentleman who was Passenger on board:

ON the 9th day July last, said vessel sailed from Londonderry, having on board 249 passengers of respectability who had with them property to a very considerable amount. They had a favourable passage during which nothing of moment occurred, the greatest harmony having prevailed among them until the night of Thursday the 1st instant, September, when at the hour of 10 o'clock it was thought advisable to try for soundings, and to their surprise they found themselves in 4 fathoms water, though at dark there was not the smallest appearance of land. The consternation and astonishment which then prevailed are easier conceived than described: every exertion was used to run the vessel offshore, but in a few minutes, she struck the ground, when it was found necessary to cut away her masts, etc. all of which went overboard. On the morning of the 2nd, they found themselves on *Mohoboa Bank near Indian River, about 4 leagues to the southward of Cape Henlopen. Every effort was made to save the unhappy sufferers who remained on the wreck during the night, although distant from the shore only about 100 yards. That evening she beat to pieces. With the sea running extremely high, the long-boats were disengaged from the deck, but before they could be manned, they drifted ashore: therefore, all relief was cut off except by swimming or getting ashore on pieces of the wreck, and we are sorry to add, that of the above, only 68 persons were saved, among whom were the master, his mates and 10 seamen. During the course of the day the inhabitants came down to the beach in numbers and used every means in their power to relieve the unfortunate people on board, among whom were about 100 women and children, only 7 women were saved. Several persons who escaped from the wreck are since dead from the wounds they received, and others are miserably bruised.

With great pleasure we learn that several humane and public-spirited gentlemen of this city are about raising a subscription for the relief of the unhappy people who were saved from the wreck of the above vessel; and there can be no doubt of their meeting with great success from the benevolent inhabitants, who have never been backward in affording assistance to the distressed.

On page 4 column 4 it was further stated:

By the papers brought by The Friendship, we have likewise the melancholy account of the loss of the ship Faithful Steward near the mouth of the Delaware. The citizens of Philadelphia generously exerted themselves in succoring the survivors and raised about £1000 for their relief.

A list of the survivors from the wreck of the ship Faithful Steward lost near the mouth of the Delaware was published in the Pennsylvania Packet on January 4, 1786 and in the Londonderry Journal, February 21, 1786.

*Mohoboa is not derived from the Scottish or Irish Gaelic language and it is not a word found in the Lenape language, therefore, the source of the word remains unknown.

The Times
Philadelphia, Pennsylvania
Sunday, December 6, 1885 – p.6

THE FAITHFUL STEWARD
General Robert E. Lee's Ancestors,
With a Strange Tale of Shipwreck

New York, December 5

Homer Lee is a tall young man with black burnside whiskers and a genial face. Persons meeting him usually express wonder at finding him so youthful. He came here from Ohio about fifteen years ago as an engraver. His success has been due to hard work. The Lee families of the country are all allied more or less closely with the Lees of Virginia. Homer Lee, who has a taste for the accumulation of odd and curious antiquities, showed me a few days ago a letter written to him by his uncle, the result of, which on its reception by him was to bring to light a long-hidden chapter in the history of the Lees.

I quote from the letter, which is signed by (Judge) Robert Lee (of Bucyrus, Ohio). It contains a glimpse of the Confederate leader which is interesting: "I met General Robert E. Lee in Philadelphia at the outbreak of the Mexican War. He was a young officer. I found him a very pleasant and intelligent gentleman, who had the genealogy of the Lee family to a marked degree. He said that during the wars or some of the revolutions in England a portion of the Lee family left England and settled in Ireland, and that many of their descendants, both from England and Ireland, emigrated to this country, but all were descendants of an original ancestry.

His narrative was very interesting but has nearly faded from my recollection. He told me of the loss of the *Faithful Steward*, which I also heard from my grandfather. A large number of the family engaged passage to this country on said ship; among the number was my grandfather, Thomas Lee, with his family. When they arrived at port the ship was crowded and they could not get passage and were compelled to wait for the next ship that sailed for Philadelphia. The Faithful Steward was a new ship, insured for more than its real value. Somewhere in the bay the captain ran the ship upon a rock and wrecked her to pieces. The passengers, alarmed, pleaded with the captain to shun the rock, but he swore he would drive the ship through or sink her to hell, and such was the terrible result. The captain, his officers and sailors

261

manned their boats, left for shore and left the passengers to perish. Among the number lost were forty-eight of the Lee family, uncles and aunts and cousins of my father, Robert Lee, and among that number was one young lady of wonderful beauty and accomplishments, called the Irish beauty. Many of the passengers secured pieces of the wreck and hoped to reach the shore but were carried out by the tide and lost."

The narrative is continued in the letter as follows: "Three men (not of the Lee family) held on to the wreck until the going-in tide. Then each put two or three guineas in their mouths and swam to shore. One of these men visited my father when I was a small boy and gave an account of the whole scene and how he felt after reaching the shore in a strange land, without friends and entirely nude, and there was a general crying scene in the family during the narrative. A few days after the loss of the *Faithful Steward* the ship which brought grandfather and family to this country arrived in port. When they heard of the loss of their friends, grandfather armed himself and hunted some days for the captain to kill him, which he would have done had he found him, for he was a spirited Irishman, but the captain had fled from the country. The ship was new and heavily insured."

The reception of this letter incited Homer Lee to make inquiries in England as to the record of *Faithful Steward*. He wrote to Sir Thomas Farrar, who caused an investigation of the old books and documents of the Public Records Office. These three memoranda were all that could be found in Lloyd's list and are extracts from the dates named:

"April 12, 1785, - Londonderry. Arrived, from Rhode Island, Faithful Stuart (sic) McCausland."

"August 30, 1785, - Captain Castle, of The Ashley, arrived in the river from Jamaica. On the first inst. spoke The Faithful Steward, McCausland, from Londonderry to Philadelphia, in Lat. 44 N. Long. About 36 W. All well."

"November 28, 1785. – The Faithful Steward, McCausland, from Londonderry to Philadelphia, is totally lost in the Delaware and 200 people drowned."

It was a curious coincidence that just one hundred years from the date of this last fatal record Mr. Lee should yesterday become possessed of it and exhibit it to me with his uncle's letter.

The Pennsylvania Packet
January 4, 1786
FAITHFUL STEWARD
Survivors List
(With Modifications Noted Based Upon the Author's Research)

Crew

Connolly McCausland
Stanfield, Mr.
Gwyn, Mr.
Linn, William
Irwin, Samuel
Quigly, John
Mourn, Patrick
McCaffrey, Edward
Brown, John
Dalrymple, William
Kelley, Robert
Hudson, Pelig
Phillips, Owen

Total Surviving Crew – 13

Passengers – Cabin

Blair, Thomas
Colhoun, Gustavus (1)
Colhoun, Thomas (1)
Dougherty, James
Hepburn, Samuel
Hepburn, John (son)
Laurence, Robert
Marshall, James
McCallister, John
O'Neill, John
York, John

Total Surviving Cabin Passengers - 11

Passengers – Steerage (Emigrant's Deck)

Aspill, James (1) (2)
Aspill, John (1) (2)
Baskin, Thomas
Beaty, James
Brocket, John
Burns, Mary (3)
Caldwell, Matthew
Campbell, Sarah (3)
Davis, John
Devin, James
Din(s)more, Robert
Elliott, James (2)
Elliott, Simon (2)
Higginbottom, Arthur
Kincade, Margaret (3)
Lee, James III
Lee, (sister-in-law) to James III
Lee, Mary (sister-in-law) to James III
Lee, Samuel (4)
Maginnis, Mary (3)
McClintock, William
McClean, Hugh
McDougal, James Dr.
McIllheney, John
McIntire, James I
McIntire, James II
McIntire, Rebecca (daughter)
McKinnon, Neal
McKinnon, Sarah (3)
McManes, Matthew
McMullen, John
McNab, John
McWilliams, Charles
Moore, Alexander
Moore, Samuel
Moore, Thomas
Munro, George
Ranolles, Thomas
Richford, George
Scott, John
Shaw, John

Smyth, James
Spires, John
Stankard, James
Watt, Andrew
Watt, James
Wright, Samuel

Total Surviving Passengers in steerage – 47

Merchants
John Maxwell Nesbitt
William Allison
James Campbell

Modifications to the Pennsylvania Packet passengers list based on research.

(1) Denotes brothers
(2) Some names in the original survivor's list have alternative spelling. Based upon family historical records, James and John Espey, brothers, survived the wreck. Could Aspill be Espey? They sound similar, however, the surname Aspill was found in the first U.S. Census – 1790. The Espey family names were used in the narrative based upon historical family research.
(3) Women surviving
(4) Based on research provided by Dorothy Ward, Samuel Lee, approximate age near ten, was with James Lee III following the shipwreck.

Lee, Samuel (4) Sources - Ward, Dorothy – Nova Numismatics, Sells, Helen

Total Survivors Adjusted – 71

U.S. Federal Census – 1790

The following names match identities of either a crew member or surviving passenger on board *Faithful Steward*. It has not been confirmed that the identity of those names extracted from the federal census are the survivors. A note of interest – there are a number on the census list who settled in Washington County, PA or nearby this location, where it has been determined others from the ship settled.

Name on Census

William Linn	Strabane	Washington Twp.	PA
Samuel Irwin	Letterkenney	Franklin County	PA

John Quigley	New Garden Twp.	Chester Co.	PA
Thomas Blair	Franklin Twp.	Westmoreland Co.	
James Dougherty	Letterkenney	Franklin County	
Robert Laurence	Bertie		NC
James Marshall	Concord Twp.	Chester Co.	PA
John McCallister	Letterkenney	Franklin Co.	PA
John York		Cumberland Co.	PA
James Aspill	Warwick Twp.	Orange Co.	NY
John Aspill	"	"	
James Beaty	Washington		PA
Mary Burns	Northumberland		PA
William Elliott		Washington Co.	PA
William McClintock	East Nottingham	Chester Co.	PA
Hugh McClean		Washington Co.	PA
Dr. James McDougal	Argyle	Washington Co.	NY
George Munro	Chartiers	Washington Co.	PA
James Smyth	Queen Annes		MD

Passenger's Perished List

No published list has been discovered, be it full or partial, of people's names who perished. The following list of names, excluding the Lee family, are attributed to the author's research and genealogical research provided by descendants of the perished.

Passenger List of Those Known to Have Perished

Campbell, Dr.
Cooke, Edward
Cooke, Edward Mrs.
Cooke, #10 – brothers and sisters (unknown forenames)
Elliott I, Simon, and wife Sarah D. Lee
Elliott, Elizabeth
Elliott, Jane
Elliott, Ann
Elliott, James
Espey, Hugh Sr. and wife Mary Stewart
Espey, Mary
Espey, Robert
Greg, Mr.
Greg, Mrs.
Hepburn, Samuel Mrs.
Hepburn, Janet (daughter of Samuel and Mrs.)

Hepburn, (unknown forename)
Lee, James I and wife Isabella Boscawen
Lee, James II and wife Mary Hamilton
Lee, Mary (Polly) (daughter to James and Isabella)
Lee, (unknown brother to James Lee III)
Lee, "
Lee, "
Lee, (unknown sister to James Lee III)
Lee, "
Lee, Isabella (daughter to James I and Isabella)
Lee, (unknown uncle to James Lee III)
Lee, "
Lee, "
Lee, "
Lee, (unknown aunt to James Lee III)
Lee, (25 cousins – unknown names) to the Lee family perished – 4 survived,
most likely some cousins to James, Simon, and William Elliott (brothers)
McIntire, Rebecca (wife of James I)
McIntire, (unknown brother to James II)
McIntire, (unknown sister to James II)
McIntire, "
McIntire, "
McIntire, "
McIntire, "
McIntire, "
McIntire, "
McIntire, "
McIntire, (unknown nephew to James II)
McIntire, (unknown brother-in-law to James II)
Total Passengers Perished as Identified – 81

Passenger Recap

Total Cabin	11
Total Steerage	47
Total Perished Per List	81
Total Passengers Accounted	139
Total Passengers Reported	249
Total Unidentified Passenger's	110 *

*Could be either an unidentified survivor or unidentified perished.

The historic marker erected by the State of Delaware to the side of Route 1 at Coin Beach states 93 women and children perished in the shipwreck. The authenticity of the number is not in question. The source for the number was not found while researching.

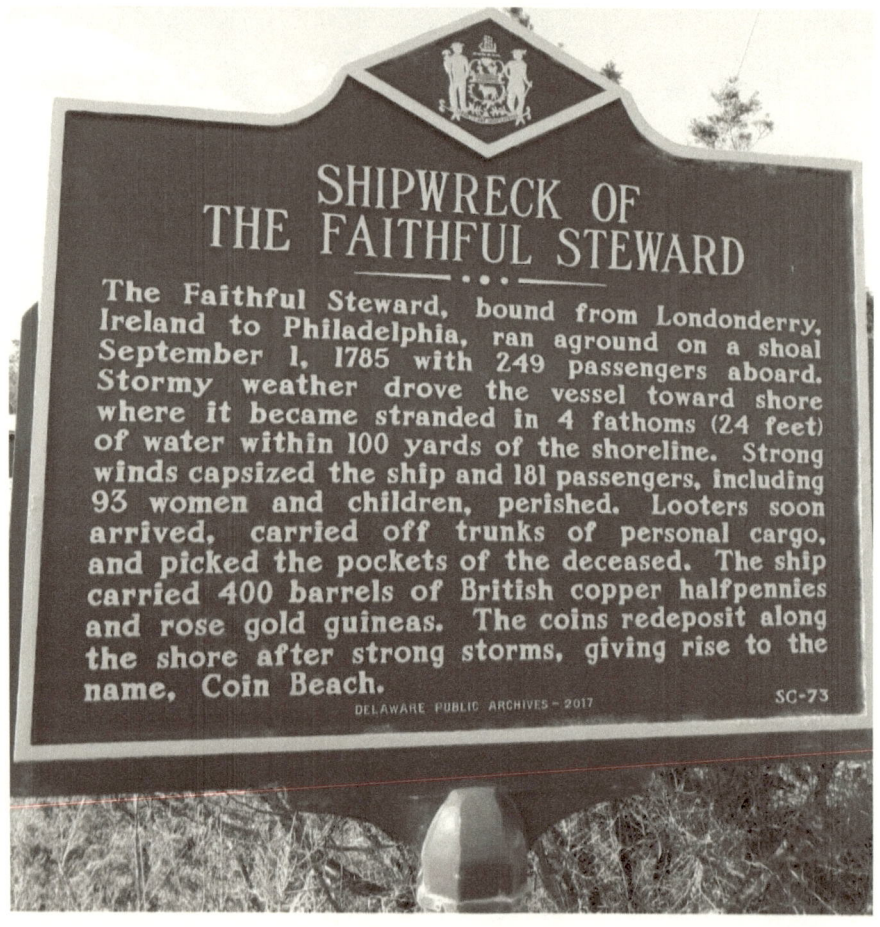

The last paragraph of the January 4, 1786 Pennsylvania Packet news article reads as follows: "The Subscribers think it necessary to give a list of the passengers (survivors) which is as correct as they have been able to make it out. Some others may also have been saved of which they have not yet had an account."

AUTHOR'S NOTES
(Alphabetical Order)

Blueskin

In accordance with one historical account, General Washington used two horses during the Revolutionary War. Always cognizant of hygiene and his personal appearance, he wore his Virginia military uniform when he called upon Martha for the first time. The Union League, with roots dating back to 1862, is located in a French Renaissance style building in Philadelphia, and considered an architectural masterpiece. Invited to the league years ago, I stood nearby the entrance only to be greeted with an impressive twelve-foot-high oil painting of the general sitting upon a brown horse, painted by Thomas Sully in 1842. Blueskin was reported to be nervous under battle.

Caldwell, Matthew

Born in Ireland in 1757. Served as an ensign in the Pennsylvania Troop during the American Revolution. Listed as a survivor in the shipwreck of *Faithful Steward*, married Mary Pinkerton (DOB 1760 DOD 1833) in 1810. No other Matthew Caldwells' were found in research and poetic license was used in incorporating his identity into the story.

Coin Beach

For those desiring an extensive discussion and analysis of the coinage washing ashore at Coin Beach, one should consult with the treatise, "The Shipwreck of the *Faithful Steward*: A Missing Link in the Exports of British and Irish Halfpence," authored by John M. Kleeberg for the Coinage of the Americas Conference at the American Numismatic Society, NY, October 28, 1995.

Mr. Kleeberg begins with the statement, a substantial portion of the halfpence in circulation in the U.S. in the 1780s was counterfeit. Further into his analysis, he reasons after presenting facts and by process of elimination, *Faithful Steward* is the likeliest of ships to have carried copper halfpence. There is no comment supporting if the copper coins were legally minted or counterfeit. Per page 61 within the treatise, he references Robert "Frogfoot" Weller's findings related to copper British halfpence found at Coin Beach with dates between 1776 – 1782. A conclusion is put forth, these coins would be counterfeit since 1775 is the last genuine date for striking of British halfpence. The basis for the statement, there was no halfpence struck beyond 1775 isn't supported by documentation, therefore, it would appear Mr. Kleeberg was stating a known fact. The treatise is dated 1995.

In 2018, archivist Susie Davis, with extensive archival experience at the National Archives, Kew, London, discovered the historic document, "Trial of the Pyx." This represents the first time a historic document dated 1784, provides irrefutable evidence British halfpence were minted in the Tower of London for the Kingdom of Ireland. And within the Trial of the Pyx there is specific reference to four mintings of halfpence consisting of twenty-five tons in 1775, five mintings totaling twenty-five tons in 1776, one minting of five tons in 1781, followed by nine separate mintings totaling forty-five tons in 1782.

Clearly, twenty-three years following the Kleeberg treatise, there now exists proof that British halfpence was minted in the years 1775 through 1782, confirming the existence of legally minted halfpence after 1775. The finding of the Trial of the Pyx provides a basis for the potential that some halfpence dated 1775, 1776, 1781, and 1782 found at Coin Beach, may be legally minted coins.

In the storyline the author determined, while not conclusive, the three brothers, Thomas, Gustavus, and Hugh Colhoun were likely sources to oversee the shipment of a cargo of thousands of halfpence stored on *Faithful Steward*. Using a process of elimination of 249 passengers – refer to the author's notes – there were 109 unidentified. It is possible the source of importing the halfpence could lie in this category, although less likely. Of the remaining 140 passengers, 82 are identified in some form in the names of the perished list. A review of the names suggests the supercargoes of the halfpence do not come from this list, given the multiple and extensive family connections, who were largely farmers and linen weavers. This leaves 58 names from the steerage or cabin list. The likelihood of a merchant/supercargo traveling in steerage is slim, therefore the remaining 11 names listed as cabin passengers could be the likely source to identify the cargo handlers.

While having no conclusive evidence, Gustavus, a merchant, and his brother Thomas, a proven mariner and cargo handler were capable of acting in the capacity of supervising the transport of the copper halfpence on the ship. Each of the three were connected to Stephen Girard, one of the wealthiest men in the United States in 1785. Several months following the shipwreck, Gustavus returns to Londonderry on the St. James. Why? Merchant business most likely.

On April 2, 1792 the U.S. Congress approved the Coinage Act, establishing the first national mint in the United States in Philadelphia. On November 26, 1792 Gustavus and Hugh Colhoun, now residing in Philadelphia, report a sale of 4,140 pounds – Warrant #31, of sheet copper at 25 cents per pound in a contract amount of $1,057.24 to the new mint. There is a connection to the Colhouns and the possibility of the transportation of copper coinage on *Faithful Steward.*

Years later, Peter Hess, a maritime attorney, shipwreck investigator, and researcher became Deputy Attorney General for the Delaware State Department of Natural Resources. Hess drafted a resolution passed by the General Assembly of Delaware commemorating the historic loss of the *Faithful Steward.* A ceremony was held where the plaque is situated, honoring the memory of the crew and passengers on September 2nd, 1985, two hundred years following the fateful horrific disaster.

Colhoun, Gustavus

Pennsylvania Gazette – March 1786

Ship passenger Notes – 152 days, on 27 December 1785 following the shipwreck of *Faithful Steward,* Gustavus Colhoun, merchant of Ireland, boarded *St. James* – owned by Philadelphia & Co. bound from Philadelphia to Londonderry. Ship Captain M. Collins reports passage was short – thirty-four days due to sailing west to east and catching the westerlies in addition to very strong winds from a storm. The ship arrived at the port of Moville located on the Lough Foyle north of Culmore Point on January 30, 1786. Many of the passengers on board signed a letter, thanking Captain Mark Collins for demonstrating skill and bravery in guiding the ship through a severe and dangerous storm. Among those attesting to the event were Marcus McCausland, cousin to Captain Connolly McCausland, and Gustavus Colhoun.

Note

Less than one-half year following the shipwreck, Gustavus, after surviving a horrific tragedy, experiencing unbelievable human suffering, embarks on a trans-Atlantic voyage to Londonderry and is involved in another storm. There is no known record of a written account of the shipwreck of *Faithful Steward* penned by Gustavus Colhoun.

Pennsylvania Gazette – 1792
Colhoun, Gustavus and Hugh

Merchants from Ireland establish an office at 37 N. Water Street, Philadelphia, next door to the Montgomery & Newbold counting house. Gustavus and Hugh Colhoun report a sale of 4,140 pounds (Warrant #31 dated November 26, 1792) of sheet copper at 25 cents per pound for a contract amount of $1,057.24 to the U.S. Mint.

Pennsylvania Gazette – June 1792
Colhoun, Gustavus

Merchant of Philadelphia marries Martha Spotswood 2 June 1792 in Pennsylvania.

Note

Gustavus was born on November 28, 1765. During the years 1808 – 1815 rented pew #43 and #94 at St. James Church, Philadelphia. In 1816, he embarked on an East India voyage, per his letter to Martha, he writes he partook of the Lord's Supper.

In 1794 he opened an office for Marine Insurance at the NE corner of Second and Dock Streets, Philadelphia. The initial capital subscribed was $500,000 in shares with $400 to be paid in dividends each February and August. Gustavus was elected as one of thirteen directors.

The Colhoun family tomb is located on the grounds of the historic Christ Church, Philadelphia, where Gustavus was interred. DOD, May 10, 1849, spouse Martha, DOD, July 8, 1856, children, Dr. Robert Harwood Colhoun, DOD, August 21, 1833, age 22 years, 6 mos. 21 d., Martha, DOD, May 20, 1862, and Ann, DOD August 18, 1862, all within yards of the burial site of Benjamin Franklin and other historic patriots of the American Revolution.

Painting of Gustavus
Colhoun Courtesy of
Tybring Hemphill

Colhoun, Hugh

Pennsylvania Chronicle – February 1795 – Naturalizations

    January 29, 1795, Hugh Colhoun, a merchant with offices at 37 N. Water St. appeared before the District Court of the United States and declared he was a native of Great Britain/Ireland. He was naturalized as a citizen declaring he would renounce any allegiance to the king and would support the Constitution of the United States.

Pennsylvania Chronicle – Business News

    Hugh Colhoun, a merchant at Girard's Wharf was elected to the Board of Directors of the Union Insurance Company of Philadelphia.

Pennsylvania Gazette – February 1799

    Colhoun, Hugh, merchant, N. Water St. weds Maria (Mary) Taylor February 14.

Note

Children of Hugh and Mary Colhoun – a son Meredith, DOB February 12, 1800, William, May 10, 1801, John Bohlen, January 28, 1803, Elizabeth Fitzsimmons, March 2, 1806, Jane Allen, October 26, 1807, Hannah Ann, July 7, 1808, and Mary Maria, date of birth unknown.

Mary Meredith, wife of Hugh Colhoun, was the daughter of Charles Meredith, a well-known and wealthy merchant in Philadelphia. Charles was friends with Benjamin Franklin as he invited Charles to become one of the incorporators of the Philadelphia Library Company. He was an Episcopalian and a vestryman at Christ Church.

The American Philosophical Society, founded by Benjamin Franklin, has many copies of original letters of correspondence between Stephen Girard and his business relationships with merchants in Charleston, South Carolina. The correspondence includes reciprocating letters praising Hugh Colhoun for his outstanding service.

Hugh's son, Meredith, apprenticed with Stephen Girard as a supercargo, sailing the seas representing Girard's business interests for many years.

Philadelphia Inquirer – October 1838
Colhoun, Hugh

Businessman and merchant passed away on October 1 at the age of seventy-one. He was buried in a black cloth coffin with a silver plate. Six carriages were hired, three from City Hall, Phila. Included in the list of items purchased for his funeral were seven pairs of silk gloves, eleven pairs of Hoskins gloves, fifteen yards of crape and pins, and ribbons. One hundred invitations were printed and delivered. Mr. Colhoun was interred in a family tomb at the historic Christ Church, Philadelphia.

Colhoun, Thomas

Pennsylvania Chronicle – Mariner News – 1796
Colhoun, Thomas

A Seaman's Protection Certificate has been issued to Thomas Colhoun, a lifetime mariner by the government of the United States expiring 1823. The purpose of the certificate is to protect his personal safety from pirating while serving on merchant vessels.

Pennsylvania Gazette – Naturalizations – January 1805
Colhoun, Thomas

On the 8th of December 1804 at the age of forty-four appeared before Benjamin Nones, Notary Public in Philadelphia, declaring he was a citizen of the United States of America has made such declaration in South Carolina. His Certificate of Naturalization was examined by the notary and declared him to be a legal citizen.

Note

Upon notarizing Mr. Colhoun's naturalization, Benjamin Nones described Thomas as 5' 9" – black hair, dark eyes, stout nose, round chin, smooth face, and a dark complexion. Scars were located on top of his head, on the back part of a hand, another on his right cheek, one above his left eyebrow, and a cherrystone mark on his left shoulder. Thomas became a master of sailing vessels, voyaging mainly from South Carolina to the West Indies. He left a will in Philadelphia dated 1806 naming his brother Gustavus as executor. He sailed as far away as Calcutta and may have made more than one trip. He was buried there on June 28, 1808 at the age of forty-eight.

Conyngham, Gustavus

Note

DOB 1744, in County Donegal to Gustavus of Largyreagh, Gentleman, and Ann Hockley. Migrated to Philadelphia at sixteen. After studies with books, he decided he was interested in the sea and apprenticed with a ship captain in the West Indian trade. Later became an American Naval Officer, investing his funds to outfit and ultimately command the cutter, *Revenge* in the Revolutionary War. Gustavus seized twenty-seven British ships, sinking an additional thirty, while operating near the British Isles south to Spain and the West Indies. An acquaintance of Benjamin Franklin, he is credited with nicknaming him, "The Philosopher." Franklin received it as the compliment for which it was intended. Gustavus, DOD – 1819, and his wife are buried in St. Peter's Churchyard, Philadelphia.

Cooke, Edward

Note

A family of ten, including Edward and his wife, reported to be passengers on the *Faithful Steward* by an ancestor. His two brothers, Lieutenant Colonel Charles Cooke and Major Robert Cooke joined the British Army. Two other brothers, one named Jacob, settled in Lancaster County. The other, Colonel William Cooke, joined the 12th Regiment Continental Line Northumberland, PA. Research (per bibliography) courtesy of Charles Thomas Cooke IV

Covenanters

Note

Over many years, Covenanters of Scottish descent fled to the northern regions of Ireland and later to pre-revolutionary British America. They signed The Covenant of the Solemn League with King Charles I promising to support him in a war against Oliver Cromwell. This was unsuccessful and King Charles I was executed. Many Covenanters fled to Ireland afterward. All swore allegiance to King James VI of Scotland, in exchange for his support of the Presbyterian Church in Scotland. Their church was a hallmark of their heritage, with some exhibiting a radical patriot leadership before and during the American Revolution.

Octorara Covenanter Presbyterian Church – founded 1754
The Oldest Covenanter Presbyterian Church in North America.

Covenanters left Ireland for Pennsylvania, settling in many locales within Pennsylvania, including Lancaster County. Today there exist many names of townships and boroughs, including some school districts, named after places in Ireland. By 1751 Rev. John Cuthbertson of Scotland served as a roving missionary and traveled throughout Lancaster County. His residence was at Bartville. A covenanter, he traveled hundreds of miles ministering to Presbyterians, maintaining a record of his marriage ceremonies and a diary outlining his travels.

The Octorara Covenanter Presbyterian Foundation was formed as a fundraising source for the upkeep and ongoing preservation of the original church. An adjacent graveyard includes burial sites of the founders of the church. While covenanters boarded *Faithful Steward*, no record has been found of survivors settling nearby and attending the Octorara church.

Octorara Covenanter Presbyterian Church – 1754

Dougal, Doctor James

Note

Of Milton, Pennsylvania, a son to Dr. Dougal, wrote how his father rescued a young man from the shipwreck of the *Faithful Steward*.

Dunlap, John – Formerly of Strabane, County Tyrone

Note

John Dunlap and business partner David Claypoole, in 1777, took over the printing of the Journals of the Continental Congress and printed the first broadsides (large one-sided copies) of the Constitution of the United States of America. John amassed considerable wealth during the American Revolution purchasing real estate owned by Tories, who were driven out of Philadelphia and sent to Virginia.

Elliott I, Simon

Note

Early members of the Elliott family left Scotland for Ireland near the same time as the Lee family departed England. He has been referred to as Wealthy Elliott by some performing genealogical research. No records have been identified to confirm his real forename. Some believe it to be William, as his eldest son was so named. Poetic license was used by the author after evaluating multiple genealogical studies from multiple people.

Elliott, John

Note

John (DOB – 1767) sailed to the colonies at the age of seventeen in 1784 on the *Lazy Mary* and settled at Remington, near Cincinnati, Hamilton County, Ohio. He built a stone house, now the oldest building in the "Miami Purchase," and is preserved as a historic site today. Together with his wife, they raised three boys and three girls – Simon, Elcy, Sarah, Isabel, William, and John.

John Jr., sent by his father to explore the middle Atlantic region, America, in 1784 on the sail ship *Lazy Mary*, met up with his two surviving brothers, William and Simon.

Years later, Mrs. Anna Martha Moss, granddaughter of William Elliott, recalled to her cousin – Simon Elliott, grandson of John Elliott, details of a song written and sung by those in their family. Mrs. Moss explained to Simon many years before, in a time when older people didn't know how to read or write, storytellers would sing songs as a means of recording and remembering family events, thus passing family history to future generations. Lyrics to the Elliott family song are listed below.

The Elliott Families
The Elliotts and the Lees and Stewarts of great fame,
They may lament and mourn, for the lands they left behind.
They may lament and mourn, as long as they have days.
For their friends and relations, lie in Mahogany's bays.
As for that lovely damsel, called Mary Lee by name,
Her beauty in particular, I mean for to proclaim.
Many handsome young men, on her did cast their eyes,
But to our great misfortune, among the dead she lies.
Author Unknown

Elliott, Simon II (DOB – 1765), William (DOB – 1764), and John (DOB – 1762), brothers.

Note

William and Simon survived the wreck. William moved to Salt Creek Township in Muskingum County, Ohio, where he raised six boys and five girls – Andrew, John, Simon, Elizabeth, Isabel, James, Mary Jane, Sarah Ann, William, Charles, and Eleanor Elliott.

Simon remained a bachelor, and after staying in Pennsylvania, later settled in Fulton County, Illinois.

Elliott, Thomas, and Margaret

Note

Thomas and Margaret Elliott, related to Simon, William, and John, left with their family from Londonderry, 1790, and settled in Jefferson County, Ohio. Additional detail of the Elliott ancestry can be found at the website for the Elliott family reunion, 1923: https://www.wikitree/Elliott-6319. Tyler Elliott, descendant of William Elliott, provided the reference – "The Elliotts – The Story of a Border Clan – A Genealogical History" Seely Service and Co. Ltd. 1974

Espey, Hugh, and Mary

Note

Hugh DOB 1735, the son of John and Jean Morehead Espey of County Down, married Mary Stewart DOB 1735 of County Londonderry. Sons, James DOB 1765, and John DOB 1760 plus Mary, a daughter, boarded *Faithful Steward* at Londonderry.

James and John survived the shipwreck while their father, mother, and daughter perished. Two older sons, Hugh Jr. DOB 1757 and William DOB 1755, having left Ireland in 1774, lived in Pennsylvania and were awaiting the arrival of their kin. William married Margaret Hemphill and settled in Fayette County, Pennsylvania. James Espey remained crippled for life due to the injuries received during the shipwreck. He married Miss McLean, a native of Scotland, and settled on a farm in Ripley, Brown County, Ohio, passing away in 1813 while attempting to save his cattle during a flood from the Ohio River. John settled nearby his brother. John Espey, DOB 1760

Londonderry, settled nearby Ripley in Brown County, Ohio. His DOD was 1822, and burial at the Stephensen Family Cemetery.

"Letter Issued by the Church for the Benefit of William Espey – 1774."

We whose names are hereunto subscribed do hereby certify that William Espey, son of Hugh Espey of Tobermore in the Parish of Kilcronaghan in the County of Londonderry, Ireland, is a Native of said Parish and during his residence has behaved himself soberly, honestly, and inoffensively, and has enjoyed the happenings of a fair and unblemished character clear of scandal or canny imputation thereof and has Received the benefits of Communion with us, is now bound for America and may be admitted into any Christian Society where Divine Providence may order his lot, certified by us at Tobermore, 20th day of May 1774.
James Whiteside, P.M. (Presbyterian Minister)
Jno. Madon C.
Sam'l Sinelery L.
John Kinnery
Thomas Jackson
Wm. Hopkinson, Clerk

Reverend James Whiteside served as minister of Tobermore Presbyterian Church from the date of his ordination, August 1, 1757, until his death, March 23, 1798.

Earlier Espeys (Josiah and Priscilla) migrated to the Plantation of Ulster, and as Covenanters subscribed to the Solemn League and Oath.
All contributions to the Espey family research are attributed to the family history authored by Florence Espey, (included in Bibliography), Jae Espey, 4 x's great-grandson to James Espy, a shipwreck survivor, and James Espey, descendant of Hugh Espey.

Eyre, Manuel

Pennsylvania Gazette – February 1760
Wed Mary Wright, daughter of Richard Wright, a Kensington, Philadelphia shipbuilder, January 8, 1760.

Pennsylvania Gazette – Shipbuilder News

Manuel Eyre and brothers, Jehu and Benjamin, Kensington shipbuilders christened the *Congress*, a merchant ship owned by Blair McClenachan to be used in Philadelphia to Londonderry trade.

Pennsylvania Chronicle – 1777

Eyre, Manuel

Shipbuilder enlists as a private in the artillery company commanded by his brother, Captain Jehu Eyre.

Pennsylvania Chronicle – 1777

Eyre, Captain Manuel

Assumes command of the Company of Artillery, First Brigade, under Gen. John Cadwalader, Philadelphia. Eyre is also a member of the Committee of Correspondence of Philadelphia and Pennsylvania Navy Board.

Note

Manuel Eyre, DOB November 10, 1736, in New Jersey, married Mary Wright, January 8, 1760, daughter of Richard Wright, a leading shipbuilder in Philadelphia. Together they had thirteen children. Manuel built some of the first gunboats under order by the Continental Congress. His first assignment was as a captain in Jehu's artillery company. After the Revolutionary War, Eyre became a member of the Pennsylvania State Legislature.

Later, Manuel formed Eyre & Massey shipbuilding, with an office at 23 Water Street, Philadelphia, nearby the merchant offices of Gustavus and Hugh Colhoun and Stephen Girard at 31 Water Street. Eyre & Massey was one of the largest, premier shipbuilding companies in the world owning upward of twenty merchant ships. One ship, *Globe,* made eight voyages to China and return, a voyage lasting over one year. Eyre & Massey never suffered the loss of one of their ships.

Manuel owned two farms nearby Philadelphia and three farms in Delaware and spent the last twenty years of his life as an agriculturalist. Manuel died in 1805.

Eyre, Jehu

Note

Born in 1738, two years younger than Manuel, at twenty-two, left the family home to apprentice with Richard Wright, a shipbuilder. In time, Jehu married Wright's daughter, Lydia, a sister to Mary, Manuel's wife.

Eyre, Benjamin

Note

Born in 1747, the youngest of the Eyre brothers left the family home in 1761 after the passing of his father and joined his brothers, apprenticing with Richard Wright. Buried at historic Christ Church, Philadelphia, his sword, epaulets, camp table, and stool are displayed at the National Museum, Independence Hall Philadelphia.

Faithful Steward

Note

No confirmation exists that the Eyre brothers, shipbuilders from Kensington, built the ship. Inquiries of historical records at the Independence Seaport Museum, Philadelphia, Mystic Seaport Museum, Mystic, Connecticut, and the Mariners Museum, Newport News, Virginia, produced no record of the shipbuilder. An article in the Londonderry Journal confirmed the ship's original owner was Archibald Stewart of Providence, and his subsequent sale of the ship to a partnership between himself and the McCauslands in 1784.

Susie Davis, Archivist from London, performed a search of British ships at the Guildhall Library and reported, paraphrased, as follows: "The absence of any record of Faithful Steward suggests there was not considered sufficient British connection. Ships from other countries might appear in these records if they made frequent voyages to British ports."

Documentation exists that *Faithful Steward* made one voyage to Londonderry under Captain Haynes and a return voyage to America under Captain McCausland (1/3 owner in a new partnership) with Captain Haynes, followed by a voyage to Londonderry before departing July 9, 1785, on that fateful voyage. The author's conclusion – an analysis of research suggests *Faithful Steward* was constructed in the United States. Research confirms there existed economic advantages for shipowners to sail American built ships, post-Revolutionary War to Ireland for resale. Based upon this research, the construction and sale of *Faithful Steward* is a realistic portrayal of what may have occurred per the storyline.

Folger Charts of the Gulf Stream

Note

Benjamin Franklin sailed for Paris in 1776, and while crossing the Atlantic, he tested the warm ocean water of the Gulf Stream. With renewed interest in the Timothy Folger (his cousin) charts, Franklin had his charts copied in Paris. The original Folger charts disappeared and were lost for nearly two centuries. In 1978 Philip L. Richardson of the Woods Hole Oceanographic Institution found two copies in the Bibliotheque Nationale in Paris. The charts were assumed obtained and saved by the French between 1776 and 1785, when Dr. Franklin was an envoy to France. In 1786, Dr. Franklin published Timothy Folger's sketch of the Gulf Stream as an article in the Proceedings of the American Philosophical Society of Philadelphia.

Genealogies

Note

The listing of shipwreck survivors, including names of passengers added to the list published in the Pennsylvania Packet of those on *Faithful Steward,* and names added in the storyline, including lineages and genealogies were comprised from multiple sources, including the author's personal research, with additions provided through research of the work of others, and descendants with family histories. As such, there is no warranty implied or expressed with regard to the accuracy of the names in the novel, as they are provided for enhancement of the story.

Girard, Stephen

Note

Girard maintained a merchant's office at 33 N. Water Street, a few doors away from Gustavus and Hugh Colhoun. Born in 1750, in Bordeaux, France, he became a mariner, then merchant, financier, and ultimately humanitarian. He sailed to New York in 1774 and, upon returning once again, on merchant business, found himself blockaded from the port, then sailed on the *L'Aimable Louis* to Philadelphia in 1776. By 1778 Girard became an American citizen residing in Philadelphia.

In 1791 he opened the First Bank of the United States, investing heavily and setting a new course for the United States by establishing a credit system and money supply. Nearly twenty years later, 1812, with congress failing to renew the bank charter, Girard bought all of the assets and reopened under Girard Bank. With the outbreak of the War of 1812, a second conflict ensued with the British. Stephen Girard singlehandedly saved the United States upon advancing a line of credit of $8,000,000 to be drawn upon to finance the war.

During the yellow fever epidemic of 1793, Girard remained in Philadelphia, assuming the role of Superintendent of City Hospital at Bush Hill. He prescribed for patients, wine and lemonade, nursing some personally, refusing to believe the disease spread from patient to patient. It was found the mosquito spread the disease.

Girard invested heavily in real estate within and outside the city in Pennsylvania. Throughout his life, he lived by a motto – "My Deeds Must Be My Life." He died at 81 years in 1831, and in his will, left more than $6,000,000 to the city of Philadelphia in a trust to establish Girard College – a school for orphan boys with no means to obtain an education. In 1998 Forbes Magazine placed Stephen Girard on its all-time list of the wealthiest men in America. Preceding him on this list were John D. Rockefeller, Cornelius Vanderbilt, and John Jacob Astor.

Hall, David Colonel

Note

Born in Lewestown, Delaware in 1752, Colonel Hall would have been thirty-three years of age if he met the McIntires at the Lewestown Courthouse. He was a lawyer and a Revolutionary War soldier, followed by a judge. Colonel Hall commanded the Delaware Line, and his unit accompanied General Washington's Continental Army to nearby Schwenksville, Pennsylvania after the Battle of Germantown, where he was wounded, followed by the historically famous 1777-1778 winter encampment at Valley Forge. Colonel Hall returned to his native Lewestown in 1779, resigning his commission in the same year. He remained a resident of Lewestown where he practiced law, and in 1802 was elected the fifteenth Governor of the state of Delaware. He was buried at historic Lewes Presbyterian Church in 1817.

Picture courtesy of the Colonel David Hall Chapter of
The Daughters of the American Revolution - Lewes, DE
and the Cape Gazette

Gravestone - Colonel David Hall
Lewes Presbyterian Church

Hepburn, Samuel

Note

May have been born in or nearby Bothwell Castle, Glasgow, Scotland
1698. Samuel's family, reported to be of high standing and good education,
was likely raised in the mercantile business. He married Janet Sinclair in 1747.
A brief time following their marriage, they may have been pressured to
migrate to Donegal, given Samuel was a covenanter. Their children, all born
in Donegal, were James Hepburn, DOB 1748, married Mary Hopewell –
William Hepburn DOB 1753, married Crecy Covenhoven – Samuel Hepburn
DOB 1755, married Edith Miller – and John Hepburn, DOB 1757, married
Mary Elliott. One story suggests Janet Hepburn remained in Ulster to settle
affairs with one of the sons. The other tale hypothesizes she perished in the

shipwreck. Samuel settled at Milton, Northumberland County, Pennsylvania, and passed away ten years after the wreck, in 1795, age ninety-seven.

Hepburn, William

Note

Son to Samuel, William migrated to Philadelphia in 1773 with his brother James, initially settled near Sunbury, and enlisted in the Pennsylvania militia due to a Native American uprising. After a time, he was promoted to colonel and became commander of Fort Munch. William was known to many Revolutionary War heroes and worked with Jacob Rush, brother to Dr. Benjamin Rush, confidant to John Adams. William purchased 300 acres near present-day Williamsport, PA and, in time was appointed a judge due to his fairness. He was known for generosity and was a founding member of the Lycoming Presbyterian Church. By 1794, he was elected to the Pennsylvania State Senate. Today, William is recognized as the founding father of Lycoming County, Pennsylvania.

Higginbotham, Arthur

Note

A survivor of the shipwreck, he was reported to have migrated to Bathurst, Ontario. John and Robert Higginbotham arrived in Bathurst after sailing from Londonderry September 9, 1817, on *Mary Ann.* Information supplied by Dorothy B. Ward.

Hudson, Pelig (Spelled Pelick in old newspaper accounts)

Note

Born in 1750 in Rhode Island, was listed in the 1774 census for Newport and 1782 listed as a resident in Newport County, Rhode Island, and again in 1790. No research of a Pelick Hudson, nor the use of the forename turned up in Northern Ireland. Minor changes in name spelling did occur; therefore, the author used poetic license, given Newport spawned many mariners, therefore, it's possible he could be the individual identified with the original crew list.

Kincade, Margaret

Delaware Gazette – September 1786

One year following a maritime disaster of great proportion, a story surfaces, a story of the heartfelt tragedy of one family and their loss during the shipwreck of *Faithful Steward*. Margaret Kincade, a young girl of fourteen years was a passenger with her father, mother, and baby brother. Margaret's older brother was waiting for the arrival of the ship at Stamper's Wharf to greet his family.

Mr. Kincade (Margaret's brother) reported a young man whose name remains unknown assisted Margaret's father by strapping a board to her and tying her baby brother to her back to save her brother's life. Margaret recalls her father was able to swim but her mother could not. Her parents promised her they would be with her as she jumped from the greatly damaged ship into the sea. Margaret awoke on the shore at nighttime with her baby brother strapped to her back. Neither her brother nor parents survived.

Note

Brian Mitchell, genealogist, and historian associated with Derry-Strabane District Council recalls in great detail when Robert Elmwood from Louisiana visited him. Mr. Elmwood was searching for the name of a relative from many years ago who survived the wreck of *Faithful Steward*. Together they reviewed the passenger survival list of women, and he knew instantly, Margaret Kincade was the name of the missing relative. Elmwood told Brian over many years; he questioned why in his family's long list of forenames Margaret was repeated many times.

Lee, Hugh*

Note

The eldest son of James Lee I and Isabella Boscawen Lee, born at Killybegs, was unable to board *Faithful Steward*. Hugh DOB 1740 Donegal, and Mary Elliott Lee, DOB 1745, and their family of five sons and three daughters, William DOB 1767, Jane DOB 1766, Hugh DOB 1773, Robert DOB 1776, John DOB 1770, Eleanor DOB 1780, and Ann DOB 1786, migrated after the shipwreck from Ireland in 1789, settling near Canonsburg, PA.

The Lees purchased a 219-acre farm from William McFarren in Cross Creek Township, PA known as "Holmes Victory." The title to their property was a Virginia Certificate issued by George Washington to James Holmes in 1774.

Hugh closely identified with the Presbyterian Church at Cross Creek Township. He and Mary raised five sons and three daughters who, upon marriage, left the homestead with one exception, a brother Hugh Lee. He remained at the farm and, upon the death of his parents, 1815, inherited the premises by will. Hugh purchased 160 acres adjoining the farm after the passing of his parents and continued farming, wheat being the principal crop. Hugh DOB 1773, son of Hugh Lee, married Hannah Orr in 1804, and they raised ten children. Hugh died in 1837.

Two years prior, 1835, Major William Lee, eldest son of Hugh and grandson of Hugh and Mary Elliott Lee, son of James Lee I and Isabella Boscawen Lee, inherited his father's homestead at Cross Creek Township. In 1876 Major Lee divided his property among his children and retired at the farm.

Major William Lee, a member of the Presbyterian Church, as was his father and grandfather, was described as a man of exactness and promptness in business – one with deep sympathy toward others and their needs – a man of his word – one who discharged his duties faithfully – one with a purpose of what was right.

The description of the character of Major William Lee, the history of Hugh and Mary Elliott Lee, and son Hugh and grandson Major William Lee, and related family genealogy were provided by Dorothy B. Ward, and the History of Washington County, Pennsylvania.

Hugh and Mary Elliott Lee

Major William Lee DOB 1807 – Grandson to Hugh and Mary Elliott Lee
Photo courtesy of History of Washington County, PA and Dorothy B. Ward

Lee I, James DOB – April 13, 1707

Note
Baptism Place – South Normanton, Derby, England
Genealogical Lineage
Sir Thomas Lee
1535 – 1585
Thomas Lee II
1556 – 1620
Lancelot Lee*
1583 – 1667
Thomas Lee
1620-1687
James Lee
1675-1711
James Lee (I)
1707 – 1785
James Lee (II)
1735 – 1785
James Lee (III)
1759 – 1842

*Lancelot Lee supported Oliver Cromwell and was granted land in Ulster.
Courtesy of Dorothy B. Ward

Lee, *(Arabella) Isabella Boscawen – Lineage, father's side

Note
Isabella's Grandparents
Boscawen, Edward (1628 – 1685)
Boscawen, Jael Godolphin (1647 – 1730)
Isabella's Parents
Boscawen, Lord Hugh (1660 – 1754)
Boscawen, Charlotte Godfrey (1662 – 1754)
Isabella's Siblings
Boscawen, Edward Admiral Honorable (1711 – 1761)
Boscawen, Ann (1703 – 1749)
Boscawen, George (1712 – 1775)
Boscawen, Hugh (1706 – 1782)
Boscawen, John (1713 – 1767)
Boscawen, Charlotte (1702 – 1745)
Boscawen, Lucy (1719 – 1784)
Boscawen, Mary (1705 – 1749)
*Baptism record reflects the forename Arabella.

Lee, James III

Note
     Born in Donegal, 1759, married in 1792 a Pennsylvanian, Elizabeth Rankin DOB 1773, and settled in Strabane Township, Washington County, Pennsylvania. Children included Thomas, Mary McBride, Jane Henderson, Elizabeth Rankin Buchanan, George Lee, James, Hugh, and John Rankin Lee. James died in 1842, fifty-seven years following the shipwreck of *Faithful Steward,* and was buried nearby his residence in Canonsburg, Washington County, Pennsylvania. In 1895 Captain Albert Lee of Uniontown, Ohio, spoke of his grandfather, James Lee III, referencing he served in the War of 1812. Captain Lee possessed the gold buttons from the uniform worn by James Lee III.

James Lee III
Oak Spring Cemetery – Canonsburg, Washington Co., PA
Small Stone to the left marks Elizabeth Rankin Lee's gravesite.

Lee, Mary "Pretty Polly"

Note

A young woman described in a written account as, of striking beauty and accomplishment, sister to James Lee II and Hugh Lee, perished in the shipwreck.

Lee, Thomas

Note

Son of James Lee I, brother to James Lee II, uncle to James Lee III, and grandfather of Judge Robert Lee of Bucyrus, Ohio, together with his family were unable to board *Faithful Steward,* due to at capacity. They waited for another vessel leaving Londonderry for Philadelphia following *Faithful Steward.*

Londonderry Journal – September 13, 1785

The ship *Congress* departed Londonderry a few days following the *Faithful Steward,* sighted the ship on August 3, longitude 42, all well, easterly wind.

Note

   Congress, owned by Blair McClenachan, a member of The Friendly Sons of St. Patrick and a privateer during the Revolution, living in Philadelphia, arrived safely at Stamper's Wharf after a passage of seven weeks, placing the arrival of his ship thereabout August 27, 1785.

McCausland, Abraham

Note

   DOB 1745, the last inscription on the family McCausland gravesite is of Abraham, died November 5, 1820, age 77. At 42 years of age was a merchant and part-owner of *Faithful Steward*, a brother to Captain Connolly McCausland, and buried at St. Columb's Cathedral, Londonderry.

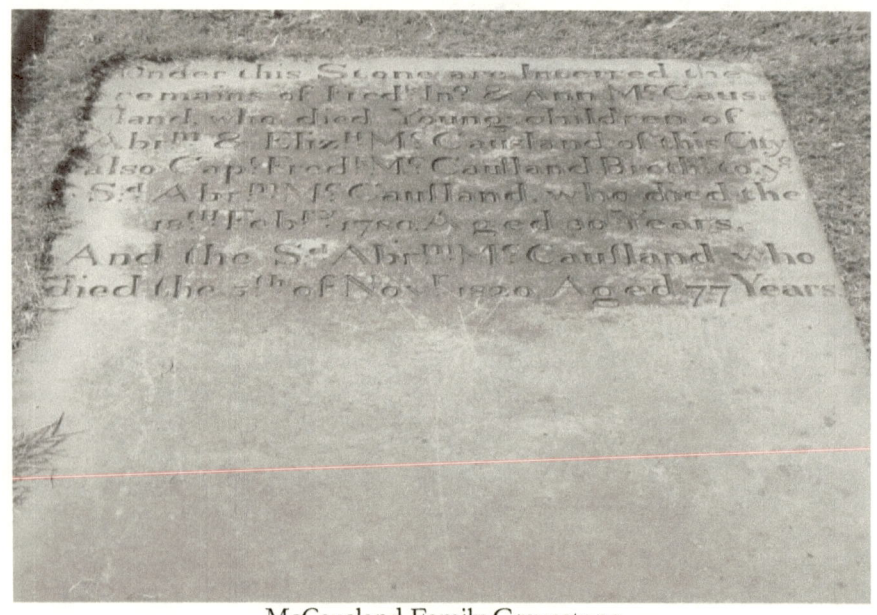

McCausland Family Gravestone
Photo Courtesy of Brian Mitchell,
Genealogist, Historian, and Author

McCausland, Captain Connolly

Note

   DOB 1750 at Fruit Hill, Limavady, was thirty-five years of age when captain of *Faithful Steward*. Of the Hillhouse family, Conolly's mother had mercantile connections to the Belfast family, a possible source of apprenticeship for the captain. It is postulated he became a seaman as early as 1768, and through 1773, commanded the *Walworth*, a joint venture of Strabane-born Thomas Barclay, a resident of Philadelphia and nephew of Samuel Carsan, born in Strabane, migrating to Philadelphia, and Marcus McCausland, cousin to Connolly. He commanded *Jane*, 1776 to 1781, in the capacity of a victualer for King George III assisting British troops in British America during the American Revolution.

A source of substantial historical research of Connolly McCausland and related family members was graciously provided through multiple researched and published articles authored by Dr. Mary Wack, Washington State University, Washington.

McIllhiney, John

Note

Born in 1760 at Londonderry, Ireland, he was twenty-five when he sailed on *Faithful Steward*. His father, William McIllheney, died in 1760 at Londonderry. John married Sarah Ann Henry and settled in Prospect, Butler County, Pennsylvania. He served in the War of 1812 and died on June 18, 1845. Source – Charlotte Sorum, 4x's great-granddaughter of John McIllhinney.

McIntire I, James

Note

Born 1728, and stated to be from Ardstraw Bridge, Parish Alt-an-Clody, County Tyrone, at fifty-seven survived the wreck. In 1785 an agreement was entered into with Native Americans allowing settlers to migrate west of the Susquehanna River. The remnant of the McIntire family may have left Maytown, staying with family near Philadelphia for one year, before settling in Bedford County, east of Pittsburgh for a time.

By 1799 the wife of James II and an infant son died, most likely in childbirth. James II lived twelve miles east of Pittsburgh in Allegheny County at the time. In the same year, James I followed his son's family to Crawford County, where James I settled near Conneaut Lake, close to Meadville. Conneaut stems from a Native American word, Konn-Knu-Yout, interpreted melted snow water lake. He died in 1800 at age seventy-two near Evansburg. Per a family account, James I brought the first clover and timothy seed to the

United States. James II recorded in his memoir his father was never able to recover from the emotional impact of the loss of his wife and children suffered from the shipwreck.

McIntire II, James

Note

James left County Tyrone at age twenty-two with his father, mother, a brother (unidentified), a sister-in-law, and a nephew, both unidentified, a sister Rebecca and six unidentified sisters. Upon reaching Lewestown, the remnant of the family, penniless and without their possessions, sailed on a schooner to New Castle paid for by a benefactor. They walked from there to Lancaster, Pennsylvania, a distance more than sixty miles, remained there and rested, then walked another twenty miles to Maytown, west of Lancaster, where they should have met Robert and settled there for a time.

Maytown, a small village, was known for provisioning those who crossed the Susquehanna River in search of land. Most likely the McIntires embarked on a journey westward over The Warrior's Path, carved out many years before by the Six Nations. The trail cut through the Allegheny Mountains, part of the Appalachian chain to Pittsburgh. It is likely this trail, years later, became the foundation for the westward extension of the Pennsylvania Turnpike. Rebecca married Robert Stanley and remained behind, while James II traveled north to Crawford County, settling in Greenwood Township. During the years 1802 – 1827, James II became the second schoolmaster, taught in adjoining townships, and was considered a strict, principled teacher.

By 1831, forty-six years following the shipwreck, Reverend William McMichael, a Presbyterian minister, and schoolteacher, met with James II, due to ill health, then sixty-eight years of age. James II provided Reverend McMichael a detailed, descriptive account of the shipwreck and his friend recorded his words, capturing his thoughts, emotions, and the memories of a young man who, at twenty-two, lost the entirety of his family except for his father and one sister.

Nearly fifty years later, 1880, the grandson of James II, Robert A. McIntire, read the entire account of near 5,000 words to the McIntire/Mason family reunion numbering in the hundreds at his East Fallowfield farm in Crawford County, Pennsylvania. In 1881 the Meadville Courier published James' previously recorded description of the shipwreck of *Faithful Steward,* and to this day stands as the only discovered historical retelling of the shipwreck.

James' account was relayed in English as spoken in 1831. His diction is most interesting as, over many years, usage of spoken English has changed. James' use of English represents a wonderful example of how people expressed themselves at the time. Upon reflecting on his account, a piece of valuable, detailed, and critical specimen of a retelling of historical events covering nearly a week in the lives of three McIntires is preserved in history.

McIntire Farm Homestead

In 1799, James II, and his family settled in Sadsbury Township nearby Conneaut Lake and Wolf Point, Crawford County, PA. Unable to obtain clear title to the land, they moved to East Fallowfield Township in 1803, settling on land described on the original deed written on sheepskin. Over the years, the family farm increased to a total of 640 acres. In 1843, after the death of James II, acreage from the farm was divided among his children from the first and second marriages. The original farmhouse, destroyed by a fire from a lightning strike in 1900, was rebuilt.

The Pennsylvania Department of Agriculture devised the Century Farm Award for farms held continuously in the name of the original founding family for one hundred years. A minimum of ten acres must be farmed. Mr. Samuel E. Hayes Jr., Pennsylvania Secretary, awarded to Mr. Raymond T. McEntire Jr., sixth-generation farmer, and owner, the Century Farm Award, commenting the McEntires doubled the Century Award to two hundred years. Today, the original farmstead has been preserved through a family trust. A caretaker is in charge of maintaining the property, and family members meet on special occasions.

Details of the history of the McIntire farm homestead and other content was provided by Suzanne Vila, 6 x's great granddaughter to James McIntire II, and Mark Tattersall, 7 x's great grandson to James McIntire II, representing today's extended family.

James Dickson McIntyre
Son of James McIntire II
Courtesy of Lucy McIntyre Jewett Historical Collection
Sarah E. Jewett Coombs – 4xs great granddaughter to James McIntyre II

On March 2, 1880, James Dickson McIntyre, born in Bedford County, Pennsylvania, 1793, father of Robert A. McIntyre, wrote a letter to his grandson, J.E. McIntyre describing family memories. In his letter, he wrote of his grandfather's family, James McIntyre I, who lived on the Kintyre Peninsula in southwestern Scotland. Years later, some of the family migrated inland to the highlands of Scotland.

The following generation was born in Ireland. Their occupations consisted of farming and weaving, and all received a good education. In 1876 Robert A. McIntyre journeyed to Coin Beach, site of the wreck of *Faithful Steward*, 101 years after the catastrophe. James Dickson McIntire wrote a letter to his grandson, Eddie, describing how his father, James II, with two unidentified friends, stripped their clothes and swam to shore, his father being the only one to reach shore successfully.

Toward the end of his letter, James Dickson McIntyre recounts of his service in the War of 1812 for ten months. In separate research, it was discovered his brother, John, also served in the War of 1812.

A copy of the letter was provided from the Lucy McIntyre Jewett Historical Collection.

Robert A. McIntyre
1820 – 1902
Grandson of James McIntire II
Courtesy of Lucy McIntyre Jewett Historical Collection
Sarah E. Jewett Coombs

Courtesy of Lucy Jewett McIntyre Family Historical Collection
Photo Courtesy of Sarah E. Jewett Coombs

Merchant's Itemization of Importation/Exportation of Goods

Note

Throughout the 1700s merchants from Ulster migrated to North America, and participated in trans-Atlantic trade with the British Colonies, Nova Scotia, and the West Indies. Examples of exported and imported goods included, sackcloth, grey-cloth, blue-cloth, linen cloth, woolen clothes, Spanish silk, bone lace, blue starch, needles, stockings, gloves, hats, purses, shoes, rings, sheets, and pillows. The list continues with apples, onions, vinegar, pepper, spices, sugar, marmalade, prunes, wine, tobacco, brass pots, iron pots, frying-pans, griddles, soap, cups, glasses, bottles, tables. Implements included hatchets, pickaxes, broad axes, files, chisels, braces, crowbars, hammers, handsaws, whipsaws, augers, spades, shovels, scythes, billows, nails, hinges and locks, iron, glass, lead and solder, nets and ropes. French pistoles, gunpowder, and horse harnesses.

Nesbitt, John Maxwell

Pennsylvania Gazette – March – 1776

J.M. Nesbitt was elected a member of the First Troop, Philadelphia City Cavalry.

STANDARD OF PHILADELPHIA LIGHT HORSE, 1776.

Standard of Philadelphia Light Horse, 1776

Pennsylvania Gazette – August – 1776

John Maxwell Nesbitt of this city is appointed Treasurer of the Council of Safety effective July 27. Mr. Nesbitt, formerly of Loughbrickland, County Down, Ireland, was appointed Paymaster of the State Navy, September 14, 1775, and a member of the Committee of Correspondence, May 20, 1774.

Pennsylvania Gazette – November – 1781

The Bank of North America is being organized by a group of city businessmen including John Maxwell Nesbitt who was duly appointed a director of the bank.

Pennsylvania Packet – December 1792

A group of investors met at the Pennsylvania State House in November to form a general insurance company naming the new entity, the Insurance Company of North America. The company was funded with $600,000 of capital and initial shares were sold to investors at $10 each. Within eleven days 40,000 shares were sold and John Maxwell Nesbitt was elected President of the company. The very first insurance policy was issued to the mercantile firm of Nesbitt & Co. for coverage on their ship, *America.*

Pennsylvania Gazette – 1793

J.M. Nesbitt appointed a member of the Committee of Merchants. The committee will collect information regarding the capture and detention of vessels belonging to citizens of the United States of America by ships of European nations at war.

Note

Nesbitt, while serving in the First Troop Philadelphia City Cavalry, was assigned to the New Jersey Campaign. He was one of the founding members of The Society of the Friendly Sons of St. Patrick for the Relief of Irish Immigrants, serving as Vice-President from 1771-73, and later as President from 1782-1796. He never married and died in Philadelphia, 1802, leaving his estate to the partners in his merchant firm.

Proctor, Thomas

Note

Proctor was the original owner of the City Tavern located at 2nd Street near the wharves in Philadelphia, where many meetings of importance took place in British America. He was appointed a Lieutenant Colonel in the Continental Army, followed by Brigadier General.

Quigley, John – Helmsman

Note

DOB 1760 Worcester, Massachusetts, enlisted in the Continental Army on September 22, 1778, and served as a Captain in March Chase's company in Colonel Nathan Sparhawk's regiment. Dippam, an Irish search engine, lists multiple voyages of the ship *Ann,* 350 tons, Captain John Quigley, from Belfast to Canadian and American ports, including Charlestown. No other mariners named Quigley, and with the forename of John, matching the same name on the crew list of *Faithful Steward* were found in research. The author used poetic license, and incorporated this John Quigley into the story.

Stewart, Archibald

Note

DOB August 18, 1727, DOD February 28, 1805, may have been near fifty-seven years of age as the original owner of Faithful Steward. There is historical data indicating Irish merchants sought to have ships built at ports in New England and Philadelphia as early as the 1730s. Archibald married Anstis Hutton in County Antrim, Ireland, in 1770, later migrating to Providence, Rhode Island.

The Society of the Friendly Sons of St. Patrick for the Relief of Irish Emigrants

Letter from George Washington (upon receipt of his medal inducting him into the society) to:

George Campbell, President
The Society of the Friendly Sons of St. Patrick
For the Relief of Irish Emigrants

Sir:

I accept with singular pleasure, the Ensign of so worthy a fraternity as that of the Sons of St. Patrick in this city – a Society distinguished for the firm adherence of its members to the glorious cause in which we embarked. Give me leave to assure you, Sir, that I shall never cast my eyes upon the badge with which I am honored, but with grateful remembrance of the polite and affectionate manner in which it is presented. I am with respect and esteem, Sir, your most obedient humble servant.

George Washington

Jefferson, Thomas

Note

While not a member of the society, he was a frequent guest to their meetings. Although he never traveled to Ireland, his knowledge of the country developed through correspondence, reading newspaper accounts, literature and music, government trade reports, reports from William Knox, U.S. Consul in Dublin, and personal contact with immigrants. In January of 1786, Jefferson recounted that nearly 50,000 emigrants came to the U.S. during 1785 (the same year as the wreck of *Faithful Steward*), mostly Scots-Irish and Irish, and the remainder German, entering through Philadelphia, Baltimore, or New York.

Scots-Irish & The American Revolution

Note

Upon researching the topic – "The history of the Scots-Irish and the Irish in the American Revolution," one finds historians who share the opinion this is the best untold story. Others have stated General Washington loved them. He knew they stood by his side and tirelessly fought enduring the perils at hand, all for the cause of winning independence for their beloved America. There were those on *Faithful Steward* with family members who migrated to British America and joined the state militias or the Continental Army.

The first Federal Census was taken in 1790, seven years following the end of the war. The first category in the census designated "Free Males of the Age 16 Upwards" in 1790 is listed herein. Benjamin Franklin estimated the population of Pennsylvania was close to one-third Scots-Irish and Irish. The below chart attempts to count the potential number of Scots-Irish and Irish available to serve in the Continental Army, or as a colony militiaman or associator, and the navies.

Free Males 16 & older	Population Rounded to 1,000
Pennsylvania	111,000 X 1/3 = 37,000 est. Scots-Irish + Irish
Virginia	111,000
Massachusetts	95,000
New York	84,000
North Carolina	70,000
Connecticut	60,000
Maryland	56,000
New Jersey	49,000
New Hampshire	36,000
South Carolina	36,000
Maine	24,000
Vermont	22,000
Rhode Island	16,000

The Ratification of the Constitution of the United States of America
Philadelphia, Pennsylvania

The thirteen colonies, now states, celebrated the ratification of the new Federal Constitution of the United States in Philadelphia. The affair was elaborate and attracted wide attention. A procession, nearly one and one-half miles long, contained about 5,000 men. State officials, Judges, members of the professions and trades, workingmen's assemblies, soldiers, all of the people turned out to celebrate the beginning of a new government.

Members of The Society of the Friendly Sons of St. Patrick filled three of nine important and leading roles in the procession. Acting in the capacity of Superintendents of the Procession were General Walter Stewart, Major James Moore, and Colonel Thomas Proctor. The First City Troop was given a lead in the parade. All members of The Society of Friendly Sons of St. Patrick, John Nixon, riding on horseback, portrayed "Independence,"

Thomas Fitzsimmons represented "The French Alliance," Richard Bache, also on horseback, depicted a herald proclaiming, "A New Era," and Colonel John Shee riding horseback, bore a banner portraying a likeness of General Washington.

The City Troop of Light Dragoons commanded by Captain William Bingham and Chief Justice McKean, riding in a carriage with other judges, represented "the New Constitution." Ten gentlemen represented the ten states that ratified the Constitution. Of these, George Meade represented Georgia and Colonel Thomas Robinson, Delaware. Thomas Barclay carried the Flag of Morocco among the representatives of Foreign Powers.

A float named "The Grand Federal Edifice" contained ten chairs. Several of those occupying the chairs were Lieutenant Colonel George Latimer, John Maxwell Nesbitt, John Brown, Tench Francis, and Benjamin Fuller. People from The Society of the Cincinnati, founded in 1783 by officers of the Continental Army, filled the remaining chairs on the float.

Trial of the Pyx

Note

The section, "Irish Half-Pence Minted for the Kingdom of Ireland" inserted in Chapter 9, Trial of the Pyx, represents an informative and profound piece of historical documentation never before published since the shipwreck.

The ceremony represents a detailed systemized procedure dating back to the twelfth century. And this procedure continues in practice today to ensure newly minted coinage in the United Kingdom conforms to specific standards.

Warrior's Path

Located on Route 6 Wyalusing, Pennsylvania overlooking an expansive valley to the south. Multiple signs of evidences of the Warriors Path are found throughout the state.

Watts, James

Note

A passenger and survivor of the shipwreck, was reported born in 1764 in Ireland, and twenty-one years old when boarding *Faithful Steward*. He married (Jane-Janet-Jeanette) forename undetermined, in 1790, in Southampton, Virginia, and died in 1805 at forty-one years, Montgomery County, Tennessee.

DISCOVERSEA SHIPWRECK MUSEUM
Fenwick Island, Delaware
Dale W. Clifton, Jr. Director

Faithful Steward
Artifacts
Salvaged coins and a cross inserted in the ship's beam

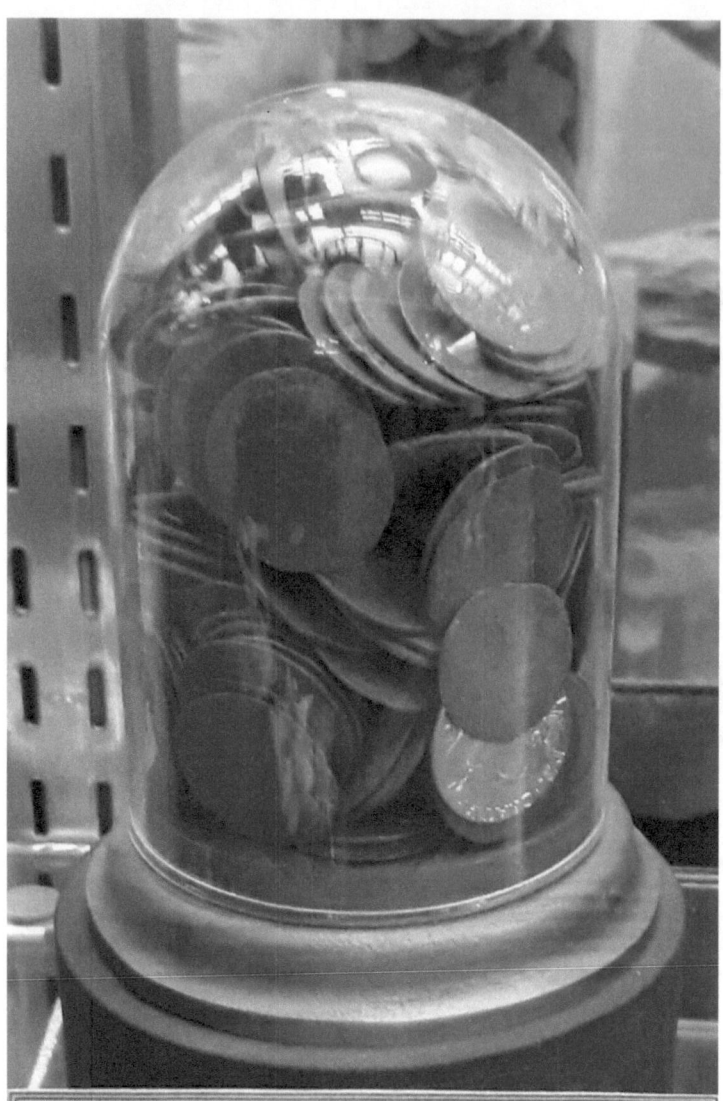

375 British & Irish Coins & 2 Gold Rose Guineas

All of these coins were recovered during Hurricane Felix on Coin Beach in about one half hour. We believe that they were part of the 400 barrels which had broken up in this storm.

Coinage Barrels

Most ships traveling to the American Colonies, carried some sort of coinage with them. These coins were carried for a number of reasons. The first and foremost reason was to buy good along the way. Sometimes in cases such as the *Faithful Steward*, British halfpennies and gold Rose Guineas, coins were being sent to the Colonies to help establish coinage at a time when we had no mints to coin our own coinage. This barrel represents a fine example of the way these coins were being shipped in the late 1700's. Barrels ranged in size from the small 30 gallon size such as this one, to some as large as a 55 gallon drum. Chests were also commonly used also to transport coinage such as th

got
that was handy
were widely used
and so many

Coin Clumps

Some of the coins recovered from Coin Beach are in the form of clumps. This is caused by the saltwater corrosion, which fuses the coins in the form of the container that once housed them. Many times they are stacked in the exact position as when placed in the barrels.

Clipped & Holed Coins

The head of King George was cut off of the coin, or, a hole was poked through the King's nose as a rebellion to the king for sending the enemy coinage.

Display of buckles

Pewter Drinking Cup

This small cup was used for everyday purposes. It was recovered from the wrecksite in 1982.

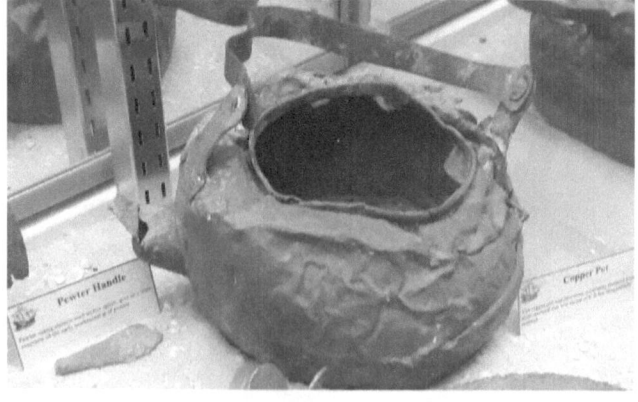

GLOSSARY

Amidships – the middle of a ship, be it longitude or latitude

Algonquians – Native American tribes linked by a common language, originally from the northeastern sections of Canada and the United States

Artificer – a skilled craftsman or a military man skilled in mechanics

Ballyboe – a term used for a small division of land, primarily in Ulster

Ballybetagh – an area under the control of a ruling Irish sept, a ruling family

Barilla – salt-tolerant plants used as a source for soda ash and sodium used in bleaching

Barony – a subdivision of a county

Basaltic – volcanic rock

Beetling – the process of pounding flax or cotton to produce a smooth finish

Boatswain – also bosun, the ship officer in charge of the cargo, sometimes can also be in charge of the crew

Buntline – a line for restraining the center portion or loose portion of a sail.

Camhouse – a box or housing built to protect people from the gears of a cam built onboard the vessel

Cassub – a product used in linen bleaching

Coercive Act – a series of laws passed by the British Parliament in 1774 restricting the rights of those in Britain's colonies in America

Companies – an organization formed in Britain during the 1600s to raise capital and invest in development

Cooper – a maker or repairer of casks and barrels

Cornet – the third and lowest grade of a commissioned officer in the military, A British term, also a sub-lieutenant

Cutlass – a short slightly curved sword

Diamond – the central meeting or gathering place in a market town

Draper – a person who deals in and sells cloth

Flaxseed – the seed from the flax plant (also linseed)

Fo'cs'le – forecastle, the forward part of a ship below the main deck used for the crew's living quarters

Glen – a narrow valley

Groggery – a slightly disreputable barroom

Guinea – a British coin minted from gold imported from West Africa

Gunwale – the top edge of the side of a ship or a boat

Hewer – a person who cuts wood, stone, and other material

Inishowen – the largest peninsula in Ireland located on the north coast of County Donegal in the province of Ulster

Iroquois – a confederacy of Native Americans – the Six Nations in the northeastern United States

Joiner – one in construction who joins articles of wood

Kelp – large brown seaweed growing in shallow nutrient-rich saltwater

Lading – the action of loading a cargo ship – also cargo

Landed gentry – individuals who were either granted land, or descendants of those granted land under the Plantation of Ulster and who leased land to be farmed

Leeward – a direction, toward the side of being sheltered from the wind, the downwind side

Lenape – pronounced La-nah-pay, a Native American tribe of Algonquian language, at one time inhabiting New York, Pennsylvania, New Jersey, and Delaware

Lieutenancy – office, rank, or commission of being a lieutenant

Ligne – a historic unit of measurement used in France before the metric

Lough – an Irish word for a lake, bay, or inlet to the sea

Lough Foyle – an estuary of the River Foyle flowing through County Londonderry, Northern Ireland

Mainmast – the primary mast, typically the second mast in a row of a three or four-mast sail ship

Maw – the oldest national card game of Ireland

Mizzenmast – the mast aft (to the rear) of the mainmast

Mull – a rounded hill, summit, or mountain, bare of trees

Muster rolls – an official list of officers and men in a military unit or ship's roll

Norman – an ethnic group stemming from Norse Viking settlers in an area of northern France and Franks and Gallo-Romans

Overseer – one who supervises property for the benefit of the owner

Packet – a smaller vessel used for mail delivery

Pearlash – potassium carbonate created by baking potash in a kiln

Peerage – the rank and title of person or peer, one holding a hereditary or genealogical title

Pinnace – a small boat equipped with sails and oars usually assigned to a warship

La poupe Deck – from the French word, la poupe – a roof formed over a cabin built aft, to the rear in a sail ship

Points – the direction of travel of a sailing craft measured by the spokes on the ship's wheel

Potash – an alkaline potassium compound

Pre-Norman – an ethnic group derived from contact with Norse Viking settlers in Normandy, France, and indigenous Gallo-Romans

Privateer - an armed ship owned and officered by private individuals holding a government commission and authorized for use in war, especially in the capture of enemy merchant shipping

Quay – a dock consisting of concrete, wood, or metal platform alongside a body of water where ships load and unload cargo

Sawyer – one who cuts wood

Schist – a coarse-grained metamorphic rock which consists of layers of different minerals

Scutch – the process of separating seeds and impurities while dressing flax, cotton, or hemp for spinning

Schuylkill River – a river running northwest to southeast into Philadelphia

Servitor – one who provides service to the king in either an administrative or military capacity

Shallop – a light sailboat often used in coastal fishing

Shawnee – a Native American tribe from eastern Pennsylvania with an Algonquian speaking language

Shipwright – a builder of ships

Siconese – Algonquian speaking Native Americans who established trails in eastern Maryland and Delaware, north to Pennsylvania

Six Nations – a league of Iroquois tribes in New York during the 1700s consisting of the Mohawk, Oneida, Onondaga, Cayuga, Seneca, and Tuscarora

Sloop – a smaller sail ship consisting of one mast with two sails

Spanish Reale – a small Spanish silver coin minted in the seventeenth century and circulated in the United States until the mid-nineteenth century

Steerage – the area below deck providing accommodations for those passengers who can afford only the least

Taffrail – the rail and ornamentation around the stern of a sailship

Termon – land owned by the church exempt from secular taxation

Trunnel-maker – a laborer who makes plates to hold the wooden sides of a ship in place

Tuscarora – Native American Iroquois community in western New York

Ulster – one of the four traditional Irish provinces in Northern Ireland

Undertaker – a person of financial means that builds defensive protective structures

Victualer – a person, a ship, employed to supply food provisions to another

Westerlies – the belt of prevailing wind in the mid-latitudes in the northern and southern hemisphere

Whist – a card game played by two in colonial times where points are scored by winning tricks

Yawl – a two-mast fore and aft rigged sailboat with the mizzenmast stepped far aft so that the mizzen boom overhangs the stern

BIBLIOGRAPHY

Books, Booklets, Pamphlets

A History of Congregations in the Presbyterian Church in Ireland 1610-1982, Presbyterian Historical Society of Ireland, 1982

American Council of Learned Societies, Dictionary of American Biography Volume XIII, Charles Scribner's Sons New York 1934 Pgs. 429-430 Nesbitt, John Maxwell

Bitter, Abraham Philadelphia and Her Merchants: As Constituted Fifty @ Seventy Years Ago, Published by Abraham Bitter 1860

Boscawen, Hugh The Capture of Louisbourg – 1758 University of Oklahoma Press, Norman, Oklahoma 2011

Burke, John Burke's Landed Gentry of Ireland 1899 Pgs. 281-282 Family Tree – Connolly McCausland

Carter, Dick, The History of Sussex County Community Newspaper Corp. 1976

Dickson, R.J. Ulster Emigration to Colonial America 1718-1775 Routledge and Kegan Paul, London 1966

Dobson, David. Scottish Emigration to Colonial America 1607-1785 The University of Georgia Press, Athens & London

Espey, Florence Mercy History and Genealogy of the Espey Family in America 1905 Pythian Printing Co. Fort Madison, Iowa

Glenn, Thomas Allen Merion in the Welsh Tract – with sketches of the Townships of Haverford and Radnor, Norristown 1896

Greenhill, Basil, Director. The Great Migration Crossing the Atlantic Under Sail, National Maritime Museum

Gillingham, Harrold E., Bland, Elias, Wilson, Edward Some Colonial Ships Built in Philadelphia, the PA Magazine of History and Biography Vol. 56 No. 2, 1932 The Historical Society of PA University of PA Press

Hanson, Ruth A. PhD, The Ancestors of Samuel McElhenney Grate Galiah Institute Publishing Arnold, Missouri.

Harrison, John History of Scots in Northern Ireland – The Scot in Ulster: Sketch of the History of the British Population in Ulster 1888 Book VI

History of Washington County, Pennsylvania with Biographical Sketches of many of its Pioneers and Prominent Men 1882 Edited by Boyd Crumrine, Published by H.L. Everts & Co. Philadelphia, PA

Kleeberg, John M., "The Shipwreck of the Faithful Steward: A Missing Link in the Exports of British and Irish Halfpence, Coinage of the Americas Conference at the American Numismatic Society, New York, October 28, 1995

Londonderry Journal 1772-1784, Genealogical Publishing Co., Inc. Baltimore, MD, Clearfield Company, Inc. 1990

Maddocks, Melvin. The Atlantic Crossing, Time-Life Books, Alexandria, VA.

MacGregor, David R., MA, FSA, FRHistS, Merchant Sailing Ships 1775-1815 Sovereignty of Sail, Naval Institute Press1985

MacMaster, Richard K. Scotch-Irish Merchants in Colonial America, Ulster Historical Foundation, Athenaeum Press 2009

Notes and Queries Historical, Biographical and Genealogical: Chiefly Relating to Interior Pennsylvania, Third Series Vol. II p. 320 Harrisburg Publishing Co.

Oberholtzer, Ellis Paxson, PhD. Philadelphia: A History of the City and its People Vol. I-IV, The S.J. Clarke Publishing Company, Philadelphia 1912

Oberholtzer, Ellis Paxson, Ph.D. Robert Morris, Patriot and Financier, The McMillan & Co., Ltd. 1903

Roberts, Priscilla H. and Roberts, Richard S., Thomas Barclay (1728-1793), Consul in France, Diplomat in Barbary, Associated University Press

Robinson, Philip S. The Plantation of Ulster – British Settlement in an Irish Landscape 1600-1670 "Baronies, Undertakers, Companies and Servitors, p. 86", "Land Grants to London Companies p. 209" The Ulster Historical Foundation Belfast, Ireland 2000

Scharf, J. Thomas, A.M. LLD. History of Delaware 1609-1888 Vol. I, L.J. Richards & Co. 1888, Philadelphia, PA

Schlegel, Donald M. Irish Genealogical Abstracts from the Londonderry Journal 1772-1784 Genealogical Publishing Co., Inc. Baltimore, MD, Clearfield Company, Inc. 1990

Shomette, Donald G. Shipwrecks, Sea Raiders, and Maritime Disasters Along the Delmarva Coast 1632-2004, The John Hopkins University Press, Baltimore

Truxes, Thomas M., Irish-American Trade 1660-1783, Cambridge University Press, 1988

Weslager, C.A., The Siconese Indians of Lewes, Delaware, A Historical Account of a "Great" Bayside Lenape Tribe, The Lewes Historical Society

Willis, J. Abbot, American Merchant Ships and Sailors, Dodd Mead & Company, The Caxton Press NY, New York 1902

Articles

Baldorf, Marcel. The Ulster Linen Triangle: An Industrial Cluster Emerging from a Proto-Industrial Region

Belfast Newsletter – Story of a Woman Survivor, March 3, 1786

Irish Genealogical Abstracts from Londonderry Journal 1772-1784 by Donald M. Schlegel

O'Malley, Eoin. The Decline of Irish Industry in the Nineteenth Century, The University of Sussex, The Economic and Social Review, Vol. 13, No. 1 October 1981, Pgs. 21-42

Mitchell, Brian, When flax and linen united Derry and the 'City of Brotherly Love' The Derry Journal October 21, 2017

Historical Journals, Newspapers, Magazines, Periodicals

Belmont Chronicle – January 14, 1886, Obituary of William Lee Sr.

Crawford Journal – Meadville, February 4, 1881, Shipwreck of the Faithful Steward, McIntire, James Jr.

Daily Universal Register of London, November 22, 1785, Shipwreck of Faithful Steward, Private Letter Collection, September 17, 1785

Londonderry Journal May 10, 1785

Meginnis Biographical Annals, Dr. James Dougal sketch, pgs. 106-108

Pennsylvania Magazine of History and Biography, Memorials of Col. Joshua Eyre Vol 3 No. 4 (1879) Pgs. 412-425

Pennsylvania Magazine of History and Biography Vol. V Publication Fund of The Historical Society of PA 1881, Philadelphia, PA

The Historical Journal, A Quarterly Record Volume II 1894 No. 2

Websites

Ask About Ireland, The Plantation of the Laggan Valley
http://www.askaboutireland.ie/reading-room/history-heritage/history-of-ireland/the-ulster-plantation/the-plantation-of-the-lag/

American Battlefield Trust, Winter at Valley Forge
https://www.battlefields.org/learn/articles/winter-valley-forge

Ardstraw-Bridge - https://www.libraryireland.com/topog/A/Ardstraw-Bridge-Strabane-Tyrone.php

Ardstraw Presbyterian Church -
http://www.ardstrawpresbyterian.org/church-history.html

Bill MacAfee's website
http://www.billmacafee.com/sourcesestaterecords.htm

Boscawen, Isabella – Relatives
https://www.ancestry.com/genealogy/records/isabella-boscawen_28345340?geo_a=r&geo_s=ca&geo_t=us&geo_v=2.0.0&o_iid=41014&o_lid=41014&o_sch=Web+Property

Brief History of William Penn http://www.ushistory.org/penn/bio.htm

Campbell, John H., Historian, Brief Account of the Society of the Friendly Sons of St. Patrick with Biographical Notes of Some of the Members and Extracts from the Minutes, Prepared by the Order of the Hibernian Society 1844, The Historical Society of Philadelphia, Published by The Historical

Society of Philadelphia 1892

Campbell, John H., History of the Society of the Friendly Sons of St. Patrick and the Hibernian Society for the Relief of Emigrants from Ireland: March 17, 1771 – March 17, 1892, Campbell, John N., Historian of the Hibernian Society - The Hibernian Society 1892 Cornell University Library https://archive.org/stream/cu31924028861974/cu31924028861974_djvu.txt

CarsanBarclay&Mitchell - https://www.google.com/search?q=Carsan+Barclay+and+Mitchell&tbm=isch&source=iu&ictx=1&fir=eAkGkBspGCx8nM%253A%252CxBGFdnKDtVyHuM%252C_&usg=AI4_-kTfkszwPFFhOFJMDRrYjhFYUHaASg&sa=X&ved=2ahUKEwi9pOrw5dndAhURjlkKHTuIBgoQ9QEwAXoECAUQBA#imgrc=XBsX6ivUhOzlyM

ContinentalNavy.com The History of the People of the Continental Navy continentalnavy.com/archives/2018/alphabetical-list-of-the-crew-of-the-frigate-alliance-1782-1783-who-received-prize-money-associated-with-the-capture-and-sale-of-the-kingston-brittannia-anna-and-commerce/

Celtic Dance – A History of Irish Dance https://www.celticsteps.ie/our-story/the-history-of-irish-song-music-dance/

Conyngham, Gustavus https://www.britannica.com/biography/Gustavus-Conyngham https://en.wikipedia.org/wiki/Gustavus_Conyngham

Cooke, Edward Family www.novanumismatics.com/the-wreck-of-the-faithful-steward-delawares-coin-beach/#comment-16171

Denominations http://umich.edu/~ece/student_projects/money/denom.html

Discover Shipwreck Museum

Dixon, Pam, Elliott Family Genealogy, Genealogy.com, Genealogy Report: Descendants of Wealthy Elliott https://www.genealogy.com/ftm/d/i/x/Pam-Dixon/GENE1-0001.html

Dorwart, Jeffrey M., The Encyclopedia of Greater Philadelphia, Shipbuilding and Shipyards http://philadelphiaencyclopedia.org/archive/shipbuilding-and-shipyards/

Dunlap, John https://www.findagrave.com/memorial/29976753/john-dunlap

Espey, Hugh https://www.findagrave.com/memorial/123773691/john-espey

Federal Reserve Bank of Philadelphia Money in Colonial Times https://www.philadelphiafed.org/education/teachers/resources/money-in-colonial-times#09

Genealogical Maps of Pennsylvania https://www.bing.com/images/search?q=genealogical+maps+of+pennsylvania&id=F4D0C0F6F86439437BB6D08BE06ADEE0ADAE2573&FORM=IQFRBA

Gulf Stream https://en.wikipedia.org/wiki/Gulf_Stream

Haynes, Joseph Captain and part owner of *Faithful Steward* https://ancestors.familysearch.org/en/MY9Q-2GZ/capt-joseph-haynes-1742-1815

Heather's Genealogy http://notheathersgen.blogspot.com/2014/11/the-faithful-steward-shipwreck.html

Hepburn, William called the 'father' of Lycoming County | News, Sports, Jobs - Williamsport Sun-Gazette April 21, 2018; Northumberland County Revolutionary War Militia (pa.gov)

Hewat, Alexander https://en.wikipedia.org/wiki/Alexander_Hewat

History of Ireland http://www.historyworld.net/wrldhis/PlainTextHistories.asp?ParagraphID=img

Higston, Sandy 12 Things You Did Not Know About Stephen Girard Philly Magazine March 3, 2016, https://www.phillymag.com/news/2016/03/03/stephen-girard-american-rags-riches-story/

History of Limavady www.limavady.org/history/newtown.html

Howton, Erica, Manuel Eyre https://www.geni.com/people/Manuel-Eyre/6000000029665121940

Humphreys, Joshua, Papers 1751-1838, Historical Society of Pennsylvania http://www2.hsp.org/collections/manuscripts/h/Humphreys306.html

Hugh Lee Family Ancestry.com

In Search of the Faithful Steward – The Story of Margaret Kincade, Robert Elmwood http://freepages.rootsweb.com/~faithfulsteward/genealogy/FaithfulStewardTemp.htm

Indian Hill Historical Society, John Elliott 1762-1843 https://www.indianhill.org/history/people-indian-hill-history/john-elliott-1762-1843/

Ireland Naming Patterns https://irelandxo.com/ireland-xo/news/irelandxo-insight-irish-naming-and-baptism-traditions

Keller, James P. McCausland Family History http://www.kelcran.com/Genealogy/sources/mccausland/rmcc.pdf

Lewes Chamber of Commerce https://www.leweschamber.com/our-town/history-lewes-de

List of Shipwrecks 1785 https://en.wikipedia.org/wiki/List_of_shipwrecks_in_1785

Littleton Coin Company Early American Coins https://www.littletoncoin.com/shop/Early-American-Coins?gclid=EAIaIQobChMIjuD30e773wIV0-DICh0mLAW_EAAYBCAAEgK-zfD_BwE

Maytown Museum House

https://maytownhistory.org/2018/03/21/museum-house-history/ Robert
Lescalette

Nova Numismatics, Packard Aaron The Faithful Steward Wreck and
Delaware's Coin Beach http://www.novanumismatics.com/the-wreck-of-
the-faithful-steward-delawares-coin-beach/#comment-16171

Nova Numismatics, Packard Aaron The Faithful Steward Wreck &
Delaware'sCoinBeach http://www.novanumismatics.com/numismatic-
essays/the-wreck-of-the-faithful-steward-delawares-coin-beach/#comment-
16173

National Underwater Marine Agency, Dale Clifton's Quest to Shake Hands
With History, Ellsworth Boyd, June 1. 2019 https://numa.net/2019/06/dale-
cliftons-quest-to-shake-hands-with-history/

Regal British Copper Coinage: Introduction
https://coins.nd.edu/colcoin/colcoinintros/Br-Copper.intro.html

Revolutionary War Records, Pennsylvania
https://www.phmc.pa.gov/Archives/Research-Online/Pages/Revolutionary-
War.aspx

Roots Chat, Genealogical James Watt

Sampson, George Vaughan. Statistical Survey of the County of Londonderry
With Observations on the Means of Improvement, Graisberry and Campbell
1802, Historical Society of Pennsylvania

Servitors and Irish Natives in the Ulster Plantation, Irish Pedigrees Library
Ireland

Shee, Colonel John
http://sites.rootsweb.com/~irlkik/history/shee.html

Shipbuilding in Colonial America
https://www.encyclopedia.com/history/modern-europe/british-and-irish-
history/shipbuilding

The Academic Studies of Ulster-Scots – Essays for and by Robert J. Gregg,
National Museum Northern Ireland
https://www.libraryireland.com/gregg/mapping-ulster-scots.php

The Counties and Baronies of Ulster,
http://billmacafee.com/admin/mapbaroniesulster.htm

The Historical Society of Pennsylvania Collection 3033 USS Alliance Ledger
1782-1783
https://hsp.org/sites/default/files/legacy_files/migrated/findingaid3033allia
nce.pdf

The Royal Mint Museum Trial of the Pyx,
http://www.royalmintmuseum.org.uk/history/history-of-the-royal-
mint/trial-of-the-pyx/index.html

The Six Nations https://ratical.org/manyworlds/6nations/

Truxes, Thomas M. Irish-American Trade 1660-1783 Cambridge University
Press

Wikipedia Articles of Confederation
https://en.wikipedia.org/wiki/Articles_of_Confederation
Wikipedia Ballintoy, https://en.wikipedia.org/wiki/Ballintoy
Wikipedia Battle of the Delaware Capes,
https://en.wikipedia.org/wiki/Battle_of_the_Delaware_Capes
Wikipedia, Charles Cadogan, 1st Earl Cadogan
https://en.wikipedia.org/wiki/Charles_Cadogan,_1st_Earl_Cadogan
Wikipedia, Denominations
http://umich.edu/~ece/student_projects/money/denom.html
Wikipedia, Donegal https://en.wikipedia.org/wiki/County_Donegal
Wikipedia, Gervase Eyre, https://en.wikipedia.org/wiki/Gervase_Eyre
Wikipedia Hearts of Steel, https://en.wikipedia.org/wiki/Hearts_of_Steel
Wikipedia List of Shipwrecks in 1785
https://en.wikipedia.org/wiki/List_of_shipwrecks_in_1785
Wikipedia, Piracy in the Atlantic World
https://en.wikipedia.org/wiki/Piracy_in_the_Atlantic_World#North_
Atlantic
Wikipedia Sheep Island
https://en.wikipedia.org/wiki/Sheep_Island,_County_Antrim
Wikipedia Sperrins https://en.wikipedia.org/wiki/Sperrins
Wikipedia, Trial of the Pyx https://en.wikipedia.org/wiki/Trial_of_the_Pyx
Wikitree – Genealogy, William Colhoun (1664-1752)
://www.whttpsikitree.com/wiki/Colhoun-13
Wilkins, Harriet Hepburn "The Hepburn Journal,
notheathersgen.blogspot.com/2014/11/the-hepburn-journal.html
https://www.battlefields.org/learn/articles/winter-valley-forge

Private Collections

Corry, Liam, Curator of Emigration National Museums, Northern Ireland
Ulster American Folk Park, Omagh "Surname Research for Locations of
Origin"
Eighteenth-Century Colonial American Merchant Ship Construction, A
Thesis, Vanhorn, Kellie Michelle Office of Graduate Studies Texas A. & M.
University, December 2004
Elliott, Simon, "The Elliott Families, 1762-1911: A History and Genealogy
with Biographics"
Espey, Jae "Personal collection of Espey Family and Genealogical Research"
Hemphill, Tybring "Personal collection of Colhoun Family and Genealogical
Research"
Jewett, Lucy McIntyre, "Personal collection of McIntire family history, letters,
and photographs", 3 x's great-granddaughter of James McIntire Jr. courtesy
of Sarah E. J. Coombs, 5 x's great-granddaughter of James McIntire Jr.

McEntire, Robert Miller, great grandson to James McIntire II, Chronology and family history; Clark, Patricia, McIntire family compiled history and information. Collections provided by Suzanne Vila, 6 x's great granddaughter and Mark Tattersall, 7x's great grandson to James McIntire II.

Mitchell, Brian, "Derry-Londonderry: Gateway to a New World, 2014"

Mitchell, Brian, "Emigration, Flaxseed Trade, Trade Ships"

Mitchell, Brian, "Redemptioners, Servants, Archibald Stewart, Stewart"

Riblet, Sarah V., "A Tempestuous Voyage at Sea and a Fatiguing One by Land: Ulster Women in Philadelphia, 1783-1812" March 20, 2014, University of Pennsylvania

Wack, Dr. Mary, "Captain C. McCausland and the Ships Walworth and Jane", "Capt. McCausland and Benjamin Franklin"

Ward, Dorothy Ball, Pedigree Chart of the Richard and Ann Constable Lee ancestry, Lee family research and ancestral photographs, Overview of Samuel Lee Research, Hugh Boscawen Research

Weir, Sir Thomas Phillip, River Roe

https://www.flickr.com/photos/16701453@N08/14916600994

ACKNOWLEDGMENTS

Researching and writing a historical fiction novel is complex and labor-intensive, but very gratifying work, requiring perseverance. The start of researching the ship *Faithful Steward* grew over six months, after pouring over names of shipwrecks identified on the map – "Shipwrecks of the Mid-Atlantic - Delaware, Maryland, and Southern New Jersey." What was behind that name? Perhaps there was a fascinating story waiting to be told. And I questioned, should I be the one to research and unearth the details. Names intrigue me, and *Faithful Steward* didn't disappoint. Writing a story would be impossible without the dedication and contribution of others – and to that end, I wish to recognize and thank those who assisted.

Liam Corry, Curator of Emigration, National Museums Northern Ireland set off a chain of events culminating in links with others. Christine Johnston, Senior Library Assistant, Libraries NI, Mellon Centre for Migration Studies at the Ulster American Folk Park provided links to websites for research and suggested books to research.

Brian Mitchell, genealogist, author, and historian, affiliated with Derry City and Strabane District Council, Northern Ireland, has been a Godsend. I discovered one whose interest in history is intense and contagious. He motivates others and readily offers genealogical research and historical reference assistance, including referrals for resource books, and information drawn from his historical files. He thinks ahead, drawing from his list of contacts, and he shared relevant names whenever he thought they would be helpful. People like Brian should be mirrored by others.

Tybring Hemphill, 4 x's great-grandson of Hugh Colhoun traces his ancestry to he and his brothers, Gustavus and Thomas. Tybring maintains an unquenchable thirst for historical research related to the Colhoun family history, and the story behind the transported copper coins. Many family references and historical facts were provided through his research and personal files.

With ancestral ties to the Colhoun family, Brian Anton assisted through his genealogical research of branches of the Colhouns, including geographical ancestral locations from his research.

Thank you to Sarah Elizabeth Jewett Coombs, 5 x's great-granddaughter to James McIntyre II, for her family's genealogical research including the Lucy McIntyre Jewett, 3x's great-granddaughter to James McIntyre II, historical accounts of the McIntyre family and photographs.

Suzanne Vila, 6 x's great granddaughter to James McIntyre II provided the Robert Miller McEntire family historical collection, including the McEntire Century Farm history.

And Dorothy Ward provided extensive genealogy and photographs from her historical collection of the James Lee family.

Contributing to the Espey family history was Jae Espey, 4 x's great-grandson to James Espey, a shipwreck survivor. Tonnie Seery, 4x's great-granddaughter to Hugh Espey Jr. contributed to family genealogy and history.

Dr. Mary Wack, Professor of English at Washington State University is a researcher and writer of history, having visited the Roe Valley, Northern Ireland. She has researched and authored valuable informative articles about Captain Connolly McCausland, and his brother, Abraham.

Special thanks to Susie Davis, an archivist with vast experience at the National Archives, Kew, London for finding the historical document, "The Trial of the Pyx." The paper, undiscovered until recently, provides historical evidence of the source and details of the minting of copper coins for the Kingdom of Ireland, with minting dates that may coincide with harvested coins from Coin Beach.

Joshua Sherrets, President of the Board of the Crawford County Historical Society, Meadville, Pennsylvania provided a valuable copy of the James McIntire II news article published in the Meadville Courier.

Joanne Kelley proofread the story, and provided feedback, including observations, opinions, and recommendations for improvement, and assisted with copy and line editing.

To Philip S. Robinson, author of "The Plantation of Ulster – British Settlement in an Irish Landscape, 1600-1670." Without his research and writing it would have been impossible to understand the geographical background and historical data and details comprising the settlement of Ulster.

Without the expertise and assistance of these, the narrative of the people, places, and events comprising the story of those who sailed on *Faithful Steward* would not have happened.

ABOUT THE AUTHOR

A business graduate of the Pennsylvania State University, Harry pursued a lifelong career in the financial services sector. He loves history and enjoys reading, researching, and studying historical events, including genealogy. These interests have led to writing historical fiction, narratives based upon the events researched. His novel incorporates the actual history of an event and becomes a fulfillment of a story that would remain a story never written; and left untold if never researched. He resides with his wife and family in the Indian Valley of Pennsylvania.

Website

harrywenzel.com

Contact

hawwriter@protonmail.com

Other books by the Author

Sindia, the Final Voyage

The tale of Sindia is based upon extensive historical research of the 326' steel-hulled four-mast square-rigged barque, aka a windjammer, built in 1887 by Harland & Wolff Heavy Industries, Ltd. of Belfast, Ireland, the same shipbuilder who years later launched *Titanic*. Sindia sailed trade routes for many years for the owner, Thos. & Jno. Brocklebank, Ltd. of Liverpool, from British ports to Calcutta and return. The barque was was sold in 1900 to the Anglo-American Standard Oil Co. of London, Ltd., a John D. Rockefeller company. The shipwreck occurred at night on December 15, 1901, close to shore near the 16th Street beach at Ocean City, New Jersey. Due to the barque's size and draft, the vessel stranded and salvage efforts to refloat the vessel failed. Ensuing beach replenishment projects over many years combined with the natural hull erosion, buried the remains of the barque underneath the sand. The saga of Sindia remains a historical commemoration in the annals of Ocean City's history today, and the Ocean City Historical Museum maintains an informative display of beautiful artifacts from the barque's cargo.

www.ingramcontent.com/pod-product-compliance
Lightning Source LLC
Chambersburg PA
CBHW022247020726
47496CB00004B/1109